Trials by Marriage

Marriages in trouble!

GW00708151

By Request

**Acclaim for Carole Mortimer,
Jacqueline Baird and Elizabeth Oldfield**

About Carole Mortimer
"Carole Mortimer delivers quality romance."
—*Romantic Times*

About Jacqueline Baird
"Readers will enjoy Ms. Baird's engaging style."
—*Romantic Times*

About Elizabeth Oldfield
"Ms. Oldfield dazzles her lucky readers…
with phenomenal characters, exciting action
and tender romance."
—*Romantic Times*

Trials by Marriage

UNCERTAIN DESTINY
by
Carole Mortimer

NOTHING CHANGES LOVE
by
Jacqueline Baird

RENDEZVOUS IN RIO
by
Elizabeth Oldfield

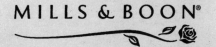

MILLS & BOON®

DID YOU PURCHASE THIS BOOK WITHOUT A COVER?
If you did, you should be aware it is **stolen property** as it was reported
unsold and destroyed by a retailer. Neither the author nor the publisher
has received any payment for this book.

*All the characters in this book have no existence outside the imagination
of the author, and have no relation whatsoever to anyone bearing the same
name or names. They are not even distantly inspired by any individual
known or unknown to the author, and all the incidents are
pure invention.*

*All Rights Reserved including the right of reproduction in whole or in part
in any form. This edition is published by arrangement with Harlequin
Enterprises II B.V. The text of this publication or any part thereof may not
be reproduced or transmitted in any form or by any means, electronic or
mechanical, including photocopying, recording, storage in an
information retrieval system, or otherwise, without the written
permission of the publisher.*

*This book is sold subject to the condition that it shall not, by way of trade
or otherwise, be lent, resold, hired out or otherwise circulated without the
prior consent of the publisher in any form of binding or cover other than
that in which it is published and without a similar condition including this
condition being imposed on the subsequent purchaser.*

*MILLS & BOON and MILLS & BOON with the Rose Device
are registered trademarks of the publisher.
Harlequin Mills & Boon Limited,
Eton House, 18-24 Paradise Road, Richmond, Surrey, TW9 1SR*

TRIALS BY MARRIAGE
© by Harlequin Enterprises II B.V., 1999

Uncertain Destiny, Nothing Changes Love and *Rendezvous in Rio* were
first published in Great Britain by Mills & Boon Limited
in separate, single volumes.

Uncertain Destiny © Carole Mortimer 1987
Nothing Changes Love © Jacqueline Baird 1994
Rendezvous in Rio © Elizabeth Oldfield 1989

ISBN 0 263 81536 6

05-9904

*Printed and bound in Great Britain
by Caledonian Book Manufacturing Ltd, Glasgow*

Carole Mortimer says: 'I was born in England, the youngest of three children—I have two older brothers. I started writing in 1978, and have now written over ninety books for Mills & Boon®.

I have four sons, Matthew, Joshua, Timothy and Peter, and a bearded collie dog called Merlyn. I'm in a very happy relationship with Peter senior; we're best friends as well as lovers, which is probably the best recipe for a successful relationship. We live on the Isle of Man.'

UNCERTAIN DESTINY

by

CAROLE MORTIMER

CHAPTER ONE

'YOU may be pregnant, Caroline,' her husband accepted coldly, 'but *we* certainly aren't. The child you're carrying is not mine!'

She stared at Justin as if he had gone insane. She had just told him the most wonderful news any wife could tell a husband, had been in a state of euphoria ever since she had gone to the doctor this afternoon and he had confirmed her suspicion that she was six weeks pregnant. She had wanted to tell Justin straight away, wanted to rush over to his office and tell him, but had known it wasn't the right place to break the news to him that he was about to become a father for the first time, deciding a candlelit dinner for the two of them at home would be a much more romantic background.

The candles still burnt on the table, the roses that adorned its centre still smelt as sweet, and she still wore the black gown she had chosen to reassure Justin that pregnant women could still look sexy.

And she couldn't believe Justin had said what she thought he had! He couldn't really have said that—could he?

But as she looked up at the coldness of his gaze, the arrogant tilt to his head, the grim set to his sculptured lips, she knew that he had.

Oh, she knew that they never discussed the possibility of having children, but even so——

'Justin——'

'You see, Caroline,' he continued dismissively, his voice deadly calm. 'I'm incapable of fathering a child, by you or any other woman.' He sipped his wine with slow deliberation, looking at her with questioningly raised brows.

She should faint, scream, anything but just sit here staring at him as if she had turned to stone. But she still couldn't believe Justin was denying their child. It had to be a joke, a sick joke—what else could it be? It certainly couldn't be the truth!

'Did you hear me, Caroline?' he bit out. 'I said——'

'Will you stop this.' Her voice was shrill. 'Just stop it, Justin. It isn't funny!'

'I didn't think so either,' he drawled, taking another sip of his wine. 'And I don't believe you saw me laughing.'

She gave a pained frown at his too-calm behaviour. 'Justin, is there a possibility you were drinking before you came home this evening?' His being uncharacteristically drunk was the only other explanation she could think of for his outrageous behaviour.

His expression became even colder, his chair pushed back forcefully as he stood up to switch on the main light with a single movement of one long, gracefully male hand. He towered over her ominously as she blinked dazedly in the sudden bright light. 'I wasn't aware that I had ever given you reason to believe I've become a secret drinker!' he rasped.

There had to be some explanation for the nightmare this evening had suddenly become—although from Justin's cold displeasure at the suggestion, she knew alcohol wasn't it.

'Justin, I'm having a child.' Her hands were tightly clasped together in her lap, her back very straight as she sat rigidly in the chair, and she knew she must have the look of a naughty schoolgirl facing chastisement. Her throat arched defensively as she looked up at Justin. 'Your child,' she added pointedly.

He was so tall and dark, as savagely handsome as any young girl dreamt her husband would be. Dark hair was brushed smoothly back from his face, a black eye-patch rakishly covering the blindness of his left eye, but his sighted eye was more than capable of glittering silver with anger or contempt—as it was doing now! The elegant black evening suit should have had the effect of taming him somewhat, but instead it did the opposite, emphasising his leashed power, giving him the appearance of a barely restrained savage being, restricted by civilisation.

Caroline had been as overwhelmed by him at their first meeting as most people seemed to be, had never ceased to be enthralled by the complex man he was. But this, this she just didn't—*couldn't*—understand!

He shook his head now, deadly calm, although

the coldness of his gaze spoke of a fiercer emotion. *'Not* my child,' he repeated softly.

'Justin, of course the baby is yours. Who else's would it be?' she said exasperatedly.

His brows rose again. 'Tony's, perhaps?' he suggested mildly.

Her face paled. Dear God, he couldn't possibly believe what he was saying!

Justin moved to pour himself a glass of brandy from the decanter in the drinks cabinet. 'I think you should have asked him to share all this with you.' He drank down the brandy as he swept an arm in the direction of the romantic dinner she had planned so eagerly, and her own appearance with her red hair swept loosely on top of her head, her throat and shoulders left temptingly bare by the style of her black gown. 'Although maybe *his* wife might have objected to that,' he bit out hardly before leaving the room in measured strides, the slamming of another door in the house seconds later telling her he had gone to his study.

Caroline had half risen to her feet as he turned to leave, but dropped back down into the chair as she realised from his flinty expression that nothing she said just now would stop him.

She leant forward to absently blow out the candles, staring unseeingly at the spiral of black smoke that trailed upwards as the acrid smell filled the air.

They should have been celebrating now, with the champagne she had asked Mrs Avery to put on ice until after she had spoken to Justin. Instead Justin had stormed out on her, and she was sitting here hardly daring to think of the fact that he had disclaimed paternity of their child.

Loving Justin hadn't been easy from the first, and even now they were married it hadn't got any easier. But she had never before wished she had never met him!

That first evening had started out well, too, but also ended abruptly . . .

'I see my dear sister has been out hunting again,' Tony drawled at her side.

Caroline gave him a puzzled frown before turning to the door of this private room in one of London's finest hotels where Tony's parents had chosen to celebrate their fortieth wedding anniversary.

Paula Hammond was one of the most beautiful women she had ever seen, tall and elegant, with midnight-black hair, and a figure that was perfectly complemented by the red gown she wore. At thirty-five, she had been married and divorced, taking full advantage of her freedom the last five years.

Caroline had seen the other woman with many men during the eight months she had known Tony, but never before with the man at her side tonight. She would have remembered if she had ever seen this man before. Any woman would.

His hair was as black as Paula's, severely styled, although that in no way detracted from his fascinating attraction. His face wasn't handsome, more ruggedly compelling, and the eye-patch he wore only added to his aura of power, his sighted eye flickering uninterestedly over the friends and relatives of the Shepherds who were gathered in the room. His mouth firmed with impatience before he turned to murmur something to the vivacious Paula. With her undoubted beauty and air of sensuality, Paula usually held her dates in complete thrall, but it didn't look as if this man were as easily seduced; Paula gazing up at him longingly as she obviously spoke to him imploringly.

Caroline turned away, finding the sight of this usually self-confident woman pleading for a man's attention, particularly that man, who didn't look as if he gave a damn whose feelings he hurt if he left now, as he obviously wanted to do, strangely unsettling.

Tony chuckled at her side. 'I think I'll have to have a word with Mum and Dad,' he drawled. 'Obviously they forgot to tell my big sister to beware of wolves!'

She turned back to the man at Paula's side, frowning a little. He was mesmerisingly attractive, and she was sure she was far from the first woman to think so, but he didn't look as if he were particularly interested in attracting women to him, his slight impatience of movement giving the impression he didn't care to exert himself for such a trivial reason. He certainly didn't seem like any of the self-centred wolves she had encountered in the past.

Before Tony. For the past eight months they had

dated exclusively. She had been looking for a man like Tony all of her twenty-three years, very handsome with his light brown hair and twinkling hazel-coloured eyes, his boyish charm captivating her from the first. She knew it was only a matter of time before he asked her to marry him. And her answer was going to be a heartfelt yes!

'I'm sure Paula is perfectly capable of taking care of herself,' she lightly chided Tony for his malicious relish concerning his sister. She had learnt early on in her relationship with Tony that although he and Paula loved each other they did like to score off each other. The thought of his sister's downfall obviously filled him with glee.

Tony shook his head. 'She's chosen the wrong man if she wants to do that. 'The Wolf' could gobble her up in one bite!' His eyes narrowed as his sister leant against the other man, her long fingernails moving coaxingly in the dark hair at his nape. 'And this wolf always walks alone.'

The Wolf? She had thought Tony meant the term as an explanation of the other man's behaviour, but this time he had made it sound as if it were the other man's name.

'The Wolf?' she prompted curiously, suddenly breathless as that silver gaze moved over her as derisively as it had the rest of the guests, before suddenly swinging back again, sweeping over her from the top of her fiery-red hair, over the delicacy of her heart-shaped face, down the length of her slender body in the blue gown that matched the colour of her eyes and somehow made her hair look redder than ever, the long length of her legs, to her tiny feet in navy blue sandals.

His gaze moved back up to Caroline's face, flushed and hot now, feeling more and more uncomfortable as he continued to watch her while Paula spoke to him so seductively. It was strangely erotic to realise that while Paula was so intent on enticing him into staying with husky promises—no doubt of how the evening would end!—his attention was focused completely on Caroline. She almost felt as if he had reached out and touched her.

' 'The Wolf'.' Tony nodded, turning away from the other couple disgustedly. 'Paula works for his law firm, de Wolfe and Partners, and he earnt his nickname by always going for the jugular,' he added drily. 'He always prosecutes, never defends, and he never loses.'

Caroline moistened her lips nervously, finding it impossible to look away from that silver gaze. 'Never?' she breathed huskily, feeling her hands begin to shake as she held her glass of wine tightly to her.

'Nope,' Tony confirmed admiringly. 'I wonder how Paula managed to persuade him into coming here tonight; it's a sure fact it's the last place he wants to be,' he derided as Paula still exerted all the charm on the other man of which she was capable—all to no avail, by the way he glanced at her so mockingly.

Caroline took advantage of his brief shift of attention to turn away from him, feeling almost weak with relief at being free from him at last.

She had felt like a prisoner while he gazed at her so compellingly, and she didn't like the way she still trembled slightly even though she no longer looked at him. He exuded a sexuality that was primitive in its demand, and for a few brief minutes he had been demanding that she be completely aware of him. His appeal was raw, savage, and yet she hadn't been able to break free of it until he allowed her to. She didn't know what was the matter with her; she loved Tony, wanted to marry him, and yet just a look from a complete stranger had affected her more deeply than anything else she had ever known.

'—so for God's sake don't call him it to his face,' Tony was muttering.

She shook off the unsettling feelings Paula's date for the evening exerted on her. 'Sorry?' She gave Tony a questioning smile.

He met her smile warmly, glancing behind her. 'I said de Wolfe is only called 'The Wolf' behind his back,' he murmured hastily. 'Whatever you do, don't call him it!' He rolled his eyes expressively.

She frowned. 'But——'

'Tony,' Paula greeted him in her huskily attractive voice that, coupled with her sensual beauty, gave a false impression of a woman interested only in her appearance and what it could get for her. Paula Hammond was one of the most intelligent, shrewd women Caroline had ever met, which made her uncharacteristically kittenish behaviour around the man called de Wolfe all the more unnerving.

'Sis.' Tony moved slightly to kiss his sister on one creamy smooth cheek.

Irritation flashed in dark green eyes as Tony deliberately provoked her with a term he knew she disliked. The anger in her gaze promised him retribution later on.

But the anger faded to be replaced by warm seduction as she gazed up at the man at her side. 'Justin, I want you to meet my brother, Tony.' She scowled at her brother impatiently. 'And his girlfriend, Caroline Maxwell.' Her smile returned warmly as she looked at Caroline. 'This is Justin de Wolfe,' she announced a little triumphantly, her hand firmly on the crook of his arm, resting possessively on the expensive material of the black evening suit.

Caroline watched as the two men shook hands, her palms feeling damp as Justin de Wolfe turned to her, her breathing suddenly constricted. It was ridiculous, the foolishness completely unlike her, and yet she had a feeling that if Justin de Wolfe should touch her even once, she wouldn't want him to stop!

She gazed at him apprehensively, feeling panicked, knowing by the mocking twist to his firm mouth that her emotions were clearly readable to him. She drew in a controlling breath, holding out her hand politely, knowing she had no choice when he arched his dark brow at her so derisively.

As his long fingers closed over her much smaller ones she felt as if he took possession of her, warmth moving like quicksilver up her arm to rapidly engulf her whole body. She could scarcely breathe, filled with a painful ache she had never known before. And to break the contact was impossible.

His gaze narrowed, his head going back challengingly as he too seemed to feel the electricity pulsing between them. 'Miss Maxwell,' he finally murmured in a throaty voice.

God, even his voice was compelling, containing a mesmerising quality that ensured everyone would listen to him, even though he only spoke softly.

This couldn't be happening to her. She was a sensible woman, a trained nurse who had been responsible for dozens of patients over the years; she didn't believe in love at first sight. Or even second sight. Love to her was something that grew from mutual respect and interests, as she and Tony had, he a doctor, she a nurse. She didn't know anything about Justin de Wolfe except that he was lethal in a courtroom, was immune to any amount of female persuasion—and that he was dangerous! And the last was all she really needed to know about him.

'Mr de Wolfe.' She determinedly extracted her hand from within his suddenly steely grip.

'Would you care to dance, Miss Maxwell?' he prompted as the small band began to play a waltz.

Her panicked gaze flew up to meet his. She was tiny, only two inches over five feet, and he was at least a foot taller; if he held her in his arms her head would be on a level with his heart. And she didn't want to be anywhere near his heart! She didn't want to be anywhere near *him*.

'I——'

He didn't give her a chance to refuse him, his hand firm against her back as he guided her on to the small dance floor, maintaining that contact as he took her hand in his and began to move fluidly among the other couples dancing.

Sexual attraction, that was what this was. What else could it be that she felt hot and cold at the same time, barely knew what she was doing as he moved her expertly around the floor? And if she felt this way about a complete stranger, a man who seemed to distance himself from everyone and everything, then she had no business believing she should marry Tony if he should ask her.

'Relax,' Justin murmured into her hair, having gathered her close against his chest long ago.

How could she relax when her whole comfortably safe world was crumbling about her ears? She wanted to run from here and never have to see Justin de Wolfe again!

He moved back slightly to look down at her, very rakish with that black eye-patch over his left eye. 'Difficult to relax when you're burning up with desire, isn't it?' he mused drily.

Caroline gasped at the statement, about to deny it, when he suddenly drew her even closer against him, making her fully aware of his own desire for her.

'That's right,' he drawled self-derisively. 'I feel it, too.'

Felt what, too? This was utter madness. He was Paula's date for the evening; she had been seeing Tony for over eight months now. Whatever she and Justin de Wolfe felt for each other, it wasn't real, was based on mere sexual fantasy.

If only he didn't feel so very real as he moulded her so snugly against him that she could feel every muscle in his body!

'Are you and Shepherd sleeping together?' he suddenly asked.

Her eyes glittered deeply blue as she glared up at him. 'If you're trying to be insulting——'

His brows arched. 'I'm not. I just wanted to know how difficult it's going to be for you to finish with him.'

She drew in a ragged breath. 'As I have no intention——'

'Caroline,' he cut in patiently, as if he were reasoning with a rebellious child. 'We want each other. We're going to have each other. Often,' he stated with casual indifference. 'But I don't intend sharing you with Shepherd. Maybe it's old-fashioned of me, but when I'm involved with a woman I like to be the only man in her life. I *will* be the only man in your life.'

She looked about them frantically, sure Paula had allowed a certifiable maniac to walk off with her. She finally caught sight of Tony, he and Paula having what appeared to be one of their not unusual arguments, engrossed in each other and not in what was going on between herself and

Justin across the room. Fond of Tony as she was, she couldn't help wishing that he hadn't felt in an argumentative mood tonight. She needed rescuing, and from the way Justin's arms had tightened about her she didn't think she was going to be able to do it alone.

'I realise you're too young for me——'

'Couldn't it be that you're too old for me?' she gasped defensively, her cheeks aflame with heated colour as he looked down at her mockingly for her outburst. It was rather stupid to be reacting this way when the least objection to their ever seeing each other again was the fact that he was at least twelve years older than she was! There were far too many other reasons why they should never meet again.

He gave a derisive inclination of his head. 'I realise I'm too old for you,' he amended in a drily derisive voice. 'That we don't know a great deal about each other yet——'

'We don't know anything about each other,' she denied heatedly.

'We know that we could go to my apartment right now and not come out of the bedroom for a week,' he drawled confidently. 'And then it would only be because we would need to eat a little to get us through the next week!' His gaze was suddenly intense on her flushed face as she gazed up at him unprotestingly. 'I want to make love to you in every way possible,' he told her compellingly. 'In ways no one else has ever made love before.' A fire burnt deep in the depth of silver-grey, primitively savage.

Caroline swallowed hard, too weakened by his verbal lovemaking to be able to move away from him. 'And then what?' Her voice was husky.

His mouth twisted into the semblance of a smile. 'And then we start all over again!'

She shook her head at the eroticism he portrayed. 'But—but we don't know each other, don't *love* each other!'

'Love!' he scorned impatiently. 'Love is a vastly over-rated emotion that brings nothing but pain to those who suffer from it,' he dismissed abruptly. 'Do you have any idea how many people I've helped send to prison because of this so-called love?' He shook his head. 'Of course I don't love you, Caroline—— By the way that's going to be shortened to Caro whenever I want to make love to you,' he announced arrogantly.

'And I suppose you'll expect me to crawl into your bed to await your pleasure at those times?' she returned angrily. How dared he think he could just walk up to her and take over her life!

His mouth twisted. 'You overestimate my control where you're concerned, Caroline.' He deliberately emphasised the full use of her name. 'I expect us to make love wherever we happen to be at the time. It's all going to be part of the excitement. And you excite me as no other woman has,' he added intensely. 'And I can also assure you that the pleasure won't all be mine,' he finished, answering her angry taunt.

She knew that, already felt fevered with a need

she didn't want but didn't seem able to fight. But he couldn't seriously expect her to meekly leap into an affair with him.

She looked up at him searchingly, at the pulse that beat in his tightly clenched jaw, at the determination in his gaze, acknowledging the aura of power he had that told her he never said anything he didn't mean. They had only met a short time ago, Justin didn't believe in love because he had seen too many people hurt and destroy in the name of that emotion, and yet he calmly expected her to put her life in his hands. The trouble was, with his closeness seducing her like this, it would be so easy to do!

'Do you know that they call you——'

'I'm well aware of what they call me,' he bit out harshly. 'And why,' he added dismissively. 'I'm good at what I do, Caroline, and I make no apology for it. If a person breaks the law they should be punished for it.'

She swallowed hard at the cold implacability of his voice. 'Can you always be so sure they're guilty?'

'I wouldn't take the case if I weren't sure of that,' he dismissed confidently.

Caroline shivered at his calm certainty in his beliefs; she would hate to be at the receiving end of his wrath. She drew in a shaky breath. 'Tony said you're a wolf that always walks alone——'

'That isn't going to change just because we're having an affair,' he cut in firmly. 'I'm not accustomed to being answerable to anyone for my actions; I relish my privacy too much for that. We'll continue to maintain separate households during our relationship, but don't expect to spend too much time in yours,' he added drily, frowning suddenly. 'You know, I didn't want to come to this party with Paula tonight, even less so once I realised it was a family occasion, but as soon as I saw you I knew why I'd come against all my better judgment. I don't believe in love——' his mouth twisted '—but even I can't fight destiny.'

She, too, felt as if she were trying to fight something she had no power over. Justin called it destiny, but she was very much aware that this destiny could prove to be as much her destruction as her future happiness. And at the moment she wasn't sure which Justin was in her life although, knowing of the contempt with which he held love, she had a very good idea!

She pulled out of his arms. 'I was also destined to meet Tony,' she reminded him firmly. 'And I'm going to marry him.' She dared Justin to deny that.

He didn't. 'I'll take you back to him,' he drawled pleasantly, his hand light on her elbow.

Caroline trusted this calm friendliness even less than she did his blunt announcement that they were going to have an affair, eyeing him warily as they rejoined Tony and Paula, the brother and sister standing together in stony silence.

'You were gone long enough,' Tony snapped with uncharacteristic bad humour. 'I was almost desperate enough to ask Paula to dance!'

His sister gave him a disparaging look. 'Don't

delude yourself into thinking I would have accepted,' she scorned.

Hazel eyes flashed. 'I suppose you intend leaving now that you've done your duty by the parents?' he accused angrily.

Paula flushed guiltily. 'Justin and I have somewhere else to go,' she defended.

'I'm sure you do,' Tony acknowledged disgustedly.

It was obvious that Paula's intention of leaving only twenty minutes after her arrival was the reason she and Tony had been arguing all the time she and Justin were dancing. Caroline suddenly found, to her dismay, that she was as disgusted as Tony at the thought of the other couple leaving so that they could make love—but for completely different reasons.

She looked up at Justin uncertainly as he squeezed her arm reassuringly.

'Caro.'

It was the softest of murmurs, barely perceptible as he spoke close to her ear so that the other couple shouldn't hear him, and yet it was enough to reassure her that he didn't intend making love to Paula tonight, that it was her he wanted.

It was ridiculous to be pleased by the realisation, disloyal when she intended marrying Tony if he should ask her. But for that heart-stopping moment she wanted to be the one to leave with Justin, wanted to hear him murmur that shortened version of her name, that no one else had ever used before, over and over again as he made love to her.

'Why don't you stay on at the party, Paula?' Justin suggested briskly. 'I really do have to leave now.'

Paula looked alarmed as it seemed he would slip away from her. 'Oh, but——'

'I did warn you I didn't really have the time for a party tonight,' he cut in in a voice that brooked no further protest to his decision to leave, alone. 'I'll see you on Monday. Tony,' he nodded abruptly to the other man. 'Caroline,' he added lingeringly, his gaze holding her captive before he turned and strode purposefully across the room.

'Damn, damn, *damn!*' Paula muttered furiously as Justin left without a backwards glance.

'You caught yourself the wrong one this time, sister dear,' Tony taunted.

Paula answered as heatedly as Tony had known she would, but Caroline wasn't listening to their conversation, still staring across the room to where Justin had left seconds earlier. He hadn't said anything about seeing her again but she knew that he was arrogant enough to try to contact her again, that he hadn't given up.

The rest of the evening was an anti-climax for Caroline, who barely noticed that Tony and Paula seemed to argue most of the time. Considering they were two mature people, Tony thirty to Paula's thirty-five, both in exacting professions, Tony a doctor while Paula was a very competent lawyer, the two of them seemed to revert to the nursery whenever they were together like this!

Caroline felt completely drained by the time the

party drew to a close, finding it extremely difficult to behave as if that disturbing conversation with Justin de Wolfe had never taken place, and finding it even more difficult to behave as if nothing had changed between herself and Tony.

But it had changed; nothing was the same, not even her response to his goodnight kisses once they reached her flat.

'You're tired.' Tony finally drew back at her lack of enthusiasm for his caresses. 'I'll see you tomorrow after work.'

Of course she was tired; it had been a long and traumatic day on the ward. Everything would look different after a good night's sleep. Most of all that conversation with Justin de Wolfe. She firmly put from her mind the fact that tiredness had never made her unresponsive towards Tony before.

But once she was in bed the memory of Justin de Wolfe and his outrageous suggestion that they had an affair wouldn't be put from her mind any longer. He was such a fascinating man, his elusiveness where women were concerned making him more so, she admitted that. And he wanted her. He hadn't said that he loved her, or that he even liked her, but he did want her.

And she didn't for one moment believe his calm acceptance of her refusal to see him again was the end of it, also knew that a little thing like not knowing her address wouldn't stop a man like him if he were really determined to see her again. And he had seemed very determined.

She——

***

'Caroline.'

She turned to the doorway, her eyes wide, shaking slightly as she saw from the cold expression on Justin's face that he was still filled with that implacable anger.

His expression darkened as she eyed him apprehensively. 'You're tired, and it's late,' he bit out, striding purposefully across the room, standing so close to her chair that the heat of his body reached out and touched her. 'It's time we were both in bed.'

'But the things you said,' she reminded in a pained voice. 'The baby——'

'I don't think anything can be gained by discussing that any more tonight.' His gaze was cold, his mouth a taut line as he pulled her effortlessly to her feet.

'But——'

'Let's go to bed, Caroline,' he prompted impatiently. 'Perhaps things will look—different, in the morning,' he added in a hard voice.

If they went to bed together tonight, would he want to make love to her? He was furious at the idea of the child she carried, but the flame she could see in the depths of his gaze told her it hadn't changed his desire for her.

But nothing would have changed in the morning; she would still be pregnant and, from the hardness of his expression, Justin would still be denying the child was his.

She shook her head, several tendrils of fiery hair

escaping the loose upsweep on to the crown of her head. 'The baby isn't going to disappear overnight,' she told him.

'Are you refusing to share a bed with me, Caroline?' He spoke softly.

She never had, not from the beginning, unable to fight the truth of his claim at their first meeting. They always wanted each other to the point of desperation; just a look from her or the murmur of her name from Justin and the two of them would be making love. It had been that way since she first went out with him.

But they couldn't make love tonight, not with the baby's existence standing so solidly between them. She would never be able to forget that Justin had accused her of carrying Tony's child; not even the mindless pleasure she could always find in Justin's arms could make her forget that.

She heaved a ragged sigh. 'I have to, Justin,' she told him emotionally. 'We have to settle the matter of the baby before I——'

He stiffened, and suddenly Caroline had a feeling much like a person in a courtroom must do just before Justin began to cross-examine them.

'The matter is settled, Caroline,' he bit out. 'The child inside you is not mine. It is a medical impossibility for it to be so.'

'But——'

'Medically impossible, Caroline,' he repeated harshly.

'Doctors make mistakes——'

'Not this time.' His voice was a cold rasp.

'But they have to have done,' she insisted desperately. 'I was a virgin that first night we were together, you know that!' She looked up at him appealingly.

He gave an acknowledging inclination of his head. 'But you did insist on seeing Tony—alone—after that, to explain that you intended marrying me,' he reminded her calmly.

Caroline felt the colour leave her cheeks, staring at him as if she couldn't believe what he was suggesting. 'Justin, you can't think, believe——'

'What other explanation can there be for your pregnancy?' He shrugged dismissively.

'You prefer to believe I went to bed with Tony just before we were married rather than that the doctor who told you you're sterile made a mistake?' she gasped in a pained voice.

His gaze was narrowed. 'Yes.'

She sat down suddenly. 'Then you're right, discussing this any further wouldn't help at all,' she said dully, blinking back the tears.

He nodded abruptly. 'I'll sleep in the spare bedroom tonight,' he told her harshly. 'We'll have to decide tomorrow what's to be done about the baby.'

That roused her from the sea of pain she had been drowning in. 'What's to be done?' she repeated slowly, reluctantly, watching him warily.

'I don't want children, Caroline,' he stated abruptly. 'I never have.'

What did that mean? That he wanted her to leave and take the baby with her, or that he just *didn't want the baby?*

CHAPTER TWO

CAROLINE awoke with a groan, pushing the hair out of her face as she rolled over to look at the bedside clock. Nine-thirty; Justin would already have left for the day.

She sat up in the bed, staring down at her still-flat stomach, already feeling an affinity with the child that nestled inside her.

How could Justin deny that child, refuse to even acknowledge its existence other than as an unwelcome intrusion into their marriage?

When she had pressed him last night to explain exactly what he meant by his remark about 'not wanting children', he had told her he thought it would be better if they slept on it and came to a decision in the morning. She hadn't wanted to wait until then, had demanded he answer her. He had completely withdrawn from her then, leaving her standing beside the table that was still set for their celebration, and when she had desperately followed him up the stairs it was to find the spare bedroom door locked against her.

He couldn't mean for her to choose between him or their baby, could he? Even if he didn't believe it was his child, he couldn't really expect her to—no! She wouldn't even acknowledge him demanding that possibility. To her it *wasn't* a possibility.

She had to persuade him to see another doctor, knowing beyond a shadow of doubt that the child she carried was Justin's. There had been no one else for her, not before or since him. How could there have been, when he fulfilled her completely, possessed her like a drug that made her body feverish and her senses so attuned to him that the mere sight of him drove her wild with need?

Their first night together, here in this very house, she had submitted herself to a far greater power than any she possessed, had known herself lost from Justin's first caress . . .

Even Caroline hadn't been prepared for his call the night they met. She was on the point of going to bed shortly after Tony had left when the telephone began to ring. Envisaging another unexpected night on duty when one of the night-staff had let them down, she picked the receiver up with a groan.

'So you and Shepherd *don't* sleep together,' came the husky greeting.

Caroline stiffened, instantly alert, moistening suddenly dry lips. 'Justin?' she said uncertainly.

'Unless some other man questioned you tonight about your relationship with Shepherd,' he acknowledged drily.

She gave an irritated frown; she had expected to hear from him, but this! 'I don't know anyone else that arrogant,' she admitted abruptly, somehow knowing that amusement had darkened his gaze.

'How did you get my number?' she prompted waspishly.

'I telephoned Paula first and asked her,' he revealed calmly.

'You——' She gasped, closing her eyes as she imagined what the other woman had made of that, the answer not a pleasant one.

'Would you like to add "bastard" after the "arrogant"?' he mused.

'Yes!' she snapped. 'And how do you know Tony isn't waiting in the bedroom for me right now?' she demanded angrily.

'Paula was only too eager to tell me that you and her brother don't sleep together,' Justin mocked. 'I believe she imagined it would deter my interest.'

Caroline gripped the receiver tightly, ashamed of how much she hoped that hadn't happened. 'And did it?' She waited breathlessly for his answer.

'Not in the least,' he answered confidently. 'I like a woman who can be a little choosy about who she goes to bed with.'

Did he also like a woman who hadn't been to bed with anyone? she wondered a little dazedly. Really, the man had no scruples at all, telephoning her in this way!

'How do you know that choice will include you?' she snapped, annoyed at the awkward situation he had put her in with Tony and his sister.

'Are you saying it doesn't?' His voice had gone huskily soft.

She didn't even know why she was having this conversation with him! He wasn't her type at all, was too worldly, too sophisticated, too experienced when it came to women. He had known exactly how to pique her interest tonight, to keep her dangling there until he decided to draw her into his web of sensuality.

'Caro?' he prompted gruffly.

Oh, God, just the sound of her name on his lips caused a shiver of awareness down her spine!

'All right,' he chuckled softly at her dazed silence. 'I don't find making love over the telephone very satisfying either. Dinner tomorrow?'

By tacit agreement she and Tony hadn't seen anyone but each other the last eight months, and no words of a permanent relationship had been mentioned between them, yet she knew it was an accepted thing between them.

She wasn't about to jeopardise her relationship with Tony just because of a mad attraction for Justin de Wolfe!

'I'll only keep asking, Caroline.' Justin seemed to realise she was about to say no; his voice was hard. 'And if Tony told you anything about me at all you have to know I never give up when I want something as badly as I seem to want you.'

Tony hadn't exactly said that, but he had told her this man never lost, which amounted to the same thing!

'Look, Caroline, if my honesty in admitting I want to make love to you is too much for you to accept, then I'm sorry,' he said impatiently at her continued silence. 'But I stopped going out on platonic dates years ago. And if you think I make a habit of picking up women at parties you would be wrong about that, too,' he added in a hard voice. 'My libido is as strong as any other man's,' he admitted derisively, 'but I rarely have the time to indulge it. Now will you have dinner with me tomorrow night?'

She had a feeling that when this man did rouse himself enough to show a preference for a particular woman he never received a lukewarm response, let alone faced the possibility of being turned down. As he was about to be!

'I'm busy tomorrow night,' she told him dismissively.

'Caro——'

'I said no, Mr de Wolfe,' she refused firmly as the silky caress of his voice threatened to once again seduce her.

'I meant it when I said I would keep asking, Caroline,' he warned grimly. 'I can't take no for an answer from you.'

Her hand shook as she slowly replaced the receiver, half expecting him to ring straight back, but realising when he didn't do so that he was wise enough to know that would just make her even angrier.

When she met Tony the next night she knew Paula had lost no time in telling her brother of Justin's interest. It didn't seem to matter to Tony that she had refused to see the other man. He was furious that Justin de Wolfe had asked her out at all, seemed to think she must have encouraged the

other man in some way—Justin de Wolfe,
reputedly not a man to exert himself for any
woman.

But he seemed determined to do so for her,
turning up at the most unexpected times during the
next three weeks, meeting her as she came off duty,
calling around at the flat, and always with the
purpose of repeating his dinner invitation.

Much as she hated to admit it, this show of
attention from a man who rarely bothered with
women at all began to affect her, and in a strange
way she began to look forward to seeing him, the
sexual tension between them building each time she
did so. Ultimately it affected her relationship with
Tony; she was no longer at ease in his company as
he seemed to regard her suspiciously. Finally he
lost his temper completely and told her he thought
they should stop seeing each other, that she should
go out with Justin de Wolfe and see how fascinating she found him when he left her after a few
dates!

She hadn't thought Tony could mean what he
had said, expecting him to come round and
apologise, but after three days of waiting she
realised he had meant every word. Her hurt turned
to anger, and the next time Justin asked her out she
accepted.

When she opened the door to him at seven-thirty
that evening she knew she had made a mistake.
Tonight even the veneer of civilisation had been
stripped from him, the black evening suit and
snowy white shirt doing nothing to disguise his

primitive savagery. Any idea she might have had about just being another conquest to him was wiped out as she met the blazing desire in his gaze; Justin was a man who usually held himself in cool control, and he no more welcomed this feeling of helplessness to desire than she did. He just knew it was useless to fight the inevitable.

Being taken into his arms was inevitable, too. Her throat arched as Justin's mouth came down firmly on hers, both of them exploding with a need that had barely been held in check since the moment their gazes first met.

She could taste him, feel him along every nerve-ending in her body, knew that Justin's veneer of sophistication had slipped because he was just as unnerved by this desire.

He kissed her deeply, hotly, his hands moving over her body with fevered insistence, cupping one pert breast to caress the pulsing nub with fiery rhythm.

Her hands were tangled in the dark thickness of his hair as she clung to him, her body on fire, knowing that if he hadn't held her so tightly she would have fallen to the carpeted floor.

Finally he drew back with a ragged sigh, resting his forehead on hers. 'Hello,' he greeted her belatedly.

She gave a shaky laugh, her hands still clinging to his broad shoulders. 'I dread to think what you could do with "Hello, darling"!'

He shook his head to clear it of the sexual haze. 'I have no doubt we'll find out,' he said gruffly.

'Are you ready to go?'

The question held much more than its surface significance, at least, for her, but one look into his arrogantly assured face when he arrived and she had known she was more than ready, that she had probably been waiting for tonight all her life. Her relief that she had waited, and not fallen into that trap a lot of her friends had by sleeping with men they were merely fond of, was immense. She knew with certainty that somehow during the last three weeks—probably instantly she saw him—she had fallen in love with this enigmatic man, that she had been fighting a losing battle.

'I'm ready,' she nodded, smiling shyly, knowing her mouth had to be bare of lipgloss by now, and not really caring. Justin was looking at her as if he would like to eat her, and her mouth felt swollen and red enough without the aid of artifice.

Later they were alone in his apartment, although Caroline doubted he had actually cooked the delicious meal they served up together. No doubt he had someone that came in to cook and clean for him, her presence unobtrusive in the extreme; Justin didn't give the impression of a man who hurried home at the end of the day to spend time cooking.

The food was deliciously prepared and cooked, smelt wonderful, too, and yet neither of them did justice to it. Caroline couldn't keep her eyes off Justin for more than a few seconds at a time, her anticipation high, and he seemed to be lost in brooding silence as he absently pushed the food around on his plate.

'I can't wait any longer!' He suddenly threw his fork down, pushing his plate away to stand up. 'Caro, I *need* to make love to you. Very badly.'

She could see just how badly by the fevered glitter of his gaze, his hands clenched at his sides. And if she were honest—and that seemed to be what Justin demanded of her—she couldn't wait any longer, either.

She stood up, too, her legs a little shaky, and then they were in each others arms, and it was just as if there had been no break from their earlier impassioned kisses, Justin's mouth wide and moist against hers, his tongue moving into her fiercely at the same time as he pulled her thighs high against him.

He was hard and pulsating against her, groaning low in his throat at the satiny feel of her thighs, his kisses becoming even fiercer, devouring, filled with hunger as he began to pull off her clothes.

Caroline felt a shiver as the cool air caressed her body as her gown fell at her feet, the feel of Justin's dinner jacket abrasive against her naked breasts, rubbing against the tips, filling her lower body with a warm ache that flamed moistly as Justin touched her there.

He suckled on her breast, drawing it hungrily into his mouth, the pleasure-pain causing her to whimper low in her throat, breathing shakily, her back arched as she pushed herself against him.

He drew just as fiercely on the other nipple while his hand cupped and caressed the breast he had abandoned, holding her up against him as if she weighed nothing at all.

She couldn't stand it any more, needing more, needing it all, pushing frantically at his jacket, their mouths fused together as Justin helped her with the removal of his clothes, sinking down on to the floor with her, lying between her parted thighs as he moved restlessly against her.

She cradled either side of his face as their kisses went on and on, moist and hungry, fevered, Caroline arching against him as he continued to caress her aching breasts.

His legs felt abrasive against her as he moved above her, increasing her passion, the ache between her thighs becoming almost a pain.

And then he came into her, slowly, not forcefully, easing her sudden tension, gently penetrating the barrier that parted and finally moved aside altogether. There should have been pain, but there wasn't, only an unfamiliar feeling of fullness, a slight discomfort that made her muscles contract at the intrusion.

And then Justin began to move within her, gently stroking her, the heat instantly returning, consuming, until her breath was coming in strangled gasps, her head thrashing from side to side as she knew she was about to shatter, to be devoured by the burning ache that filled her whole body now.

Suddenly her back arched, her thighs thrust fiercely against Justin, her eyes wide with wonder on Justin's face as the pleasure exploded, imploding in a million different places in her body.

Justin continued to thrust against her, and as one wave of pleasure ended another began, until she felt it would never stop, awestruck as she watched the savage beauty of Justin's face as he grimaced as though in pain, groaning loudly, suddenly even more fierce against her, driving her over the edge again as she felt his own fevered release.

He gently lowered his weight against her, burying his face in her perfumed hair, his breath deep and rasping. 'It was more,' he finally groaned, 'so much more than I even imagined!'

She could never have imagined anything as devastatingly shattering as the passion they had just shared. She didn't need to be experienced to know that it had been something special. She hadn't known whether she would be able to feel pleasure at all the first time they made love, but it had been never-ending, and even now she wanted him again. As she felt him stir against her she knew that it was what he wanted, to.

He looked down at her questioningly as his passion rekindled. 'Are you all right?' His voice was husky.

A delicate blush darkened her cheeks. 'I don't hurt at all,' she assured him softly, finding her shyness utterly ridiculous considering the intimacy of their positions.

He frowned. 'You'll probably be a little sore tomorrow,' he warned sympathetically. 'But as long as you feel OK now?' Still he hesitated about repeating that fiery splendour.

'I feel fine,' she said gruffly. 'I feel better than fine,' she added determinedly. 'And I want you again, too.'

He smiled his satisfaction with her answer, and it made him look more rakish than ever, his hair tousled, the eye-patch giving him a devilish look.

She tentatively touched his cheek near the black patch. 'What happened?' She frowned her concern.

'A dissatisfied client,' he dismissed shruggingly, bending to move his lips against her throat.

Her frown deepened, even though his lips sent a delicious thrill down the length of her spine. 'I thought you always won?'

'Not *my* dissatisfied client,' Justin gently mocked. 'I made sure he was put away.'

Her fingers stilled against his cheek. 'But if he was put in prison . . .'

'They all get out eventually,' Justin explained tautly. 'I do my job, Caroline,' he added softly as she shivered in reaction. 'This man just happened to believe there was something personal in my prosecution of him. When he got out of prison he paid me a little visit.' He frowned.

She was still trembling. 'Where is he now?'

Justin's mouth twisted. 'Back in prison, for attacking me this time.' He shrugged dismissively. 'It really isn't important.'

'But he—he blinded you in one eye!' she gasped.

He nodded. 'And it isn't a pretty sight. But then

knife wounds never are,' he murmured almost to himself. 'But let's not talk about that now, Caroline.' His gaze moved over her hungrily. 'I want to make love to you again. And this time we might even make it as far as the bedroom,' he added self-derisively.

Caroline blushed as she looked around them and realised they were still in the dining-room.

Justin's mouth quirked. 'Don't look so embarrassed, Caro,' he teased throatily. 'At least it wasn't *on* the table!'

He carried her through to his bedroom, beginning to make love to her again, more slowly this time as neither of them were so feveredly desperate, but it was just as intense, just as shattering, the two of them lying damply together as their hands still moved caressingly over each other, unable to stop the touching.

As the night passed swiftly by, Justin was indefatigable, making love to her again and again, groaning his protest when she had to leave him in the morning to go to work.

He watched her as she dressed in the gown that seemed so out of place in the brightness of the sunny Sunday morning. After the intimacies they had shared it was a little ridiculous to feel shy in front of him, but the way he watched her so steadily unnerved her, and she heaved a silent sigh of relief as she zipped up the back of her gown.

'Can you be available on Thursday?' He sat back against the coffee-coloured pillows, his chest bare as the matching sheet lay draped across his thighs. He was so completely male, his body all hard muscle, and he knew how to use that body to the satisfaction of both of them. 'If not next Thursday——' he frowned at her silence '—it will have to wait a couple of weeks; I'm going to be very busy until then.'

Caroline suddenly realised what he had said, shaking her head to clear it of the sensual spell this man seemed to exert over her without even trying.

What did he mean, could she be available next Thursday, if not it would have to wait a couple of weeks? She knew she had behaved like a wanton the night before, but she had thought the passion more than returned; she didn't expect him to try and fit her in among all of his other social engagements now that he had taken what he seemed to want!

Her face paled as she realised what a fool she had been to imagine that what was between them was special. How many other women had told themselves the same thing, only to realise that what was love on their side was merely lust on the side of the man?

She was twenty-three years old and had received more than her fair share of sexual proposals over the years, mainly from medical students who believed a nurse was fair game, but she had behaved like a fool last night, had become totally infatuated with a man who saw taking a woman to bed as no more than another conquest he had to make.

A sob caught in her throat as she turned away to search for her shoes where she had placed them on the floor, tears blinding her. She stiffened as she felt Justin's nakedness behind her as he pulled her back against him.

'Don't you want to marry me?' His voice was silkily soft against her ear.

Marry? She turned slowly to face him, her eyes wide, searching the derisive amusement of his face. His derision seemed to be self-directed, as if he, too, found the prospect of marriage surprising, even if he were resigned to it.

'Destiny played a dirty trick on me three weeks ago,' he drawled ruefully. 'The moment I saw you I wanted you,' he told her calmly. 'And after only one night with you I know that no other woman has ever matched me in passion the way you do.'

She blinked, still dazed that he had meant he wanted to *marry* her next Thursday. 'You want to marry me because—because we make love well together?' she said disbelievingly, the tender ache in her body reminding her of the night that had just passed, of just how well they made love.

'Not the sort of marriage proposal you were ever expecting to hear, was it?' he mocked, cupping her chin to caress her cheek lightly with the pad of his thumb. 'But it isn't just how well your body fits to mine,' he said ruefully. 'It's because I know, realised as I waited for you the last three weeks, that I don't ever want any other man to have you. Even less so now.' His smile was gentle at her self-conscious blush at his reference to her virginity. 'No, I'm not in love with you,' he seemed to read the uncertain question in her eyes, 'I've already told you my opinion of that emotion,' he scorned. 'But I do know this wanting isn't going to go away in a hurry, that it probably never will, and that I want my claim on you to be a public one. Is that going to be enough for you?' He looked down at her steadily, his gaze narrowed to a silver slit.

Because she was too much in love with him to say no, it had to be enough.

They had been married four days later, Justin having no family of his own to invite, only her parents, her brother and sister—Simon and Sonia—and a couple of her friends in attendance. Until he met her Justin really had been a wolf that preferred to walk completely alone.

Almost seven weeks of marriage hadn't seen too many changes in her husband. When they made love they were completely attuned, but the rest of the time Justin chose to hold himself aloof, rarely talking about his work to her, only agreeing to socialise with her family because he knew she expected it of him.

And now he seemed to think she had conducted some sort of experiment with Tony in between his proposal and their wedding, to see if she and Justin really were so unique in their passion for each other, and that the baby she carried was the result of that experiment. She hadn't needed to make love with another man to be sure of that!

The baby she carried was Justin's, no matter what he believed about his being sterile. My God, why hadn't he told her he believed he could never give her children? It wouldn't have changed her decision to marry him, but he should have told her, damn it! What sort of man married a woman without telling her something as important as that? A man like Justin, she acknowledged dully. He didn't want children; why should he bother to explain that he could never give her any?

Dear God, where did they go from here? What were they going to 'decide' about the baby today?

She sat up straight against the pillows as a soft knock sounded on the door, and forced a tight smile to her lips as Mrs Avery put her head around the door, before entering with a bright smile as she saw Caroline was awake.

'Mr de Wolfe told me to let you sleep this morning.' She put a tray of coffee down on the bedside table. 'But I thought I heard you moving around a few minutes ago.'

Justin's 'unobtrusive' housekeeper had turned out to be this friendly little woman with warm blue eyes. She had confided in Caroline shortly after she moved in as Justin's wife that the Mrs part of her name was merely a cursory title, that she had never married but felt it was necessary to be a Mrs in the job she chose to do. Mrs Avery was almost sixty, and Caroline sincerely doubted that Justin would ever feel the inclination to chase her around the apartment, but if the other woman felt happier being thought a married woman then she wasn't about to spoil that for her. The two of them had become firm friends over the weeks, Mrs Avery treating Caroline just like the daughter she had never had. She had no doubt the housekeeper was going to be thrilled when she was told about the baby. But she dared not tell anyone about that yet, not until she had sorted things out with Justin. He had to be convinced that the baby was his!

'I have to be on duty in just over an hour.' She accepted the coffee gratefully.

Justin had been very amenable about her continuing with her career, although she had cut down on her hours slightly, knowing Justin wouldn't appreciate her working late into the evening or during the night. She couldn't help wondering now, a little bitterly, if he hadn't encouraged her to continue with her career because he had known she would never have children to occupy her time. Children of his, that was.

Bitter reproach on her part wasn't going to help this situation, she inwardly reproved. She had to try and look at this from Justin's point of view. For years he had believed himself sterile, had probably come to terms with that fact; of course he was going to find it difficult to believe now that she was carrying his child. Perhaps the hours he had spent alone in bed last night, the first time they had slept apart since their marriage, had given him a chance to think, to realise that a mistake just could have been made.

Yes, she was sure that by the time he got home this evening he would have realised she could never have made love with any other man but him, that the child had to be his. His decision that he didn't want children had probably been a defence mechanism because he didn't believe he could ever have any. By the time he got home this evening they would be able to discuss all this rationally.

Some of the despair left her as she went to work on that happier note, putting her troubles from her mind as for the rest of the day she concentrated on her patients.

She was going to miss her work on the wards once she had the baby. Being a nurse had been the only thing she had ever wanted to do, all her educational qualifications gained for just that reason. It had been a wonderful five years, but no doubt the baby would help compensate for what she lost. She wanted this baby so much, wanted to give Justin the son he had thought never to have.

He wasn't home when she got in, so she went through to have a soak in the bath before dinner, frowning her puzzlement when she returned to the bedroom an hour later to discover he still wasn't home.

He wasn't usually this late home. Unless——

She hurried out to the kitchen; Mrs Avery was just in the process of putting the finishing touches to dinner—for one. Whenever Justin was going to be late, or not going to make dinner at all, she had requested that the housekeeper serve her dinner on a tray rather than going to all the trouble to lay the table formally; Justin wasn't coming home for dinner tonight!

She moistened her suddenly dry lips as the housekeeper looked up at her curiously. Justin hadn't called her at work today as he usually did when he was going to be late or miss dinner, but it was obvious that he had let Mrs Avery know of his plans. How to find out what those plans were without making an absolute fool of herself!

She forced a tight smile to her lips. 'It's as well Justin isn't in for dinner tonight as we have steak pie,' she remarked lightly.

Mrs Avery smiled mischievously. 'Not one of his favourites, is it?' she acknowledged. 'But I know how you enjoy it, so as soon as Mr de Wolfe telephoned me this morning to say he would be away for a few days I decided to prepare all your favourite meals to cheer you up. No wonder you were looking a bit peaky this morning when I brought in your coffee. Such a pity he had to go away so soon after you were married. But I——'

Caroline was no longer listening as the woman chattered on. Justin had gone away for a few days. Was that the decision he had come to during the long night hours they had been apart, separated by the thickness of a wall? Were those 'few days' going to turn into a week, and then a month? Did he ever intend coming back?

CHAPTER THREE

CAROLINE still felt numb the next day, didn't know whether Justin expected her to leave during his absence or wait until he returned and told her to go.

Justin might have married her for all the wrong reasons, but she loved him very much, had hoped the desire he felt for her would eventually turn into love, too. The fact that he had gone away, without even bothering to call and tell her, seemed to say that he could never accept the child she carried as his, that he no longer wanted her because of it.

But if that were the way he felt, he was going to have to tell her that to her face, was actually going to have to tell her to leave. She didn't doubt that he was capable of it; she had realised as she lay awake for the second night in a row that she was no closer to him emotionally than she had been six weeks ago. She had come to know him, however, and if he still stubbornly believed her to be carrying another man's child, Tony's child, he wouldn't hesitate to end their marriage. Like someone expecting the axe to fall, she waited.

The last thing she needed later that morning was a visit from a friend of Justin's she had never met before and whom he had never mentioned.

In his mid-thirties, the same as Justin, Don Lindford seemed nice enough, but, with Caroline so worried about her relationship with Justin, he couldn't have called at a worse time!

He shook her hand politely. He was a couple of inches under six feet, good-looking in a pleasant sort of way, with his sandy-brown hair brushed neatly to one side, and warm brown eyes.

'I was sorry I missed the wedding,' he smiled. 'I was away at the time and couldn't make it.'

'That's all right.' She indicated he should sit down. 'I'm afraid Justin hasn't spoken of you,' she admitted awkwardly as they sat across from each other.

He chuckled softly. 'That sounds like old Justin,' he mused. 'We go back a long way, but Justin more than lives up to his reputation of being a lone wolf.'

'Yes,' she acknowledged dully, wondering if that was what Justin was considering going back to. It was a certainty he didn't think this 'cub' was his!

'I have to admit to being surprised when I heard he had married,' Don Lindford said ruefully. 'Although since I've met his bride for myself, perhaps it was understandable,' he added warmly.

'Only perhaps?' she teased, starting to relax in his company. Justin never had spoken about any of his friends, but she had known he must have made some over the years; this man came as a pleasant surprise. Somehow she had been expecting any friend of Justin's to be as arrogantly aloof as he usually was.

'Definitely understandable,' he grinned conspiratorially. 'Your housekeeper said she isn't expecting Justin back today?' He frowned.

Caroline drew in a ragged breath. 'No.'

He pulled a face. 'He's taking a chance leaving you alone so soon after the wedding. If it had been me I would have taken you with me on my business trip.'

She smiled her gratitude at the compliment, giving a rueful grimace. 'There are some occasions when a wife would just be in the way,' she excused evasively.

'Hm,' Don Lindford acknowledged thoughtfully. 'Oh, well.' He stood up. 'I won't keep you any longer. I just thought I'd drop in and say hello to Justin's bride once I learnt he wasn't available. It's been nice meeting you.'

'Caroline,' she encouraged, also standing up. 'Could I offer you a cup of tea or—or anything?' she said awkwardly.

'No, thanks,' he refused warmly. 'If you could just tell Justin I called, and that I'll be in touch again soon?'

'Of course.' She walked him to the door. 'I really am sorry he wasn't here, I'm sure the two of you have a lot to talk about as you haven't seen each other for some time.'

'Yes,' he nodded. 'Once again, it's been nice to have met you, Caroline.'

She closed the door once he had left, turning with a thoughtful smile. She had been beginning to wonder if Justin had any friends after six weeks and not a mention of one; Don Lindford wasn't half as awesome as she had imagined friends of Justin would be. She would have to get Justin to invite him over for dinner sometime.

If she was still here. Well, she wasn't leaving without a fight; of that she was certain.

It seemed to be her day for unexpected visitors, her sister Sonia calling that afternoon.

Caroline had spent most of the afternoon pretending an interest in the book she was currently reading, knowing that if she looked too forlorn Mrs Avery would only offer her sympathy, and that was the last thing she needed, feeling particularly tearful today. She was well aware of the fact that her emotionalism was due to her pregnancy, but that didn't make it any easier to cope with. And the last thing she wanted today of all days was a confrontation with her sister.

She stood up stiffly as her sister was shown into the room by Mrs Avery.

Three and a half years her junior, Sonia was nevertheless possessed of a self-confidence that precluded her feeling uncomfortable no matter what the circumstances. And despite the awkwardness between the two sisters the last month, Sonia crossed the lounge to kiss Caroline warmly on the cheek.

'I called the hospital and they told me it was one of your days off,' Sonia explained dismissively. 'You're looking very beautiful,' she complimented easily. 'Married life is just wonderful, isn't it?' Her own eyes sparkled with happiness as she sat down without being invited to do so, a tall, blue-eyed blonde who moved with all the natural grace and beauty that had made her such a highly successful model the last two years.

No one looking at the two of them would ever believe they were related, but then that wasn't surprising; Caroline was an adopted child who had been almost four when her 'mother' suddenly produced twins, a boy and a girl. No one could have been more surprised than her parents at this startling event, having been told years earlier they would never have children of their own. But the appearance of Simon and Sonia had proved them wrong, and with Sonia and Simon's charming effervescence it was impossible not to love them.

It seemed ironic that what had happened to Caroline's parents twenty years ago was now happening to her and Justin—only, unlike them, Justin refused to believe a miracle had happened.

Caroline gave a grimace at the way her sister attacked the awkwardness between them with her usual bluntness. 'How is Tony?' she asked drily.

'Doing very well considering I'm not the world's best housewife.' Sonia gave a grin as Caroline smiled acknowledgement of her lack of talent in the home. 'I would have fared much better married to someone rich like your Justin.' She shrugged light-heartedly. 'But even if I do say so myself I'm doing OK as a doctor's wife.'

It had come as a shock when, two weeks after her own wedding to Justin, Sonia and Tony had gone off together and quietly got married. Sonia had admitted later to being attracted to Tony from the first, although not for anything would she have poached on Caroline's boyfriend. But as soon as Caroline had shown that she was in love with Justin, Sonia had felt free to pursue Tony, and she had chased him mercilessly once she knew Caroline no longer wanted him. From the haste with which he had married her sister he hadn't needed much chasing! After all the bitterness he had shown towards Caroline in the weeks before they had broken up, she couldn't help feeling resentful towards him for the abrupt way *his* affections had changed.

It hadn't been an easy situation the last month, with Tony still obviously angry about the way she had married Justin so suddenly, and Caroline slightly disgusted with the haste in which he had married Sonia, so the two couples had been avoiding each other. It had been a very awkward situation for their parents, doubly so as they had always been a close family before this. From the determined glint in Sonia's eyes she had come here to try and make it like that again.

But it wasn't Caroline she should be speaking to. Tony being the one to do most of the avoiding, still very angry about a love that she hadn't been able to do anything about.

Perhaps she had been a little angry with Sonia, too, for the way in which she had run after Tony, but considering the state of her marriage to Justin that anger now seemed petty and unimportant. What did it matter that Sonia had married Tony when she could be about to lose Justin?

'I'm glad.' She gave a strained smile.

Sonia gave her a considering look. 'Are you? I got the impression a month ago that you would be pleased to see me fall flat on my face.'

Caroline frowned at this uncharacteristic attack by her sunny-natured sister.

'Forget I said that,' Sonia dismissed self-disgustedly. 'I can't believe I did say that.' She grimaced, her lovely face smooth and creamy. 'I came here to invite you and Justin over to dinner tomorrow night.' She arched questioning brows.

Caroline was still frowning over her sister's accusation. There had always been rivalry between the two of them, but she had always thought that was natural between two sisters. She certainly hadn't wished for the downfall of Sonia's marriage to Tony, no matter how stunned she had been by it at the time.

'Caroline?' Sonia prompted at her silence, uncertainty clouding the usually laughing blue eyes.

She focused on her sister with effort. 'What does Tony say about that?'

'It was his idea,' Sonia announced happily. 'I think I must have passed the wife-test and so he's now ready to forget all the—unpleasantness of the past.'

'Sonia, are you really happy with Tony?' she probed worriedly.

'Oh, yes,' her sister answered without hesitation. 'Of course, he was still in love with you when we got married—he was, Caroline,' she insisted at her pained gasp. 'But all that's changed now,' she said confidently. 'I wouldn't be making this invitation if it hadn't,' she admitted bluntly.

Sonia had to be wrong about Tony's feelings a month ago. Oh, he had been angry about her decision to marry Justin, had accused her of wanting the other man for his wealth, had hauled any number of other bitter assaults on her during their last conversation, most of them concerning Justin's feelings for *her*. He certainly hadn't been in love with her then, if he ever had been; only his pride had been hurt.

'Do say you'll come, Caroline,' Sonia prompted at her silence. 'Mummy and Daddy would be so pleased if we all patched up our differences.'

Caroline's expression softened as she thought of the two people she had always known as her parents, knowing they had continued to love her as their own even after Sonia and Simon were born. The mend in the rift between their two daughters would please them, she knew. But she was still troubled by what Sonia had said about Tony's feelings for her.

'Sonia, you're wrong about Tony and me,' she frowned. 'We had already finished before Justin and I went out together.'

Her sister nodded. 'Tony told me all about that. For a while he was convinved that if he hadn't lost his temper over what he thought was going on between you and Justin, you would never have gone out with him and then married him. But that isn't true, is it?' Sonia shrugged.

No, it wasn't true. Eventually, she knew she would have gone to Justin anyway, without Tony finishing with her. Looking back on that time now, she was surprised she had managed to hold out the three weeks that she had!

'Tony realises that now?' she said anxiously.

'I think his pride was hurt more than anything,' her sister nodded. 'But he wants to make amends now, told me to invite you and Justin over for dinner.'

Her mouth twisted. 'Sure he doesn't just want to gloat about the success he's made of his marriage?'

'Maybe a little,' Sonia conceded, mischief lighting her eyes. 'But as you and Justin are so happy together, too, it doesn't really matter, does it?'

Caroline's humour left her as abruptly as it had appeared, a shadow darkening her eyes. She wasn't even sure she had a marriage any more.

Sonia was instantly attuned to her unhappiness. 'Everything is all right between you and Justin, isn't it?' She frowned her concern.

A lot of women, in the same circumstances, might worry that she would try to play upon Tony's past affection for her if her marriage was shaky, but Sonia wasn't like that, genuinely concerned for Caroline's happiness.

'Fine,' Caroline evaded; she wasn't ready yet to talk to anyone about the strain that existed between her and Justin. 'I'll have to talk to him first before making any arrangements to come over for dinner,' she thankfully excused. 'But I doubt we can make it tomorrow; Justin is away at the moment, you see.'

'I didn't realise,' Sonia said slowly.

'It's just a business trip,' she dismissed lightly. 'But we'll make arrangements for coming over to dinner as soon as he gets back,' she promised, willing her sister to leave now that she had said what she came here to say. Much more of Sonia's sympathetic looks and she would be crying all over her sister's silky dress!

'If you're going to be on your own this evening, why don't you come to us, anyway?' Sonia suggested eagerly. 'I'm sure it can't be any fun eating alone.'

She could just guess what interpretation Justin would put on her going to Sonia and Tony's for dinner! 'I'm really not sure when Justin is going to get back, and I'd like to be here when he does,' she refused with an apologetic smile.

'OK.' Sonia stood up to leave. 'But remember, you owe me.' Her eyes twinkled mischievously.

Caroline gave a start of surprise. 'I do?'

Sonia grinned, a perfectly natural smile that was nothing like the poses she affected in front of a camera. 'Paula hasn't exactly welcomed me as a member of the family, as my sister stole Justin right from under her nose. At least, I think it was her nose,' she added derisively.

Caroline couldn't help smiling at her sister's mischievous humour. 'She'll get over it,' she predicted with a relaxed smile, walking out with her sister to the door.

Sonia arched dark blonde brows. 'I don't know too many women that would "get over" a man like Justin!'

Caroline's smile remained fixed on her lips as she said goodbye to her sister, but her cheeks actually hurt from the strain of it by the time she returned to the lounge alone. Sonia was right; not many women would get over wanting someone like Justin. *She* would certainly never stop loving him!

She was in her room showering before dinner when she heard the apartment door opened, followed by Mrs Avery's surprised greeting, her pleasure obvious.

Justin. He had come home after all.

Her hands shook as she fastened the belt of her robe about her slim waist, putting up a self-conscious hand to her damp hair, its thick vibrancy drying in disordered waves. She had been going to blow-dry it into style as she usually did, but right now talking to Justin was of paramount importance. What did it matter that he would see her hair in its naturally wayward state for the first time? She doubted he would be much interested in her appearance anyway.

She faced him with wide eyes as the bedroom door opened seconds later and he stepped inside. He was dressed as he usually was for a day at work, his charcoal-grey suit perfectly tailored, his shirt pristine white, a silver-grey tie knotted at his throat. Had he been at work today after all?

'Caroline.' He nodded abruptly, putting his

briefcase down beside the bedroom chair, straightening his cuff as he turned to face her. 'Why do you look so pensive?' he regarded her coldly. 'Do you imagine I've returned home to beat you?'

She swallowed hard, hating it when he took on the guise of the successful lawyer he was. The man she loved was the fiercely gentle, always considerate lover that she had known in her bed every night since they had married—except for the last two nights.

She breathed raggedly. 'Have you?'

His mouth twisted as he loosened his tie, throwing off his jacket to place it over the back of the chair, an unusual thing for this usually fastidiously tidy man to do. 'Do I have reason to?' He arched dark brows.

'No,' she answered him unhesitantly.

He sat down in the chair, leaning back against his jacket, his eyes closed, seeming to forget her existence for the moment.

Caroline took the opportunity to look at him, to really look at him. He looked strained, lines of tiredness beside his eyes, his face paler than it usually was. In that moment he looked all of his thirty-six years, and Caroline longed to go to him, to kneel at his feet as she soothed the tension from his face. But there had been too much bitterness between them the last few days for her to be sure of her welcome, and she would break down completely if he rejected her.

Finally he roused himself, one hand moving to

the back of his nape to ease the pressure there, his gaze dark and disturbed as he looked at her across the width of the room.

Caroline was able to see the pain in his gaze then, the deep and utter despair that was so unlike the confident man she was used to.

'No,' he confirmed grimly.

She gave a puzzled frown, looking at him searchingly. 'No what?' she finally prompted in a voice husky with emotion.

He sighed. 'No, I have no reason to beat you.'

She didn't understand, puzzlement grooving a frown between her eyes. 'You aren't—angry, about the baby any more?' she questioned hesitantly.

He stood up so suddenly that she took a step backwards, receiving a mocking grimace at the involuntary movement. 'What's the use of being angry about the baby?' he dismissed harshly. 'It's a fact, isn't it?'

Her head went back in challenge. 'Yes.'

He nodded. 'That's what I thought,' he drawled uninterestedly. 'You—what have you done to your hair?' he frowned suddenly.

She put up a hand to the unruly swathe. 'I haven't had time to—to style it yet. Justin——'

'I like it.' He watched her, completely still, although restless energy permeated from him. 'It makes you look like a——Hell!' He swore viciously to himself. 'It's because I want you every damned time I look at you that we're in this mess in the first place, and as soon as I get home all I can think about is lying you back on that bed and feeling you shudder against me!' He shook his head disgustedly, striding to the door to wrench it open. 'Get some clothes on,' he instructed coldly. 'I'll be waiting in the lounge for you so that we can finish this conversation.'

Caroline couldn't move for long minutes after he had left, a small bud of hope pushing itself steadily forward. Did his words mean that he accepted the baby as his after all?

God, it was only a slight hope, but it galvanised her into action. Quickly pulling clothes from the cupboard to dress, the fawn loose-knit top she wore a perfect colour match for her tailored trousers, she left her hair as it was, not wanting to waste the time on it just now.

Justin stood at the lounge window looking out over London, dropping the curtain back in place to turn and face her as he heard her entrance. He had his thoughts and emotions completely back under control now, his expression one of aloofness.

Caroline could only sigh for the passing of his earlier lapse, knowing she couldn't hope to do more than maintain her dignity when Justin became this cold stranger.

She regarded him warily. 'Where were you last night?'

He shrugged. 'At a hotel,' he dismissed curtly. 'It wouldn't have been a good idea for me to come back here then,' he explained heavily.

Her lids lowered to hide the tears that suddenly blurred her vision. 'At least you have come back,' she said shakily.

'Yes,' he acknowledged derisively, 'but then this happens to be my apartment,' he reminded drily.

She looked at him accusingly. 'Our apartment,' she corrected firmly. 'If you're asking me to leave I would advise you to do it in a less subtle way than that,' she added in a hard voice. 'Because whether you believe it or not the child I'm carrying is yours. And I'll be damned——'

'I know,' he said quietly.

'—if I'll let you just——' Her voice trailed off weakly, and she stared at Justin with widely disbelieving eyes. She swallowed hard, so tense she felt as if she might snap in half. 'Did you just say—did you——'

'The child inside you is mine,' he confirmed flatly, his expression grim. 'Yesterday I returned to my doctor so that he could carry out tests to see if it were possible. Today,' he bit out harshly. 'he told me that the operation I had several years ago had somehow reversed itself, that I'm more than capable of fathering a child.' His mouth was tight with anger, boding ill for the doctor that had imparted this news to him.

Caroline's joyous relief at Justin's admission to being the father of her baby was quickly superseded by what he had said after that. She shook her head uncomprehendingly. 'I—operation?' she repeated dazedly. 'You don't mean a—a——'

'A vasectomy,' he supplied coldly, nodding abruptly. 'That's exactly what I do mean, Caroline,' he said impatiently.

Stunned disbelief was too mild a description of her emotions at that moment; she felt as if the breath had been completely knocked from her body, as if someone had dealt her a severely debilitating blow. Coloured spots of light danced before her eyes, and for a moment she felt as if she might faint.

'But—but *why?*' she cried when she at last found the strength to speak.

'Surely that's obvious?' Justin drawled.

'Not to me!' she groaned, her arms cradled about her stomach where their child nestled so innocently.

He gave an impatient sigh. 'I've already told you, I don't want children. The operation was supposed to ensure that I never had any,' he added with grating anger.

But what of the child she now carried?

CHAPTER FOUR

JUSTIN'S mouth twisted as he seemed to read the horrified question in her eyes. 'Yes,' he drawled, 'your pregnancy does seem to be rather a problem, doesn't it?'

The numbness fell away to be replaced by searing pain; Caroline knew without needing to be told that Justin still rejected their child. He was an aloof man, yes, often arrogant, but he could be kind, and he was always completely unselfish when they made love; what had made him dislike children so much that he had taken the drastic step of a vasectomy to ensure that he never had any? She knew that his own childhood had been happy, that he still deeply missed his mother who had died four years ago and his father who had followed her six months later, so it couldn't possibly be for that reason that he had decided never to have a family of his own.

She looked at him as if seeing him for the first time; she had never before known a person who simply disliked children, especially to the extreme Justin had gone to to avoid having any of his own.

He returned her gaze steadily for several seconds, and then pain clouded his gaze and he turned away. In that moment he looked completely vulnerable, as if a wound had opened up inside him and he didn't known how to stop the bleeding.

There was more, so much more to his decision not to have children than he was prepared to tell her, and she wanted so badly to know what it was, to be able to help him. But already his expression had become closed, as if he regretted even that tiny lapse in his guard.

'You want to have the baby, of course,' he bit out uninterestedly.

She stiffened. 'Of course.'

He nodded, as if he had never doubted what her answer would be. 'Then it would seem——'

'Justin, I don't want a divorce,' she cried, crossing the room to look up at him pleadingly. 'We don't talk about our feelings for each other, just seem to accept what we have——' her voice broke emotionally '—but I love you, Justin,' she told him raggedly. 'And I love your child that I carry inside me. Don't ask me to choose between the two of you!' She clasped his hands in entreaty, her eyes awash with tears.

He made no effort to return the clasp of her hands, but the didn't pull away from her either, his gaze dark as he looked down at her. 'I wouldn't do that,' he finally answered her gruffly. 'I don't think any woman's love should ever be tested to the extreme where she has to choose between her husband or her child. Besides,' he added self-derisively, 'I know I would lose.'

Her eyes clouded blue-grey. He was right; she would do anything he asked of her—except give up her child. Her hands dropped away from his, her cheeks ashen as she turned away. 'Do you want me to leave now, or—or will the morning do?'

'I don't want you to go at all.'

She spun around to face him, frowning heavily. And then she sighed. Of course he didn't want her to go, but they both knew she had to.

Her mouth twisted sadly. 'I hope I haven't disrupted your life too much the last few weeks. I tried not to——'

'Caroline, I said I don't want you to go,' he pointed out harshly.

'Yes, but——' She shook her head dazedly at his determined expression. 'What about the baby?' she reminded him softly, frowning.

He drew in a ragged breath. 'Isn't there room in your life for both of us?'

'Of course.' She shook her head in puzzlement. 'But you said——'

'And I meant it,' he cut in harshly. 'The child is yours, Caroline, and you must make what arrangements are needed for it. As long as it doesn't disrupt or disorganise my life, things can stay as they are,' he announced arrogantly.

Caroline gave an inward groan; babies were notorious for disrupting even the best laid plans, and they had a habit of disorganising on sight.

'We'll get a house outside London,' Justin continued distantly. 'That way the baby will be able to have its section of our living accommodation and I'll be able to have mine.'

And never the twain shall meet, thought

Caroline with a frown. What was *she* supposed to do. Distribute her attention between the two? She knew that was the general idea. Justin could have no idea of the amount of time that needed to be spent on a new baby, on a toddler, an infant; according to her mother the worrying and caring never stopped, even when the 'child' was as old as she was!

How could she agree to Justin's outline of the rest of their lives with any idea of being able to keep to it? What would it do to the child to grow up knowing its father was in the house but wanted nothing to do with it? But there was plenty of time before it would come to that, and in the meantime she might be able to persuade Justin into loving his child. From the coldness of his expression now that didn't look like much of a possibility, but it was all she had to hope for, loving him as much as she did.

'What if it doesn't work out?' she hesitated.

He sighed his impatience. 'I've made my compromise, Caroline, I can't offer any more.'

It was so much more than she had expected, but she knew the way he imagined them living would never work out, that children couldn't live by those rules. Maybe by the time Justin had realised that, he would have come to love his child after all. What choice did any of them have, unless she asked for the divorce without even trying to make her marriage work. That wasn't even a possible consideration. Once Justin had a child of his own, a son who looked like him, he might change his mind about not wanting children.

'I'll take it!' She gave a self-conscious grimace at his mockingly raised brows. 'I'm sorry, I didn't mean to make our marriage sound like a bargain I've just made.'

'We both know that a bargain is definitely something I'm not,' he derided. 'Now that that's settled I think I'll go to our bedroom and try to catch up on some of the sleep I missed the last two nights.' He looked at her warily. 'Caro?'

A blush of anticipation darkened her cheeks. 'I thought you said you wanted to catch up on your sleep?' she teased.

'I can do that later.' His gaze was intent. 'At the moment I need to make love to you. I don't want dinner,' he told her firmly as he guessed her intent to remind him they hadn't eaten yet. 'The sleep can wait. But I need *you* very much.'

That need was as close as he ever came to feeling anything for her, and with a man like Justin, a man who regarded most emotions as a weakness, it was the most she could expect for the moment.

'I need you, too,' she admitted softly. 'Justin——'

'Let's take one day at a time, Caro,' he advised gently. 'Starting with tonight.'

Their two nights apart had made them more eager for each other than ever, clothes landing where they were thrown, the two of them merging together without delay as they reacquainted themselves with each other's bodies. For Caroline, moments joined with Justin like this were the happiest in her life, a time when she felt truly one with him, when nothing could ever separate them.

Her own pinnacle reached, she loved nothing better than watching Justin as he lost all control, moving fiercely against him to increase his pleasure, loving the near-agony on his face as he shuddered into her in wave after wave of ecstasy. Tonight she joined him in this burning pleasure, knowing they had reached the ultimate in lovemaking.

'That was—that was——' Justin rested his damp forehead against hers, still moving spasmodically in lingering pleasure. 'I didn't hurt you?' He voiced his concern, knowing their lovemaking had been wilder tonight than ever before.

Caroline knew this would be his only acknowledgement of the baby she carried, that even though he didn't want it he wouldn't deliberately harm it. It was a start.

She caressed the sleek dampness of his back. 'Pain doesn't feel good,' she murmured throatily, 'and that felt very good!'

He chuckled softly, rolling to the bed at her side, taking her with him as he rested her head against his shoulder. 'I certainly didn't marry a shy virgin,' he said with satisfaction.

She had felt shy with him in the past, disturbed by his physical pull on her, but tonight she was filled with a new self-confidence.

'I like your hair like this.' He nuzzled against the wavy tresses. 'It makes you look like a wanton.' He laughed huskily as she buried her face against his chest. 'Not quite so wanton after all,' he murmured indulgently.

They lay quietly together, each savouring the aftermath of their passion, the new closeness that seemed to have sprung up from what Caroline had believed would be the end of them.

Suddenly Justin rolled over on to his stomach, his long fingers entangled in the softness of her hair as he gazed down at her intently. 'I still want you more than I have any other woman,' he told her intently.

Caroline smoothed the hair from his forehead, running a caressing finger over the black velvet eye-patch. 'I don't think I need to be assured of that at this moment,' she murmured indulgently, loving his weight on her.

'No,' he acknowledged heavily. 'But you said you love me, and I——I don't want to lose that love.'

Even though he couldn't love her in return. It was the first acknowledgement he had made of her admission earlier, and although her outburst had seemed to mean little to him at the time she could now see that it mattered to him very much, that he deeply regretted not being able to feel the same emotion for her. But she had gone into this marriage with her eyes wide open, and besides, she knew that he did feel something for her, otherwise he would have ended the marriage as soon as he found out about the baby. Instead he had chosen to find a compromise, one that was going to be difficult to live up to, certainly, but he had been determined to keep her in his life, as his wife.

'Has knowing I don't want our child made you hate me?' he ground out intently.

Her expression softened, but Justin wasn't looking at her; his gaze unseeing, he was lost inside himself.

'Children are such vulnerable creatures, you see,' he murmured raggedly. 'The most vulnerable things in the world . . .' He trembled against her. 'I can't love our child, Caroline; I'm sorry.' He lay his head against her breast, just like the vulnerable child he was so afraid of caring about.

Caroline continued to hold him, feeling very protective at that moment. Justin was afraid of love, and loving; she would just have to surround him with so much of it he couldn't escape feeling the emotion himself. She could do it, could do anything now that she knew he cared for her enough not to let anything end their marriage.

A lot of women in Caroline's situation would have felt miserable over the sudden change that had come over their life, but all mixed up with Justin's aversion to their child was his new-found tenderness with her. In some strange, elusive way, they were closer than they had ever been.

They never talked about the baby, and yet Caroline knew they were both very aware of its existence, that it made Justin softer and more approachable.

For three days they lived in a romantic glow, Caroline filled with an inner peace that had her running to greet Justin when he arrived home from work in the evenings, both of them eager for the time they could close the bedroom door behind them and just forget everything but each other.

It couldn't last, of course, and the intrusion came in the form of a telephone call from her sister.

'Well?' Sonia demanded without preamble. 'You can't tell me Justin is still away on business!'

The invitation for dinner! She had forgotten all about it in the tension of Justin's return and his subsequent decision to carry on with their marriage and ignore the fact that she carried his child.

'Er—no——'

'Then why haven't you called?' Sonia reproved impatiently. 'I know it isn't going to be the most pleasant of evenings,' she conceded with a sigh, 'but for the sake of the family we can't go on avoiding it.'

When Simon had called around briefly yesterday evening he had seemed to find the whole situation rather funny. Sonia's twin in every way, he couldn't bring himself to be serious about anything for more than two minutes, and the predicament of his two sisters, with Sonia marrying Caroline's ex-boyfriend, really seemed to amuse him. Having been the brunt of his practical jokes most of her life, and having taken them all in good humour, Caroline couldn't feel angry with him over something that had been of Sonia's and her own making. Justin seemed to consider her young brother needed a year's hard labour to make him see the serious side of life!

'No,' she accepted softly. 'OK, I'll talk to Justin about it tonight.' She grimaced at the thought of bringing this note of disharmony into their new rapport.

'You mean you haven't even spoken to him about it yet?' Sonia groaned.

'You and Tony haven't been our main topic of conversation recently, no,' she answered impatiently.

'That's a pity,' Sonia drawled drily. 'You and Justin have been ours.'

'Why?' she asked bluntly.

'Tony said he's seen you around the hospital a couple of times recently and you seem very distracted.'

She smiled. 'So you and he have been speculating as to whether or not the honeymoon is over?' she derided without rancour.

'Well . . . not exactly.' Sonia's squirm of discomfort could be heard in her voice. 'But we have been concerned about you, yes.'

'Well you needn't be,' she dismissed briskly. 'Justin and I are very happy together,' she said with a confidence she had only known the last three days. 'However, I do have something I want to talk to you about when we come over,' she added enigmatically, deliberately obscure, knowing the enjoyment of teasing her sister as she imagined Sonia's impatience to know what she wanted to talk about.

As a child, Sonia had always found it impossible to keep a secret, either her own or anyone else's, and she hadn't changed over the years, always hating having to wait for anything.

'Tell me now,' she predictably encouraged, her eagerness evident in her voice.

'I'd rather not,' Caroline dismissed lightly, mischief shining in her eyes as she smiled to herself. She was going to see her parents after work that evening to tell them about the baby; dinner with Sonia and Tony would be the ideal time to tell them about it, too. 'It's rather—personal,' she added confidingly, still smiling teasingly.

'Do you want me to call round tonight?' her sister instantly offered. 'It wouldn't be much out of my way, and if it's so urgent——'

'Oh, it isn't urgent,' Caroline assured her softly. 'It can wait until Justin and I come over for dinner.'

Although she doubted her sister could, she acknowledged indulgently as she rang off. Christmas had always been an exhausting affair with Sonia around, her young sister refusing to let anyone go back to sleep on Christmas morning after she had woken up, demanding that she see everyone else's presents besides her own. Waiting until Caroline went over for dinner before knowing what she wanted to talk about was going to be a severe strain on her.

Her parents, as she had known they would be, were ecstatic at the thought of becoming grandparents, and as she listened to them chattering about the exciting event she was glad to be able to give them something back, besides her love, for all that they had given her.

An older version of Sonia, tall and blonde and beautiful, her mother, at almost fifty, still retained the elegant slenderness that her younger daughter had also inherited. The love between her and her tall and handsome husband was a tangible thing. That love had surrounded Caroline, Sonia and Simon when they, too, had lived at home, but like all parents theirs had realised when it was time to let go so that their children could seek out loves of their own. Caroline knew that they found Justin a little aloof, that they were even a little in awe of him, but they did approve of him, of the happiness he had given their eldest daughter. And they were overjoyed at the thought of the baby.

Her smile turned to a niggling frown during the drive home as she wondered how best to approach Justin with the idea of dinner with Sonia and Tony. She knew without being told that he wouldn't be thrilled at the idea; he hadn't forgotten yet that she had been involved with Tony when the two of them had met, his bitter accusations when she first told him about the baby proof of that. But they couldn't go on avoiding her sister and her husband for the rest of their lives, not unless they wanted to continue making things unpleasant for all her family. Except Simon, of course, who would no doubt carry on finding it amusing.

Mrs Avery had left for the evening, the dinner almost ready, when Caroline heard her husband's key in the lock. She tensed as if for a fight. Damn, and things had been going so well for them lately!

'Mmm.' Justin drew back slightly after accepting her kiss hello, his linked hands at the curve of her spine bringing them into intimate contact. 'How long can dinner wait?' he urged with husky intent.

'It can't,' she said regretfully.

'Pity,' he drawled as he went to their bedroom to freshen up, his arm about her waist as she accompanied him.

Perhaps it was a little early in their marriage for Justin's desire for her to have waned, but even so, his way of always making her feel desirable filled her with a warm glow.

She watched with unashamed enjoyment as he undressed before stepping under the shower, loving the lean beauty of his body, an excited heat coming to her cheeks. She was waiting outside the shower cubicle with a towel for him to drape about his hips when he stepped out from under the hot spray, and she sat on the side of the bath as she watched him take his second shave of the day, a dark shadow left on his jaw even after this was accomplished.

Their gazes met often in the mirror as Justin drew the blade smoothly over his chin, a fire kindling there, becoming a flame, finally raging into burning desire, hungry for each other as Justin finally turned to sweep her up in his arms and carry her through to the bedroom.

'I don't care what's going to spoil for dinner,' he muttered as he threw off her clothes with practised ease. 'You can't look at me like that and then expect me to meekly sit down and eat dinner!' he growled in a voice that spoke of his arousal.

This man had never been meek about anything, and she revelled in his fierce lovemaking, matching his passion as she was the one to take them both into that swirling vortex where she could only cling to Justin as her stability to stop her floating away completely.

They dressed slowly and leisurely, sharing intimate smiles, laughing softly together as they served up the dried chicken and overcooked vegetables; Caroline was sure that neither of them noticed what they were eating anyway as they ate without taking their gazes off each other.

'Will you—will you ever show me under that?' Caroline looked pointedly at the eye-patch. 'It doesn't matter if you'd rather not,' she rushed into speech as she realised what she had done. 'I realise it must be very painful for you to look at and—oh!' She stared at him transfixed as he moved one slender hand up and brought the black velvet patch up on to his forehead.

A scar ran from just below his eyebrow to his upper cheek, a thin silver line that looked deceptively harmless, the real damage the blade had done as it sliced through his flesh obvious as he looked at her with his sightless eye, the iris so light a grey it seemed almost colourless, the pupil that same void.

It wasn't an ugly scar to look upon; it was the thought of the wound that caused the cold shiver down her spine. She knew every inch of Justin's body intimately, knew that he had no other scars but this one, which implied that the damage that man *had* done he had done deliberately. To deliberately try to blind Justin——! The thought made her feel ill.

Justin settled the patch back into place, calmly pouring more wine for both of them, watching with satisfaction as Caroline took a swallow of hers. 'Did you go and see your parents this evening?' he asked conversationally—just as if he hadn't, in effect, bared his pain to her.

'Yes,' she confirmed dismissively, her hand covering his as it rested on the table top. 'Justin, I'm not repulsed by your scar,' she told him earnestly. 'I'm just—sickened by the thought of what you suffered!' Her voice told him of the pain she now suffered with him.

He shrugged. 'It happened some time ago now. You've seen it, now let's just forget it,' he advised harshly.

She should never have asked this of him tonight, should have realised, when they were both trying so hard to make their marriage work, that he wouldn't be able to say no!

'I'm sorry, Justin.' She squeezed his hand. 'I shouldn't have pried.'

His gaze was very tense. 'Some things are better left as they are,' he agreed in a hard voice. 'Do you want a piece of burnt apple pie?' His mood softened slightly as they both recalled the reason the food had been over-cooked. 'Or shall we go through to the living-room and have coffee?' He quirked dark brows.

She nodded, standing up. 'At least that won't be burnt!'

Justin was glancing through some papers from his briefcase when she entered the room with the coffee things, putting them away as soon as he heard her approach, although it would take a little longer for him to put his role as lawyer away, she knew from experience. It could be a little unnerving living with a man who could be both harsh stranger and tender lover, but she was learning to cope with it.

'Mum and Dad send their love,' she began to chatter as she poured their coffee. 'Dad is in the middle of some business deal at the moment, and Mum is coping with seeing him through it, as usual. Dad makes the worst salesman I ever knew.' She smiled indulgently, relieved to see the tension was leaving Justin as she continued to chatter her nonsense. 'But somehow he seems to be successful at it.' At forty-five her father had been forced to make a career change, and for the last five years he had been involved in the sale of computers. He was an easy, charming man, able to put most people at their ease, and yet he seemed to go to pieces every time he made a large sale. It was a cause of great teasing from his family.

'He has charisma,' Justin said drily.

'Yes.' She sobered, looking across at him uncertainly. 'I told them about the baby.'

He nodded; not by so much as a flick of an eyelid did he show that the subject disturbed or displeased him. 'I thought that you might,' he acknowledged distantly.

'They're thrilled for us,' she added awkwardly.

He gave an inclination of his head. 'I expected that, too.'

She felt a stab of pain at his lack of interest, and then berated herself; it was too soon for him to feel anything else. They had months yet before the baby was born.

She looked at him beneath lowered lashes, unable to gauge his reaction to her next announcement. 'Sonia telephoned me at work today.' She waited breathlessly for him to say something, anything; when he didn't, just raised questioning brows, she rushed into speech again. 'She and Tony have invited us over for dinner.'

Once again he showed no emotion. 'Did you accept?' he said curiously.

A blush darkened her cheeks. 'I wouldn't do that without talking to you first.' She shook her head.

'And is that what you were doing earlier—talking to me?' His voice was harsh.

Her eyes widened at his implication that their love-making had been in the form of a bribe on her part.

His mouth twisted at her pained incredulity. 'Isn't that the way all wives get around their husbands?' he derided. 'Give him a little of what he wants and then you can take a whole lot of what you want?'

She was hurt that he could think she would be that devious, very much so, and her first instinct was to tell him to go to hell. But they had come such a long way the last three days; she didn't want to lose that because of a cynical misunderstanding on Justin's part.

'I didn't say that I particularly *want* to go to dinner with Sonia and Tony,' she returned, her eyes steady on his.

His gaze narrowed. 'Why not?'

'But then again I didn't say that I *didn't* want to go either,' she said lightly. 'I'm going to leave that decision completely up to you.'

'Damned if I do and damned if I don't?' he drawled ruefully, his mood softening slightly.

Caroline smiled. 'Not really. It's going to be awkward for all of us, and if you would rather not——'

'We'll go,' he decided with his usual arrogance. 'It's time the awkwardness was brought to an end,' he added determinedly.

She nodded. 'I'll call Sonia tomorrow and tell her. In the meantime,' her eyes glowed with mischief, 'could I offer you another—bribe?'

Justin gave a groan of self-disgust as he stood up and crossed the room to her side, coming down on his haunches, touching her cheek gently. 'That was a hell of a thing for me to have said,' he admitted with a sigh. 'I'm sorry, Caroline.'

She met the intensity of his gaze, smoothing back the dark swathe of his hair. 'Not Caro?' she encouraged in a husky voice.

'*Always* Caro,' he admitted ruefully. 'Let's leave all this for Mrs Avery to clear away in the morning and go to bed, hm?' he encouraged softly.

She shook her head, laughing huskily as Justin frowned his disappointment. 'I meant I'll get up early in the morning and clear these things away,' she mocked, standing up. *'Not* that I didn't think it was a good idea to go to bed. You know what they say about pregnant woman——' She broke off, looking up at him with stricken eyes.

'No,' he returned smoothly, his arm about her waist as they walked to their bedroom. 'What do they say?'

Caroline's breath left her in a relieved sigh. She had been so afraid . . . But it seemed the subject of her pregnancy wasn't a taboo one; only Justin's enthusiasm for it. Well, she had never thought these next months were going to be easy!

She stood up on tiptoe and whispered in his ear exactly what was said about the hormones of pregnant women.

His gaze widened teasingly as he straightened, humour glinting in the depths of silver-grey. 'You mean you're going to get even *more* demanding?' he sighed. 'Try and remember I'm an old man, Caroline.'

She smiled at his reminder of what she had told him the night they met. 'Older men make the best lovers,' she said pertly—and then held her breath as she realised she had once again said the wrong thing after Justin's recent suspicions that Tony had been her lover.

His expression softened as he saw her self-reproach. 'How would you know?' he teased softly. 'You've only ever had one lover!'

She needed no other assurance that he believed her about that now.

But that wasn't going to make having dinner with Sonia and Tony any easier; she wasn't looking forward to it at all.

CHAPTER FIVE

TO ALL intents and purposes they were just two couples about to spend the evening together, but beneath the surface politeness of their initial greetings Tony's mood was slightly morose, and Justin watched them all with a speculative gaze.

Sonia had lost no time in making the arrangements for that very evening once Caroline had telephoned her and told her she and Justin accepted her invitation. Maybe she had thought they might try to get out of it if she allowed any time to elapse. Whatever the reason for her haste, they were all together now, and it was left to Caroline and Sonia to keep the conversation going, chatting about general things while the two men eyed each other in male challenge.

Sonia was looking her usual beautiful self, and the apartment they had bought and that she had decorated reflected her sunny personality, the bright oranges and lemons in the lounge only slightly subdued by small touches of brown. Tony seemed very well, as if married life suited him, too, although his dark frown ruined his charming good looks slightly; he obviously still hadn't quite forgiven Caroline for marrying Justin, despite the fact that he had found happiness with her sister!

'Having you back certainly seems to suit Caroline,' Sonia told Justin mischievously. 'She looked quite wan while you were away on business.'

'I seem to remember your telling me I looked beautiful that day,' Caroline reminded drily.

'Well, you did, darling,' her sister nodded. 'You always do. But you looked a little lost, too.'

She cast Justin an uncomfortable look, knowing by the teasing glitter in his gaze that he found her sister's chatter amusing.

'I wasn't lost at all,' she told Sonia impatiently, avoiding Tony's somewhat scornful gaze. 'I had plenty to keep me busy. And you came to call. And so did——Oh!' She gave a stricken groan as she realised she had forgotten to tell Justin about the visit from his friend, Don Lindford. 'Oh dear! Justin, I'm so sorry.' She gave a rueful grimace. 'With all that was happening I just forgot, and——'

'Darling, what are you talking about?' he prompted with indulgent humour.

'You had a visitor while you were away, and I completely forgot to tell you.' She shook her head in self-disgust. 'And Mr Lindford seemed so nice, too——'

'Mr who?' Justin prompted quietly, sitting forward in his chair.

'Don Lindford,' she explained awkwardly. 'I really am sorry I forgot to tell you. But he did say he would be in touch again soon, and that—that he was sorry to have missed you,' she ended lamely.

She knew very well why she had forgotten to tell Justin that the other man had called: Sonia's visit coming shortly afterwards, and then Justin's own traumatic return. Under the circumstances it wasn't really surprising she had forgotten Don Lindford's visit, but even so it was a little shameful when he was the first and only friend of Justin's she had ever met!

'I *am* sorry,' she said again, grimacing.

Justin seemed lost in thought, his expression harsh. She knew it had been thoughtless of her to omit telling him about the other man, but he really didn't need to look so angry about it; Don had said he would come back!

'Did he stay long?' Justin finally bit out into the uncomfortable silence, Sonia looking puzzled by the exchange, Tony regarding them with narrow-eyed speculation.

Caroline's cheeks burnt as she hurriedly looked away from Tony's mocking expression. He seemed to be saying, 'Are you still sure you married the right man?'

'Only a few minutes,' she answered Justin. 'He didn't seem to have a lot of time. I offered him a cup of tea, but he refused, and——'

'What did he talk about?' Justin prompted harshly.

'Nothing, really.' She shook her head dismissively. 'I told you, he didn't have a lot of time. Was his visit important?' She looked at him frowningly.

For a moment it didn't seem that he would

answer, and then he drew in a ragged breath, shaking off his stormy mood with effort. 'No, I don't suppose so,' he grated. 'I'll try and get in touch with him myself, although he can be a little elusive. But if he calls around again perhaps you could let me know immediately?' He arched dark brows.

He was displeased with her omission, that was completely obvious, and the last thing she had wanted was to show any sign of dissension between the two of them in front of Sonia and Tony. She took the only way she could to cover up the strain she now felt under.

'Justin and I have some wonderful news,' she smiled brightly, ignoring his frowning look. 'I'm going to have a baby!' she announced at their questioning looks.

'How lovely!' Sonia cried enthusiastically, missing her husband's sudden loss of humour as she threw her arms about Caroline and hugged her. 'When's it due?'

Caroline turned sharply to Tony as he addressed her directly for the first time this evening, aware of Sonia's sudden tension as she still stood with her arms about her. Things were obviously still far from perfect between her sister and Tony!

Her head went back challengingly as she met Tony's mocking gaze. 'In just over seven months' time.' Her expression dared him to dispute that.

'A honeymoon baby; how wonderful!' Sonia recovered quickly, smiling at Caroline with genuine pleasure.

'Not exactly,' Justin drawled. 'Caroline and I never actually had a honeymoon.' He looked at her. 'Maybe now would be a good time for it,' he murmured softly.

She blushed at the warm desire in his gaze, feeling hot all over at the thought of several weeks alone with Justin, with nothing to do but please each other. It sounded like heaven!

'Champagne!' Sonia announced excitedly. 'We have to have champagne to celebrate. Tony, pop down to the off-licence and——'

'It really isn't necessary,' Caroline put in hastily before he could come back with some cutting retort, knowing that, in the mood he was in tonight, he was more than capable of it. 'I probably shouldn't be drinking alcohol in my condition, anyway,' she dismissed lightly.

'One glass of champagne isn't going to hurt you—or the baby,' Sonia insisted. 'Tony?' she prompted again, her voice firm.

Caroline held her breath, knowing that Justin wouldn't stand for it if the other man said anything insulting.

'Why not?' Tony drawled, getting slowly to his feet, very handsome in black fitted trousers and an open-necked green shirt. 'Why don't you come with me, Justin?' he suggested as he pulled on his jacket. 'I'm sure the women would welcome the chance for one of those girl-to-girl chats they seem so fond of!' He looked questioningly at the other man. 'Especially as they have something so interesting to chat about,' he added tauntingly.

Justin stood up, coldly meeting the other man's gaze. 'A short walk while the women finish preparing dinner sounds like a good idea,' he nodded.

Tony gave him a scornful look as the two of them walked to the door. 'We'll be lucky if we get any dinner at all tonight after Caroline's announcement! After you.' He held the door open with a flourish.

'Don't wives, especially pregnant ones, get a kiss goodbye any more?' Sonia teased them both.

Tony walked towards her. 'There isn't anything you're not telling me, is there?' He kissed her briefly on the lips.

'Believe me, the day I find out I'm carrying your child I'll be shouting it from the rooftops,' Sonia assured him huskily.

Caroline turned away from the intimacy of the moment, grimacing a little as Justin frowned down at her, obviously unhappy with being put in this position, a man who could only show his affection in private. And she knew he was still a little angry with her about Don Lindford.

She moved up to kiss him lightly on the mouth, frozen for an instant as he deepened the caress before moving abruptly away again, as if he regretted the impulse.

She stared after him a little dazedly as he left with Tony.

Sonia giggled at her side. 'It hasn't been half as bad as I'd imagined,' she admitted at Caroline's questioning look. 'I thought the two of them might resort to pistols at dawn, fisticuffs at least,' she reported happily. 'I think I'm a little disappointed that they've gone off together to buy champagne instead.' She wrinkled her nose prettily.

'Sonia!' Caroline reproved in a shocked voice; the last thing she needed was any more turbulence because of her marriage to Justin.

Her sister sat down, patting the sofa at her side for Caroline to do the same thing. 'Not that I would have wanted them to hurt each other or anything like that——' her eyes gleamed with mischief —'but I'd simply love to see your Justin without his usual control!'

Caroline couldn't help returning her smile as she settled down next to her on the sofa. 'Believe me, it doesn't happen very often.'

'Really?' Blonde brows rose over laughing blue eyes. 'And I would have said, just from looking at him, that he's a very sensual man!'

Caroline gave her a reproving look. 'That's for me to know—and no other woman ever to find out!' she added teasingly.

Sonia laughed softly. 'We don't need to; anyone looking at you can see you're very—satisfied, with your marriage.'

'Liberated as Mum and Dad are, I think they might be a little shocked at the way their "baby" is talking right now,' Caroline drawled.

Sonia sobered. 'I can't believe my big sister is going to have a baby of her own very soon.' She shook her head sadly. 'It doesn't seem that long since we were playing with our dolls!'

'No.' Caroline became lost in those happy memories, too.

'Is Justin pleased?'

She focused frowningly on her sister. 'Sorry?'

'Is Justin pleased about the baby?' Sonia repeated lightly. 'He didn't say a lot, so I wondered . . .' She looked at Caroline questioningly.

'Oh, you know,' she shrugged. 'Men are always a bit flattened by pregnancy,' she evaded.

'Hm,' Sonia nodded, her attention already wandering from Justin and his reaction to becoming a father. 'I wonder if that's what Tony and I need?'

Caroline's hand covered Sonia's restless one; she saw the bewilderment in her sister's eyes as she allowed her cheerful guard to slip for a brief moment. 'Don't have a child expecting it to hold the marriage together,' she advised gently. 'Often it does the opposite.'

Sonia shrugged off her despondency, her dazzling smile back in place. 'I don't need anything to keep Tony happy but little old me,' she grinned. 'Let's surprise them and have dinner ready when they get back.' She stood up to pull Caroline to her feet. 'Another few months and you'll need a crane to do that,' she announced cheerfully on her way to the kitchen she had decorated in blue and white; she had told Caroline when she showed her around on their arrival that, as it was the room she intended spending the least amount of time in, it could have more conservative colours.

'Thanks,' she said drily as they set about draining the vegetables and carving the meat.

They had barely placed the food on the table when the men arrived back, the two of them arguing good-naturedly about their taste in literature.

It was the fact that it was good-natured banter that surprised Caroline, who gave the two men puzzled glances as there no longer seemed that tension between them that had been all too evident earlier in the evening.

'A toast.' Tony stood up once the champagne had been poured. 'To Caroline and Justin—and the cub they're expecting,' he added teasingly.

Caroline barely had time to register his mocking humour before she became aware that Justin was standing up, his champagne quickly dampening his trousers, his glass on the floor.

Her first thought was had he done it on purpose, so that he didn't have to drink a toast to a child he didn't want and couldn't love? And then she knew he wouldn't be so petty, that it had to have been a genuine accident.

Only seconds had passed by the time she reached that conclusion, but it had been long enough for Sonia to have brought him a towel from the bathroom so that he could mop up the surface dampness.

'Never mind, old chap,' Tony mocked. 'I'd be a nervous wreck, too, if I were about to be a father.'

Justin handed the damp towel back to Sonia. 'I think we'll have to go, Caroline,' he announced regretfully, grimacing as he pulled the damp material away from his thighs.

'Borrow a pair of my trousers,' Tony offered as he

saw how disappointed Sonia looked. 'We're about the same size, and I won't mind if you won't.' He looked challengingly at the other man. 'It was probably my fault anyway,' he pulled a face. 'Alluding to the fact that everyone calls you The Wolf. Behind your back, of course,' he added drily.

Justin turned to an ashen-faced Caroline. 'Not always behind my back,' he murmured softly, rewarded with the delicate blush that tinged Caroline's cheeks. Since that first night, when she had learnt that he knew of the nickname after all, she had always cried out that name when they made love!

'I see,' Tony drawled suggestively. 'Well, let's not break up the evening just because of a little spilt champagne,' he dismissed.

Caroline stared down at her hands after the two men had gone into the bedroom. It had to have been an accident—didn't it?

'Don't look so upset,' Sonia cajoled gently. 'Personally I'm glad of a good excuse for the food being awful,' she confided with a grimace.

She couldn't help chuckling at her sister's self-derisive humour, and was still smiling when Tony rejoined them.

It was several minutes before Justin came out of the bedroom, too, and Caroline's eyes widened as she took in the grey pair of trousers that Tony had leant him. Much more modern than anything she had seen Justin in before, with their fitted waist and baggy style, they nonetheless made him look more rakishly attractive than ever.

'I should watch it, old man,' Tony drawled as he

looked at Caroline knowingly. 'I know that look from living with her sister; it means your wardrobe is about to undergo a complete change!'

Justin returned the smile, resuming his seat at the table. 'I don't think they would be very suitable for the courtroom,' he mocked.

'Oh, Caroline won't be sending you to work in them,' Tony informed him confidently. 'Some other woman might appreciate that more than she would like. No, she'll be more interested in getting you *out* of them when you're at home.'

'Tony!' his wife scolded as Caroline could only blush. 'Propose the toast again and keep your thoughts to yourself.'

'See what I mean,' he told the other man resignedly. 'It's wicked when you're just a sex-symbol.'

Caroline shared her laughter with Justin; when Tony was in this mood he was irresistible!

'Let me propose the toast,' Justin spoke softly, holding up his glass that Tony had refilled. 'To my beautiful wife.'

Her blush deepened at the obvious pride in his voice.

'Don't forget the baby,' Sonia reminded him impatiently.

He only hesitated for a fraction of a second, not enough for Sonia and Tony to see his reluctance, but too long for Caroline to be unaware of it. 'And the baby,' he added abruptly, sipping the bubbly wine.

Caroline needed more than a sip, but the bubbles tickled her nose and made her eyes water.

'I'm afraid the dinner is going to be ruined now,'

Sonia announced with an innocently regretful voice.

Caroline took one look at her sister, Sonia glanced back, and the two of them burst into laughter.

'It's all right, Justin,' Tony said drily when he saw him looking at them in surprise. 'If you had eaten your dinner while it was still hot you would have found that my wife had ruined the meal long ago. I usually advise people to bring along something for indigestion!'

'Tony Shepherd! How dare you!'

'Don't worry, she isn't really mad,' Tony assured them confidently. 'If she were really angry she would have called me "Anthony Graham Shepherd",' he said knowingly. 'She can't really be angry with me when she knows I'm telling the truth, you see.' He shrugged.

'Tony!' Sonia groaned in acute embarrassment. 'What's Justin going to think?'

'Before or after I've tried the food?' Justin drily joined in the teasing.

'Caroline, you never told me Justin can be cruel.' Sonia pretended to be hurt by their humour at her expense, although the laughter in her eyes belied the impression a little.

What she had expected to be a disaster of an evening, Caroline had found pleasantly enjoyable. The food wasn't half as bad as Sonia had claimed it would be; in fact it was rather nice, despite being a little cold. And the company was certainly scintillating. There had been a few awkward moments, but in the circumstances that was only to be expected; all in all it had been a successful evening.

Justin was very quiet on the drive home, and Caroline glanced at him searchingly several times.

'It went well, I thought.' Finally she couldn't stand the silence any longer.

He frowned. 'What? Oh—yes,' he nodded vaguely.

She grimaced, putting her hand on his thigh, instantly feeling him tense beneath her touch. 'Are you still angry with me?' she coaxed. 'Because I forgot to mention your friend's visit,' she explained at his puzzled expression.

Justin gave a heavy sigh. 'I'm not angry with you at all. I wish you had remembered to tell me sooner, but I'm certainly not angry with you.'

'Then why—never mind,' she dismissed with a strained smile. 'What did you say to Tony when the two of you went out for champagne?' she probed teasingly. 'He certainly seemed in a better mood when he got back.'

His mouth twisted. 'We didn't fight it out, if that's what you mean.

She sobered. 'No, of course that isn't what I meant,' she said impatiently. 'He just seemed— different, when the two of you got back.'

Justin shrugged. 'Maybe he realised he no longer has a chance with you. How would I know why he was different—if he was,' he muttered irritably.

Tony *had* been much more amenable after he and Justin went out for champagne, and even Justin had to have realised that. But if he didn't want to talk about that change, or the reason for it, she knew there was nothing she could do or say to make him do so.

Justin's strangely taciturn mood persisted even once they had showered and prepared for bed, and for the first time since they were married Justin turned out his bedside lamp and lay with his back towards her.

She tentatively touched his bare shoulder. 'Justin?'

'Go to sleep, Caroline,' he told her harshly, his back still towards her.

'But——'

'I'm tired, Caroline.' He turned on her angrily, his gaze glittering in the darkness. 'We don't have to make love every night!' he added scornfully.

She drew her hand away as if she had been burnt, blinking back the tears, her throat aching as she tried to stop them flowing. 'I'm sorry,' she said in a choked voice. 'I didn't realise. I thought—it's just that this is the first time you haven't wanted me . . .' Her hurt was reflected in her eyes.

Justin looked angrier than ever. 'And after almost two months, isn't it due?' he attacked.

Her tongue ran along the dryness of her lips. 'I suppose so . . . I—of course.' She turned away blindly, lying in the darkness with her eyes wide open, finding it more and more difficult to hold back the tears.

If she had expected him to relent, to apologise for his bad humour, she was out of luck. The only movement he made in the bed was to settle down with his back towards her once again, and within minutes the deep evenness of his breathing told her that he had fallen asleep.

She at last allowed the tears to fall. Why had she assumed Justin would always want her? Maybe she was being unreasonable expecting him to make love to her every night; after all, he didn't have to want her all the time, and maybe he really was tired.

But he didn't have to be so cruel about it, could even have held her in his arms until they both fell asleep. He had wanted to hurt her for some reason.

Maybe he had changed his mind about accepting the baby because he wanted her so much. Maybe he no longer wanted her. But that didn't ring true, not after the way he had tried to persuade her into bed when she was all dressed and ready to go to Sonia's and Tony's for dinner! He had been eager enough then, teasing her when she almost forgot Sonia and Tony completely and gave in. As he had drawn away from her he had promised to make love to her later until she begged for mercy. Instead he had rejected her, turned his back on her, and then fallen asleep. It didn't make sense to her at all.

She glanced longingly at the golden smoothness of his back, hungering for contact with him, but fearful of rejection once again. Instead she lay on her back staring sightlessly up at the ceiling, sure that she wasn't going to be able to sleep.

She awoke to the realisation that something was wrong, very wrong.

It took her several seconds to shake off the disorientation of a deep sleep, to realise that it was still dark outside, that she could feel the warmth of Justin's body beside her own.

Then what had awoken her, because something surely had? Could it be that——

'No, damn it!' Justin suddenly ground out fiercely at her side, his tension a tangible thing. 'No!' he groaned again. 'You çan't. I won't let you. Oh, dear God!'

Caroline had scrambled into a sitting position at his first outcry, moving to soothe his brow now, murmuring reassuringly to him as he seemed in the grips of a horrific nightmare.

'It's all right, Justin,' she crooned. 'It's all right darling. Justin——'

'Penny!' He gave an anguished shout.

Caroline recoiled as if he had struck her. Who on earth was Penny?

CHAPTER SIX

'SO IF you can think of somewhere you would like to go, I can arrange to be free all of next week.' Justin looked at her indulgently.

Somehow trying to think of where they could go on their belated honeymoon didn't hold all that much appeal for Caroline when she wasn't even sure they had a marriage any more.

It wasn't just that Justin hadn't made love to her for three days, and nights; it was that he was still having those dreams at night, and each time he did he called out for the woman called Penny. She still had no idea who the other woman was, but the love and anguish in Justin's voice when he spoke of her was obvious.

Love. Yes, the emotion Justin had warned her he could never feel for *her,* she knew he felt for the other woman.

Caroline's own anguish had begun the very first time he had cried the other woman's name, an emotional torment that didn't leave her day or night. If Justin loved this woman called Penny, why wasn't it her he had married? Unless, she had guessed, when no other explanation seemed to make sense, Penny was already married and so unnattainable to him? It made his decision to marry *her,* when he admitted to only feeling desire for her, rather more understandable.

The last thing she felt like doing now, however, was planning a honeymoon trip for herself and Justin. What was the point of a honeymoon when the two of them didn't even touch any more unless it was by accident? And she couldn't bear the idea of the two of them going off to be alone somewhere with Justin's thoughts of Penny being a very intrusive third.

God, she was glad he hadn't tried to make love to her the last three days; she wasn't sure she would have been able to respond even if he *had* touched her!

He hadn't told her he had had a vasectomy, and he had lied when he scorned love; he was definitely in love with this Penny. Maybe even his initial decision not to have children had something to do with the other woman, or perhaps that was the reason the two of *them* weren't married; it would be difficult for any woman to accept Justin's decision not to have children, and the steps he had taken to ensure it never happened.

Whatever the reason, Justin wasn't with the woman he loved but was married to her instead, and she didn't feel as if she could go on a honeymoon with him as if nothing had changed between them. Oh, her love for Justin would never change, she had known that when she had been able to accept his conditions concerning her having the baby, but it was no longer a love she felt able to give unreservedly.

'I'm really not worried about going anywhere, Justin,' she dismissed shruggingly. 'I would have to take time off from the hospital, and—and it seems rather silly to go on a honeymoon when we've already been married two months,' she added lamely, evading his suddenly concerned gaze.

She couldn't stand his concern, not when his night-time ramblings about another woman had broken her heart!

'Every woman should have a honeymoon she can look back on,' he gently reproved her lack of enthusiasm.

'And who told you that?' she said sharply, embarrassed colour darkening her cheeks as Justin raised his brows in surprise at her vehemence.

'Darling, I married you so quickly, you didn't have time to arrange the grand wedding you must have really wanted. At least let me give you the honeymoon,' he softly cajoled.

'I'm really not interested in going away at the moment.' She picked up her napkin from her lap to fold it precisely and place it next to the cup of coffee which was all she had had for breakfast. 'We've very busy on the ward, and——'

'Caroline, what's wrong?' Justin's hand clasped hers as it still rested on the table. 'You've been very jumpy the last three days. I thought you would welcome the idea of some time away——'

'And so you decided to indulge me!' she flared resentfully, glaring at him. 'I'm not a child, Justin, who has to be spoilt and petted when I fall down and graze my knee! I'm a trained nurse, responsible for people's lives; I certainly don't expect my husband to treat me like a moron!'

Justin gave a pained wince. 'I see one of the other characteristics of a pregnant woman is surfacing,' he said drily.

Her eyes flashed. 'And what's that?'

He shrugged. 'The uncertain temper.'

'And just how would you know?' she challenged, pulling her hand away from his as she stood up. 'I do not want a honeymoon, either now or in the future. And now, if you'll excuse me, I have to go to work.'

'No, I won't.'

She turned sharply at the door to the dining-room at his softly spoken words. 'No, you won't what?' she prompted impatiently.

He stood up slowly, towering over her as he joined her at the door. 'No, I won't excuse you,' he told her firmly, his hand under her chin as he made her look up at him.

'Caro——'

'Don't you dare!' she cried vehemently, wrenching away from him. 'Don't you dare try and seduce me, you—you——'

'Caroline, for God's sake, what is the matter with you?' He lost all patience with her seemingly unreasonable behaviour.

'I'm going to work.' She threw open the door. 'I don't want to talk about this any more!'

She ran out into the hallway, rushing past a wide-eyed Mrs Avery on her way to see if they wanted more coffee, and, grabbing her jacket off the hall-stand, hurried from the apartment as if she were being pursued.

She heartily thanked the fact that nursing didn't give a lot of time for private thought as she somehow managed to get through the morning without a crack in her well-formed defences showing. But by lunch-time she felt drained, both physically and mentally, and, ignoring the hungry cry of her stomach, she went for a walk outside, where she hoped the freshness of the day would help to clear her head.

The hospital grounds were lovely, kept that way by the full-time gardeners they employed, although the beauty of the flowers didn't reach her today, her thoughts immediately returning to that scene between herself and Justin this morning. She was behaving like a shrew, she knew that, and yet his suggestion of a honeymoon had just seemed to be the final straw.

For three days she had done her best to pretend that everything was as it had always been between them, that Justin didn't call out for another woman in his sleep, but this morning she just hadn't been able to pretend any more!

She had accepted so much from Justin because she loved him and wanted to be with him: the fact that he couldn't love her, that he didn't want their baby; she just felt she had come to the end of the disillusionment she could take and still love him that unquestioningly.

'Slow down! For God's sake, Caroline, I'm not

as young as I was, and I'm not sure you should be walking at that pace in your condition!'

She turned to find Tony hurrying after her, panting with the effort of trying to catch her up. One look at the man she would have married if she had never met Justin, one look at his uncomplicated face, and the tears she had been repressing all morning burst out in a flood, her body racked by deep sobs.

'Hey, women don't usually cry as soon as they see me,' he gently rebuked as he took her into his arms, Caroline's tears instantly wetting both of them. 'Caroline, what on earth has happened?' he demanded in a concerned voice.

She just cried all the harder, burying her face in his white coat.

'Has something happened to Justin?' he prompted worriedly.

She let out a loud wail before burying her face in his coat again.

'Caroline, we'll have to go somewhere more private if you're going to carry on like this,' he warned with feeling.

She roused herself enough to look around them, realising as she did so that these gardens were visible from several of the wards. 'Get me away from here!' she groaned in embarrassment.

With his arm about her shoulders to shield her from prying eyes, Tony took her to one of the private lounges, shooing out the only other occupant, a student nurse, so that they could be completely alone.

He sat down in a chair with her on his lap. 'Now tell me what's wrong,' he encouraged gently, removing her crumpled cap so that she could be more comfortable against his shoulder.

'You were right, Tony,' she sniffled self-pityingly. 'You warned me I could never hold Justin's interest——'

'I didn't exactly say that,' he denied uncomfortably. 'Anyway, I was angry that night; I said things in the heat of temper.'

'And sometimes they can be all too truthful,' she sobbed.

'Have the two of you argued?' Tony guessed with some relief. 'I shouldn't worry about it. Sonia and I do it all the time, and the making up can be——'

'Justin has someone else,' she told him flatly.

'What?'

She swallowed hard, still shaking quite badly. 'Justin is in love with someone else,' she stated much more calmly than she felt.

'No.' Tony shook his head.

She gave a start of surprise, blinking dazedly at his absolute certainty she was wrong. 'He has another woman, Tony,' she insisted firmly. 'I even know her name,' she added shakily.

'From where?' he prompted patiently.

'From his dreams,' she answered defensively. Somehow she had expected Tony to sympathise with her, to be her ally, not to have him flatly refuse to believe in Justin's duplicity. 'He calls her name in his dreams!'

'Oh, well, that doesn't mean anything,' Tony scorned. 'I dream about——well, never mind who I dream about,' he dismissed ruefully. 'But I can tell you I usually want to do more than talk to her!'

Caroline shook her head. 'This isn't that sort of dream, Tony,' she said confidently. 'Justin cares for this woman. Very much.'

'I don't believe it. I'm sorry.' He held up his hands defensively as she stood up to frown down at him. 'I may still think he did a dirty thing by making my girlfriend fall in love with him,' he grimaced, 'but I can say with all honesty that I don't believe he's interested in any other woman but you. You can't really believe otherwise, Caroline,' he rebuked. 'Have you asked him about this woman?'

She turned away. Asking Justin about Penny was the one thing she had put off doing—she was afraid of the answer. Once she knew, irrevocably, that he loved someone else, she wouldn't be able to stay with him, no matter how much she might love him.

'No, I can't; don't you see that?' She looked at Tony anxiously.

He shook his head. 'I can see that you're probably putting yourself through a lot of unnecessary pain.' He sighed. 'Caroline, I have the most reason to want to believe Justin is an out and out bastard, to have you leave him, but the truth of the matter is I like the man, I respect his honesty, and I truly don't believe he would stay married to you if he were in love with someone else.'

'Even if that someone were unnattainable?' she questioned uncertainly.

'Even then,' Tony confirmed. 'Damn it, Caroline, the night of my parents' anniversary party he was dating my sister; by the end of the evening he had told her he no longer wanted to see her because he wanted you. He isn't a man to mince his words, or his emotions, and if he wanted this other woman he would have told you—and her.'

She still looked uncertain, wanting to believe what he said was the truth, but the memory of the way Justin cried out the other woman's name kept haunting her; he was like a man in torment.

'Caroline, if it really distresses you that much then ask him about her,' Tony advised impatiently. 'But don't keep letting the thing fester and grow in your mind.'

She gave him a wan smile. 'I'll think about it. You know, you aren't bad as a brother.' She bent down to kiss him on the cheek.

'Caroline,' drawled a pleasant voice. 'Tony?' Justin added questioningly. 'And please, don't either of you say "this isn't what it seems",' he murmured derisively as they both turned to him with stricken faces. 'What it "seems" couldn't possibly be taking place here!' He looked pointedly around the lounge that anyone could walk into at any moment—and had!

Tony stood up. 'I'm glad you said that,' he said with some relief. 'I might have found it a little difficult explaining to Sonia what I did to merit having you put me in one of my own wards!'

Justin gave the ghost of a smile, his gaze bleak. 'I try never to jump to conclusions,' he bit out harshly. 'So what *were* you doing?' He looked at them both coldly.

All Caroline could do was stare at him; Justin was the last person she had expected to see here today. Oh, he knew his way around here OK, had sought her out several times when he was trying to persuade her to go out with him, but what was he doing here now, and looking as if he hadn't been to work, wearing a casual grey shirt and denims that hugged his waist and thighs? She never failed to receive a jolt of physical awareness whenever she saw him in clothes like this, and today was no exception.

'I——'

'Aren't pregnant women emotional?' Tony cut in dismissively to the other man. 'All my medical training and I never realised they all fall apart at the seams. I'm going to make sure Sonia knows exactly what she's letting herself in for before she gets pregnant,' he grimaced. 'I don't fancy walking around damp from tears all the time.' He pulled his damp jacket away from him pointedly. 'And the slightest little thing sets them off.' He shook his head disgustedly. 'I only told Caroline I thought she should slow down a little and she started blubbering all over me. Very embarrassing, I can tell you,' he confided in Justin.

He was doing his best to smooth things over for her, and at that moment Caroline could have kissed him all over again. Only she very wisely didn't!

'Don't worry, Tony,' Justin drawled. 'The only person Caroline will be "blubbering" all over in future is me.' He turned to her, complete awareness of the real situation in his gaze, although he said nothing. 'I've come to take you out to lunch,' he told her softly.

Her eyes widened, and then she gave a groan of disappointment as she looked down at her fob-watch. 'I've got to be back on duty in a few minutes,' she said regretfully.

'Hm,' he murmured, looking pointedly at the other man. 'If you'll excuse us . . .'

Tony grinned. 'You know, you dismiss a man even better then my old tutor used to—and he was an expert!'

'Thank you.' Justin gave an acknowledging smile.

Tony winked at Caroline before leaving, his tuneless whistle echoing up the corridor seconds later.

'You know,' Justin spoke softly, 'in a way I regret what I did to him two months ago.'

Caroline frowned; he regretted marrying her?

'No,' he mocked her unspoken question. 'I don't regret marrying you, only that I had to hurt Tony to do it. But I think he and your sister are going to make it, don't you?' he prompted lightly.

She didn't trust his calmly pleasant mood, was sure he must really be angry at finding her and Tony in such a compromising situation; he had to be biding his time before making his displeasure felt.

'I think so,' she answered his question, sure from the amount of times Sonia entered Tony's conversation that he did really care for her sister. 'Justin, just now really wasn't what it seemed.' She decided that attack was the best form of defence.

'On reflection,' he drawled slowly, 'it seemed like an old friend giving comfort because you were upset. Wasn't that what it was?'

'Yes,' she challenged, picking up her crumpled cap from the small coffee-table beside the chair she and Tony had been sitting in, staring down at it as she waited for Justin's icy anger to wash over her.

'And *I* was the reason you were upset,' he said softly.

Her head went back, her eyes wide as she stared at him. 'Yes,' she confirmed tremulously.

He drew in a ragged breath. 'I'm sorry, I've been—preoccupied the last few days,' his voice was gruff.

He was as aware as she that that preoccupation included not making love to her, not even touching her unless it was accidentally.

Justin sighed at her lack of response. 'I've had—something on my mind. Will you let me make it up to you?' he urged gently.

Caroline frowned. How could he possibly make up to her the fact that he talked of another woman in his sleep, that he spoke of her with love?

And yet this man, his gaze soft, his mouth curved into a gentle smile, wasn't the same man who had so cold-bloodedly asked her to marry him. That man had been cold himself, his emotions firmly held in check, only relaxing his rigid control when they were in bed together. The Justin standing in front of her now was the same man she loved when he made love to her, except they weren't in bed. She didn't know what it meant, after the last three days she was afraid to even hope, but surely it had to mean something?

She swallowed hard. 'How?'

His gaze warmed even more. 'By first of all taking you out to lunch——'

'I told you,' she groaned. 'I have to be back on duty in a few minutes.' She shook her head.

'And if you recall I said "hm",' he teased. 'Are you going to be angry if I tell you that I haven't just arranged for you to take the rest of the day off but the next eight days as well, that as you couldn't seem to make your mind up about a honeymoon I've made it up for you?' He eyed her questioningly.

Angry because she didn't have to come to work for a week and try to put a brave face on things? Angry that she was going to be alone with Justin for that time and possibly straighten out the tension between them? Angry that he had cared enough to behave so arrogantly?

'Caroline?' he prompted with a pained wince.

'Ordinarily I would be very angry at your arrogance,' she told him abruptly. 'Ordinarily I might even have told you what you could do with it. But then,' she added lightly, 'pregnant women aren't "ordinary"! When do we leave? And where are we going?'

His expression had changed only slightly as she mentioned the baby she carried, and he tried to mask even that, only Caroline's extreme sensitivity on the subject making it obvious to her.

'We leave as soon as you've been home to change,' he said briskly. 'Mrs Avery is even now doing your packing for you. As to where we're going, that's to be a surprise, but I will tell you, just so that you aren't disappointed, that you aren't going to need your passport.'

'That's good.' Her eyes glowed with laughter. 'Because I don't have one!'

'You don't?' Justin laughed in disbelief. 'Then thank God I didn't whisk you off to the Bahamas as I first intended. I only decided against it because seven days isn't long enough to get over the jet-lag and start enjoying yourself. We'll have to do something about getting you a passport, Caroline,' he told her as they left the lounge on their way out of the hospital. 'Who knows what I might arrange for Christmas!'

The woman called Penny still stood between them, perhaps she always would, but Caroline couldn't resist this Justin, a light-hearted, indulgently teasing Justin—and perhaps she didn't want to!

She felt as excited as a child as Justin put their luggage in the boot of the car. But they hadn't been driving for more than half an hour when Justin turned into a small car park.

'I never did give you lunch,' he reminded her ruefully as she looked at him enquiringly.

It was a delightful country inn, authentic by the look of the low beamed ceiling; Caroline chuckled as Justin had to bend his head not to crash into the beams.

They had never done any of the things other newly married couples had, no drives out into the country, no quiet lunches together in quiet inns like this one, no walking along a beach hand in hand——She brought herself to an abrupt halt on the last image; she just couldn't imagine Justin on a beach, getting his trousers damp and sand in his shoes! But then she hadn't married any ordinary man, and she had known that when she fell in love with him.

And she didn't feel that Penny was with them now. It was as if Justin had left his thoughts of the other woman behind in London, that the woman no longer intruded on their relationship. Oh, God, she hoped so!

They dined on typical bar fare, indulging Caroline's sweet tooth afterwards with a huge bowl of trifle.

She gave a sigh of satisfaction as they emerged out into the sunshine. 'That was wonderful!' A shadow clouded her eyes. 'Er—have you been there before?' She couldn't bear the thought of being with him in the same places Penny had.

'No.' He turned on the ignition. 'Just a lucky guess.'

'Oh, yes,' she beamed at him, leaning back

against the head-rest. 'I think I could fall asleep now.' She laughed.

'Then why don't you?' Justin tuned the radio into a station playing softly romantic music. 'We still have quite a way to go.'

She didn't mean to fall asleep at all, meant to enjoy every moment of being with this man who was making her fall more and more in love with him by the minute, but three virtually sleepless nights, the warmth of the day, and the soft music all resulted in her being asleep within minutes of their resuming their journey.

She only woke up when Justin brought the car to a halt. Sitting up to look dazedly about her, she saw that they were parked in front of an old manor house that was approached by a long gravel drive that wound through picturesque gardens, the house itself old and beautifully maintained, the whole place having an unreal appearance about it.

She turned curiously to Justin as he sat watching her reaction.

'It is a hotel,' he assured her, turning to smile at the doorman as he opened the car door. 'We'll be there in a moment,' he instructed distantly. 'If you could see that our luggage is taken to our room. Mr and Mrs de Wolfe,' he supplied as he handed the keys to the car boot to the other man.

'But where are we?' Caroline demanded excitedly as she looked at the beauty around her, the immaculate gardens that seemed to go on for ever, the mellow grace of the manor house.

'Devon,' Justin supplied indulgently, enjoying

her pleasure in their surroundings. 'This place probably once belonged to a member of the aristocracy who fell on hard times. Whatever the reason, it's now a hotel.'

'It's lovely.' She stepped out of the car as he held her door open for her.

'So are you.' His gaze darkened as he looked down at her. 'Are you feeling rested now?' he prompted in a husky voice.

'After all that sleep, I should hope so!' she dismissed ruefully.

'Good,' he murmured as he clasped her elbow, and they walked up the steps together. 'Because when I requested our suite here I intended it should be a honeymoon in the full sense of the word.'

When Caroline saw the four-poster bed that took up most of their bedroom, she knew exactly what he 'intended'!

CHAPTER SEVEN

'I'M SURE the waiter thought we were newlyweds,' Caroline chuckled as the two of them entered their suite later that evening. 'He started to offer me confetti instead of dessert!'

Justin smiled, darkly handsome in his tailored evening suit. 'We are newlyweds; two months doesn't exactly make us a staid married couple.'

Caroline laughed happily, feeling more light-hearted tonight than she ever had before. 'I don't think coming up to bed at nine-thirty dented the impression!'

Justin put the keys to their suite on the low drinks cabinet. 'I only got through until that time because you insisted on having coffee,' he drawled, throwing off his jacket, and loosening his bow-tie.

She leant into his body as she unfastened the top button of his shirt for him. 'When you made the booking here did you check that they do room-service?' she murmured throatily. 'Because I have the distinct impression that Devon is going to be wasted on us!'

'I checked.' He curved her tightly against him, making her aware of every hard muscle in his body. 'It's a twenty-four hour service, just in case we lose track of time,' he murmured before feasting on her mouth.

Three days without his kisses and caresses made Caroline's response all the more fiery, her fingers clenched in his hair as she more than returned his passion.

'Oh, Justin, I've missed you,' she groaned as his lips moved feveredly down her throat.

'I'm sorry, darling. So sorry. I never meant——'

'Just love me, Justin,' she urged with feeling. 'Just love me as if you'll never let me go.'

He became suddenly tense, raising his head to look at her. 'I never will let you go, Caro,' he ground out fiercely. 'Never!'

She could see the savage pride of possession in his gaze, knew that he meant every word. Penny was losing and she was winning! Maybe *that* was why the other woman had been on his mind so much lately; his subconscious had already been saying goodbye to that other love, allowing Caroline into his heart instead. Oh, he still hadn't said the words, and perhaps he never would, but he was different with her now, and it could only be because he had come to care for her in spite of himself. What had started out as a depressing day now seemed full of possibilities.

'Then love me, Justin,' she encouraged with a slight sob in her voice. 'Love me!'

Even his lovemaking was different tonight, just as fiercely intense, more so after the last three nights of loneliness, but tonight he was intent on pleasing her as never before, raising her again and again to the heights only to deny her release at the last possible moment.

Caroline felt as if she were going insane as he once again denied her, moving restlessly against him, finally unable to bear his slow, tormenting caresses any longer, becoming the aggressor as she pushed him down beneath her, the one to do the possessing, controlling their passion, and Justin, until they both reached a shuddering release.

She lay exhausted against his chest, their bodies clinging together damply, their breathing moving in ragged harmony.

'I always wondered what it must feel like to be ravaged by a woman,' Justin murmured lazily into the silence.

Cheeks warm with embarrassment, Caroline lifted her head to look at him, reassured by the sated satisfaction in his face. 'And?' she teased throatily.

'And——' he stretched like a contented kitten, almost dislodging Caroline from her more than comfortable position above him '—I think I might grow to like it.' He grinned up at her.

Her face burnt from the deliberate provocation of his remark. 'Justin de Wolfe, you are——'

'Uh-uh, I know you aren't really angry with me,' he said languidly. 'What was it Tony said about your sister? When she's really angry she launches into his full name!'

'Justin David James Charles de Wolfe is too much of a mouthful for anyone—let alone when I'm feeling so very tired.' She watched him beneath lowered lashes.

His brows rose in disappointment. 'Not too tired, I hope; this *is* supposed to be the first night of our honeymoon.'

'Oh, I think I might manage to find a little more strength from somewhere,' she teased him. 'Of course, if you're going to let me do all the work again . . .'

'My darling Caro——' he rolled over so that she lay beneath him '——this time you won't have to do anything but just lie there and——'

'Justin David James Charles de Wolfe!' She frowned warningly, rewarded by his throaty chuckle. 'Have you ever known me to "just lie there"?'

'No,' he said with satisfaction. 'It isn't in that passionate nature of yours. But I do think we should at least try the bed out once while we're here, don't you?' he added derisively.

For the first time she realised that, as on that first night together, they had made it no further than the carpeted floor, this time in the beautifully decorated and furnished lounge to their suite.

She smiled up at Justin. 'I think everyone should make love in a four-poster bed at least once in their lives.'

Justin looked around the room appreciatively. 'I suppose there are endless possibilities for the rest of our stay here.' He stood up, lifting her up easily into his arms. 'But right now the experience of a lifetime awaits us!'

Devon definitely was wasted on them this time around; they rarely left their suite, and when they did it was only to walk on the beach they discovered on walking down a cliff-path at the back of the hotel. To Caroline's surprise Justin enjoyed nothing better than taking off his shoes and socks, rolling up his trousers, and paddling in the surf with her at these times.

It was as if she was seeing yet another Justin, an even more endearing one, an infinitely more loveable one. And, when she already felt as if she loved him to bursting point, that seemed impossible—yet it was happening. Never more so than on the last day of their stay when she awoke to the worst feelings of nausea she had ever experienced.

The nausea didn't really hit her until she moved away from Justin's sleeping body, intending to use the bathroom before he even woke up. As soon as she stepped out of bed, the feelings of sickness washed over her in waves, and she swayed unsteadily on her feet as she tried to swallow down the feeling. Realising she wasn't going to be able to do that, she made a mad dash for the bathroom before she disgraced herself all over the luxuriously expensive carpet!

Her stomach kept heaving even once it was empty, and tears streamed down her face. Morning sickness! How were she and Justin going to carry on as if nothing was changing in their marriage when she couldn't even lift her head off the pillow in the mornings? The tears began to fall even harder.

'It's nothing to cry about.' Justin was suddenly

at her side, bathing her face, soothing her. 'Come on back to bed,' he encouraged gently. 'I'll get you some tea and dry toast sent up. Or would you prefer biscuits?' All the time he was talking he helped her back into the bedroom, tucking her in firmly beneath the covers before going to the telephone and placing their order.

All the time he spoke on the telephone, Caroline watched him miserably over the top of the bedclothes, sure her morning sickness had ruined what had been a perfect honeymoon so far.

'They're sure to realise why you asked for dry toast,' she sniffled miserably once Justin was off the telephone.

Smiling gently, he came to sit on the side of the bed, careful not to pull the covers tightly across her sensitive stomach. 'What difference does it make?' he cajoled, bathing her face once again.

'They're all going to think—going to think—'

'That we can't keep our hands off each other,' he teased softly. 'Besides, *we* know we've really been married two months, and that the baby is perfectly legitimate.'

She swallowed hard. 'That's the first time you've mentioned the baby without—wincing.' She looked up at him searchingly.

His gaze lost all its humour, suddenly evasive. 'Caroline, I——' He broke off as a knock sounded on the door, and stood up with what seemed to Caroline to be relief. 'That will be our breakfast,' he said lightly. 'Just stay where you are and I'll bring it through to you.'

As if she was going to go anywhere in her condition! Oh, damn it! Being bad-tempered about this wasn't going to help the situation at all. Justin couldn't help not wanting the baby, and she couldn't help her morning sickness either. She would just have to put a brave face on it if she weren't to make him impatient with the whole thing.

She was attempting to sit up against the pillows when Justin came back into the room with the breakfast tray.

He frowned as he saw what she was trying to do. 'I told you to stay where you were,' he reproved, putting the tray down to cross the room to her side.

She forced a bright smile to her lips, not realising it came out looking more like a grimace against her pallor. 'I'm feeling much better——'

'Like hell you are,' his voice rasped. 'Don't be a damned fool. Get back down in that bed before I decide to put you over my knee instead!' He settled her back down.

She frowned up at him from the lying position he had gently, but firmly, pushed her into. 'Stop swearing at me,' she said in a disgruntled voice.

'That isn't easy to do when you're behaving irresponsibly,' he scowled. 'You look like hell, you obviously feel even worse, and you have the nerve to try and tell me you're feeling better!'

The tears threatened to overflow again. 'I was only——'

'I know what "you were only".' He sat on the side of the bed again. 'Darling, you're my wife, and when you feel unwell, whatever the circumstances, I want to know about it,' he told her abruptly. 'You don't have to put on some sort of act with me, as if you're afraid to admit to feeling ill.' His gaze darkened as she gave a guilty blush. 'I'm not some sort of ogre, Caroline.' He stood up to move away from her. 'Now drink your tea and chew on your toast,' he encouraged gently as he handed them to her. 'You'll start to feel better in no time.'

She didn't exactly make a miraculous recovery, and as she fought down the nausea for the rest of the day, she had a feeling her sickness wasn't going to be confined to just the morning, but Justin was marvellous with her, knowing exactly the right moment to sit down and take a rest, or hand her one of the biscuits they had gone into the nearest town to buy. But he never again alluded to the fact that her sickness was caused by her pregnancy, once again ignoring its existence.

When she turned to him that night he gently took her in his arms and just held her against him, the caress of his hand on her back soothing rather than arousing.

She looked up at him with shyly encouraging eyes. 'I really am feeling much better now,' she assured him truthfully. 'And I'd hate to waste the last night of our honeymoon,' she added enticingly.

His gaze was searching. 'It isn't going to be wasted if we just hold each other,' he finally told her gently, obviously not satisfied with what he saw in her face.

'But I don't want to just hold you,' she protested impatiently. 'I really am all right, Justin,' she added enticingly, playing with the dark swirls of hair on his chest, knowing by the sudden unevenness of his breathing that it was having the desired effect. 'I have the feeling I'm going to be a night person with this pregnancy,' she said happily.

Justin's arms closed about her. 'How fortunate,' he murmured with satisfaction before his mouth claimed hers and all conversation ceased.

Their honeymoon had changed their relationship yet again. Justin seemed more relaxed with her than ever, and while he didn't openly mention her pregnancy again he was very considerate of her condition, always managing to waken before her so that he could bring her the tea and dry toast in bed. Usually this managed to ease the nausea, which seemed to be lessening as her pregnancy progressed anyway. By the time she was three months pregnant the sickness had stopped completely, something Caroline was more than grateful for.

Their social life had picked up, too, in recent weeks; they saw Sonia and Tony often, going out to the theatre and dinner occasionally, too. But Don Lindford hadn't called again, and when Caroline asked Justin if he had managed to contact the other man he had muttered something about him being out of the country at the moment.

It was on a return invitation to Sonia and Tony's one evening that the first moments of awkwardness since their holiday occurred. The last five weeks had been such happy ones, her relationship with Justin closer than ever. He no longer dreamt about the woman called Penny, or called out for her in the night, so Caroline could only assume that her guess at Justin fighting to hold on to that old love had been the right one; and that Justin had lost. The woman Penny was out of his mind and out of his heart now; she was sure of that.

But as soon as she saw that Sonia and Tony's other guests for dinner were Paula and a handsome blond-haired man, she knew that the evening wasn't going to go as smoothly and as pleasantly as she had hoped when she and Justin had set out earlier.

'I hear congratulations are in order,' Paula drawled as soon as they had been introduced to the man who was her partner for the evening, Brian Pendleton seeming to be a pleasant man.

'Thank you,' Caroline accepted abruptly, wary of the other woman on this, their first meeting since the night she and Justin had met for the first time.

'I can't say I exactly envy you,' the other woman mocked. 'Waddling around the place for the next few months!' She ran her hands pointedly over the perfect smoothness of her waist, very beautiful in a blue and silver gown that showed more silver as she moved.

Caroline opened her mouth to make a cutting reply, looking up at Justin as his arm came possessively about her waist.

He smiled at her encouragingly. 'Caroline is much too graceful to ever "waddle" anywhere,' he derided.

Paula gave a bitchy smile. 'You mean you'll still love her when she's so rounded with your child that you can scarcely share a bed!'

Justin's gaze hardened. 'There will never be a time that Caroline and I don't share a bed, Paula,' he told her softly, a warning in his voice.

The older woman's mouth tightened resentfully, but she was wise enough to say no more on the subject.

The evening was completely ruined for Caroline; how could she relax and enjoy herself when Paula Hammond seemed determined to make sure she didn't? Not that she could blame the other woman for still being upset about the way Justin had ended their relationship, but it had been five months ago, and Justin was very much the married man now.

'I'm sorry,' Sonia groaned, having asked Caroline to help her in the kitchen so that the two of them could talk alone. 'She more or less invited herself once she knew you and Justin were coming tonight, and Paula has enough arrogance for ten women!' she added with feeling. 'I would have put you off, but in the circumstances that might have looked too obvious.'

'It's all right.' Caroline squeezed her arm, seeing that her sister was really upset about the situation. 'I don't have anything to fear from Paula,' she said confidently, sure of Justin in a way that a woman like Paula could never make her doubt.

'Except her tongue!' Sonia reminded her drily. 'I feel sorry for poor Brian Pendleton; he's obviously only been brought along as an afterthought. Tony is absolutely disgusted by Paula's behaviour.' Sonia sighed. 'That's all we need to complete the evening: the two of them having one of their not unfamous arguments!'

Caroline chuckled softly. 'Justin could act as referee!'

Her sister nodded absently. 'I'm not even sure I have enough food; Paula only invited herself an hour ago.'

'You always cook too much anyway,' Caroline assured her lightly. 'I doubt if any of us will go hungry.'

Sonia squeezed her eyes tightly shut. 'I can't believe Paula actually publicly challenged your place in Justin's bed,' she groaned disbelievingly, shaking her head. 'Anyone with any sense—and that seems to exclude Paula in this case—can clearly see he can't take his eyes off you.'

Caroline laughed softly, warmed by the knowledge. 'Please don't worry about it; I'm not going to.' And surprisingly she knew that she wasn't, these few minutes she took to collect herself renewing her confidence in the marriage she and Justin were trying to build together. Nothing a woman like Paula Hammond could say could damage the relationship they already had together.

Her smile was completely natural as she went back into the lounge, sitting on the arm of Justin's chair as she leant into him, looking up to meet

Paula's scathing glance with questioningly raised brows.

'Isn't it perfectly nauseous to observe newly-weds together?' Paula spoke drily to no one in particular. 'But then I suppose you know all about nausea at the moment, don't you, Caroline?' she prompted with a sweetness that didn't fool anyone—and wasn't supposed to!

'Paula——'

'Actually,' Caroline cut across Tony's anger with an apologetic smile in his direction, 'I'm feeling in the best of health,' she told the other woman derisively. 'But then that's as it should be when I'm feeling so happy,' she added challengingly.

Paula gave a disgusted snort, but was prevented from further comment by Sonia's firm announcement that dinner was ready.

Caroline smiled at Justin as they took their seats, but although he returned the smile she could see from the anger in his gaze that he was at the end of his patience where Paula was concerned.

Paula hadn't got where she was in her profession by not being able to read people, and as they ate dinner she chatted amiably with them all, just as if her bitchiness had never occurred.

Caroline shared a conspiratorial smile with Tony, could see by his grimace that he could cheerfully have strangled his sister if he had been allowed to.

It wasn't until they were all sitting together in the living-room, drinking coffee, that Paula's self-control lapsed once again.

'Isn't this all very civilised?' Again she spoke to no one in particular. 'My brother is married to the sister of the woman he once intended marrying, and that sister is married to the man I——'

'You what, Paula?' Justin prompted in a dangerously soft voice.

Her eyes flashed deeply green. 'Whom I admire very much,' she answered challengingly.

'The professional admiration is reciprocated,' he bit out. 'Otherwise you wouldn't be working for my law firm.'

Paula flushed angrily at the veiled threat. 'I was only pointing out how curious it is that Tony should now be married to Caroline's sister instead of Caroline!'

'Not curious at all—when you consider the fact that he happens to be in love with Sonia,' Justin grated harshly.

'As you are in love with Caroline?' the self-assured woman taunted.

Some of the colour left Caroline's cheeks. She had never dared to openly voice that question, and she knew Justin would deeply resent a third person intruding in this familiar way. She could only hope he wouldn't deny the emotion in his chilling anger!

'Paula, why don't you go home?' Tony burst out furiously. 'You've done some stupid things in your time, but this must surely rate as the stupidest!'

His sister's eyes flashed again. 'You——'

'More coffee, anyone?' Sonia broke in brightly.

Paula wasn't to be put off. 'You——'

'No?' Sonia continued as if no one had spoken. 'In that case it's time for the part everyone dreads; washing-up! Paula,' she spoke coldly, 'you can come and help me.'

Surprised brows rose over mockingly appreciative green eyes. 'So the little mouse can roar,' Paula drawled, standing up.

'She can do more than roar,' Sonia told her sweetly, 'so don't push it, hm?' Her saccharine smile matched her tone.

Paula gave a huskily appreciative laugh. 'What a lot of champions you have, Caroline,' she said softly. 'Obviously "roaring" isn't a family characteristic. But then, of course, it wouldn't be; the two of you aren't really sisters, are you?' she dismissed with a shrug. 'Poor Caroline; first Sonia superseded you with the people you considered your parents, and then she came along and took the man in your life, too.' She gave a feigned sigh. 'Life can sometimes be such a bitch, can't it?'

'Not half such a bitch as you!' Tony sprang angrily to his feet. 'For your information, Caroline finished with me long before I first went out with Sonia,' he bit out contemptuously. 'And Caroline has always been her parents' much-loved eldest daughter. Now you can take yourself, and the poor man who is stuck with you for the evening——' he gave Brian Pendleton a pitying glance '—and get out of my home,' he told his sister harshly.

Furious green eyes turned on Caroline and Justin as Caroline once again sat on the arm of his chair.

'You don't need to tell me to get out of my office, too,' Paula rasped. 'I couldn't go on working there, anyway, watching you make such a fool of yourself over a woman who obviously knows a meal-ticket when she sees one.' She gave a scornful laugh as Caroline paled. 'She even made sure of it by getting pregnant straight away. But can you ever be sure it isn't my brother's baby?' Her head went back in challenge.

Caroline was barely aware of the shocked gasps around the room. She stared at Justin, a coldly furious Justin that she had never seen before, a nerve pulsing in his jaw as he slowly stood up.

'If you'll excuse me?' He spoke softly to their host, receiving a nod from the still-stunned Tony. Justin reached the door in two strides and wrenched it open, his silver gaze ripping into a now pale Paula as she realised, by the fact that she had succeeded in infuriating a man who could usually remain calm through any situation, that she had finally gone too far. 'Don't come near either Caroline or myself—but especially Caroline —again, or I'm not going to be answerable for the consequences. Do I make myself clear?'

'Very.' Paula picked up her clutch-bag with a calmness that defied him to think his threat meant anything to her. And maybe it would have looked convincing if her hand hadn't been trembling so badly. 'Come along, Brian,' she instructed haughtily.

The slenderly handsome man stood slowly to his

feet. 'I'll see you to your car,' he nodded politely.

Green eyes widened. 'But I drove you here,' she reminded lightly.

He nodded. 'I'll see you to your car,' he repeated tautly.

The three left sitting in the room, once Paula and the not-so-amenable Brian Pendleton had left, all looked shattered by the vitriolic attack, Justin standing beside the lounge door, breathing deeply in his anger.

Tony was the first to recover. 'My God, I didn't realise she was capable——I hope you don't believe there was any truth in that wild accusation she made about the baby.' He shook his head. 'Because it *was* wild,' he insisted firmly. 'Caroline and I never—we never——'

She was barely conscious of Justin's, 'I'm well aware of that,' although she was grateful for it, had hoped Paula's provocative taunt wouldn't make him reconsider the initial doubts he had had about the baby being his.

'Caroline.' Suddenly Justin appeared in her line of vision as she stared down at the floor; he was down on his haunches in front of her. 'Darling, it's all over now,' he soothed gently, pushing her hair back from her forehead.

'She was right,' she said in a pained voice, looking up at Justin with bewildered eyes. 'For years I've denied it, but—but I always felt pushed out by the fact that my parents had children of their own. I just——No one has ever put it into words before.' She shook her head.

She could see an emotion much like love in his eyes as he moved forward to pull her head down against his shoulder. 'Darling, of course you felt that way,' he said understandingly. 'Any four-year-old would feel resentment, let alone one who had been brought up to believe she was special because she was adopted.' His hands moved caressingly across her back.

She blinked back the tears. 'But I felt that way again when Sonia married Tony. I didn't love him myself, I—I just didn't like the idea of her marrying him.' She turned to her sister, pain etched into her face. 'I'm sorry. I—I'm sorry.' She could no longer hold back the tears.

'Caroline, you have nothing to feel sorry for,' Sonia chided gently, at her side, too, now. 'Do you think I didn't realise how you felt? God, in your place I would have refused to have anything to do with Simon and me. But you didn't, you were like a second little mother to us.' She smiled at the memory. 'And if you had even once guessed how I felt about Tony before the two of you finished you would probably have backed out and let me have him! Caroline, you don't have a selfish bone in your body, and we all love you.'

Years of hiding a resentment she had thought no one else knew about were suddenly stripped from her, leaving her free in a way she had never known before. Until Sonia and Simon were born she had known she was a very special person in her parents' life, but once she knew there was to be a baby of their own, even worse, *two* babies together, she had never felt as secure of their love again, had spent the rest of her life trying to prove herself to them. And now she saw it wasn't necessary. Sonia was right; all of her family did love her.

She gave a wan smile. 'You're right, Tony.' She smiled at him over Sonia's head. 'Pregnant women are much too emotional.'

He returned the smile affectionately. 'I think this pregnant woman's emotionalism was long overdue,' he said gently.

She turned back to Justin, warmed by the concern in his gaze. 'Paula must have wanted you very much, to have risked everything in that way,' she said sadly.

'Not really,' his mouth twisted. 'She had already handed in her notice, and was due to leave at the end of the month.'

'That's Paula all over,' Tony dismissed disgustedly. 'Even her "grand gesture" turns out to be not quite what it seemed.'

The touch of humour lightened the atmosphere, and they all smiled a little with relief at the passing of the awkwardness Paula had so wantonly caused.

'I think we should leave now.' Justin straightened up.

Caroline shook her head. 'I'll help Sonia with the clearing away first.'

'Don't be silly,' her sister dismissed lightly. 'Tony can help me do that.'

'Yes,' he grimaced, 'I can help her do that.'

Caroline was completely poised again now, and she stood up with a shake of her head. 'You two men enjoy a brandy together while Sonia and I tackle the washing-up.'

'I——'

'That sounds like a good idea,' Justin agreed firmly, deftly cutting off the other man's protest, sharing a look of complete understanding with Caroline as he realised she wanted to talk to her sister alone before they left. 'Make mine a large one.' He scowled, sitting down, stretching his long legs out in front of him in a completely relaxed pose.

As soon as the kitchen door closed behind them Sonia and Caroline were in each other's arms.

'I never realised—— I thought I was very ungrateful—— Do Mummy and Daddy know?' Caroline groaned at what a fool she had been all her life.

'I'm sure they know how you felt, yes,' Sonia nodded emotionally. 'But they knew you would feel worse if they spoke to you about it. Do you know that when we were younger Simon and I always envied you? Yes, we did,' she insisted at Caroline's sceptical look. 'We never thought it was fair that you had been especially chosen by Mummy and Daddy and we had just been born to them!' her sister told her ruefully. 'It was only when we got older that we realised perhaps you didn't see it that way.'

She shook her head. 'I suppose children always want what isn't theirs; I wanted to *be* Mum and Dad's, and you and Simon wished you could be adopted so that you could be "special", too!' She sighed ruefully. 'I think it's mainly due to Mum and Dad's sensible loving that we've turned out as level-headed as we have.'

Sonia hugged her again before stepping back. 'You're going to be just as sensible with your baby, you'll see.' She began to tidy up. 'And Justin is such a nice man, he deserves to be happy this time.' She ran the steaming hot water into the sink, putting in the plates to soak.

It took a few seconds for what she had said to sink in, but once it did Caroline stared at her back with puzzled eyes. This time?

She swallowed hard. 'I'm glad you and Tony like him so much,' she answered dazedly. *This time?*

Sonia turned to give her a brief smile. 'Once you get past the surface coldness you can't help but like him. And I suppose it's only natural that he should have built up defences after what happened,' she chattered on.

'Yes,' she agreed hollowly. *After what happened?* She had completely lost her grip on this conversation, had no idea what Sonia was talking about.

'I know how unhappy I would be if anything happened to Tony and me.' Sonia shook her head. 'And she could only have been young,' she added sadly. 'It seems such a waste.'

The evening had been too long, been too fraught with tension already; Caroline swayed tiredly as she tried to make sense of the conversation. It had something to do with Justin's past, of that she was certain, but the little he had told her himself, about his childhood, his parents' death, didn't include any 'she'. Except the Penny he spoke of in his dreams. Could this puzzling conversation have anything to do with her?

'It must have been a terrible time for Justin,' Sonia continued, completely unaware that Caroline had no idea what she was talking about as she did the dishes without looking round.

'Yes,' Caroline agreed again, desperate to know what she had so far been afraid to ask Justin, fearing the end of their marriage if she did.

'But now he has you.' Sonia turned to smile at her. 'He has a whole new life with you and the baby you're expecting. He already seems so much more—relaxed than he did when the two of you were first married.' She resumed washing the dishes. 'I hope you didn't mind Tony telling me about the death of Justin's first wife.' She frowned. 'It's such a private thing, really, but Paula told Tony, and so Tony told me . . . I just——'

Caroline was no longer listening to her sister's chatter. *Justin had been married before!*

CHAPTER EIGHT

CAROLINE hadn't wanted to look at it, hadn't wanted to see the indisputable proof which told her that not only had Justin lied to her about believing in love, he had also not told her of his first wife, a woman he *had* loved.

She hadn't seen their marriage certificate since Justin had slipped it into his pocket after their wedding, but there under the marital status column for Justin was the word 'widower'!

Caroline didn't know how long she had been staring at it, feeling completely numb. Widowers were elderly gentlemen, men who had lived a lifetime with the woman they loved, not men of Justin's age who hadn't had a life at all! She couldn't think how she had missed this tangible evidence on their wedding day, except that she had been so ecstatically happy that day she hadn't really seen anything at all except Justin.

She had somehow managed to get through the last of the previous evening, agreeing eagerly when Justin suggested they leave shortly after she and Sonia returned from the kitchen. And if Justin had noticed that she was a little quieter than usual he had obviously put it down to a reaction to Paula's bitchiness, also seeming to understand when she had been the one to suggest she was too tired for lovemaking.

She had barely slept, still too numb from what Sonia had unwittingly revealed to her, too stunned to confront Justin for the truth just then. But this morning, after he had left for work, she had found their marriage certificate locked away in Justin's desk along with his other private papers—although a heartbreaking search had revealed no previous marriage certificate for Justin. To Penny.

Penny had to have been Justin's first wife; it was too obvious not to be the truth. And if, as Caroline suspected, Penny was also the reason Justin had had a vasectomy, preferring not to have any children at all if they couldn't be the children of the woman he had loved, then it would mean the end of *their* marriage. While she had still held out hope that Justin would eventually come to love their child, she had been willing to try anything to keep their marriage intact, but she wouldn't —couldn't—subject her child to a lifetime of rejection by its father because it wasn't the child of the woman he had loved. That would be a cruelty to them all.

She felt for Justin, knew he must have suffered terribly after his first wife's death, even sympathised with his decision not to allow love into his life again. But there had been so many things he had never told her about himself that she was beginning to wonder if they had ever really had a marriage. Marriage had to be more than pleasing each other in bed! Where was the sharing, the confiding, the *trusting?*

She felt betrayed, deeply let down, was hurting so badly she wanted to cry and never stop. But the tears wouldn't come, and neither would the release from the numbing pain. Only Justin could help her now, and she doubted that he would want to, not in the way she needed to be helped. For that he would have to tell her he no longer loved Penny; and she knew that wasn't true. He would have to tell her he wanted the child she carried; and she knew that wasn't true either.

The dream that had begun so fragilely now seemed set to shatter into irretrievable pieces.

It wasn't the ideal time for Don Lindford to pay his return call, but when Mrs Avery came into the living-room later that day to tell her he was outside in the hallway she knew she would have to see him, if only to tell him how sorry Justin was to have missed him the last time he called.

'Mr Lindford.' She rose smilingly to greet him, doing her best to put aside her despair at least for the duration of his visit.

'Don,' he gently reproved, taking the hand she held out to him.

He was just as charmingly handsome as ever, slightly more tanned than he had been the last time she had seen him, but then Justin had said he had been out of the country. After the typically British summer they had just had he would have had to have been to have acquired a tan at all.

'Don,' she returned. 'Won't you sit down?' she

invited politely, sitting in the chair opposite his as he
did so. 'I'm afraid Justin isn't here again,' she
explained apologetically.

'So I understand.' He nodded slowly.

'He will be in his office all of this afternoon
though, if you would like to——'

'I can't, I'm afraid,' he said regretfully, his brown
eyes warm, his sandy-coloured hair slightly ruffled
from the breeze outside. 'I just called in on the off-
chance on my way to the airport.'

'You're going away again?' Her eyes widened. She
didn't know why she had, but she had presumed Don
Lindford was a lawyer like Justin; if he were he had
some very strange clients to need to go out of the
country so much. 'Justin tried to contact you after
your last visit,' she explained at his questioning look,
'but apparently you were out of the country then,
too.'

He smiled. 'Didn't Justin tell you I'm in the
import/export business?'

'No.' That explained so much!

'It can sometimes make me—elusive,' he added
enigmatically.

'That's what Justin said,' she acknowledged
ruefully.

'Did he?' Don chuckled. 'He knows me so well.'

'It would seem so.' She returned his smile ruefully.
'I gather the two of you have been friends for a long
time.'

'And I gather,' he said teasingly, 'that the "pack"
is about to increase by one. It is just one, isn't it?' he
prompted mischievously.

Because she was so naturally slender her pregnancy had begun to show almost immediately, and now at four months she had a definite 'bump' to clearly reveal her condition.

'As far as we know,' she said drily.

'Your brother and sister are twins, aren't they?'

Her eyes widened. 'How did you know that?' she asked curiously.

He frowned, shrugging. 'Someone must have mentioned it,' he dismissed. 'Justin's unexpected marriage to you caused quite a lot of gossip at the time, you know,' he added teasingly.

'I can imagine,' she acknowledged disgustedly; how much more speculation it would cause if their marriage came to an abrupt end! 'I can't bear gossip,' she snapped impatiently.

'Most of it was from jealous women who would have given anything to be in your place,' Don pointed out.

Like Paula. 'I can understand that,' she accepted heavily. 'Can I offer you a drink this time, Don?' She gave a wan smile.

'Afraid not,' he answered ruefully. 'I really am, literally, on my way to the airport. But I'll take a raincheck, though, for the next time I come to see Justin.'

'Perhaps he'll even be here next time.' She sighed. 'The weekend is really the best time to find him at home,' she advised.

'Right.' He stood up. 'It's been nice meeting you again, Caroline.'

'And you.' She walked out to the door with him.

'You must come to dinner when you return from your trip abroad.'

His grin widened. 'As soon as Justin feels up to sharing the company of his wife!'

Her smile didn't quite reach her eyes. 'He's looking forward to seeing you again, I can assure you.'

'We'll see,' Don said non-committally.

'Where are you off to?' Caroline enquired politely.

'A few days here, a few days there.' He shrugged dismissively. 'In my business you're never quite sure where you're going to be tomorrow.'

'Obviously.' She gave a rueful smile. 'Well, I wish you success on this latest business trip.'

'Thanks.' His gaze was warm. 'And you take care of your wolf and cub, OK?'

'OK.' She laughed softly.

His fist lightly grazed her jaw. 'Justin is a very lucky man,' he murmured admiringly.

Her eyes were suddenly shadowed. 'I'll tell him you said that.'

Don straightened, looking at his narrow gold wrist-watch. 'You do that,' he nodded absently. 'I have to dash if I don't want to miss my plane,' he said regretfully.

Caroline turned slowly away from the closed door once he had left; she would make sure she didn't forget to tell Justin about his visit this time! It was unfortunate that they kept missing each other.

She couldn't help wondering if part of Don's initial surprise at finding Justin had married her was because he had known Penny, known how much Justin loved the other woman.

'Has Mr Lindford gone?'

She drew in a deep breath before raising her head to look at Mrs Avery, frowning deeply as she saw how worried the other woman looked. 'What is it, Mrs Avery?' she asked, voicing her own concern at how pale the elderly woman looked. 'What's wrong?'

'I'm not really sure.' The housekeeper shook her head. 'Mr de Wolfe told me that if ever Mr Lindford called again I was to telephone him straight away and let him know. But——'

'What on earth for?' Caroline was puzzled now: did Justin want to see the other man so much, and was he afraid she would once again forget to tell him of his visit?

'I don't know,' the older woman returned, 'but I did just as he asked, and now Mr Lindford's left before Mr de Wolfe returned, and——'

'Justin is coming home?' Caroline was even more puzzled.

'Yes. But I——' The housekeeper broke off as she heard a key put in the lock.

Caroline stared at Justin in some surprise, although she had known it had to be him; she had never seen him quite so distraught before, his hair looking as if he had run his fingers through it many times, his face pale beneath naturally dark skin.

She also knew he must have driven as if the devil were at his heels to get home in the short time since Mrs Avery must have called him. What on earth had made him so upset about Don Lindford's visit that he had risked having an accident in this way?

'Where is he?' His voice was grim.

'Justin——'

'Where is he, Caroline?' He prompted in a fiercely hushed voice.

'He's gone. But——'

'Damn!' Justin slammed his clenched fist against his thigh. 'Damn him!' He closed his eyes in frustrated anger.

'Justin.' She shot a pointed glance in Mrs Avery's direction, the poor woman looking more bewildered than ever. As she was. But she wasn't about to satisfy her curiosity out here in the hallway; she and Justin had too much to discuss for that.

He relaxed only slightly, attempting to give the housekeeper a reassuring smile. 'Thank you for calling me so promptly,' he told her gently. 'Could Mrs de Wolfe and I have some tea in the lounge now, please?'

Mrs Avery seemed glad of something to do and hurried off to her kitchen, where her pots and pans didn't cause her half so much worry as the two humans she worked for.

Caroline turned back to Justin. 'Perhaps now you wouldn't mind telling me what all that was about?' she said irritably, disturbed by the way Justin had burst in here asking for the other man.

He sighed. 'Let's go through to the lounge,' he suggested firmly.

She preceded him into the room in tight-lipped

frustration, even though she realised they couldn't carry out their conversation in the hallway.

'Really, Justin,' she turned to him impatiently as soon as they were in the privacy of the lounge, 'why on earth did you rush home in that way just to see Don Lindford? Or was it just to see him? She frowned suddenly. 'You didn't think I was attracted to him, did you?' She was horrified at the thought.

'Of course not,' Justin grated abruptly. 'Damn it, Caroline, I—what did he want?' he demanded, his gaze narrowed.

'To see you again, of course.' She moved restlessly about the room.

'Caroline.' He spoke slowly, worriedly. 'Hasn't it ever occurred to you that Lindford calls at very strange times if he expects to find me at home?'

She ceased her pacing, looking at him questioningly. 'Well, yes, of course it has,' she confirmed hesitantly. 'But last time he just called on the off-chance, and this time he said he was on his way to the airport and thought he would just drop in——'

'The airport?' Justin echoed sharply. 'He's going out of the country again?'

She nodded. 'So he said. He said he's in the import/export business, so I——'

'Did he indeed?' Justin snorted derisively. 'I doubt very much——' He had come to an abrupt halt next to the tiny table that stood beside the chair Caroline had been sitting in earlier, and slowly picked up the folded piece of paper there. He shot Caroline a puzzled look as he held their marriage certificate in his artistically slender hands.

Caroline stiffened. She had left the certificate out, intending to talk to Justin about his previous marriage, only they had become side-tracked by the subject of Don Lindford. Now she felt like a child caught with her hand in the cookie jar. Which was ridiculous. It was their marriage certificate, for goodness' sake! And she wasn't the one who had been keeping secrets . . .

'There's no need to look at me like that,' she snapped defensively, her nerves strung out to breaking point. 'It's *our* marriage certificate.'

'Yes?' he prompted calmly—too calmly!

'I wanted to see it!'

'Obviously.' Justin nodded, his gaze narrowed on her in slow speculation.

Caroline sighed. 'I think you can guess why,' she bit out impatiently, hating being made to feel on the defensive like this, feeling very much as she had at their first meeting when she had felt at such a disadvantage by his blunt honesty.

'Guess why you went into my desk, looked through the papers there?' he queried pleasantly. 'Actually, no,' he said harshly. 'I can't imagine why you would feel this sudden urge to see our marriage certificate. Perhaps you doubted its legality?' he derided harshly. 'Or maybe you were just hoping there had been some sort of mistake?'

'Why on earth would I hope a thing like that?' she gasped in a pained voice.

He shrugged broad shoulders. 'Things have always been strained between us,' he grated.

'Maybe you realise this marriage wasn't such a good idea after all.'

Her eyes widened. 'Is that the way you feel about it?'

'We weren't discussing me,' Justin said abruptly.

She gave a ragged sigh. 'Of course I don't want to end our marriage,' she dismissed impatiently. 'I just—— I wanted to see our marriage certificate. I—something Sonia said last night made it—necessary,' she finished awkwardly.

He stiffened warily, suddenly tense. 'Something *Sonia* said?' he repeated softly.

Caroline swallowed hard, her heart fluttering nervously now that she could no longer put off discussing the fact that he had been married before. 'She mentioned your first marriage,' she told Justin in a rush, colour burning her cheeks at the same time that his seemed to pale. 'Quite—casually, innocently.' She shrugged awkwardly. 'She thought I already knew, you see,' she added emotionally, wishing she could remain calmly in control, but the subject was still too new to her for her to cope with it in the way she had all the other surprises her marriage had revealed.

Justin gave a weary sigh, the marriage certificate fluttering back down on to the table as he moved his hand to run his fingers distractedly through his hair. 'Yes—I do see,' he finally answered in a raggedly disjointed voice. 'The marriage certificate confirms that I was married before,' he conceded flatly.

'Yes,' she nodded, her eyes pained.

'And now you want to know about——'

'Penny,' she put in firmly.

He frowned darkly. 'How do you know her name?' he demanded suspiciously.

'Dreams. *Your* dreams,' she revealed. 'When you called out for her.' She deliberately kept her voice devoid of emotion, not wanting it to sound like an accusation, even though his calling for the other woman had made her feel betrayed.

'Oh, God.' He groaned, his gaze momentarily hidden from her as he squeezed his eyes tightly shut. The memories were all there in the silver-grey depth once he looked at her again. 'I'm sorry for that,' he told her heavily. 'I thought they had all stopped. I—I am sorry you had to find out about Penny that way.'

Caroline moistened her lips. 'All I learnt from your dreams was that you had a woman in your life called Penny. I didn't realise until last night that she had been your wife.'

His gaze widened. 'Then what——' He broke off abruptly as Mrs Avery bustled in with the tray of tea.

'Sorry I took so long.' She seemed unaware of the tension in the room, her flushed cheeks telling of her own flustered mood. 'The telephone rang. And then I realised I had forgotten to put the kettle on. And then—but you don't want to hear all this.' She suddenly seemed to realise that the silence in the room was fraught with an expectant tension. 'I'll go and see about dinner,' she awkwardly excused herself.

'Poor Mrs Avery.' Caroline gave the ghost of a smile as the tiny woman hurried from the room. 'She isn't used to all this.'

'I don't think any of us are,' Justin bit out, seeming more in control after the brief interruption. 'If you didn't know Penny had been my wife, what *did* you think she was?' He watched her closely.

Caroline drew in a ragged breath. 'I believed that—that she was the woman you loved. I didn't know she was dead.'

'If I loved another woman, why did I marry you?' he demanded impatiently.

'Any number or reasons.' She shrugged ruefully. 'Penny could have been married to someone else. Or maybe she couldn't accept your decision about not having children. Or perhaps——'

'I get the general idea,' Justin bit out raspingly. 'When did these—dreams start?' he frowned darkly.

She sighed. 'The night we first went to dinner with Sonia and Tony. The first night you hadn't— hadn't——' She couldn't put into words the start of her disillusionment when he had rejected her so cruelly.

'Oh, my God,' he groaned emotionally. 'And when I called out for Penny later that night you thought it was because I loved her!' He grasped Caroline's arms painfully, forcing her to look at him. 'Darling, it wasn't that at all——'

'Don't call me that.' She wrenched away from him, her eyes dark with pain. 'You loved her. I could tell that you loved her!'

'Of course I did,' he admitted dismissively. 'But it was twelve years ago, Caroline. I'm not even the same person now that I was then!'

'I know that,' she choked. 'The man you are today is incapable of feeling love!'

The hands he had been raising to grasp hers suddenly clenched into fists instead, Justin recoiling as if he had been struck.

He turned away from her, his breathing ragged. 'Can't you see,' he finally bit out forcefully, 'how much loving someone hurts?'

'I know exactly how much it hurts,' she choked, her love for him clearly revealed in her pain-filled eyes if he would only care to turn and look at her.

And he did turn, flinching back from her as if she had dealt him a physical blow. 'I never asked for your love.' He shook his head, coldness in his gaze now. 'I told you from the first how I felt about it.'

'But you didn't reject my love when I first offered it to you!' she reminded him raggedly.

'No,' he conceded heavily. 'I'd hoped— wanted——' He breathed harshly. 'Where do we go from here?'

Caroline felt as if part of her had curled up inside her and died. What had she expected, that Justin would suddenly get down on his knees and declare his undying love for her, tell her that no matter how he had felt in the past he could no longer deny his love for her and their child? Those were the things that dreams were made of, and when a man was as determined as Justin never to fall in love again they were destined to remain just that, dreams.

'*You* don't go anywhere,' she sighed shakily. 'But I have to go. You must see that.'

No emotion showed on his face; she might just as well have told him she intended going out shopping, not that she was leaving him and not coming back!

'Like all women, I had foolish dreams,' she dismissed self-derisively, her heart breaking inside. 'But now I think it would be best, for all of us——' she had to think of her child, and the man standing before her could never love anyone '—if I just left.' She held her head up proudly in defiance of the pain that threatened to rip her apart.

Justin still stood unmoving—and unmoved. 'I can't let you do that,' he murmured softly.

As if any of them had a choice any more! She had to believe they would all be better off her way, she because she would no longer be constantly seeking the unattainable, her baby because it would grow up knowing only love, and Justin because he was happiest when he wasn't forced to acknowledge emotion. It didn't matter that she would always love him, not when she had her child to consider, too.

She gave a dismissive shake of her head. 'I wasn't asking your permission, Justin,' she stated huskily. 'This is the way it has to be.'

'No.'

'Justin——'

'Not yet, Caroline,' he insisted harshly. 'If you still want to go in a few months' time then I'll help you set up your new home. I'm sure Mrs Avery will be only too pleased to accompany you wherever you want to go,' he added drily. 'Her loyalties had changed by about the second day you moved in,' he conceded ruefully.

'I'll be pleased to have her,' Caroline accepted distractedly, 'but I'm most certainly not waiting a few months before I leave.'

'I can't let you go just yet.' Justin shook his head.

'And I already told you I don't need your permission!' She was becoming deeply agitated; why couldn't he at least let her leave with her dignity intact! 'Justin, don't let's prolong this. Let's just end things while we're at least still friends.'

He gave a tight, humourless smile. 'I'm not asking this to hurt you any more. I just—Caroline, why don't you sit down? You've been under enough strain for one day.' He frowned. 'All this can't be good for the baby.'

'Please don't pretend that it matters to you,' she said sadly. 'That would be too cruel.'

'I certainly don't want you to lose it, and if I——' He broke off, breathing harshly. 'You have to stay here!'

Caroline looked at him searchingly. 'Why?' she finaly prompted huskily.

'Is your pregnancy going well?' he probed anxiously. 'Is the doctor satisfied that everything is—normal?'

'Very normal,' she confirmed warily. 'Justin, tell me what's wrong?' she urged with a sudden certainty that something definitely was wrong!

He drew in a deep breath. 'You once asked me about—well, about this.' He put a hand up to his velvet-covered eye.

'Yes?' She felt a strange churning in her chest.

Justin nodded abruptly, seeming to be searching for the right words. 'There is no easy way to tell you this,' he finally bit out harshly. 'You're sure nothing is—going to happen, to you or the baby?' He looked at her anxiously.

'I can't promise.' She shook her head. 'But if it's something that I have a right to know, something that affects my leaving today, then I think you should tell me.'

'At least sit down,' he encouraged softly.

She couldn't see how having her sit down was going to make any difference if what he were about to tell her was so disturbing, but she did as he requested anyway, sensing that he really was anxious nothing should happen to the baby.

'The tea is probably cold by now, but——'

'Justin, I don't want any tea,' Caroline told him patiently. 'I just want to know what's bothering you.'

'Lindford is what's bothering me!' he bit out forcefully.

'Don Lindford?' she repeated in a bewildered voice. 'But what does he have to do——' She broke off, paling as she remembered what Justin had said a few minutes ago. 'You mean he——' She swallowed hard, nausea quickly rising. 'He's the one——'

'——who blinded me,' Justin finished grimly, his fingers moving absently against the black velvet that covered the unseeing orb. 'Yes, he's the one,' he confirmed harshly. 'And until I find out what he intends to take from me this time, I can't let you leave here!'

CHAPTER NINE

CAROLINE looked up at him with bewildered eyes. 'Take from you?' she repeated dazedly.

Justin came down on his haunches beside her chair, taking her chilled hands in his. 'Surely you can see that he's been coming here for a reason, that his friendly little promises to "see me again soon" are no more than veiled threats?' he explained grimly.

Yes, she could see that now, now that she knew the other man had deliberately injured Justin in the past because of the wrong he considered he had done him.

She would never have guessed that the pleasantly attractive man was responsible for blinding Justin, his ready charm having lulled her into a false sense of security where he was concerned. It gave her a shiver down her spine to recall how friendly he had seemed, how he had talked to her teasingly as if he were an old friend of Justin's who had just heard of his marriage. She didn't need to be told where he had been 'away' so that he was unable to attend their wedding as he had claimed. It would have been a little difficult for him to have got out of prison for the day!

God, how he must laughed at her for her

ignorance about him. And Justin was right about those veiled threats; she recognised them for exactly what they were now. She also realised what Justin had already known, that the other man's visits while he was at work hadn't been accidental at all, that Don Lindford had been well aware of the fact that Justin wouldn't be at home at that time of the day.

Last time he had taken the sight of one of Justin's eyes as his retribution; what did he intend to take this time?

'Oh, God, Justin!' She paled even more as realisation hit her. 'He knows about the baby.' She clutched at him frantically. 'He realised this afternoon that I was pregnant, and congratulated me on the fact.' Her eyes were wild. 'He wouldn't try to—try to—— God! Justin,' she choked again. 'The man's dangerous, his vindictiveness is a sickness. Can't you do anything to stop him?' She gazed up at him anxiously.

'The police already know of his last visit——'

'They do?' she pounced eagerly.

He nodded slowly, his gaze gently apologetic. 'I was afraid to tell you before who he was in case anything happened to the baby. I didn't want to risk causing you to miscarry,' he told her grimly. 'But I had to stop you leaving me, and leaving yourself open to Lindford's schemes.' He looked at her searchingly. 'Maybe I should call your doctor now and get him to check you over. This must have been a shock to you, and——'

'Justin, babies, and pregnant women, are much

stronger than you realise,' she sighed. 'I don't even feel a twinge of discomfort. And no doctor would thank you for bringing him here for no reason other than your own worry.'

'I don't give a damn whether he would thank me or not,' he rasped. '*You're* what's important.'

She could see that she was important to him, that although Justin still didn't want their child—*his* child—he couldn't bear to see anything happen to her or it. She didn't know which it was worse to feel, the futile love she had for Justin, or his own inability to recognise love, to acknowledge it even if he did recognise it.

'You should have told me about Don Lindford, Justin,' she frowned. 'It's been weeks since his last visit.' She gave an involuntary shiver as she realised he had been as close to her in this room as Justin was now.

'I've alerted the police, although there isn't anything they can do unless he actually commits a crime, except warn him to behave himself, and they've already done that.' He grimaced. 'Paying a visit and congratulating you on your pregnancy can't be considered a threat. But Mrs Avery knew to call me if he came here again.'

'You've been treating me like a child who had to be protected from the truth, Justin——'

'It was *your* child I was concerned about. Can't you see that?' he interrupted angrily. 'I knew you would never forgive me if anything happened to the baby because of who and what I am,' he said bitterly. 'You've forgiven me a lot of things, but even you wouldn't have been able to accept that!'

'You still should have told me, shouldn't have kept this to yourself.' Her eyes suddenly widened as she realised Don Lindford knew all about her family too, and now that she knew who he was, and what he had done to Justin in the past, she very much doubted that he had acquired that knowledge through gossip about her and Justin, as he had claimed he had. He seemed to have an obsessive need to know all about Justin, and the people who were close to him. 'My family have to be warned——'

'Tony already knows to take care of Sonia, and your parents are sensible people, too. Unfortunately, paying me social calls can't be considered a crime,' Justin grated, his gaze bleak.

'But he didn't come to see you. I'm sure seeing me here alone was deliber—— What do you mean, Tony already knows about it?' She looked puzzled as she realised what he had said. 'You told him?' she frowned.

Justin gave an abrupt nod of his head. 'The night we first went over there for dinner. You had mentioned Lindford's visit, and Tony saw my reaction to it. He realised something wasn't quite right about Lindford's visit. In the circumstances I thought it best that he know.' He shrugged.

'So that's why he seemed different when the two of you got back from buying the champagne,' Caroline said slowly.

'Yes,' Justin sighed. 'As soon as we were out of the door he started asking questions.' He looked at

her ruefully. 'Once he knew the truth about
Lindford he agreed with me about not telling you
yet, something to do with the early months of
pregnancy being the most delicate. As it turned out
it was the best thing; it saved you six weeks of
unnecessary worry. When anything might have
happened,' he added pointedly.

For someone who proclaimed to care nothing for
their child he had been very anxious that no harm
should come to it! Unless that really was because
he believed she would blame him if she miscarried
because of a past he could do nothing about. She
suddenly felt too tired to battle with her own
thoughts any more today, feeling weak and ill.

She sighed wearily. 'It seems I have no choice
but to stay here until we find out what—game this
man Lindford is playing with us.' Worry etched
her brow. 'I wish—oh!' She gave a start of surprise
as she clutched instinctively at the slight swelling
that was the baby.

Justin was instantly at her side, his face very
pale, his gaze darkly shadowed. 'What is it?' he
demanded anxiously. 'Is it the baby? Oh, my God,'
he choked. 'I didn't——'

'It is the baby, Justin.' She spoke calmly,
soothingly, her expression serene. 'But nothing is
wrong. I just felt a fluttering movement, like the
gentle beat of a butterfly's wing.' Tears of
happiness glistened in her eyes as she looked up at
him emotionally. 'I felt our son or daughter move
inside me for the first time!' she told him shakily.

He seemed to pale even more, shaking his head

as he moved away from her. 'You couldn't have done,' he gasped. 'It's too soon, surely?'

'About sixteen weeks the doctor told me it can occasionally be felt, and I'm just over that, although it is usually about twenty weeks.' She gazed up at him yearningly. 'It's the strangest sensation, and yet the most beautiful too. I——'

'I think you should go and lie down,' he cut in abruptly, keeping his gaze averted from where her hands still rested lightly against their baby. 'I'll have Mrs Avery prepare an early dinner and then I think you should get some rest. And you don't need to worry, I'll be sleeping in the guest-room from now on!'

Caroline watched in dismay as he strode briskly from the room. Nothing was going to change, it never would change; she had been a fool to hope that it ever would. She could only hope she wasn't forced to stay here too much longer.

But their lives did change irrevocably after that day, with not even the physical closeness there now to prevent Justin and herself from becoming complete strangers.

They went about their lives separately, often not seeing each other for days at a time, Justin often eating dinner in his study while Caroline had a tray in her room. If Mrs Avery was aware of the estrangement she wisely said nothing.

They heard nothing from Don Lindford in the weeks that followed, and it seemed that he was still out of the country. Justin had his own ideas as to the purpose of these 'business trips' but proving it would be difficult, although it almost seemed as if the other man was daring Justin to try and prove anything against him by telling him of his 'import/export' business.

Neither of them had any doubt that he meant to keep to his promise to see Justin again!

Caroline was dismayed when she realised that she and Justin never had finished their conversation about his first wife, about how and why the other woman had died. Not that it really mattered, Caroline acknowledged, not when Justin's ability to love had died with her. She didn't need to know anything more about his first marriage than that.

Despite the worry about Don Lindford, and the state of her marriage, the pregnancy was going well. The baby moved all the time now, seemed extremely active. It was an experience she should have been able to share with Justin, but after the last time she had attempted it she didn't dare. As a result, the baby was growing nicely and *she* was losing weight. By the end of her fifth month she felt too dispirited to continue working. She was sad to let her career go and to say goodbye to all the wonderful people she had come to know at the hospital, but really felt she wasn't doing her patients or herself any good by continuing. But the extra time at the apartment that no longer seemed like home to her didn't bring her any comfort.

After two weeks of wandering about the perfectly neat and tidy rooms, when she was even beginning to get on Mrs Avery's nerves with her constant listlessness, Caroline knew she couldn't stand living like this any longer, that it was time for her to start getting on with the rest of her life.

'No!' Justin bit out furiously that evening when she told him she was going to start looking around for somewhere else to live.

She sighed brokenly at his implacability. 'I can't live like this any more!'

His mouth tightened as his gaze flickered over her finely etched features and too-slender body. 'And what about Lindford?'

She made an impatient movement. 'If he's that dangerous why don't the police arrest him?' She knew she was behaving unreasonably, but she just couldn't cope any more.

'There's a little matter of evidence, Caroline,' Justin reminded her in a rasping voice. 'He hasn't committed any crime—that they're yet aware of,' he added grimly.

If the last weeks had been hard on her, Justin hadn't fared any better, his face thinner, lines of tiredness beside his eyes, no sign any more of even his arrogant humour. They were making each other more unhappy than was necessary by this enforced continuation of their sham of a marriage. Anyone looking at them could see they were unhappy together.

'He could go on like this for years,' she pointed out restlessly.

'He won't,' Justin said with certainty. 'Sooner or later he's going to get tired of playing.'

'And if it's later?' She sighed her frustration with the situation, not even caring at that moment that, when Don Lindford did tire of playing, someone might get hurt. She was too tired and angry to think rationally.

Justin shrugged. 'I can't see that it's going to harm you to continue living with me like this,' he bit out, his eyes narrowed. 'What's really changed, Caroline?' he derided. 'Only that we no longer share a bed!'

She flinched. 'You're right.' She was suddenly very still. 'We always were strangers anywhere else but there.'

He frowned darkly. 'I didn't mean it like— Caroline!' he called after her as she fled the room.

He made no effort to follow her to the bedroom she now slept in alone, and for that she felt grateful. These damned tears, she cursed the flood that cascaded down her cheeks; the morning sickness had passed only to be replaced by tears that fell at the slightest provocation. And living with Justin the way that she was at the moment there was all too much of that! She cried because she was bored and restless, she cried because there seemed too much to do, she cried because she loved Justin, she cried because she hated him a little, too. Anything could make her cry, even the fact that it was raining outside.

Justin was right, she couldn't leave here just yet. And that made her cry, too!

The socialising they had to do made matters even

worse. Her whole family seemed to like Justin, and when they dined with her parents Simon usually managed to be there now, his admiration for Justin so great that he was contemplating becoming a lawyer, too, once he had left university. Even being with Sonia and Tony was a strain, although Tony, at least, was aware of the situation concerning Don Lindford.

The situation also seemed to have brought out Tony's protective instincts where Sonia was concerned, to have shown him his true feelings for his wife, his love for her now undoubted. And if nothing else good had come out of the mess, Caroline could at least be glad that had. Tony and Sonia's marriage was going to last; she was sure of it.

Although she wasn't quite so certain of that when Sonia turned up at the apartment swearing and cursing about her husband.

'How dare he!' She marched into the apartment after Caroline, having nothing else to do, had opened the door to her ring. 'Treating me as if I'm six years old, like I have no sense at all—yes, just as if all I have between my ears is fresh air!' She glared across the width of the lounge at Caroline, who watched her rather bemusedly. 'And you're no better,' she suddenly accused, her blue eyes blazing furiously. 'I realise I'm your "baby sister", but how could you keep something like this from me? I thought we were close, closer than ever before after admitting how guilty we felt about our jealousy of each other as children. And now you——'

'Sonia, would you calm down and tell me what's wrong?' she prompted ruefully. 'Let me ask Mrs Avery to get us some tea,' she said persuasively. 'And then——'

'Tea!' her sister echoed explosively. 'I don't want any tea, I just want an explanation!'

She held up her hands in a defensive shrug. 'For what?' Caroline was completely puzzled by her sister's outburst. 'Darling, you aren't still imagining that Tony is in love with me, are you? Because——'

'Of course not,' Sonia dismissed impatiently. 'Although at the time I wasn't imagining it,' she added firmly. 'What I am talking about is the fact that no one troubled to tell me about this man Lindford!' She glared.

'Oh.' Caroline turned away with a sigh. 'That,' she grimaced.

'*That?*' Sonia exploded. 'Some man has been going around threatening you, issuing obscure threats to all of us, and all you can say is "Oh—that"!'

Caroline sighed. 'I gather Tony told you about him?'

Her sister nodded impatiently. 'He's been like an old mother hen lately, wanting to know where I am all the time, when I'll be home, things like that. At first I was quite flattered that he seemed to be acting jealously,' she admitted ruefully. 'Then I began to feel as if he didn't trust me for some reason, and I didn't like that.'

She could see by Sonia's mutinous expression that she hadn't. 'The poor man told you out of self-defence!' she realised with a shake of her head.

'So what if he did?' her sister said unrepentantly. 'He should have told me what was going on weeks ago.'

Caroline sighed. 'I only found out myself a short time ago.'

'But you didn't say a word about it to me,' Sonia rebuked her. 'He could have—could have——You shouldn't have kept it to yourself, Caroline.'

'Justin and Tony ganged up on us,' she said ruefully. 'But they only did what they thought was best, although I have to admit I was as angry as you to start with,' she reasoned as her sister seemed about to protest again. 'Look at it from their point of view,' she pointed out gently. 'They didn't want to worry either of us.' The last thing any of them needed was Sonia becoming so angry about the situation that she continued her argument with Tony!

'Of course not,' Sonia agreed slowly, looking ruefully at Caroline's obvious pregnancy. 'I'm sorry, love, for coming here and going on like this, but I was just so angry at being treated like a child——'

'So was I.' She smiled.

'Gave Justin hell, hm?' As Caroline had intended, Sonia began to relax, the fire dying out of her eyes as she sank down into one of the armchairs.

'Do you think that's possible?' Caroline sat

down, too, now that the danger had passed; Sonia could be totally unreasonable if she allowed herself to stay angry.

'I think it's possible for you to do anything where Justin is concerned.' Sonia wrinkled her nose prettily. 'He's obviously very much in love with you.'

She remained outwardly calm, but inside she was dying a little more. She didn't know how Justin felt about anything any more, but even if he did love her she knew that even to keep her with him he wouldn't ever tell her of that love. And even if he could admit to feeling something for her, there was still the baby to consider, the child he didn't want.

'I was—a little angry with him at the time,' she admitted dismissively.

'Like I was a "little angry" with Tony,' Sonia said teasingly.

Her mouth quirked in amusement. 'Probably.'

'Men!' Sonia shook her head. 'When will they learn that women aren't made of delicate china?'

'I can't say I altogether mind being protected,' Caroline said thoughtfully, remembering the warm glow she always felt in Justin's arms. 'Even if that is disloyal to the liberated female.'

'It is, but I'm afraid I feel the same way,' her sister confided. 'Although don't, for goodness' sake, tell Tony that!'

Caroline laughed softly. 'I won't. Would you like that tea now?'

'Why not?' Sonia accepted lightly. 'In view of the fact that you shouldn't drink anything stronger

I think it will do as a celebration drink.'

She rang for Mrs Avery. 'What are we celebrating?' She frowned her puzzlement, briefly breaking off the conversation to ask for the tray of tea before turning curiously back to Sonia.

'Why the fact that it's all over, of course,' her sister commented with impatient indulgence for her puzzlement.

Caroline became suddenly still, her heart beating faster, her mouth dry. 'Do you really think it is?' she said enigmatically.

'Of course.' Sonia scorned her lack of confidence. 'The American authorities have this man Lindford now; they've charged him with everything from illegal parking to arms smuggling. Justin says he's in real trouble.'

She swallowed hard. 'Tony told you that, too?'

'I'd have killed him if he hadn't,' her sister told her lightly. 'Justin told him the good news a couple of days ago; it was because Tony suddenly *stopped* asking me where I was going that I became suspicious!' she added ruefully. 'Personally I hope they put him away for a long time——'

Caroline was no longer listening. Justin had known for at least two days that Don Lindford no longer posed a threat to any of them, and *he hadn't told her!*

CHAPTER TEN

WHEN Caroline had asked Justin about Don Lindford on the few occasions they had talked together he had told her the other man was still proving elusive. If Sonia were to be believed, and Caroline had no reason to believe Tony would lie to her sister—every reason to be sure he hadn't now that he was familiar with her sister's temper!—then that was no longer true.

Why hadn't Justin told her that?

The only answer that seemed possible was that he hadn't wanted her to leave. But that didn't sound like the Justin she knew, the Justin who had assured her that once this was over he would help her find somewhere else to live, that he was only keeping her here for her own safety.

He was late home that evening but Caroline was waiting in the living-room for him, having assured Mrs Avery that she could see to serving dinner for the two of them tonight. If they wanted any. Personally she didn't think she could eat a thing.

'Justin?' she called to him before he could disappear into his study for the rest of the evening.

He was frowning heavily when he appeared in the doorway, tall and dark, the eye-patch giving him the appearance of a misplaced pirate. 'Yes?' he prompted abruptly, his manner not forthcoming.

He was more a stranger to her now that he had ever been, but she still loved him more than he seemed to believe it was possible to love anyone. Her hands rested self-consciously on the rounded swell of her body, the same swell that prevented her putting her hands anywhere else. 'I want —need—to talk to you,' she told him huskily.

His brows rose. 'Can't it wait until I've had a shower and changed?'

'No,' she said flatly.

Justin put down his briefcase in one of the armchairs with forceful movements, striding into the room to look down at her, his gaze hooded. 'You didn't see the doctor today, did you?' he frowned. 'I thought that wasn't until next week.'

The fact that he was aware of her routine check-ups with her doctor at all came as something of a surprise to her; that he knew when they were stunned her.

His mouth tightened as he saw her reaction to his question. 'Mrs Avery chatters on about them as if I should be interested in every twinge!' he bit out dismissively.

Dull acceptance darkened her eyes to the colour of sapphires. For a moment she had actually believed he had taken an interest in her pregnancy. She should have realised that Mrs Avery, as excited about the baby as if it were her own grandchild, and not realising Justin's feelings, had talked to him about her visits to the doctor; she always asked for full reports when Caroline returned home.

When was she going to realise, once and for all, that Justin just didn't care about this child?

'I'm sorry you've been bothered,' she told him bleakly. 'I'll tell her not to worry you with it. But that won't be necessary now, will it?' She looked at him challengingly, her eyes narrowed, her hair a blaze of tumbling curls about her shoulders. She could sense his tension at her question, although not a nerve pulsed to show he was in the least disturbed by it. 'She'll realise you don't care about this pregnancy as soon as I move out and ask her to go with me,' she added at his lack of response.

His hands were thrust into the pockets of his suit trousers. 'And when is that going to be?'

She shrugged, forcing herself to remain calm when what she really longed to do was get up and shake some sense into him, some feeling! 'Tomorrow, I think, don't you?' She looked up at him questioningly, willing him to tell her he didn't want her to go at all. But of course, he didn't.

His breath left his body in a ragged sigh. 'Was it Tony or Sonia who told you about Lindford?'

At least he wasn't attempting to prevaricate about the other man's arrest. 'Does that really matter?' She shook her head. 'I know, and so there's no reason for me to stay on here. Why didn't *you* tell me about him?'

Justin turned away, taking his time about pouring himself a drink.

'Justin!' she finally prompted when she could stand the tension no more.

He turned slowly, a look of utter defeat on his

face, his drink remaining untouched on the side-table. 'Why don't you stay on here until you've found somewhere else to live?'

He wasn't going to say why he hadn't told her about Don Lindford's arrest in America; she could see that by the determined thrust of his jaw. If she weren't so angry with him for his obstinacy she could have cried for what he was so wantonly throwing away. 'I can always stay with my parents for a while,' she said firmly. 'I'm sure they won't mind.'

His mouth twisted into a bitter smile. 'Anything but staying on here!'

'Yes!' Anger flared in her eyes, her struggle to stand up most undignified; Sonia had been right about the crane! Finally she managed to stand across the room from Justin. 'The way things are, I can't stay here!'

He sighed. 'I wish I could say things will change——'

'But you can't,' she finished dismissively, walking to the door.

'Where are you going?' he called out to her.

She stopped, but she didn't turn, too aware of the tears burning to be shed, of too many wasted tears, to put either of them through that again. 'I've already packed my things,' she told him softly. 'I think it would be best if I went to my parents tonight——'

'Don't go!'

She closed her eyes as the pain of parting from him ripped through her. 'Please don't make this any harder than it already is!' she groaned, taking another step out of his life.

'For God's sake, don't go, Caroline!' He stood behind her now, spinning her round to face him, his hands painful on her arms. 'Don't leave me!'

She gazed up at him searchingly, at the pain etched into his face, pride and arrogance stripped from him in this moment of pleading. He was hurting just as badly as she was, but she dared not allow even that to change her mind about leaving. They couldn't go on without love between them, a shared love, a love that included Justin caring for his child.

She shook her head. 'I'm sorry, Justin—oh, don't!' she choked as a silver-wet trail fell unheeded down his grooved cheek at her refusal. 'Oh, my darling, no!' she groaned as she wiped the wetness away with her fingertips, only to find his cheek was instantly wet again, the patch over his unsighted eye rapidly dampening, too. 'Justin, don't!' Her arms were about his waist as she pressed her cheek against his heaving chest.

He held her fiercely to him, his body racked by sobs. 'I love you, Caroline,' he rasped. 'Dear God, how I love you! Don't leave me,' he begged again. 'I'll do anything, anything you want, but don't leave me!'

It broke her heart anew to know that she had done this to him, reduced him to this. But what of their child? As if aware of her thoughts the baby moved impatiently inside her, indignant at the way it was being squashed between their two bodies.

Justin drew back with a pained gasp at the
fleeting movement, staring down at the swell of
their child, his gaze widening incredulously as he
saw an elbow or a knee move against the
smoothness of Caroline's dress. He swallowed
convulsively, one hand moving tentatively towards
her, barely resting against the tautness of her body,
but nevertheless receiving a healthy kick in response to his touch.

He looked up at Caroline in wonder, his hand
more firmly against her now, feeling the strong
movements of his child.

Caroline could see the battle he was fighting with
himself, and stood utterly still, barely able to
breathe as she waited for the outcome. Since that
first time, the baby's movements had grown
stronger and more frequent, but she had never
again mentioned it to Justin, accepting his lack of
interest. But the expression on his face now told
her that he hadn't been uninterested at all, that he
had been—afraid! Strange as it was, unbelievable
as it seemed, she could see the naked fear in his
silver gaze.

'Justin?' she prompted dazedly.

He fell to his knees in front of her, his face
buried against the child as it nestled so snugly
within her. 'She thought I didn't care either.' His
voice was muffled against her body. 'She thought
because I—because I couldn't cry, that I hadn't
loved them. Or her. I wanted to cry,' he choked,
fresh tears on the hardness of his cheeks, 'but
somehow until I saw you were going to leave, too, I

couldn't seem to! I never wanted to hurt her, Caroline,' he told her raggedly. 'I never wanted her to do *that!*'

His words were too disjointed for her to know exactly what he was talking about, but she did understand that he was crying now as if he would never be able to stop. And they were cleansing tears. How she loved him; God, how she loved him! They would work something out for their future so that they could be together; they *had* to.

'Tell me, Justin.' She smoothed the hair back from his sweat-dampened face, dislodging the eye-patch in the process, gasping slightly as Justin reached up to rip it off completely to throw it across the room, leaving himself completely vulnerable.

'This is what I am, Caroline,' he choked. 'Scarred inside and out!'

'Tell me, my love,' she encouraged again, sitting down on the sofa, Justin at her side as she cradled his head against her shoulder. 'I love you,' she reassured him softly.

He drew in a ragged breath. 'Penny and I were both twenty-two when we got married. I—I had wanted to wait before having children, but—we took risks.' He shrugged. 'And within six months of being married Penny was pregnant. She was only three months along when—when she lost it——'

'Oh, Justin . . .' She closed her eyes in pained denial, only now beginning to realise what he had suffered in the past.

He shook his head. 'The baby had barely begun to seem real to me when—when it was gone again,' he said harshly. 'I was upset, naturally I was, but Penny was devastated. It hadn't been a planned baby, but as soon as the doctor declared her fit enough Penny wanted to try again.' He gave a ragged sigh. 'I wasn't so sure. The last time had—well, it had frightened me, and this time I was afraid I might lose Penny, too. But she was ecstatic when she found out she was pregnant again, began to plan the nursery straight away, buying things for the baby, as if doing so would ensure nothing went wrong this time. She had the nursery decorated and ready for occupation by the time she was five months along,' he remembered dully. 'I tried to tell her she should wait, that it would be best to wait until—until we were sure everything was going to be all right. But by the time she reached her fifth month I had begun to hope, too. At night we would—I used to lie beside her waiting for the movements of the baby, and then Penny and I would laugh at how strong he was.' He swallowed hard, lost in the memories.

It was all becoming clear now: Justin's knowledge of pregnancy, of pregnant women, when he had supposedly never had anything to do with them, didn't *want* anything to do with them. Why hadn't she realised that earlier?

'Penny used to call him our little cub.'

As Tony had that night Justin had spilt his champagne, and she had thought it might be because he didn't want to drink a toast to their baby!

That had also been the night he had first dreamt

of Penny, the first time he hadn't made love to *her*. But she could see even that differently now, knew how disturbed he had been about learning of Don Lindford's visit, could see that his distraction had been because he had been worried about her, and that worry had brought forward his nightmares of losing Penny. It even explained his sudden desire for them to go away on a honeymoon; he had been afraid for her when the other man came back. What a fool she had been!

'Penny was just over five months along when the premature labour began,' Justin continued flatly. 'They tried to stop it, but nothing could be done. Our son was too small to survive, as small as one of my hands,' he remembered emotionally. 'They let us see him, and he—he was perfect in every way, except that he was too small!' He shook his head, closing his eyes, his cheeks wet once more. 'Damn it, why couldn't I have cried then!' he groaned forcefully.

'They told Penny she shouldn't risk having any more babies, that more pregnancies would probably end up the same way. Penny begged me to share her pain, for that, and for the babies we had lost, but somehow it was all locked up inside of me and I couldn't let it out. Instead I buried myself in my work. And then one day, I—I came home from work to find Penny in the nursery she refused to redecorate, a bottle of sleeping pills at her side.' He spoke distantly. 'I've often wondered if things might have been different if I just could have cried!'

It was all so obvious now: Justin's reluctance to love, his decision not to have children; to the extent that he had taken the necessary step to ensure that he never did, his lack of interest in their child once he knew he hadn't succeeded. He had been afraid to love this child in case it were taken from him, too. She should have made him talk to her earlier, could have shared the pain and anxiety he couldn't even acknowledge. All those disjointed incidents, Justin's vasectomy, his comment that children were too vulnerable to love, his refusal to accept her pregnancy; they would all have made sense if she had only sat down and thought about them logically, instead of assuming he was still in love with his first wife.

'Justin.' She touched his face tenderly. 'I'm thirty weeks along now; even if I went into labour there's a very good chance they could save the baby. You do want it?' she probed gently.

His eyes darkened. 'That was something else I felt guilty about. I really wanted this child, right from the moment you told me you were pregnant and I first began to hope it could be mine. I loved Penny, but our babies never quite seemed this real to me.' He frowned.

'Possibly because you were too young to appreciate the miracle of them,' Caroline comforted. 'Also this child——' she put his hand against her again, a lump in her throat at the tender fascination on his face '—this child seemed an impossibility to you.'

'*You* seemed an impossibility to me,' he

admitted gruffly. 'After Penny I shut love out of my life, and for twelve years I succeeded. But the first time I looked at you I felt a jolt right where my heart should be. I cold-bloodedly decided it was lust raising its ugly head, and I've learnt that the best way to deal with that is to let it take its course. But you wouldn't let it.' He frowned. 'You were determined to remain faithful to Tony, wouldn't even accept my invitation for dinner until after you had an argument with him. By that time it was more than lust—maybe it always had been,' he acknowledged ruefully. 'Once I had made love to you I knew I couldn't let you go, that I had to hang on to you any way that I could. Even if it meant marrying you. I had no right marrying you believing I was sterile, probably had no right marrying you at all.' He shook his head. 'The night you told me you were pregnant I almost collapsed. Then I began to hope for a miracle. And when that miracle became a reality I was so damned scared I couldn't think straight. What if we lost this baby, too? What if I lost you?' His face was haunted. 'It seemed that if I rejected the baby, ignored its existence, then I didn't have to acknowledge that anything could go wrong.' He gave a bitter smile. 'You see what a coward you've married.'

A coward wouldn't have survived losing the babies and Penny the way that he had, and she knew beyond a shadow of a doubt that it hadn't been because he was cold and unfeeling; that he had loved his wife and children very much. If anything, Justin felt things too deeply, and because he knew how badly he could be hurt he locked his emotions away inside himself and refused to let them out, conquering them instead of letting them defeat him.

Allowing himself to love her meant he could no longer do that, but with the vulnerability had come a chance for a new happiness for him. She would make sure he never knew anything else.

'Our child doesn't think you're a coward, and neither do I.' She looked at him with all the love she had for him showing in her over-bright eyes.

He gave a low groan at her unquestioning acceptance of him. 'That night Sonia told Tony she would be shouting it from the rooftops if she were pregnant with his child I felt so damned guilty for denying you that pride in our child.'

'It doesn't matter,' she assured him huskily. 'The night the baby is born, *you* can go and shout it from the rooftops. Whatever happens, Justin,' she told him warmly as his eyes once again became shadowed at the thought of her having the baby. 'We'll get through it together, because we love each other.'

He looked at her uncertainly. 'You aren't leaving?' he said hesitantly.

'Never,' she promised with feeling. 'Never, never, *never!*' She threw herself into his arms.

She had been wrong that day she denied that pain could be good; the pain Justin had allowed to flow today had cleansed his heart and soul. They could only go forward from here, would look to the future and not the past. And she would give him a healthy child, someone else to fill the great capacity he had for love.

'Darling, what are you doing?'

Justin chuckled against her nape. 'Well, if you don't know I must have been doing it wrong all these years!'

Caroline turned slightly to return the intimacy of his smile, her back arching as his lips moved lower, travelling the length of her spine where he had unzipped the gown she had just put on. 'I thought we were going out for lunch,' she reminded him faintly, Justin's touch inciting its usual magic; lunch was the last thing she felt in the mood for now.

'I didn't say that,' he murmured softly, his fingers playing lightly at the base of her spine. 'I merely asked Sonia and Tony if they would take the children for lunch so that we could celebrate alone.'

She turned in his arms, her hands linked behind his head, nuzzling against his hair-roughened chest, damp still from where he had just taken a shower. 'I assumed we were going out for an anniversary lunch.' She could hear the accelerated beat of his heart, feel his desire against her.

'I intend having a feast.' His tone left no doubt as to who he intended feasting on!

She laughed softly. Four years of marriage hadn't changed their instant awareness of each other, even their children not doing that: their beloved first-born Katy, two-year-old and already independent Aaron, who was so much like his father, and adorable six-month-old James. All the children openly adored their father, and Justin couldn't have been a more gentle or caring parent, especially so because he knew what he had already lost. The night Katy had been born they had both cried with happiness, and their wonder and delight in their children hadn't lessened over the years.

Sonia and Tony expected their first baby in five months' time, and Caroline had a feeling that taking Katy, Aaron, and James for lunch today was their way of seeing how they were going to cope as parents. Knowing her mischievous trio, she had a feeling the other couple might wonder what they had let themselves in for with approaching parenthood by the time they picked the children up in a couple of hours!

The last three and a half years had been happier than Caroline had ever imagined they could be, filled with love and laughter, and most of all with knowing how important she and Justin were to each other, no longer any secrets or shadows between them. Although she would never have wished for it to happen that way, the last remaining shadow to their untroubled happiness had been removed three years ago when Don Lindford had been killed during a knife fight with another prisoner. She hated all kinds of violence, but she loved Justin and her family too much to be genuinely sorry that the man wouldn't be able to come back and threaten them once again.

She now had no doubts as to what her destiny

was to be: unimagined happiness with Justin and their children, for the rest of their lives.

As her gown fell softly to the carpeted floor, she knew she and Justin were fated to be destiny's lovers, for eternity . . .

Jacqueline Baird began writing as a hobby when her family objected to the smell of her oil painting! She immediately became hooked on the romantic genre, which proved to be successful as her first romance was published by Mills & Boon® in 1988 and she has since sold over four and a half million copies of her books worldwide.

Jacqueline loves travelling and worked her way around the world from Europe to the Americas and Australia, returning to marry her teenage sweetheart. She lives in Ponteland, Northumbria, the county of her birth, and has two teenage sons. She enjoys playing badminton, and spends most weekends with husband Jim, sailing their Gp.14 around Derwent Reservoir.

NOTHING CHANGES LOVE
by
JACQUELINE BAIRD

CHAPTER ONE

LEXI opened her eyes and for a moment was completely disorientated. White walls, a narrow bed, white sheets, and the smell . . . antiseptic!

She moved to sit up, and the full horror of the past night sliced into her heart. She groaned with the unaccustomed pain and dragged herself up to a sitting position, her small hands clutching the white weave of the coverlet.

Her baby, the tiny being growing inside her only twenty-four hours ago, was no more. She had miscarried; after all the expert care and bed rest, nothing had been able to save her precious child. Moisture flooded her violet eyes, and with the back of her hand she brushed it away.

'Now, now, Lexi, try not to upset yourself too much.'

She looked up at the familiar figure of a Dr Bell, a tall, balding man; he had been her doctor for all her twenty years, but even he had been helpless to prevent her losing her first baby, a boy . . . She tried to smile but it was a watery effort.

'Some things in life, child, are just not meant to be.' He took one of her small hands in his, his world-weary eyes scanning the small, beautiful figure in the bed. He could remember the day she was born, tiny and squalling, with a shock of brilliant red hair. She had developed into a bright, incredibly beautiful young woman and she did not deserve the grief she had borne for the past few years. He had hoped that with her marriage not a year ago her luck had finally turned, but in that it seemed he was mistaken; her high-flying husband had not even bothered to attend the hospital last night, although he had been informed of the imminent loss of the baby.

'But I so wanted my baby,' Lexi moaned.

'It is tragic to lose a baby at fourteen weeks, but there is always a reason, nature's way of letting us know something is not quite right. But you're young and perfectly fit; there will be many more babies for you. The important thing is not to worry about it.'

'If you say so.' But the flat, toneless quality of her voice told the doctor the poor girl was not convinced.

'Anyway, that handsome husband of yours will be here shortly. I have spoken to him personally.'

'Jake knows?' she queried quietly.

'Yes, and the two of you together will soon see this as a sad memory, nothing more, once you fill Forest Manor with a few healthy children.' He smiled and, straightening up, he let go of her hand. 'Believe me; after all, I am the expert.'

A commotion, raised voices in the corridor outside the small private room, prevented Lexi making any reply. The door swung open and a tall, dark man rushed into the room. Pushing Dr Bell aside, he sat down on the side of the bed, and gathered Lexi's small hands in his much larger ones.

'God! Lexi, I'm so sorry, I know how much the baby meant to you; I can't believe it has happened.'

'Jake.' She murmured his name. 'It wasn't my fault.' She wanted to explain, but couldn't find the words. Her violet eyes roamed over his handsome face, the night-black hair curling haphazardly over his broad brow, as though he had never had time to brush it. His dark eyes that at first glance looked brown but on closer inspection were almost navy blue, were fixed on her small face, the concern in his expression undeniable. Jake, her husband; he looked so dynamic, so vitally alive, and she felt dead inside. An aching void where her child should have been.

'Shh, darling, don't try and talk. I'm here now, I will look after you.'

But would he? The question popped into her mind, she did not know from where. Lexi had needed him last night, had cried out for him in her agony, but where had he been? Giving a dinner party for clients...

'Did your meeting with the Americans, the Stewarts wasn't it, go well?' she asked quietly.

Jake sat up straighter, his clasp of her hands loosening. 'More or less.'

'Which was it?' Lexi queried, somehow aware the worried frown marring his brow wasn't solely for her.

His hand tightened on hers but his smile was forced as he answered. 'One or two problems, but nothing I can't handle. Don't concern yourself, Lexi. Let me worry about the business. The important thing is for you to get better and out of this tiny cottage hospital as quickly as possible.'

'What kind of problem?' she asked mechanically.

Jake turned his dark head to Dr Bell and deliberately changed the subject with, 'I wanted Lexi to go to Harley Street, but she insisted on you, and I want some answers, and I want them now. Why wasn't I informed last night when this happened?' And, getting to his feet, Lexi ignored for the moment, the two men stood face to face.

'According to our records, the sister on duty telephoned the manor at nine last night. You were unavailable at the time, but my sister was assured you would be given the message.'

'I don't believe it; I demand to see the administrator, and I'll make damn sure heads roll for this.'

Lexi closed her eyes briefly, trying to block out the image of a furious Jake, but it was impossible. She looked at him, all six feet plus of bristling male aggression. He was wearing a short-sleeved knit shirt in pale blue that fit snugly across his wide shoulders and broad chest. A black leather belt slung low on his hips

supported well-washed denim jeans that clung lovingly
to his long, muscular legs. The father of her baby, and
yet, when he had arrived, he had said he knew how much
the baby meant to her. How she wished he had said,
'us', and swept her into his arms; she ached to lay her
head on his broad chest and forget yesterday had ever
happened.

She tuned back into the conversation in time to hear
Dr Bell demand, 'Do you really think this is the time or
the place for this discussion, Mr Taylor?'

Lexi's bemused gaze went from one man to the other,
not sure who to believe; she wanted to believe Jake.

'You're right, Dr Bell,' Jake agreed curtly. 'But don't
think you have heard the last of this.'

'Please, Jake,' she reached out a trembling hand 'No
recriminations, I couldn't bear it.'

'Oh, hell! I'm sorry, Lexi,' and swooping down, at
last he cradled her in his strong arms. 'Forgive me
darling, it's just I'm so angry, I wasn't here when you
needed me. No business deal is worth a fraction of what
you mean to me.' He tilted her head back to look into
her bruised eyes. 'You do know that, darling?' With one
long, tanned finger he traced the soft curve of her cheek,
the dark circles under her eyes, then softly his sensuous
mouth brushed lightly against hers.

'Yes, Jake, of course,' she murmured huskily, her
voice thick with tears. But did she? the errant thought
flashed in her mind. She glanced up at him and was
stunned to see moisture glistening on his thick black
lashes.

'I called last night, after midnight, and they told me
you were asleep. If only I'd known.' His deep voice shook
with emotion.

'It's all right.' But he could have asked about the baby;
if he weren't such a workaholic he might have done. She
banished the disloyal thought and added, 'You're here
now and that's all that matters.'

For a long moment their eyes clung. Pain, regret and deep sorrow; the message passed between them, too agonising to put into words.

'There will be other children, love.' Jake cradled her head against his broad shoulder, his strong hand smoothing the wild tangle of red curls back from her face and gently down her back in the age-old gesture of comfort. 'Cry if you need to, Lexi, let it all out.' His deep, rich voice murmured soft words of comfort and consolation.

To Lexi it was the care she needed and, held close in Jake's arms, the familiar scent and feel of him enveloping her, she cried as though her heart would break. Finally, all cried out, she hiccuped and raised swollen red eyes to his handsome face.

'I'll be all right now.'

'We both will be; together we can beat whatever the world throws at us.' His dark head lowered and his mouth claimed hers in an achingly gentle kiss.

Lexi curled her slender arms around his neck, needing him as never before. His sensuous lips, warm and mobile, moved seductively over hers, his tongue slipping erotically into her mouth. Surprised by his turning the kiss from gentle to passionate, she tensed, inexplicably revolted. Jake groaned against her mouth, a flare of desire sharp and instant tautened his huge frame, and, pulling back, he looked down into her pale face.

'God! What am I doing? You're ill, you need rest.' He pressed her back down against the pillows, and shifted his tall body uncomfortably on the bed. 'It never fails. From the first day I saw you, I only have to look at you to want you.' A rueful self-deprecating smile twisted his firm lips. 'I shall have to learn to control my baser instincts around you, at least for a while,' he teased lightly.

Lexi attempted a smile, but unsettling questions niggled at the edge of her mind. Was that all Jake wanted from her? A warm body in his bed? Was that all he had ever wanted? Their baby, a mistake!

Half an hour later, after Jake had left, promising to return in the evening, Lexi was informed by Dr Bell that she could leave the next day. She should have been pleased, instead all she felt was a mind-numbing exhaustion and physical weakness that made the thought of leaving the security of the hospital for their apartment and the bustle of the hotel, and the inevitable condolences of the staff, a terrifying prospect.

A deep, drawn-out sigh escaped her. It was so unfair, she thought hopelessly. On Friday afternoon she had been a happy, pregnant mum-to-be. She had driven into York to keep an appointment at four with Dr Bell, just routine, but first she had gone shopping for something glamorous to wear at the dinner party she was hosting the following night with her husband at Forest Manor. The manor, once her childhood home, had been converted by Jake's property company into a country house hotel. Now only the west wing was home.

Unfortunately, it had started to rain, and, dashing to keep her doctor's appointment, she had slipped on the wet pavement and fallen. She had jumped to her feet and run on, arriving at the surgery late and rather upset. Dr Bell had examined her, and said she was spotting a little, and insisted she stay in the local hospital for a day or two just as a precaution.

Lexi, slightly in awe of her sophisticated, dynamic husband, had dreaded telling him. She knew Jake was hoping to make a deal with Mr Stewart, an American tycoon who owned, among other things, his own airline, along with a tour firm that ran regular trips to England. Jake had explained that if Mr Stewart agreed to use the new Forest Manor hotel as a regular stop for his clients, the hotel was assured of being at least half-full all year, even if it never got another customer. A great deal if Jake could get it.

She need not have worried, because Jake had arrived on the Friday night from London and been a tower of strength, telling her not to worry, his PA, Lorraine, could host the party and all Lexi had to do was look after herself and the baby.

Lexi turned restlessly on the narrow bed. How could life change so drastically from Friday to Sunday? All her hopes and dreams squashed by a wet pavement. It seemed so pointless...

'Come on, Mrs Taylor. Cheer up.' The sister who had attended her the night before walked in. 'You're young, and time heals all wounds. I know you don't think so at the minute, but it is true. And it's also true that I did ring your home last night; a woman answered and promised to give your husband the message.'

Lexi looked at the sister, and she knew Jake's hand was in the unsolicited statement somewhere.

'The young woman sounded supremely efficient; I never doubted for a moment she would pass the message on.'

It could only have been Lorraine, Lexi thought resignedly. 'It's all right, Sister, I believe you. My husband has been in this morning. Everything is fine.'

'I wish you would tell him that.'

Lexi heard the sister mutter under her breath as she left the room, and felt sorry for her. Lexi knew personally just how intimidating Jake could be if he thought he had been wronged in any way. She still shuddered to think of the way he had dismissed the foreman on the hotel project last Christmas, frog-marching the man to his car and tossing his gear in with him. Jake was not the sort of man one argued with. Lexi had never tried; far too much in love with him, she would do anything to appease him.

Now, why did that thought make her feel even more depressed? she mused. Maybe losing the baby had made her realise once again how fragile life was, and question her slavish acceptance to everything Jake said or did. She tossed her head to dispel the unsettling notion, and the bedroom door swung open to reveal what looked like a walking basket of flowers.

The junior nurse dropped it on the floor with a sigh of relief and a huge smile. 'Somebody out there loves you,' she teased.

Lexi eyed the huge basket with wonder. Masses of roses tastefully arranged with babies' breath and the message on the card was simple. 'Love always, Jake.' The briefest of smiles curved her lips. Just like him: larger than life.

Alone once more, Lexi turned over on to her side, her violet eyes fixed firmly on the flowers. The aching sense of loss was still there, but somehow it did not seem quite so devastating, as long as she had Jake. She smiled softly remembering the first time they met, perhaps it was the mind's way of dealing with a hurt too hard to face, she mused, as she drifted in a dream-state, recalling the past in minute detail. At nineteen years of age, and having just completed her first-year exams in languages at St Mary's college, London, Lexi had been called back to her home, Forest Manor, because of her father's sudden death. Her mother had died three years earlier, only weeks after her father had retired from the Diplomatic Corps. Laughtons had for generations entered the foreign service, and between postings lived in Yorkshire.

The house was a beautiful old stone-built manor. E-shaped, with mullioned windows, oak floors and beautiful hand-carved panelling and situated seven miles from the cathedral city of York, mid-way between the tiny villages of Sand Hutton and Stockton-on-the-Forest.

But on the death of her father his substantial pension had ceased, and the lawyer had informed Lexi that his personal debts were quite large. As one of the Lloyds names her father had enjoyed a good private income for years, but a few years previously he had changed syndicates hoping to make even bigger profits.

Unfortunately the reverse had happened, and Lexi had had no alternative but to put the house and its extensive parkland on the market to cover the debt.

Lexi turned over on to her back and stared sightlessly up at the blank white ceiling. It seemed incredible to believe it was under a year since she had first met Jake. She felt as if she had known him a lifetime, so much had happened.

It was a beautiful July day. Lexi waited in the entrance porch of her home, and watched as a sleek black car drew to a halt in front of the door and the tall figure of a man stepped out.

'Mr Taylor?' she queried as the man bounded up the stone steps to stop only inches away from her.

'Yes, and you must be Alexandra Laughton. Your solicitor said you were young, but he didn't mention beautiful.'

'Lexi, please. No one calls me Alexandra,' she said nervously and blushed scarlet, embarrassed by his frank compliment, and also by the overpowering effect the man had on her. He looked about thirty, and was dressed in a plain white shirt, dark tie and an immaculate three-piece business suit, the jacket stretched taut across broad shoulders and a massive chest. His hair was black and thick, and his face alert and hard. There was no mistaking the fierce predatory expression on his roughly hewn features. A broad forehead, deep dark eyes, high cheek bones and a straight blade of a nose above a wide, firm mouth. His skin was the colour of polished mahogany.

'I'm afraid I'm in rather a hurry. So, shall we proceed?' he said briskly, all business.

'Y-yes. Yes, of course,' she stammered, leading him into the panelled entrance hall. 'You're very brown. Are you English?' God! Where had that come from? She cringed; it was totally out of character for Lexi to pass personal comments and she turned red with embarrassment. 'Please...'

To her surprise he started to laugh and, catching one of her small hands in his, he said, 'Jake Taylor, luv... Born within the sound of the Bow Bells. A cockney, a tanned cockney, though I believe my father was a foreigner.' He drawled the last word teasingly.

He was laughing at her but she could not blame him; so far she had not managed to make much sense. Lexi shook her head in a vain attempt to clear her brain, and her long red hair spun around her face in a glittering cloud before settling back on her slender shoulders. She had dressed with care, expecting the first prospective buyer for the house, in a plain, shirt-style straight-skirted cream summer-dress. She had added a minimum of make-up to her golden skin; she was one of those very rare redheads with a skin that actually tanned. Her full lips were carefully outlined in a soft coral lip gloss and a touch of mascara on her long lashes completed her make-up and she'd thought she appeared quite adult, until this man had looked at her.

'I'm sorry, that was presumptuous of me. Please, follow me, and I'll show you around.' Her violet eyes met his once more, and she felt the intensity of his gaze to the soles of her feet. She again shook her head, but nothing could clear her mind and she spent the next hour leading him around the half-dozen reception rooms, up the grand staircase, all around the upper floors until finally they arrived back in the hall with Lexi still in a bemused state.

'Are you free for the rest of the day?'

'What? Oh, yes.' Lexi had to get her brain in gear, but it seemed to be an impossibility. 'But why?' she asked, standing once more in the front porch. Common sense told her he should leave: he was too dynamic, too male, and certainly too sophisticated for her. She felt oddly threatened by him, but her foolishly fast-beating heart wanted him to stay.

'Good. I had only allowed an hour for our meeting; now I think I'll make a day of it and you can show me around the countryside, then I can get the feel of the place. You understand.'

She didn't understand at all, but her heart leapt in her breast at the prospect of spending the whole day with the man. Before she could agree or disagree Jake had ushered her into his car and slid in beside her. He made a call on the car-phone to someone called Lorraine, who seemed less than pleased at his extended visit, Lexi thought, then he turned to her.

'Now, I am your willing tourist until late this evening, or, if you prefer, tomorrow morning.' And, flicking her a blatantly sensual smile, he asked, 'Which way to Castle Howard? I've heard it's worth seeing.'

The faint spicy tang of his aftershave teased her nostrils, and for some reason his sexy grin appeared to heighten her awareness of him in a way no other man had ever managed to do before. She was not a complete innocent; she had a good social life at college and she had had her fair share of dates, but Jake Taylor was something else again, and she found the emotion he aroused in her enthralling.

Twenty minutes later they were driving up the impressive drive through the entrance gates and into the large field-like car park of Castle Howard.

'Good, it's near your place,' she heard Jake murmur as he helped her out of the car, his eyes darting all around, taking everything in.

Jake flung a casual arm around her shoulders. 'I think this might just be the clincher,' he opined and, paying the admission fee, urged Lexi through to the courtyard while she was still trying to fathom out what he meant.

For the next few hours she walked around in a dream. Jake strode around the elegant house, his hand never leaving her shoulder as he talked non-stop to her, pointing out the things that really grabbed his interest, from the magnificent domed roof in the grand hall, unique in all of England, to the quaint child's high chair. Castle Howard was magnificent: the furnishings, the restoration, works of art—everything about the place was exquisite. A superb example of eighteenth-century architecture, it was built by the Third Earl of Carlisle, and to the present day was still owned by the same family of Howards. Lexi had visited many times before, but today the awesome grandeur of the place was overwhelmed by her intense awareness of her companion.

To Lexi's surprise Jake seemed almost as impressed by the wide variety of tourists—Americans and Japanese rubbed shoulders with continentals—as he was with the house itself, and finally, when they walked back outside into the summer sunshine and strolled around the extensive grounds, Jake had no compunction in striking up conversations with dozens of people, while Lexi looked around at the wonderful landscape, long lawns, magnificent lakes, summer house, and, high on one hill, the family mausoleum. It wasn't hard to see, she thought, why it had achieved worldwide recognition as the location for the television serial *Brideshead Revisited*. Perched on the Howardian Hills, it had to be one of the best stately homes in England.

'Penny for your thoughts.'

She looked up and smiled into Jake's darkly handsome face. 'They aren't worth much, but I am hungry,' she stated. 'Walking gives me an appetite.'

'You give me an appetite,' Jake growled huskily and, before she realised his intention, he had turned her into his arms, and brushed his hard mouth gently across her full lips. It was like being touched by lightning; a shiver trembled the length of her spine and her full lips parted helplessly beneath his. The breath hissed out of him. 'God!' he exclaimed, as he broke the kiss.

He held her away from him, studying her flushed, be-mused face. 'I've been aching to do that from the minute I set eyes on you. You have a very unsettling effect on me, little girl. But this is not the place.' Knowing full well how he affected her, he grinned reassuringly down into her wide violet eyes, and, curving her arm under his, led her back to the car.

She wasn't used to a handsome sophisticated man like Jake flirting with her and, during the journey to the city of York where Jake had insisted they visit next, she couldn't think of a word to say. But somehow the at-mosphere between them was a companionable one, and by the time they arrived in York and found the car park Lexi had recovered some of her poise.

It seemed quite natural to walk hand in hand around the mighty cathedral, and then follow the narrow streets around the Shambles. Finally, they ended up in a small French restaurant with the original name of Number 19 Grape Lane, and, over a lovely meal of pan-fried salmon on a bed of pasta in a red wine sauce—Jake's choice—he enthusiastically explained his plan for Forest Manor. He wanted to buy it and turn it into a hotel, and shrewdly he asked her if she would take it off the market for a week or two while he had a feasibility study carried out.

He could have knocked it down for all Lexi cared; for the first time in her life she was in love. Hopelessly, helplessly in love. Her gaze lingered on his striking fea-tures as he set out his ideas for the conversion; he looked years younger as, with a sheepish grin, he ended with, 'Sorry, I can get quite boring when I start discussing business.'

'No, you're fascinating,' she said softly, and the deepening gleam in his dark eyes set her heart ablaze. Jake was everything she had ever dreamed of in a man, and best of all he appeared to feel the same way, if the goodnight kiss he pressed on her lips when they parted at her door was anything to go by, and his promise to return the next day.

The only slight hiccup in her headlong flight into love was her solicitor. On Monday morning she called Mr Travis and told him what had happened and that she did not want anyone else viewing the house for a while. Mr Travis was not convinced it was the right thing to do, and insisted he had friends in the city and a few discreet enquiries were called for. Taylor Holdings was not a company he was familiar with, nor did he know much about Jake Taylor; the sensible course was to check out Jake's financial position—after all there were a lot of time-wasters in the housing market. Lexi reluctantly bowed to his superior judgement, while not for one moment doubting Jake.

How could she, when they had spent a wonderful Sunday together and she was expecting him back again on Monday?

At the sound of the car drawing up Lexi dashed out of the front door to welcome Jake. Her step faltered when she saw he was not alone. A stunning brunette was hanging on to his arm. He introduced her as Lorraine, his PA and right-hand man, but Lexi saw the possessive gleam in the other woman's eyes, and her heart plummeted in her breast. But she need not have worried...

Jake, accurately reading her mind, shrugged off Lorraine's hand and, stepping forward, pulled Lexi into his arms and kissed her thoroughly, then whispered, a hint of laughter in his deep voice, 'Strictly an employee, little one; you're the only woman for me, understand?' And she did...

Lexi turned a beaming smile on the other woman, and quite happily fell in with Jake's suggestion that she show Lorraine around while he made a couple of phone calls; he would catch them up in a few minutes.

Leading Lorraine from one room to the next, Lexi, her jealous fear dispelled, chattered on quite freely, virtually giving Lorraine her life history, and learning in return that the other woman had known Jake from school and had worked for him almost six years. By the time they were viewing the bedrooms, Lexi was feeling quite at ease with the other woman.

'This is a lovely house, and I can see why Jake is interested. But I'm surprised you want to sell it.' Lorraine offered a question in her tone.

'I don't, not really.' Lexi grinned back at her. 'But unless I marry a millionaire real quick I have no choice,' she joked, but she did not see the contemptuous glint in Lorraine's eyes as she led her back out into the hall and down the grand staircase.

'You never considered working, but then your sort never do, born with a silver spoon in your mouth.'

Lexi's head swung around in surprise at the sneering resentment in Lorraine's voice, but before she could answer Jake was with them. The conversation became general, and she put the unsettling comment from her mind.

She was reminded of it abruptly a week later. The next weekend Jake asked her to marry him and Lexi ecstatically accepted. Only to have Lorraine telephone her on the Monday as soon as she heard the news.

'You think you're clever Miss Laughton. "Marry a millionaire real quick," you said. But I've heard of your solicitor Mr Travis's enquiries, and when I tell Jake everything he will be far from pleased. No one has ever questioned Jake Taylor's financial viability; the last thing he needs is his merchant bank asking questions because some gold-digging little hick from the sticks is looking for a wealthy husband. I wouldn't count on marrying him if I were you.'

Lexi did not know what she said in reply—she was too shocked at the other woman's allegations. But she could not deny she had jokingly made the comment about marrying a millionaire. Later, when Lexi repeated the conversation to Jake and explained about her teasing comment, he dismissed her fear, saying that he understood Lorraine! She had a chip on her shoulder due to her upbringing along with a suspicious nature, but there was no way she would ever convince him that Lexi was anything other than a beautiful, pure young woman who had agreed to be his wife. After reinforcing his opinion with a long, sweet kiss he added that Lorraine was a great PA—loyal to a fault, but a bit over-protective where his business interests were concerned. As for Mr Travis checking his credit rating, it was no more than any efficient lawyer would do for his client, and she was not to worry; nothing could prevent their marriage.

They were married in a civil ceremony at the register office in York, three weeks from the day they met, and flew off to Paris for a brief honeymoon.

Lexi stirred restlessly in the narrow hospital bed. It had been so beautiful. August in Paris—sparkling blue skies, and by night, dinner at Maxim's and back to an exquisite little hotel overlooking the river Seine and Notre-Dame.

Jake laughingly carried her over the threshold of the suite and slid her gently to her feet. 'Ready for our dirty weekend, Miss Laughton?' he teased, as he kicked the door closed behind him. Lexi smiled and laughed with him.

They had arrived at Heathrow airport and Jake had presented the tickets to the check-in clerk, to be informed that Lexi's passport was in the name of Miss Laughton, while the tickets were in the names of Mrs and Mrs Taylor. The only way she had been allowed on the plane was by Jake changing her ticket back into her maiden name. Jake had thought it was a huge joke, but Lexi had cringed with embarrassment, even more so when Jake had handed the passports to the hotel receptionist, while taking the key for the honeymoon suite. She was sure everyone must think she was a woman of easy virtue. Jake had howled with laughter and called her old-fashioned.

'The first thing I'm going to do when we get back is change my passport,' Lexi said with a chuckle. Later she was to be glad she didn't...

Jake gathered her into his arms, and with a husky growl declared, 'At last you are mine, and mine alone for always, my beautiful, gorgeous girl. My wife.' She knew no document could bind her more surely to her husband than the love she felt for him.

With gentle hands he removed the turquoise silk dress she wore, sliding it down over her hips to pool in a pale cloud at her feet, all the while pressing tiny kisses to her eyes, her face, her throat.

Sighing, she wrapped her slender arms around his broad shoulders, quivers of sensation darting through her body as she melted helplessly in his hold. He was her husband, her love, and she wanted him with every fibre of her being.

Tenderly, he swung her into his arms and carried her from the sitting-room to the bedroom and carefully laid her down on the huge, old-fashioned four-poster bed. She stared up at him, her love and longing highlighting the pure beauty of her fine features.

Jake, his blue eyes darkened to almost black, reverently bent over her and removed the slight wisps of lace that passed as her underwear and she felt her whole body blush, suddenly overcome with shyness and an unexpected, virginal fear.

'You're my wife, my love; I will never hurt you, I promise,' Jake said throatily, while he quickly divested himself of his clothes.

A gasp of sheer female appreciation escaped Lexi's softly parted lips. Jake was magnificent; she couldn't help staring. His broad shoulders gleamed like polished mahogany in the dim light of the bedside lamp, the musculature of his chest was somehow exaggerated by the downy covering of black hair that arrowed down over his flat stomach to brush out at the apex of his thighs. Her blush deepened as she realised he was fully aroused. She closed her eyes, and felt his lips brush across her mouth.

'Don't be afraid.' He kissed her long and slow. 'Trust me, my darling.' And she did, as his long body covered hers.

When he finally took possession of her pulsating form with one quick thrust, a brief pain was swiftly overtaken by sheer ecstasy. 'Jake.' She cried his name, and her love for him, as they reached the pinnacle together as one. Afterwards, Jake murmured husky rasping avowals of love as he buried his face in her throat...

Slowly, she opened her eyes, a soft sensuous smile curving her lips 'Jake.' Her violet eyes, the lingering traces of sensuality clearly visible, fastened on the dark face looming above her. She stretched up a small hand, and then blinked. He was wearing a sweater... She closed her eyes for a second and it all came flooding back. Jake was sitting on the side of her bed. She was in hospital. The smile vanished from her face. Her baby gone...

'Lexi, are you all right?'

'Yes, yes, I'm fine. I was asleep,' she murmured and, pulling herself up the bed, she sat up.

'Lorraine sends her apologies,' Jake said abruptly. 'Apparently she took the message last night when Stewart and I were in the study. She forgot to tell me afterwards with the pressure of discussing some——' he hesitated, his mouth twisting grimly '—slight alterations Mr Stewart suggested. I know I should fire her for it, and I will if you say so. But I feel it was partly my fault. The discussion became quite heated, and Lorraine isn't like other women. She would never forget a business message, but anything else she doesn't see as important.'

'Don't fire her for my sake, Jake,' Lexi responded quietly. She knew Lorraine did not like her, hadn't from the beginning when she'd tried to convince Jake that Lexi was only after his money and that he was making a mistake in marrying her. 'Tell her I accept her apology.' She looked up and saw Jake was looking somewhere over her left shoulder, his expression oddly evasive, and she wondered, not for the first time, just what relationship Jake had with his PA.

'You're very generous, Lexi. I've done some investigating today and I should have asked about the baby last night, when I phoned, but I assumed it was all right, while the young nurse I spoke to assumed I already knew you had lost it.'

'It.' He called their baby 'it'. How could he be so insensitive? '*It* doesn't matter, as long as your business was successful, all is not lost,' she said with a biting sarcasm that was wasted as Jake glanced down, and leaning forward, kissed her lightly on the lips.

'Thank you, Lexi, you're very forgiving. I want you to get better and come home. I miss you.' His dark eyes searched her still pale face. 'Everything will be fine, I promise.' And, lifting one long finger, trailed it down her cheek. 'How about a smile, hmm?'

'I'll be coming home tomorrow,' she offered with a pitiful attempt at a smile.

'Good, and perhaps now you can return to London and college, if you like.'

Lexi felt like screaming. When they were first married they had lived in London and Jake had suggested she stay at home, saying she had no need for a degree in languages, he would give her a degree in love instead. Many a lunchtime he dashed back to the apartment and they spent hours in bed. Or they drove up to Yorkshire to oversee the renovations on the manor. Then, when the hotel had been completed by the Easter, they moved permanently to Yorkshire, Jake saying he could work as easily from his study in the apartment. Lorraine could look after the London office. The new apartment was a delight, and Lexi had quite happily spent the past months helping out in the hotel reception.

But had she been happy, she suddenly questioned, or had the feeling of resentment towards Jake started long before she lost the baby? When only weeks after having her pregnancy confirmed Jake suddenly, because of 'pressure of business' he had said, took to spending all week in London, returning to Yorkshire only at the weekends, while insisting she stay in the country; it was better for her, he had said, as a mum-to-be.

Now Jake was calmly suggesting she go back to London and college as though nothing had happened.

She hid her anger and resentment as he arranged to collect her the next day and kissed her goodbye. But after he had left it hit her. Jake had avoided telling her whether his deal of the previous night was successful or not. But then he had been very evasive the last few weeks about his business; no doubt Lorraine would know!

Lexi wondered yet again how close her husband and Lorraine were. On their honeymoon Lexi had asked Jake if he had ever had an affair with his PA and Jake had said 'Good God, no!' and burst out laughing, but Lexi had never been able to see the joke...

CHAPTER TWO

LEXI, dressed in the same blue jeans and soft T-shirt she had worn on Friday before her accident, was sitting on the edge of the hospital bed waiting for her husband. The necessary discharge papers had been signed an hour ago. She glanced out of the window for the hundredth time; the sun was rising high in the sky, embracing the utilitarian lines of the hospital building in a rosy glow, but its warmth could not pierce the coldness in Lexi's heart.

Jake entered the room in a rush, full of apologies for the delay. 'Sorry, darling, Lorraine and I were tied up on a conference call. You would not believe the inefficiency of the telecommunications here. We were disconnected half a dozen times.' He frowned. 'In today's climate of recession, speed and efficiency are essential to sustain success.'

Did it matter? she wondered bleakly as five minutes later she was comfortably seated in Jake's car as he eased it out of the hospital gates.

'Lorraine has arranged for Meg to come in every day for the next week or two.' He shot her a quick sideways glance. 'I don't want you doing anything at all until you are completely recovered.'

Lorraine seemed to be arranging an awful lot in her life lately, Lexi thought bitterly, and was stung into replying, 'She needn't have bothered. What is there to recover from? I've had a miscarriage, not lost a limb. In fact, the quicker I can get back into Reception and working, the better I'll like it.' Lexi knew she was being deliberately antagonistic, but she couldn't help it. It was either anger or tears, and she had cried enough to last a lifetime.

'Lexi, please. Lorraine was only trying to help, to make up for forgetting the message the other night. You're in shock, you need...'

'Jake,' she cut in, 'I know what I need and it is to get back to normal as quickly as possible. So please, just leave me alone.' And she wished flaming Lorraine would vanish in a puff of smoke...

The car came to an abrupt halt outside the entrance to their private wing. Jake turned towards her, his eyes narrowed faintly as they took in her pale, determined expression. 'You need a rest.' And before she could protest he had lifted her from the car and carried her into the house and up to their bedroom, and laid her gently on the bed.

'The doctor told me to be prepared for rapid mood swings, darling, and you can complain as much as you like but you will do as I say,' he commanded arrogantly, and then he leant over her and brushed his lips along her brow. 'Is there anything you want?'

Her baby back...but the words were never said as, wretched, she flopped back against the pillow, listless and lifeless. A faint sigh left her lips. 'No, I'm fine. I'll join you downstairs later.'

'Good girl.' He straightened, his dark eyes smiling compassionately down at her. 'We will have other children, Lexi. We have plenty of time.'

She managed a weak smile, but, for the first time since meeting Jake, she was actually relieved to see him leave the room.

Meg, bless her, was all sympathy with Lexi as she woke her with a cup of tea and the information that dinner was almost ready. Lexi smiled weakly at the small, grey-haired woman who had been the daily at Forest Manor as long as she could remember.

'Nothing ever seems to work right for me in this house, does it, Meg? My mother died here, my father, and now my baby. Maybe if I had stayed in London and never come back here I wouldn't have lost my baby.'

'Don't be ridiculous,' Meg said shortly. 'Losing a baby has nothing to do with where one lives. You're just clutching at straws, my girl. Now come on, up, dressed, and down, and look after that husband of yours. We don't want that black-eyed witch latching on to him, now, do we?'

Lexi chuckled. Meg's opinion of Jake's PA was on a par with her own. The woman might be tall and sophisticated and a brilliant businesswoman, but she gave Lexi the creeps, and, even though Jake denied any involvement with her, Lexi had a suspicion that it wasn't for the want of trying by Lorraine...

Sitting at the dinner-table half an hour later with Jake and Lorraine was hardly a relaxing experience. Although Jake made a great effort to keep the conversation flowing, Lexi found it increasingly difficult to answer in anything but monosyllables, until the other two began discussing a Docklands development Jake was involved in, and Lexi was no longer required to speak at all.

Lorraine, as if forgetting Lexi's presence altogether, became quite explicit. 'Really, Jake, you have to decide if you want the deal and go for it. A conference call is not going to do the trick. You'll have to be in London tomorrow at the latest.'

'Not now, Lorraine.' Jake said curtly, shooting the dark woman a warning glance, and, turning to Lexi, added, 'I'm staying here. Don't worry, darling.'

'Please, Jake,' Lexi pleaded softly, she could sense the undercurrent in the air there was something going on she knew nothing about, and right at the moment she did not care. 'I'll be OK with Meg, in fact I think I would like to be on my own for a while. If you're needed in London I really think you should go.'

'No way.' He reached across the table and caught her small hand in his. 'You need me.'

The tenderness in his gaze was almost Lexi's undoing, her lips began to tremble but with a great effort of will she pulled her hand free. 'I'd rather you went, honestly, Jake.'

'That's settled, then.' Lorraine spoke up. 'You're being over-protective, Jake. I'll get back to London after dinner and set up a meeting for tomorrow.'

Jake's dark eyes caught Lexi's, a query in their depths. 'You've had a very traumatic emotional experience; you need my support.'

His support was a little late in coming, Lexi thought bitterly. He had barely mentioned their child. It had been a boy. Did Jake know that? She had no idea. The same as she had no idea what perverse sense of justice was motivating her angry resentment.

Lexi looked into her husband's dark, serious face and wanted to reach out to him and beg him to stay, hold her, comfort her, but somewhere deep inside she felt an aching guilt. It was her fault she had lost their baby; she did not deserve the tender loving care in his eyes; she had failed him in the one thing a woman should give her husband, and, because of that, the very least she could do by recompense was not get in the way of his business. She glanced across at Lorraine and saw the impatience in the other woman's eyes.

'Really, Jake. Lexi has only had a miscarriage. It happens to women every day and they get over it. In fact, it might be a blessing in disguise. We are going to be frightfully busy over the next few months. You wouldn't have much time for a child just now. Next year would be much better.'

Lexi couldn't believe the insensitivity of Lorraine, but she did catch a glimpse of something that looked very much like relief in her husband's eyes, just before he exploded.

'For God's sake, Lorraine. Keep your bloody opinions to yourself,' Jake swore violently. 'You might be a brilliant businesswoman, but in the feminine stakes we both know you're a non-starter. Can't you see you're upsetting Lexi? How can you be so heartless? It was my child as well...'

'Sorry-y.' Lorraine drawled and, pushing back her chair left the table. 'If I'm driving back to London tonight, I'd better get started. Give me a ring at home later and tell me what you decide.' And she left the room.

Lexi, with head bowed, pushed the remains of her chicken chasseur around her plate, too choked to speak. She felt a hard hand curve around her shoulder and looked up. Jake had walked around behind her and was leaning over her.

'I'm sorry, Lexi. Ignore Lorraine. She's a great PA but home and family are of no importance to her. She doesn't mean to be callous, she just doesn't think unless it is business... Come on, I'll take you back upstairs.'

'I can manage on my own.'

'I know, darling, but indulge me, hmmm?' And lifting her to her feet he swung her up into his strong arms, his deep blue eyes riveted on her own. 'I don't like feeling helpless, Lexi, and losing our baby has left me that way.'

She felt the tears fill her eyes. Jake was hurting just the same as her, and she made no demur when he carried her back to the bedroom.

Gently he let her slide down the long length of him, linking his arms behind her back and holding her steady against his hard body for a long moment. She let her head drop against his chest and felt the firm, steady beat of his heart beneath her cheek, and found it oddly reassuring.

'I'll always be here for you, Lexi, you know that, don't you?'

She raised her face to his. 'Yes. Yes, I know, but Lorraine is right. I'll be fine; your business is important in London, please go.' And, forcing a smile to her soft lips, she teased, 'After all, you will only be a telephone call away, and surely British Telecom can get a single call right.'

'Shhh, sweetheart, I'm not going anywhere.' His dark head swooped and his firm lips covered hers in a gentle kiss. 'Everything will work out,' he murmured against her mouth. 'But now get into bed, and rest. I'll join you later.'

Lexi turned away and, slipping out of her clothes, she headed for the bathroom. Everything would work out. Jake had said so... but somehow, for the first time since her marriage, she wasn't quite so sure.

A couple of hours later, Lexi woke from a light, troubled doze to the sight of Jake striding across the room from the bathroom, completely naked. Her violet eyes slid over his hard-muscled body almost with dislike. He was perfect, so alive, all virile male, but her son was dead and she felt a failure.

When he slid into bed beside her and drew her into his arms, she didn't offer any resistance, needing his protective embrace, until she realised, with something very like disgust as he folded her into the heat of his body, a hard thigh over her slender limbs, that he was sexually aroused. She pushed him away with an angry snort. 'My God, Jake. How can you?'

'Hush, Lexi, I don't want to do anything, just hold you, but you know you always have this effect on me. You don't have to do anything: a look, a smile, you just have to be there and my body reacts... and it has been a few empty nights without you,' he drawled softly, adding, 'Just lie still and soon I'll relax.'

She tilted her small head back and looked up into his shadowy features, barely visible in the moon's silvery light beaming through the window. His dark eyes burned down into hers, a sensual, teasing gleam in their indigo depths. 'Unless, of course, you want to help me relax,' he murmured throatily, kissing her softly parted lips.

She knew exactly what he meant; until she had become pregnant they had enjoyed a full, totally erotic sensual relationship. He had taught her everything she knew about sex and also how to please him, but in the circumstances she found it distasteful, and, pushing herself out of his arms, she slid to the far side of the bed.

'My God! Surely you can control your insatiable appetite for once? You disgust me.' She felt the instant tension in his large body at her words but she didn't care if she had hurt him. She was hurting too much herself.

'I was only teasing, Lexi, trying to cheer you up. This is as hard for me as it is for you, darling, and I don't know how to handle it.'

'Try using the spare bedroom,' she said curtly. 'I need my sleep.'

'Do you mean that?' He sat up in bed, his hands grasping her slender shoulders and pinning her to the bed. 'Is that really what you want? You know I'll do anything to make it easier for you.'

It wasn't what she wanted; she wanted to be held in his arms and sleep with her head on his chest, have him tell her how much he loved her, tell her it wasn't her fault they had lost the baby, but she couldn't say any of those things. Instead, in a small, tight voice, she looked straight up into his puzzled eyes and said, 'Yes, I would prefer to be alone, if you don't mind.' She noticed the flash of pain in his expression before he quickly controlled it.

'Dr Bell said to pamper you, so all right.' His dark head lowered and she knew he was going to kiss her but deliberately she turned her head away and his lips brushed her cheek. 'Goodnight, darling,' he said softly. She felt him leave the bed and a few seconds' silence before the door closed with a soft thump.

What had she done? And why? She didn't know. The huge bed was lonely without Jake, and slowly the tears trickled down her cheeks. She didn't recognise the person she had become, and, as she sank into an exhausted sleep, her tired mind gave up trying to find an answer.

Over the next few weeks, Lexi seemed to move through the days in a world of her own. Oh, she functioned all right on a purely practical level, but on an emotional level she was numb, haunted by guilt because she had lost the child. Not even Jake could get through to her.

The first morning back at Forest Manor, he had been all concern, refusing to leave for London, until on the Wednesday evening he insisted on taking her out to dinner, trying to cheer her up. They dined at Number 19 Grape Lane in York, the first place they had ever shared a meal together, but the exquisite food tasted like sawdust in her mouth, and she heaved a sigh of relief when Jake finally suggested returning home.

As she slipped her nightdress over her head, a soft confection of satin and lace, Jake walked into the bedroom. She lifted her head, and eyed him across the wide expanse of the large bed. He was fresh from the shower, his dark hair slicked back across his proud head, his body gleaming golden, naked except for a short white towel slung around his hips, his long sinewy legs planted slightly apart. He looked like every woman's dream of a lover, but to Lexi he appeared as a threat to her blessed numb state. She watched wary-eyed as he walked around the bed to stand in front of her.

His strong hands curved around her upper arms and he eased her towards him. 'Lexi, we have to talk. You've slept alone long enough; it's becoming a habit.'

She tensed her body rigid in his hold.

'Don't get me wrong, sweetheart. I know it is too soon for lovemaking.'

'How thoughtful,' she snapped curtly.

'Give me some credit, Lexi, but you have to understand, separate beds are not the answer to your problem. You need care and comfort.' His dark head bent towards her.

'Not now,' she said starkly, and watched as Jake's proud head reared back.

'Then when, Lexi? You hardly talk any more.'

'I do, I worked in Reception today for a couple of hours, and thoroughly enjoyed it.' And she had. Jake had been working in his study and she had walked through to the hotel just as a party of French tourists arrived. She had felt quite animated for a while, getting back to work.

'You can talk to strangers, but not to your husband?' he queried silkily, his mask of concern slipping to reveal his frustration. 'For God's sake, Lexi, you have to snap out of it.' His fingers dug into her flesh and she winced, her head lifting fractionally in time to catch the flare of frightening anger in his dark eyes, quickly controlled.

'It's hard, I know, Lexi, but we have to try and forget. When I first met you the one thing I noticed, above your beauty and your voluptuous little body——' his dark eyes swept lingeringly over her from head to toe and then back to her upturned face '—was your eager appetite for life, your vibrancy; don't let this one set-back knock all the life out of you. I want my wife back as she was. I want us to get back to normal as quickly as possible,' he declared frustratedly.

'If what you say is true,' she opined with remarkable calm, considering his naked chest was scraping gently against the delicate fabric of her nightgown over her softly rounded breasts, 'I think you should return to London tomorrow. After all, for the past couple of months you've worked in the city all week, only returning home at weekends. That's normal for us.' Her huge violet eyes held his gaze and she watched his eyes darken almost to jet, feeling the tension in his hard body.

She thought she heard him murmur, 'I need you,' but she must have been mistaken as, with a faint sigh, Jake slid his hands up her throat and cupped her small face.

'Yes, whatever you want.' And, holding her head steady, he closed his firm, sensuous mouth over hers in a hard, possessive kiss. He straightened abruptly. 'And God knows the business certainly needs me, even if you don't.' And he left, a defeated slant to his broad shoulders.

After that night, Jake returned to the London apartment and his head office, and Lexi slipped into a regular routine: she worked a few hours every day in Reception, and at weekends Jake returned home.

He took her out for dinner, and to the theatre in York; he even insisted on them spending a day at Castle Howard, but nothing could snap her out of her lethargy, and the separate bedrooms remained... Meg tried as well, warning her that she was a fool to leave her husband alone with the lovely Lorraine all week—she was just asking for trouble. But Lexi refused to listen. If Jake slept with Lorraine, it was no more than she had always suspected, she told herself, and refused to admit there was anything wrong.

She worked, didn't she? So what if she was a bit quiet? Surely it was allowed after all she had suffered. And she wrapped her grief around her like a shroud.

Lexi opened her eyes slowly and turned over in the large bed, just for a second she felt a pang of something like regret that Jake's hard masculine body wasn't there beside her. She sighed deeply and, pushing the tangled mass of her flame-coloured hair from her small face, she stretched and sat up. She looked around the room. A few short months ago, when the renovations were first finished, this room had been her pride and joy; she had chosen the decoration, a soft blend of peaches and cream saved from being too feminine by the heavy antique mahogany furniture. The summer sun streamed through the window, dancing into every little nook and cranny. It was a gorgeous summer day, and then she remembered the date—it was a Wednesday, her day for a check-up with Dr Bell, but also it was the day before her first wedding anniversary.

Dr Bell took one look at her and demanded to know what was wrong. Lexi broke down and told him: her guilt over losing the baby, her distaste for sex, even her suspicion that Jake was having an affair with Lorraine. Three hours later, after much good advice, such as 'try taking a holiday', Lexi found herself sitting on the afternoon train heading for London, and Jake.

She watched the patchwork of the countryside sliding past the carriage window in the hot summer sun and she felt as if she had awakened from a long sleep. Not so much sleep as nightmare, she admitted ruefully. Dear Dr Bell had explained everything: she had been suffering from hormonal depression and the fact that she had lost the baby and was consumed with guilt about it had made her worse, prone to suspicion, irrational... But once the doctor had convinced her it was a quite common reaction to a miscarriage, she had suddenly felt rejuvenated.

Lexi had taken great care with her appearance, for the first time in weeks. Her red hair shone like living flame and cascaded down her back in lavish curls. The smart, sleeveless plain mint-green silk sheath she wore clung lovingly to her slender curves and ended just above her knees, revealing a goodly amount of shapely legs; on her feet she wore high-heeled white pumps and she carried a small white clutch bag in her hand containing her passport. A hastily packed suitcase was on the rack above her head. She was going to surprise Jake, and persuade him to let his super-efficient Lorraine look after the business while he accompanied Lexi to Paris for the rest of the week, a repetition of their honeymoon a year ago. It would be perfect...

The first hint that Lexi's plan was not going to go smoothly came as the train ground to a halt, half an hour away from King's Cross station. Lexi heard with dismay that the train was delayed because of a bomb scare at the station, and to make matters worse a glance out of the carriage window showed the blue sky turn to black and the heavens open in a storm that would have rivalled Noah's. She consulted the slim gold watch on her wrist and sighed. She would not catch him at the office, but still, she told herself, it didn't matter. She would catch him at the apartment; they had spent many a happy hour there when they were first married.

Dreamily she recalled the first weeks when they were so close. Jake had told her all about himself. He was a self-made man, and a bastard, he had declared on their second date, but luckier than most. Apparently, his mother had fallen in love with a married man when on holiday on the continent, and Jake was the result. The married man, to give him his due, had provided for the mother and child. He had paid for a Victorian terraced house in London for them, and every month a cheque arrived, though the man himself never put in an appearance. When Jake was sixteen the money had stopped coming, and they had only been able to assume the man had died. Jake had left school and begun working on building sites and, after the death of his mother four years later, he had taken his first step into the business world, by converting the three-storey house into apartments.

Lexi smiled reminiscently; they had been lying naked in bed in their Paris hotel and she had teased him about being a self-made millionaire at thirty. Laughingly he had responded, 'If you married me for money, as Lorraine would have me believe, you're in for a shock. Every penny I make I reinvest; a paper millionaire need

not necessarily have spare cash floating around. But
don't worry, I won't see you go hungry.' And, leaning
over her satiated naked body, he had murmured throatily,
'Take a bite of me any time, darling.'

The train started with a jolt, jerking Lexi out of her
reverie; she was surprised to note they had been delayed
well over an hour. Still, soon she would see her husband,
and she hugged the thought to her with secret delight.

Before getting a taxi from the station she took time
to purchase from one of the small boutiques a bottle of
Jake's favourite aftershave. Kindly the assistant gift-
wrapped it for her. Not a very exciting or original anniversary present, but the best she could do at short notice.
Ten minutes later, she was sitting in the back of a taxi
speeding through the streets of London.

With a light step she dashed across the pavement and
into the entrance of the mansion block that housed Jake's
apartment, dodging the sheeting rain. The lovely summer
day had deteriorated into a very wet and windy night.
Still, nothing could dampen her spirits and, with suitcase
in one hand and bag and gift in the other, she dashed
up the flight of stairs to the first-floor apartment.

She placed her suitcase on the floor and, taking her
key from her bag, let herself into the cosy flat. A short
hall with a telephone table and cloak cupboard was
thickly carpeted in a deep, dark red. Silently she moved
along the hall; she stopped at the hall table and deposited the parcel on it and the suitcase at her feet, and
then took a step further to the living-room door. She
reached out to open it but it was not closed and swung
half-open at her touch, and then she froze.

Jake was already at home, and not alone. A small
balcony with various large green houseplants partly ob-
scured the door from the two people sitting side by side
on a large, curved, black hide sofa in the sunken lounge.
But Lexi could see all too clearly. Jake and Lorraine, a
bottle of wine, and two glasses on the table beside them,

but, more damning than that, they were both wearing only towelling robes.

She stood numb with shock, the rainwater dripping from her long hair, running icily down her spine, her thin dress no match for the storm outside. But the storm in her heart was worse. She listened in open-mouthed horror as her life dissolved around her.

'It's no good, Lorraine, I just can't tell Lexi. At least not yet. She's just lost a child, for God's sake! She will be so hurt...' Jake's deep voice sounded harsh in the stillness of the room.

'You're being ridiculous, Jake. She has to know some time and if you don't tell her she'll find out anyway, and that will hurt her a hell of a lot more. It is impossible to keep a thing like this secret.' Her scarlet-tipped nails reached out and curved around Jake's arm, and Lexi, from her vantage place at the door, flinched as though she had been struck.

'I've told you before, Jake, you're far too protective of Lexi. She is a twenty-year-old woman, she has lost a child; she knows the world is not all sweetness and light. These things happen and there's nothing anyone can do about it. You cut your losses, and try again.'

'You don't understand, Lorraine. I made a promise to Lexi when I married her. What am I supposed to say to her? "Sorry, darling, but circumstances have changed, and it's a tough old world out there. Sorry I've got to break my word, but I'm sure you understand..."' he drawled sarcastically.

'She will understand, Jake, and it's not as if you're leaving her with nothing; she's a sleeping partner in the business—half of all you make is hers. Personally, I always thought she was a gold-digger anyway. I told you so when you insisted on marrying her. She might jump at the chance of being rich in her own right...I know if I was in her position I would.'

'Lexi has been protected all her life; she's not like you.' Jake's dark head turned to the woman at his side. 'That's why you make such a damn good PA: you're as tough as any man and mercenary to boot, but fortunately Lexi is not.'

Lexi had seen and heard enough. 'It's not as if you're leaving her with nothing,' echoed in her head. How could she have been such a fool? Her husband and his PA were having an affair; they were actually discussing how he was to divorce her. For all Lexi knew it had been going on since long before she had met Jake. Suddenly it was blatantly obvious, she realised with numb acceptance. Jake had only married her for Forest Manor.

She recalled their wedding-day, when she had mentioned eventually settling at Forest Manor and Jake's look of shocked surprise. She had naïvely assumed, with their marriage and Jake's promise to pay her father's debts, that the house would stay a house. But Jake had quickly put her straight. It was still essential that the place be turned into a hotel, though he did promise they could keep a private wing for themselves. Lexi, so in love, had of course agreed.

So many little things suddenly made sense. At first, when the hotel was completed, Jake had insisted he could work as easily in Yorkshire as London. But almost as soon as her pregnancy was confirmed suddenly business was hard and he needed to be in London all week. Now she realised Jake must have wanted out of the marriage from the minute the hotel was up and running and making money for him. No wonder the pair sitting on the sofa before her had been so negative about Lexi's pregnancy. While she was devastated at the loss of her child, her swine of a husband had probably been laughing with relief. It was this thought more than anything that gave Lexi the strength to do what she did next.

Straightening her shoulders, she walked out on to the small balcony but did not descend the steps to the couple below. Standing above them gave her some sense of superiority, even if it was just an illusion.

Jake saw her first and jumped to his feet, swinging around to look up at her. 'Lexi, what are you doing here?' His dark face was flushed, and for once he looked less than in complete control as his strong hands tugged at the belt around his waist holding his robe together.

Lexi's violet eyes narrowed to mere slits of purple ice. 'I called to tell you I'm going on a little holiday with Cathy, a friend from school, but I couldn't help overhearing your conversation.' By this time Lorraine had stood up next to Jake. Lexi almost choked. The woman was wearing Lexi's robe, and it was too small for her, or perhaps, from a man's point of view, it was perfect, barely covering the other woman's large breasts.

'Lexi, let me explain.' Jake moved towards the stairs.

Imperviously, Lexi held up her small hand. 'There is really no need, Jake. I heard everything, and I hate to disillusion you, but you are wrong about me, and Lorraine was right. I really don't care about you breaking your promise to me. I would much rather have the money.' If Lexi had any lingering doubt about the perfidiousness of Jake it vanished, as she recognised the look of pure undisguised relief that spread over his handsome face.

'You heard it all, everything, and you really don't mind...?' He smiled up at her. 'Thank God for that! I was dreading telling you. You've been so down lately, losing the child and everything; I just never imagined you would be so sensible. I think this calls for a drink. Champagne even.' And holding up a hand to her he said, 'Come on down, and we can all celebrate.'

Celebrate! The heartless swine, but then, why was she surprised? She had never been a match for the sophisticated couple in front of her, and perhaps in her heart of hearts she had always known that. Only once had she mentioned to Jake that he seemed very close to his PA and he had burst out laughing, though he was flattered that Lexi was jealous. The bastard! She swore under her breath, but not by a flicker of an eyelid did she reveal her true feelings; instead she responded smoothly, 'I'm afraid I haven't time, the taxi is waiting downstairs...'

In three steps Jake was beside her. 'Don't be ridiculous. You can't leave just like that! Lexi, I knew nothing about you taking a holiday.' His strong hands reached out for her but she took a hasty step back into the hall, she grabbed her suitcase and headed for the door. Jake caught her as she opened the door.

'Wait, Lexi, I refuse to let you go off like this; we have things to discuss,' he declared adamantly. 'You've been ill, for God's sake!'

'You have no say in the matter any more. You broke your promise, and now I'm breaking mine. Go back and celebrate with Lorraine.' Her face a cold mask, she stared straight at him. 'As for me, I never want to see you again.'

If she had slapped him, she couldn't have shocked him more. His hand fell from her arm and all the colour drained out of his face. 'You don't mean that, Lexi, you're being childish. I thought you said you understood... Sit down, have a drink and...

'Call my solicitor in York with the divorce papers,' she cut him off, and spun around.

'My God! You don't care, not for me, the hotel...Lorraine was right all along, you mercenary little bitch...'

But Lexi barely heard him. She was free, out of the door, and running down the staircase, her suitcase banging against her leg as she moved and the tears streaming down her face. She vaguely heard Jake's harsh voice shouting after her but she did not stop running until she had put a couple of streets between herself and her louse of a husband.

Finally she waved down a cab and collapsed in the back seat. 'Just drive around, please,' she murmured.

'You're the boss,' the driver said flatly.

The tears dried on her face, her violet eyes huge and blankly staring inward... 'Childish,' Jake had called her for not accepting that he wanted to divorce her with the sophisticated *élan* he expected from his women.

Hormonal depression, she thought with dry irony, What a joke! Deep in her subconscious, hadn't she always wondered what the dynamic London businessman saw in her? Why a man of Jake's obvious wealth and charm would marry a naïve young woman from Yorkshire? She had always sensed the ruthless streak in him but had convinced herself it would never be turned on her. Jake loved her! And that was the biggest joke of all. He had swept her off her feet, used her body in lust, and even that hadn't satisfied him for long.

She groaned, a small whimper of sound. All her suspicions about Jake and Lorraine had been confirmed in one horrendous evening. Jake had probably been making love to Lorraine every time he was in London, while Lexi, as the little wife, was in happy ignorance, working in the hotel miles away. Lexi closed her eyes briefly to shut out the pain; she would not give in to it, she vowed silently.

Dear heaven! While she was losing her child Jake and Lorraine had most likely been in each other's arms... She couldn't bear to think about it, and, opening her eyes, her mouth a tight white line, she made a silent promise. Jake had hurt her for the last time...

Her mind was made up. She had used her old school chum's name on the spur of the moment earlier, but actually it was a good idea. The thought of Cathy was comforting. They were both children of diplomats and had spent five years together at the same convent school in Sussex. They had shared a flat in London for a year but had not been in touch since Lexi had dropped out of college. But Lexi was pretty sure Cathy still had the same apartment. She gave the cabbie her friend's address, and half an hour later Lexi was being warmly welcomed by an amazon of a girl with green hair into an Earl's Court apartment that looked like a bomb had hit it.

'Hey, you hardly look the happy mum-to-be. What's happened?'

Lexi collapsed on the beaten-up sofa, and between her tears told Cathy everything...

The following day she made a long phone call to her solicitor in York, advising him that soon he would be receiving divorce papers from her husband, and instructing him to act on her behalf, to accept whatever Jake said without query, but on no account to let her husband have the new address she would forward to Mr Travis as soon as she was settled.

With the old man's condolences ringing in her ears she replaced the receiver, and, with a grim smile for Cathy, said, 'Right, to your parents', and then as far away from England as I can get, and if by any remote chance you bump into Jake Taylor you have never seen me, and have no idea where I am. Promise...' And Cathy did.

CHAPTER THREE

LEXI stepped out of the lift at the ground floor, her glance sweeping professionally around the elegant marble foyer, lingering slightly on the view of the dining-room through large double doors. Yes, all was serene; the few guests who had opted to lunch in the hotel were being attended to with the expert efficiency expected of the staff at the Hotel Le Piccolo Paradiso.

As manager of the small, exclusive hotel it was Lexi's job to make sure everything ran smoothly, and even now, when she was off duty and on her way down into Sorrento for the rest of the day, she could not help checking everything was in order.

Today it was slightly more than that, she admitted to herself with a wry smile. She was meeting Dante for lunch and he would be expecting to hear if she was going ahead with the divorce. It was still a niggling puzzle to Lexi why Jake Taylor, in almost five years, had never instigated divorce proceedings. It just didn't make sense. The last night in London she had heard Jake and Lorraine discussing how to break the news to his wife of their involvement and they had even got around to discussing the money side of divorce, and wondering if Lexi would accept it. When she had faced Jake he had made no attempt to deny anything, was delighted she had overheard and was going to be sensible and actually suggested she join them in a drink.

For years she had been expecting to hear from Mr Travis, her solicitor, that Jake had approached him for a divorce but it had never happened. When Dante had asked her out a few months ago, she had decided it was

44

time she got back into the world of male-female relationships, and to do so she had to be free. Finally, a week ago she had rung Mr Travis in England and, after a long conversation with the lawyer, she had confirmed in writing her desire to start divorce proceedings on the five years' separation statute. This very morning she had received a letter from her solicitor confirming that the proceedings were progressing on her behalf.

Dismissing the problem from her mind, she strolled over to the reception desk and in her usual fluent Italian asked Franco, her young assistant manager, if everything was in order.

'*Si*, Lexi.' His dark brown eyes swept over her appreciatively, taking in the rich tumble of golden-red curls flowing down her back and the seductive silhouette of her voluptuous figure outlined in a brief blue cotton jersey scooped-neck shift dress. Her shapely legs were bare and golden as was the rest of her exposed flesh. Five years in Sorrento and she had matured into a stunningly beautiful woman from the slim, rather solemn girl who had first arrived. Franco sighed dramatically. 'Meeting Signor Dante? I think he is a very lucky man.'

Lexi grinned in acceptance of the compliment. 'Forever the charmer, Franco,' she quipped. '*Ciao.*' And her strappy blue sandals tapped out her jaunty step as she crossed the marble floor and stepped outside into the brilliant blaze of midsummer sun.

She stopped for a moment beside the little Fiat Panda—it was a company car but Lexi considered it hers—she stared out over the roof of the car at the view before her. It never failed to lift her spirits, she thought musingly. The hotel was perched high on a hill overlooking the bay of Naples. The isle of Capri was visible on the left, an exquisite jewel set in a sea of azure. With a contented sigh, Lexi opened the car door and sat in the driving seat.

Why worry? she told herself. According to the solicitor, in six weeks' time she could divorce Jake Taylor on the grounds that they had been apart for five years; she didn't even need her husband's consent. Dante should be satisfied with that. Very soon she would be officially free...

She started the little car and spun along the elegant drive lined with orange and lemon trees and turned right at the main gates on to the road down into Sorrento. She was singing softly to herself as she swung the wheel expertly around the first of half a dozen hairpin bends that zig-zagged down the hillside, only to gasp as, with lightning speed, a black Bugatti sports car swerved violently to pass her, only missing her car by inches.

The same blasted car again! Stupid macho oaf, she thought scathingly, as she registered the brief outline of a dark, greying man behind the wheel of the gleaming monster of a car. But, once more steadily driving along, she had the same uncomfortable feeling that there was something vaguely familiar about the driver of the Bugatti. She had seen the car a few times in the past few months. It was hard to miss; at first she had thought the driver might have been a guest at some time. But the hotel was small—only twenty luxuriously appointed suites, strictly for the very wealthy and discerning traveller, and she knew virtually all the guests, past and present.

She had never actually got a good look at the driver. But somehow she had the strangest feeling she knew the man on a more personal basis. Which was ridiculous when she thought about it; people with the sort of wealth that could afford a Bugatti were not in her social circle. Dante, her boyfriend, was comfortably off, owning two jewellery shops—one in Sorrento and another in Amalfi. He was a good, hard-working, serious-minded man and would make her an excellent husband and father to her children.

A shadow darkened her violet eyes, as she realised with a sense of shock it would be exactly five years to-night since she had lost her child. She had never completely got over the miscarriage, and sometimes in her darkest moods she couldn't help asking herself if she had finally instigated divorce proceedings herself and was contemplating marrying Dante, more because she still had a desperate longing for a child, than through any great love for the man himself.

She dismissed the unsettling thought from her mind. Anyway, Dante hadn't actually proposed yet, she smiled wryly, counting her chickens again! A bad policy, she remonstrated with herself, as she manoeuvred the car through the hectic lunch-time traffic in Sorrento and down to the Marina Piccolae. She had arranged to meet Dante at the Dolphin restaurant, a long wooden structure that stretched out on wooden stilts from the steep cliffs into the sea and served excellent fish dishes. She parked the car on a small cobbled side-lane and walked around the curve of the old port.

A tender smile curved the corners of her full mouth as she watched the local children playing in the sea. It didn't seem to bother them that there were fishing boats tied up haphazardly around the water's edge; in fact it appeared to add to their enjoyment as, like fish themselves, they jumped and dived off the boats.

Sorrento was a stunning town, built over a flat plateau that rose precipitously from the sea. On the top of the steep cliffs the big hotels had lifts cut through the rock and down to the base and the sea. Small beaches with large rectangular wooden pontoons greatly increased the available sunbathing areas and, for the swimmer, access to the sea itself, but at quite a substantial charge to the public. Certainly more than local children could pay.

Lexi glanced at her watch. Oh, hell! She was late. Putting a spurt on, she dashed the last hundred yards to the restaurant, and breathlessly walked through the dining-room and out on to the open-air deck. She glanced around and smiled as she caught sight of Dante. He had not seen her and for a moment she allowed her gaze to linger on his downbent head. He was such a nice man. At forty-two he was beginning to get a little heavy, maybe, but nothing could take away from his friendly smiling face as he looked up and caught her gaze. Of medium height, with the black curling locks of a true Neapolitan and huge thick-lashed dark brown eyes, he reminded Lexi of some lovely cuddly spaniel.

He stood up as she approached. 'Late again, *cara*.' And holding out her chair for her he brushed her cheek with his lips. 'But you are worth the wait.'

She had not seen him for over a week and his husky compliment did wonders for her self-esteem. She sat down with a contented sigh, and looked out over the sea with complete satisfaction. Yes, she had made the right decision. England had no appeal for her any more. Her life now was in Italy with Dante and in a few weeks she would be free to marry him, and turning her attention to her companion she smiled brilliantly. 'Dante, have I ever told you? You are a truly lovely man.'

His broad, tanned face split in a huge grin. 'In that case, let's eat quick and go back to my place for siesta.'

She chuckled. 'You never miss a chance.'

Suddenly serious, Dante caught her hand in his across the table. 'I don't intend to, I've waited months for you. Have you heard from England?'

Lexi withdrew her hand from his as the waiter arrived with two plates of superbly grilled langoustines in garlic butter. Dante knew her taste so well and had already ordered. 'Yes, yes, I have, and I've checked the law with my solicitor and he has told me that in a few weeks' time, when the separation has lasted five years, I can have a divorce with or without my husband's consent. I got a letter this morning and the wheels have already been set in motion. No problem.'

'You're sure?' he demanded sceptically.

'Absolutely,' she confirmed.

'In that case, how about a November wedding? Most of the tourists have left by then and we can take an extended honeymoon.'

Not the most romantic proposal in the world, she thought, her lips twitching in a wry grin, but in the past few months Dante had let her know in countless ways that marriage was on his mind. Which was why she had finally got the courage to apply for a divorce herself. After all, five years without sight or sound of her husband was enough proof for any court in the land that the marriage was over. But until meeting Dante she had been reluctant to do anything about it, perhaps deep down she had been afraid of maybe having to face her ex-husband again. Stupid, she knew, but even now she still couldn't seem to throw off a niggling unease...

Dante was watching her with dark, pleading eyes; his proposal might have sounded casual, but she knew he was a hundred per cent sincere. 'Yes' was such a simple word, but suddenly Lexi shivered. A ghost walking over her grave; it couldn't be anything else—the temperature was a boiling ninety-five degrees. But somehow, with the mention of honeymoon and the thought of the irrevocable step she was about to take, she was no longer so sure.

'*Cara*, say something.'

'Yes, yes, that will be fine. November.' She said the words and smiled as Dante reached across the table and, catching her hand in his, gently squeezed her fingers, before planting a kiss on the back of her hand.

'Thank you, *cara*, I promise you won't ever regret marrying me.' Then his lips parted in a cheeky grin. 'Signor Monicelli will be delighted to stand with you; I took the liberty of asking him, on your behalf, last week.' And, letting go of her hand, he picked up his fork and continued eating.

Lexi shook her head, and smiled at his confidence, then followed suit, but her mind wasn't on her food, delicious though it was. The mention of Signor Monicelli had sent her thoughts spinning back to when she had arrived in Sorrento for the first time. She had stayed in London one night with her friend Cathy, after the painful betrayal by Jake. The following day Cathy had whisked her off to her parents' house in Surrey, and two days later Lexi had found herself travelling with Cathy's parents to Italy, where Cathy's father was taking up the post as British consul in Naples. Mr Clarke-Smythe had introduced her to Signor Monicelli, the owner of the Piccolo Paradiso and the Italian, once assured of her gift for languages and former brief stint in the Forest Manor hotel, had given her a job as a receptionist...

She had been lucky. Because of the haste of her first marriage her passport had not been changed from her maiden name of Miss Alexandra Laughton, consequently, with the exception of Signor Monicelli—she had mentioned it to him because it had seemed the right thing to do—and Dante, of course, no one else knew she had once been married.

Dante had been, and still was, a great friend of Signor Monicelli's son Marco, and that was how Lexi had got to know him. Up until last year Marco had been the hotel manager until a horrific car smash had left him paralysed from the waist down. Now he lived on the paradise island of Ischia with his parents and Lexi had been promoted to manage the hotel. But she knew Signor Monicelli was in the process of selling the hotel. Still, she thought musingly, even if the worst scenario occurred and the new owners did not want to employ her as manager, would it matter that much, now she was committed to marrying Dante?

She would regret losing her job, and she knew without any false pride that she was very good at what she did. But as there was some hope, if Signor Monicelli took his son to America, of Marco being taught to walk again, and he wanted to give Marco every chance, her own worries about unemployment were of no account.

Later, as dusk was falling, Lexi manoeuvred her little car back up the road to home, if not exactly ecstatic, she was feeling happily content at the future before her. Dante adored her. Admittedly, his kisses did not set her on fire, but they were loving and pleasurable, and she had no doubt when they finally married she would discover that his lovemaking was equally nice. Much as he teased her about going to bed with him, he was quite content to wait until they were married. Another big plus in his favour.

She shook her head as she got out of the car at the entrance to the hotel. What was she thinking about, adding up the plus signs like an accountant? And with a light step she ran up the stairs and into the foyer. It was a shame Dante had had to curtail their day out, but unfortunately the manager of his Amalfi shop had taken suddenly ill and Dante had to leave her to go and look after the shop himself.

Actually, she was relieved in a way; tonight she had a feeling she would not have been the best of company, as thoughts of the past flickered through her mind again. She stopped at the reception desk with a smile for Franco that did not quite reach her eyes and asked automatically, 'Any messages?'

Somehow all day she had been swinging between the past and present with alarming frequency, and she knew the cause; it was the same every year on the anniversary of her miscarriage, she thought ruefully, knowing she was being stupidly sentimental. Turning all her attention on Franco, she listened as he told her Signor Monicelli wanted her to call him urgently.

Picking up the telephone on Reception, she quickly dialled her boss's number. Five minutes later she replaced the receiver her lovely face wreathed in smiles. Apparently, the hotel sale had gone through, and the good news was that all the staff, herself included, were to remain in their jobs. She did not question why only minutes earlier she had accepted that she would leave work on her remarriage. She didn't dare admit even to herself the possibility that she loved her work more than Dante, but the lightness in her heart told its own story as she turned back to Franco, still grinning. 'Everything else OK?' she asked.' No more double-booking, I hope!' she teased with a mock frown.

Poor Franco, only the week before, had discovered a booking made by Anna, a junior, for a honeymoon couple registered to stay in a suite already occupied by a very important Arab guest. Luckily Lexi had been able to sort it out, but she had had to give her own, the manager's suite to the young couple, and spend the next few days sharing a room with Anna, the trainee receptionist.

'Not double-booked exactly.' Franco replied quite seriously.

'What? You haven't, not again!' Lexi's eyes narrowed keenly on his attractive face. When it came to business she was a hundred per cent efficient and she expected the same from her staff. Piccolo Paradiso was a favourite of a few seriously rich clients. People who appreciated the peace and quiet, the first-class service and absolute discretion of the management.

'No, no,' Franco responded, but Lexi noticed he avoided her eyes. 'But the gentleman was most insistent about seeing you...'

'I wouldn't take no for an answer,' a deep harsh voice echoed in her head.

Lexi swung around and the air left her lungs in a rush; she paled beneath her tan, her small hand reaching out to curl around the edge of the reception desk to give herself some support as her eyes widened to their fullest, extent in horror on the man before her. Of course, she

should have known; it was the man in the black Bugatti.
Jake . . . her husband.

'Why the surprise, Lexi? Surely you must have been
expecting me,' he opined hardly, his dark blue eyes, as
cold as the arctic wastes, sweeping her from head to toe
with insulting sexual insolence. 'The curt note from your
solicitor to mine informing me you were divorcing me
was bound to elicit a response. That was your intention,
was it not?'

She straightened her shoulders and let go of the desk.
'No, Mr Taylor.' Her chin tilted defensively as she held
his hard gaze. 'In fact, I'm amazed you even know about
the divorce.'

'My solicitor heard from yours yesterday, and immediately faxed me. What did you expect?' His smile
was chilling. 'That'd I'd let you?' he drawled, and a
frisson of alarm skidded down her spine.

'I never expected to see you again.' Her eyes dropped,
slanting over his tall frame. If anything, he was even
more arresting then she remembered. His handsome face
was a little thinner, the lines bracketing his sensuous
mouth slightly deeper, and his once night-black hair was
now lightly sprinkled with grey, but it did nothing to
detract from the potent, almost animal sexuality of the
man. His broad shoulders and fine-honed frame were
clad in hip-hugging jeans and a soft-knit shirt that only
served to reinforce his lethal attraction.

A shiver of, not fear, but something more shaming
made the fine hair on her skin stand erect. She felt
nineteen again and stunned at the immensity of her reaction to this man. She hated him, but was horrified to
realise he was still able to elicit an instant sexual response in her feminine body.

She was suddenly conscious of her skimpy blue jersey
dress and bare legs, her long hair falling down her back
in wild disarray. She knew she looked as though she had
just walked off the beach and wished like hell she was

attired in her uniform, a neat black suit and crisp white shirt. With a shaking hand she defensively tucked a few wild tendrils of hair behind her ear.

'Do I pass?'

His deep voice rasped along her overstretched nerves. She couldn't believe what a fool she had been! It had never occurred to her that Jake would respond to her solicitor's formal notification of the impending divorce in person. Her brows drew together in a puzzled frown. Why on earth would he want to? They had had no contact in almost five years. Surely Jake would be as happy as her at the ending of the marriage.

'If that frown is anything to go by, don't bother to answer—I probably wouldn't like your reply. Instead, let's find somewhere to talk.' He stepped towards her. Lexi tried to step back, his great height intimidating her, but was brought up hard against the reception desk.

'That will not be necessary,' Lexi managed in a taut voice. 'We have nothing to say to each other.' Her gaze once more met his and her violet eyes widened at the dark threat she saw in the deep blue depths of Jake's.

'You might find my presence abhorrent, Lexi, but I, I am not finished with you, not by a long way,' he told her in a hateful drawl. 'The next few weeks should be entertaining.'

'If you were thinking of staying here, Mr Taylor...the hotel is full.' She desperately tried to hang on to her business persona, but the shock to her system made her voice shake.

'So you say, but...'

'I am the manager, I know...' Her violet eyes sparkled with barely controlled anger, as some of her self-control returned. 'I think you should leave.' She gestured with her hand towards the entrance, and she bit her lip as Jake's strong hand caught her wrist in a painful grip.

'Let me go,' she hissed, her eyes stormy with pent-up anger as she tried to wrench her arm free.

'Nobody dismisses me with the wave of a hand, and certainly not a mercenary little bitch like you...' Jake snarled. His face hardened into an expression that made Lexi wish she hadn't tried so cavalierly to dismiss him as he continued. 'Now, if you wish to discuss our marriage in the foyer of the hotel, I really don't mind,' he informed her ruthlessly. 'I'm sure the rest of the guests will enjoy it.'

A chill shivered its way down the length of her spine as he dropped her wrist. With her other hand she rubbed where he had touched her, and what did he mean, mercenary? She didn't have a mercenary bone in her body, and she had never taken a penny from Jake since the day she left him.

'Is everything all right, Signorina Lexi?' Franco's voice intruded warily.

'Yes. Yes, fine,' Lexi confirmed swiftly as she glanced quickly around. Oh, God! The guests were on their way to dinner, and here she was looking like something the cat dragged in, arguing in the middle of Reception.

'Signorina Lexi... Odd, I could have sworn you were my wife,' Jake prompted with sardonic cynicism. 'Still, I suppose I should be grateful you appear to be working for a living. I fully expected you to have some wealthy lover looking after you.'

Lexi's head swung back to look at Jake, her mouth falling open in stunned amazement. 'Why, you...' Words failed her, which was probably just as well, she thought a moment later, remembering where she was.

'Or perhaps you're between keepers, hmm?'

Lexi registered the gasp of astonishment from Franco behind the desk. 'You are married to this man?' Franco exclaimed, and then broke out in a torrent of Italian, mostly about what Dante would say.

Lexi groaned inwardly and tried in a few words to calm her excitable assistant down. But finally she had no other course than to admit Jake was her husband.

'When you two have quite finished.' Jake's curt command stopped them both, his piercing gaze fixed on Franco. 'Perhaps you would arrange for my luggage to be taken to my wife's suite.'

For Lexi it was the last straw; she wanted to scream at Jake to shut up, but she knew she had to get him out of the reception before the whole damn place heard his revelation. 'Follow me,' she snarled between clenched teeth.

'I knew you would see it my way, Lexi, sensible girl,' he goaded mockingly.

She was too angry to take the lift, but preceded Jake up to the third floor and along to the far end of the corridor, her rage mounting at every step. She turned the key in the lock and opened the door. She didn't bother to look if Jake was behind her, but stormed across the room, flinging her bag on to a convenient sofa, and turned with her back to the window.

'Now, what the hell do you think you're playing at, Jake? How dare you come here and insinuate about my morals, or lack of them, in front of my staff and guests? Then to announce to the world we're married! You've got some damn nerve.' She was in a full-blooded fury, years of anger and frustration racing to the forefront of her mind.

'Is it so strange that I object to hearing my wife addressed as Mi-ss...?' Jake emphasised cynically.

'Dear God! You're mad. We have been separated for five years—five years, Jake. In fact, I can't understand why you didn't divorce me years ago, or why the hell you are here now, instead of cavorting around London with your faithful Lorraine,' she grated furiously.

'Then let me enlighten you, my sweet,' Jake drawled, a thread of steel in his voice. 'I have come to reclaim my wife.'

Her breath caught in her throat at his sheer arrogance. Her body trembling with fury, she cried, 'Don't be ridiculous.' Her voice shook with the force of her anger. 'You can't just walk into my life and say you're going to reclaim it.' She had hated this man for years; he had taken her girlish dream of love and family and forever and ground it in the dust beneath his feet. She was older now, a mature working woman, and no way would she put herself back in the subservient position of Jake's wife. 'I won't tolerate it.'

Jake, his dark eyes fixed on her flushed and furious face, slowly strolled across the room to stop only inches away from her. 'No more than I will tolerate some curt note from a solicitor telling me I am to be divorced.' The deadly intent in his softly voiced comment was more frightening than if he had shouted at her. 'You, Lexi, are my wife, and divorce is not an option, not now, not ever. Do I make myself clear?' he prompted silkily.

She had taken as much as she could stand; he was much too close, much too threateningly male. Without warning, her hand flew in a wild arc towards his mocking face, and she yelped with pain as he stopped her before she could make contact. His strong hand like a manacle around her wrist, in one deft movement he forced her hand down and behind her back, bringing her slap up against his hard body. In a second he had both her hands pinned by one of his much larger ones behind her back, and his dark head was swooping down.

Lexi tried to fight, but his arm was like an iron girder around her slender waist. She attempted to kick him, but was quickly trapped between his powerful thighs. Heat, totally unexpected, flooded through her body at their intimate entwining, and she could do nothing to prevent Jake using his free hand to grasp her chin and tilt her small face up to his.

'I will not tolerate violence, not even from you, Lexi.' Then his hard mouth crushed down on hers.

Fiercely she pressed her lips together, but the savagery of his kiss was not to be denied. His teeth nipped her bottom lip and her lips parted on a startled gasp of pain. His tongue plunged into her mouth, seeking out the moist dark corners with erotic expertise that took her breath away.

She vowed she would show no response—she hated him, had done for years. His hand slid from her chin to caress her throat and lower, the kiss gentled into an evocative, teasing caress and she felt something inside her leap to instant life as she threw her head back to avoid his kiss! No—to give him better access to the soft skin of her throat. His lips found the vulnerable hollow at the base of her neck, and her pulse-rate leapt alarmingly as her body responded with long-denied passion.

His free hand stroked down and edged inside the soft cotton neckline of her dress, to caress the soft, creamy mound of her breast—she was not wearing a bra—and, as his fingers stroked the burgeoning tips, bringing them to hard aching nubs of desire, she was helpless, drowning in a sea of passion she had thought lost to her forever. She felt the force of his masculine arousal, hard against her stomach, and a low moan escaped her.

'That's it, Lexi, let go.' His throaty voice quivered across the soft curve of her cheek, before his lips once more claimed hers. Fire coursed through her veins, lighting every nerve and sense, until she moved restlessly in an attempt to assuage the desperate hunger consuming her.

She was hardly aware her hands were now free, so lost in her abandoned descent into passion was she, nor that her dress had been slipped down her shoulders. She cried out as his mouth closed over her aching breast to tease the rigid tip with his teeth and tongue, and her own small hand grasped his muscular bicep as he bent her over his arm, his sensuous mouth suckling, grazing, teasing her into insensibility. Her other hand tangled in the thick silk hair of his head, urging him closer.

Then suddenly she was free. Her violet eyes, deep purple with passion, stared up into his darkly flushed face. 'Jake...?' she queried, still enslaved by his passionate assault.

Jake straightened, and with insultingly steady hands slipped her dress back up on to her shoulders. His dark eyes seared triumphantly down into hers. 'Later, Lexi; there's someone at the door. My luggage I expect.'

Only then did she hear the rat-tat-tat at the door. Her face burned with shame. God! What had she done? Jake had only had to touch her and she had burst into flames...

She was trembling, her legs would barely support her and, taking a few faltering steps, she collapsed on the sofa. She looked across the room as Jake opened the door to admit the young man with his luggage.

'Put it in the bedroom, please,' he commanded, and not a flicker of emotion disturbed the even tenor of his voice.

Lexi gazed in something like despair as the bellboy walked straight across the room and through into the bedroom, avoiding looking at her. She had employed the young man herself last year and it hurt to see him ignore her and to see the obvious embarrassment on his face. God, what had she done to deserve this? she wondered helplessly. And, resting her head in her hands, her elbows on her knees, it took every bit of will-power she possessed not to burst into tears. She could feel the moisture pricking at the back of her eyelids; she swallowed hard on the lump that formed in her throat and, slowly lifting her head, she ran her hands through the tumbled mass of her Titian hair, shoving it ruthlessly behind her ears.

She was a two-time loser, she thought bitterly. She hated Jake with a passion that had not dimmed in five long years... Yet her traitorous body still yearned for him. She cursed silently under her breath; how had she allowed the arrogant swine to walk in and walk all over her, yet again? Would she never learn?

Worse, her job was very important to her, but how was she going to be able to keep the respect of her staff after this? Even supposing she could get rid of Jake immediately, already the rumours must be rife. The manager ensconced in her suite with a husband nobody knew she had. It was a mess, a complete and utter disaster...

She felt the brush of a hand across her head, and she jumped in her seat.

'Take it easy, Lexi; we'll talk later. First I need to wash and change.'

She didn't answer, she couldn't; instead she watched with a kind of detached fascination as Jake strode across in front of her and into the bedroom. She stared at the door long after he had closed it behind him, heard the faint sound of running water, and her mind presented her with a memory of herself and Jake in the shower. She blinked furiously to dispel the image, and gazed around her.

This was her sanctuary: the pleasant lounge tastefully decorated in blue and gold, the ornate antique Italian-style furniture. The elegant desk, the two soft blue velvet sofas, a hotel suite, but also her home, with her own books on the shelves. She was happy here, and in less than an hour Jake had destroyed her peace, her contentment, her life. It was so unfair, all she wanted was to be free of the man.

Then it hit her: she had nothing to worry about, Jake's agreement was not necessary; in a few short weeks she could divorce him whether he liked it or not. Firmly, she took herself to task. She had been reacting, not acting, and it had to stop... She would hear Jake out, and then send him off with a flea in his ear. Maybe sexually he still had power over her. Who was she kidding? Never mind maybe, he did: her breasts were still tender from his touch; she ran the tip of her tongue over her swollen lips and the taste of him was still in her mouth. She was like a moth to his flame and always had been ...

But she was twenty-five, a mature adult woman; surely she could resist him for the short time he would be here? Or perhaps the lovely Lorraine would appear on the scene and Lexi's troubles would be over. She sighed. Why hadn't Jake married Lorraine? When Lexi had settled in Italy and informed her solicitor of her address she had watched the post, expecting any day Jake's request for a divorce. When it had never arrived she'd worried, but as the months turned to years she had gradually put it out of her mind.

Suddenly it hit her! Jake was a ruthless businessman. He had married Lexi to get his hands on the manor and turn it into a paying venture, but Lorraine had no asset Jake coveted other than her body, and he wouldn't waste a marriage vow on that.

CHAPTER FOUR

'YOUR turn for the bathroom.'

Lexi jumped to her feet as Jake walked back into the room, and she had to stifle a gasp at his appearance. His black hair was still wet from the shower and brushed severely back from his broad forehead, giving his ruggedly attractive features a harder, more ruthless definition. He was dressed in a conventional black dinner-suit, the perfectly tailored jacket emphasising the width of his broad shoulders, the white silk shirt contrasting sharply with his sun-bronzed skin. Pleated trousers fitted snugly over his hips. He looked magnificently male yet somehow predatory as he casually strolled across the room and lowered his long length on to the sofa.

He glanced up at Lexi, his dark gaze sliding lazily over her. 'I've been travelling all night and half the day; I'm hungry, so be quick,' he commanded. 'And leave your hair loose; I like it that way.'

'Now wait a minute.' Lexi finally found her voice, he was not moving in on her and taking over her life, not again...'

'Really, Lexi, you never used to be so argumentative. Run along and get ready, unless of course you prefer we eat here.' His hand went to the tie at his neck. 'It might be more intimate, at that,' he opined mockingly.

Fuming, Lexi picked up her bag from the sofa and dashed to the safety of the bedroom. She flung her bag on the bed and stopped, her eyes widening in furious amazement. The devil had deliberately laid out a pair of black silk pyjamas on the bed—a blatant statement of intent. Well, she would show him, she vowed, marching across to the bathroom, pulling her dress over her head as she went. Jake might think he had won, but he had a rude awakening coming. She would have dinner with him, and if he refused to see sense about the divorce and go quietly, he could keep the damn suite and she would share with Anna again.

Naked, she stepped into the shower and turned on the tap, telling herself there was no way she was going to jeopardise her chance of a divorce. Another six weeks and Jake could do nothing to stop her, provided they stayed separated...

Standing under the soothing spray, she was tantalisingly aware of the lingering trace of Jake's cologne, the vital male scent of him still pervading the air from his recent occupancy of the bathroom. She was forced to admit it was far too big a risk being in the same room as the man. She shivered and, turning off the water, stepped out. It was only fifteen minutes ago that she had been putty in his hands. His lethal male charm still had the power to make her quake, and she couldn't afford to give in, not now. Not when she was so close to her goal.

Picking up a large, soft towel, she briskly dried herself, and walking into the bedroom opened a drawer and pulled out a flimsy cream lace bra and matching briefs. She slipped them on, and, crossing to the fitted wardrobes, extracted a pair of cream silk, softly pleated culottes with a matching sleeveless silk blouse. In seconds she was dressed, and, straightening the gold-trimmed collar that complemented the gold leather belt she cinched tightly around her small waist, she silently vowed that there was no way Jake was sharing her bed—not now, not ever, even if she ended up sleeping in the laundry cupboard! She hated him with a depth of feeling she had not believed herself capable of.

Briskly she brushed her hair and casually twisted it into a loose chignon on top of her head. The addition of a moisturiser to her face, a touch of dark mascara to her long lashes and the use of a soft pink lip-gloss to her full lips completed her toilet.

Finally she slipped her feet into high-heeled gold sandals, and, efficiently transferring a few basics from her bag on the bed to a small gold shoulder-bag, she straightened her shoulders and, taking a deep breath, re-entered the sitting-room.

The sofa was empty. She looked around; Jake was standing at the darkened window, his body in profile as he stared out into the night, seemingly unaware of her presence. For a moment she allowed her eyes to linger on him; was it tension she sensed in his huge frame? No, it couldn't be... His hard, chiselled features were curiously still, almost brooding. He turned, and his eyes locked with hers. His expression was impossible to define, and for some unknown reason Lexi felt menaced by the fraught quality of the silence between them, but she could not tear her gaze away.

Jake broke the contact; his dark eyes lowered, conducting a slow, sweeping survey of her feminine form before returning to her face, and she sensed a hint of disapproval, but why she had no idea. It was a designer outfit she had bought in the winter sale at an exclusive boutique on the isle of Capri.

'Very elegant, and expensive, no doubt.' Jake commented distastefully, his face hard with something like disgust as he moved towards her. 'But I told you to leave your hair loose.' And before she could object his strong hands had deftly unpinned her hair so it fell in a red cloud around her shoulders.

'Your days of telling me what to do are long gone,' she snapped, bitterly resentful, her hatred burning brighter as she remembered the months and years it had taken her simply to stop dreaming about the swine. She bit down hard on her lip. She would not let him taunt her into losing her temper; instead she deliberately swept her long hair back off her face. 'Don't you realise I have my position as manager to think of?' she informed him caustically.

'Not for much longer,' he declared arrogantly.

Lexi knew she should demand an explanation for his remark but he was standing within inches of her, and she could almost feel the warmth of his body; the sheer animal magnetism of the man had the power to stir her senses as no one else she had ever known. Shocked and greatly disturbed, she made no comment. Instead she headed for the door; retreat was the only option she was capable of pursuing.

The dining-room of the hotel was luxurious and intimate, and, as Lexi walked across the room with Jake at her side, his large hand firmly clasping her elbow, to the casual observer they looked like the perfect loving couple. The man tall and strikingly attractive and the woman small and exquisite, her eyes sparkling and her face flushed with pleasure. Only a very close observer would see that it was rage that put fire in her eyes and colour in her face.

By the time they were finally seated at Lexi's usual table she was so furious she wanted to hit Jake. As she had spoken to various guests, Jake had delighted in introducing himself as her husband, completely ignoring her acute embarrassment.

'What the hell do you think you're playing at?' she hissed as she carefully folded her napkin on her lap. Her eyes flashed angrily across to her companion. 'I suppose you think that was a huge joke telling Miss Davenport you're my husband. Only last week she met my boyfriend; what on earth is she going to think? And she's one of our best customers.'

Jake's mouth curved derisively. 'Hardly my fault, Lexi, my dear; you should have had more sense than to acquire a boyfriend when you still have a husband.'

She flung up her head, fury leaping in her eyes. 'I don't have a husband, I haven't...'

'Had me in years. I know, but tonight I intend to correct that,' he drawled smoothly, his glance sweeping down to the deep V of her shirt, and lingering on her exposed creamy cleavage with lascivious intent.

'That was not what I meant and you know it, you...you...pervert,' she shot back, the colour in her face almost matching her hair.

His dark features hardened immeasurably 'I will not tolerate opposition, Lexi. I have let you run free far too long, but not any more.' His eyes held hers with unwavering scrutiny. 'Fight me and I will fight back, and I can assure you I always win.'

Her eyes warred angrily with his. This was one fight Lexi had to win, to keep her self-respect, her pride. Her life. How would she have answered? She never knew, as the waiter appeared at the table.

'Would madam and sir like to order now?' The pointed use of madam only fuelled Lexi's anger.

'A pasta Genovese, followed by steak, medium, for me, and shall I order for you, Lexi darling? I know your taste so well.' Jake's question was a silken-voiced taunt that made her see red.

'I'm not hungry,' she snapped at the poor waiter. 'No starter, and anything. Veal Marsala, whatever.'

Jake sat back in his chair, his dark eyes resting on her flushed face. 'Is that any way for the manager to treat staff? The man was only doing his job.'

'I never lose my temper with staff.' Lexi managed to keep her voice low. 'It's only you, and your presence here, that makes me lose my temper.'

'Funny, when we first met you never argued with me. In the beginning I used to wonder when the famous red-headed temper would show itself, until I married you and discovered you saved all your fire and passion for making love.'

Suddenly, kaleidoscopic images of herself and Jake in bed together filled her mind with erotic clarity. She briefly closed her eyes to dispel the images, and when she opened them again, Jake was slowly assessing every one of her features, from her red face to the small hand that lay on the table, the fingers clenched in outrage, and, when he returned his gaze to hers, she had to fight to keep herself from trembling. Luckily the wine waiter intervened and the next few moments Jake spent choosing the wine, a rather good Barola, while Lexi fought to regain some self-control, which unfortunately deserted her immediately Jake opened his mouth again.

'Your present lover—Dante, isn't it?' He smiled but the smile never reached his eyes, as the intensity of his gaze nailed her to the spot. 'It seems he does not take after his namesake. Dante's *Inferno*. It is obvious he lights no fire in you, Lexi; if he did, you wouldn't have the passion to cross swords with me, or melt in my arms as you did earlier in the bedroom.'

'Will you shut up...? People will hear...' Lexi cast a frantic glance at the tables around them. Thank God no one seemed to have overheard. 'This is a very exclusive hotel, and I am responsible for it.' She took refuge in her professional role, mainly because she had a nasty feeling there might have been some truth in Jake's jeering remark and she did not want to examine her own emotions too closely.

Jake slanted her a sardonic glance. 'But of course you're quite right. I would hate the hotel to lose any custom because the manager went crazy in the dining-room. Terrible for business, especially now.'

Sarcastic pig! She muttered under her breath, but, fighting down the urge to retaliate, Lexi forced herself to remain calm. She heaved a sigh of relief when the wine waiter returned with the requested bottle and after allowing Jake to taste it filled both their wine-glasses.

Jake raised his glass to her. 'Well, isn't this nice? Quite like old times, Lexi. You and I sharing an expensive, intimate meal together.' And, lifting the glass to his firm mouth, he swallowed the rich red liquid. But the mocking light in his dark eyes belied his innocent comment.

For a moment Lexi had felt a brief regret for the past. When they were first married, and lived in London, they had used to eat out a lot, sampling the meals on offer in some of the best restaurants in the capital. She had been so in love, filled with such hope for the future... Hastily, she picked up her glass and took a gulp of the wine in an attempt to steady her nerves and dismiss the painful memories. She ignored Jake as another waiter placed a plate of pasta in front of him. That will shut him up, she thought thankfully. But what did he mean, 'especially now'? She banished the irritating thought, and began to get her mind in gear. How did Jake know about Dante? She hadn't told her solicitor why she wanted the divorce. In fact, she had given her solicitor strict instructions not to tell anyone, especially not Jake, where she was living.

'How did you know where to find me?' The question slipped out involuntarily. Her mind was spinning like a windmill and it was all Jake's fault. She cast him a baleful glance across the table. His dark head was bent and there was no doubt he was enjoying his food; he made love with the same wholehearted enjoyment as he relished fine food, enjoying every taste and... Annoyed, she clamped down on the wayward thought.

'I asked...' she began.

'I heard you.' His dark head lifted, his blue eyes clashed with hers. 'I have known for years where you were.'

'But how?' she asked, taken back by his revelation.

'We have a mutual acquaintance. Mr Carl Bradshaw.'

Her brow furrowed in a frown as she searched her memory; the name rang a bell.

'He was a regular customer at this hotel, before he married. Apparently he was staying here the spring after you arrived. By sheer coincidence I had business dealings with the man. We were sharing lunch when he showed me a photograph of you taken by the swimming-pool here. He was bemoaning the fact he had met a gorgeous girl who had actually said no to him. I recognised you immediately, but I didn't bother telling him you were my runaway wife,' he offered cynically. 'You slipped up there, Lexi; Carl Bradshaw is one of the wealthiest men in Europe.'

Lexi remembered the man, and he had asked her out, but at the time she had been still raw and bleeding from Jake's betrayal. But what did Jake mean, she had slipped up? She heard the words and assimilated them but it made no sense. All this time Jake had known where to find her and yet only now had he bothered. And what did he mean, she had run away? He had freely admitted he wanted out of the marriage, she had heard him with her own ears declare to his mistress, Lorraine, his intention of breaking their marriage vows. Her nerves stretched to breaking point, she lowered her head to escape his gimlet-like gaze, and, picking up her glass, took a sip of the soothing wine.

Carefully, she placed the glass back down on the table, and, regaining her self-control, she glanced up. 'So why turn up now?' she demanded coldly.

For a long moment he just looked at her. A muscle tautened along the edge of his jaw, and his eyes darkened with icy bleakness. 'I do not appreciate my wife acquiring a permanent boyfriend and suing me for divorce. I decided to put a stop to it,' he declared arrogantly.

'Some hope; we're engaged.'

'Not any more, you're not.' His dark eyes narrowed on her mutinous face. 'Tell me, Lexi, why do you think your so-called fiancé was called away this evening?' he questioned with thinly veiled mockery.

'You—you arranged it.' She looked at him in horrified amazement. 'But how? In fact, how did you know about Dante?'

'I had you investigated, months ago.'

Months ago, but he couldn't have known then that she was suing for divorce, she hadn't known herself.

'As for your friend, as you know better than most——' contempt lurked in his eyes '—people will do anything for the right price. Hence your friend's manager took conveniently ill, and I did not have to waste time waiting around for you.'

'Bu...bu...but...' As she spluttered with rage, Lexi's violet eyes flashed fire. 'How dare you?' she finally cried, rather inanely.

'I dare anything to get what I want, Lexi, and make no mistake, I want you.' His steely gaze seemed to sear through to her soul. 'And now I can afford you.'

'Afford me...' she burst out. Of all the hypocritical swine, he took the biscuit. It wasn't enough that he had married her in the first place simply to take over her family home; he had the audacity to insinuate that she was mercenary. She picked up her knife, longing to stick it in his hateful, mocking face.

His dark head angled towards her. 'Don't even think it, Lexi,' he hissed with sibilant softness. 'And I suggest, unless you want the whole of the restaurant to know your business, that you shut up and eat up.'

How did he walk into her mind like that? Lexi thought, but before she could form a reply the waiter placed the main course in front of her. She had been so caught up in her own emotional turmoil that she had not noticed the man's arrival...

Oh, what was the use? she thought wretchedly, her shoulders slumping dejectedly as she picked up her fork and began to push the food around her plate. Jake was a master at getting his own way. If she had any sense at all, it would pay her to spend the rest of the meal ignoring the man and marshalling her thoughts into some kind of order.

Lexi picked at the superb food; it could have been ashes for all she cared. She drank the wine and that helped to restore her confidence a little, but it was false courage and she knew it. She glanced across at Jake, who was eating his steak with every sign of enjoyment. He caught her look and his firm mouth curved in the briefest of smiles.

'The food is exquisite; I must compliment the chef,' he offered smoothly.

'Do that,' Lexi grunted, and looking at her watch she noted it was almost ten. The sooner she could get the confrontation with Jake over and done with, the quicker she could get him out of her life.

'Shall we adjourn to the lounge for coffee?' his deep voice queried, meticulously polite.

Not deigning to look at him Lexi shoved back her chair and stood up, determination in every line of her small frame. 'No, we can have it in my suite. We've spent long enough this evening avoiding the real issue. Shall we go?' And, not waiting for his response, she picked up her bag and walked through the dining-room, a stiff smile plastered on her face for the benefit of the few guests who bade her goodnight, and headed for the lift.

'Right, say what you have to say and leave,' Lexi demanded, standing rigidly in the middle of the room. Nervously she rubbed her damp palms over her hips. She was no way as in control as she sounded, but Jake couldn't possibly know that, she reassured herself. He was standing with his back to the door, his dark eyes slow and analytical as he swept her stiff body and back to her face.

'Sit down, Lexi.'

'That won't be necessary; I don't intend you will be here that long. I am a working girl; I have a busy day tomorrow, and I want to get to bed.'

'By all means, Lexi; we can talk in bed if that's what you prefer.'

He sounded amused, damn him. 'In your dreams, buster,' she burst out, her temper bubbling over. 'You have no right to come barging back into my life, telling everyone you're my husband, completely destroying my credibility with my staff. Just where the hell do you think you get off? I have had just about as much of you as I can stand, and if you don't leave in the next minute I will call the porter to throw you out. In fact, I can't understand why I didn't do it in the first place.'

In two strides Jake was beside her, his large hands closed over her slender shoulders, his fingers biting into the soft flesh. 'Enough, Lexi, screaming like a fishwife will get us nowhere.' He was right and, taking a deep breath, she fought down the *frisson* of awareness his touch aroused, and stepped back. He let her go...

'Have you finished shouting?' Jake asked quietly, subjecting her to a slow and intent appraisal that left her feeling wanting.

She had gone over the top a bit, and raising a hand to her brow she smoothed back the tangled strands of her long hair, and swallowed on her anger. 'Yes,' she said curtly. She had been finished with Jake long ago and yelling at the man wasn't going to solve anything. 'Please tell me what you came for, and go.'

'Sit down, Lexi.'

She subsided into the nearest chair and watched warily as Jake sat down on the sofa, his long legs stretched out in front of him in negligent ease.

'Now, isn't this more civilised, darling?' he drawled mockingly, while never taking his dark gaze from her flushed face.

'Get on with it, Jake.' She was in no mood for polite chit-chat.

'It's perfectly simple, Lexi, I told you earlier. I want you back as my wife, reinstated in my bed.'

It took a tremendous strength of will to retain a degree of civility, but somehow she managed it. 'Is that all?' she quipped lightly while her mind spun on oiled wheels. He was up to something, but what? He had said earlier that he wanted her back, and now he had reiterated the request, yet she knew it wasn't true. He didn't love her, never had, and why the thought should bring a flash of pain, she did not question. So what other reason could he possibly have . . . ?

'I get it!' Lexi exclaimed. Of course, why hadn't she thought of it before? She sat back in the chair, a sigh of relief escaping her. It was so obvious; in a flash of blinding clarity she saw it all. Jake was a very wealthy man, and she knew to her cost that he would do anything for money. Divorce must have terrified him, because according to the law his wife could take half of his money half his business. No wonder the swine came hot-foot to Italy.

'Good, I am pleased. Then let's get to bed, it's been a long day,' Jake drawled facetiously.

'No, I understand, Jake.' She bent forward, her elbows on her knees, her serious gaze fixed on his face. 'You have nothing to worry about; I've instructed my lawyer. I don't want any alimony, not a penny. Your business, your investments, everything is safe. I don't want it. I'll sign a contract now, tonight, if you like.' And for the first time since meeting Jake again his lips parted in a genuine smile, even if it was a little self-satisfied.

There was no returning smile on Jake's handsome face. Instead his gaze became hooded and he rose to his feet to tower over her. 'Nice try, Lexi, but it won't work.'

'But——' she flashed him a puzzled look '—surely . . .' Perhaps he hadn't understood.

'You took me for a fool once, but never again. 'He reached down his strong hands, and grasping her upper arms, he hauled her to her feet, and, tilting her head back with one large hand, his chillingly bleak eyes locked on hers, trapping her in his gaze. 'You would no more give up a fortune than pigs would fly, and as for signing it away, forget it.'

'Why, you arrogant...' Before she could complete the sentence his dark head bent, his mouth covering hers in a harsh, bruising kiss. She twisted her head in a frantic effort to get away, her hand clawed at his shoulder while she kicked out at him with her feet, but with insulting ease Jake ground his mouth down on hers, the relentless pressure forcing her lips apart.

There was nothing she could do to prevent his plundering invasion, and to her horror she felt the betraying curl of desire ignite in her stomach. In a desperate effort to get him to desist she lifted her hand to his face and scratched the hard jawline.

Jake jerked his head back, and his dark eyes flared with inimical rage. 'You shouldn't have done that, Lexi,' he said with icy menace. He shifted his weight, trapping her helplessly against him; she tried to strike out at him, but with consummate ease he trapped both her hands in one of his between their two bodies.

Lexi's eyes widened to their fullest extent as she recognised the intention in Jake's black gaze. 'No, Jake.' She was powerless, held hard against him; she could feel the heat of his body through the fine fabric of her clothes, and to her horror she could feel his masculine arousal. Then she had no more chance to think, as his mouth once more took hers in a kiss that went on and on, becoming a ravaging, passionate possession that violated all her senses but paradoxically set her body on fire. She wanted to cry, 'Stop!' in shame and disgust, but instead her body softened, moving of its own volition to accommodate Jake's hard length.

She trembled uncontrollably as she felt his strong hand slide insolently over her shoulder and down into the open neck of her shirt. With a savage wrench, her blouse was open to her waist and his hand cupped the fullness of her breast. In seconds the bra was pushed from her breasts and his long fingers dragged tantalisingly over one rigid nipple; catching the aching peak, he nipped it between his finger and thumb as his mouth slid down to her throat, closing over the madly beating pulse in a wild lover's bite that took her breath away. She whimpered, a fierce pleasure, almost pain, burning through every nerve in her body, her stomach clenched in heated excitement. She was lost, a fierce primeval need sending the blood surging through her veins like molten fire.

Incredibly, it was over. Jake, with a muffled curse, shoved her away from him, and she fell in a crumpled heap on to the sofa behind her. For a moment she did not know what had happened; one second they had been clawing at each other in desperate sexual need and now she was collapsed on the sofa, his tall dark form towering over her. Lexi did not dare look at him. The traitorous response of her body filled her with bitter humiliation. She hated him, even as she still ached for his touch. But even worse was the knowledge that Jake must know her body had betrayed her.

'Cover yourself, woman,' Jake snarled contemptuously. 'You disgust me, and, God knows, I disgust myself.'

His words killed all trace of desire in her trembling body in an instant. An icy chill shivered along her skin and, struggling, she adjusted her tattered clothes. So, she disgusted him ... Why did the words hurt? she wondered bleakly.

'I won't take you tonight.' Her head shot up at his words; he was standing about a foot away, his dark eyes glittering with an unholy light, his face flushed with the force of his rage, and the marks of her nails carved his jaw. Her gaze dropped to his strong hands curled into fists at his thighs, as if it was the only way he could stop himself lashing out at her.

'Chance would be a fine thing.' She tried to sneer. He hated her... it was there in every taut line of his large body, in the black depths of his eyes, and the cruel twist of his hard mouth. She could almost taste the hatred, an evil aura in the air.

'Chance has nothing to do with it. The way I feel right now it would be more an assault than making love.' The harsh, guttural comment froze her blood. 'That's what you drive me to, you little witch.'

Lexi gasped, and clenched her hands together at her breast in a futile gesture of self defence. Jake's glance dropped to her hands, and his mouth twisted in a bitter cynical curve.

'Don't worry, Lexi, you have nothing to fear. I will not sully the anniversary of our son's death by taking you in anger.'

'You remembered...' she whispered, stunned to realise that Jake had actually known this was the anniversary of her miscarriage, and, even more surprisingly, he had known the lost child was a boy. Her gaze flew to his dark, forbidding face, and she realised he had controlled his earlier rage.

Hooded lids dropped over his deep blue eyes, masking his expression as, with a negligent shrug of his broad shoulders, he said 'Of course, that's the main reason I'm here.'

Lexi didn't understand any of this. She supposed she should be thankful he was not going to share her bed. 'But...' she began, only to have the question stop in her throat as Jake went on.

'I want the child you owe me, but I also intend to make sure it's mine.'

He could not have hurt her more if he had tried. Once she would have given anything to have his child, but now... 'No... never...' She murmured the words more to herself than to him. She found it incredible that he could be so arrogant, so lacking in any moral conscience.

'Yes, my dear Lexi, though in the present circumstances I am going to have to wait a few weeks to be assured of the parenthood,' he said cynically 'I have no intention of being stuck with your boyfriend's offspring...'

'Why, you...' Lexi leapt to her feet as the meaning of his words hit her. 'I...'

'Not again, Lexi.' His arms swept around her and held her hard against him. 'Tomorrow you are coming with me, and I intend to watch you every minute of every day until the time is right, and then, my dear Lexi, you and I will resume our marriage fully. Understood?'

'You can't make me.' Though once more held firmly in his arms, she had a horrible feeling he probably could.

'If I let you go, will you endeavour to behave like a lady for a change and listen?' He smiled mockingly down into her once again flushed and furious face.

'Yes,' she got out between clenched teeth: she would do anything to escape his all too familiar embrace.

'Good.' And, lifting her off her feet, he deposited her once more on the sofa and sat down beside her, his hard thigh pressing lightly against her slender limbs. She eased along the sofa putting a little space between them. He shot her a cynically amused glance and then, leaning back in the seat, he steepled his long fingers in front of him, for all the world as if he was about to give a lecture.

'It is really quite simple, dear Lexi. I have bought this hotel. You are now employed by me.'

She couldn't believe it. 'You own... Then I'll resign...'

Ignoring her comment, he continued in a voice devoid of all emotion, 'Unless you do as I say, I will cancel the sale, and Signor Monicelli will not get the money, and his son will not recover.'

Her head spun as the implications of his words sank in. She flashed him an angry glance, hating him in that second more than she had in all the years they had been apart. 'There are other people in the world who might buy the hotel,' she shot back sarcastically. 'You are not the only businessman on the planet, even if you like to think you are,' she lashed out in fear. She did not like where the conversation was going.

'True,' he agreed silkily, his gaze never wavering from her taut, rebellious features. 'But aren't you forgetting an important factor?' he prompted smoothly, but the underlying steel in his tone was unmistakable. 'Time is of the essence for young Marco. This place has made only a modest profit in the last couple of years and I have the power to make it known that it is not a viable proposition,' he elaborated cynically. 'If young Marco's trip to America is delayed or cancelled, who knows?' He turned his hands palms up in a negligent gesture. 'It will be a great shame if he is condemned to a wheelchair all his life, simply because the money is not available for his treatment.'

Lexi stared in horror at his hard, chiselled features. Not a flicker of compassion lightened his indigo eyes. No! her mind screamed silently, she couldn't do it, tie herself to this man once again when she knew there was only hatred between them. 'Why—why me?' she asked dazedly. It didn't make any kind of sense...

One eyebrow arched sardonically. 'You're my wife. I'm a very wealthy man, I need an heir and I don't believe in divorce. Nor do I appreciate hearing my wife is thinking of marrying another man.'

He might as well have added *so there*, Lexi thought in stunned amazement. Obviously it must have been a blow to his pride to discover she had a boyfriend. How typically chauvinistic. It was all right for Jake to have an affair with his PA but the slightest rumour that his estranged wife might do the same and he was hot-foot to Italy to put a stop to it. Talk about double standards! But why was she so surprised? she asked herself sadly. This was the same man who had broken his marriage vow to her and then expected her to toast him and his girlfriend in champagne. The so-called civilised sophisticates, but Lexi had never been one of them.

With a jerky movement she staggered to her feet and walked across the room to gaze sightlessly out into the dark night. How could she be responsible for Signor Monicelli's losing the sale? For young Marco's perhaps being tied to a wheelchair for life? She spun around.

Jake had followed her and was standing a step away. She looked up at him, and it was a stranger's face she saw. 'Would you really condemn a man...?'

'Believe it.' Jake brutally cut her off, and she did... It was there in his mocking smile and the ruthless glint in his eyes. 'Technically, Lexi, it is only you who can condemn the man to his chair, not I,' he said callously, adding, 'Yes, or no, Lexi?'

It wasn't fair, she raged inwardly, Jake must know damn fine there was no way she could let the Monicellis down; they had virtually saved her sanity five years ago, and she owed them. Why now, she fumed, just when she had got her life in order? Dante...Dante; she had today promised to marry him.

'Dante... What can I tell him?' she cried in dismay, unconsciously giving her answer.

She did not see the flash of triumph in Jake's eyes before his expression hardened fractionally. 'You can ring him before we leave in the morning, but I will not allow you to see him,' he warned icily.

'Leave? I can't leave, I have my job...'

'Not any more.' And striding across the room he picked up the telephone receiver and dialled a number. 'Lorraine, get over to the Piccolo Paradiso first thing in the morning. I want you to take charge until a permanent manager can be found. OK... Goodnight.' Jake replaced the receiver and turned, a smile of triumph curving his hard mouth. 'Your replacement arrives in the morning.'

Lexi stood as though turned to stone at the mention of the other woman's name, her violet eyes blank as her thoughts turned inwards; Jake had it all arranged, must have been planning it for weeks. The fact she had started divorce proceedings had little or nothing to do with it.

'The divorce didn't matter?' she said to herself.

'No, not really. I had every intention of reclaiming you. The fax from my lawyer simply made me speed up the proceedings.'

'Lorraine.' She almost choked on the name. 'Why didn't you divorce me and marry her years ago?' she demanded. After all, it was what he had intended—she had heard them discussing it. She raised angry eyes to Jake's. 'She's still with you. Let her give you the heir you say you want,' she prompted sarcastically.

'Lorraine is much more valuable to my business than she could ever be as a wife and mother,' he offered casually.

'And that's it?' Lexi stared into his harsh face, unable to believe what she was hearing. 'You expect me to crawl back into your bed and provide you with a child.' She could not keep the shock and horror out of her voice. 'And at the same time, your mistress——'

'Why so surprised?' Jake cut in cynically. 'You've lived in Italy for years, you were planning on marrying an Italian. It's quite common in this part of the world for the wife and mother to be revered, while the mistress provides the fun.'

He meant it, he actually meant what he said. 'There is no way on this earth I will put up with an unfaithful husband. You should know that better than most, Jake,' she said scathingly. Hadn't she left him because of his infidelity?

'Should I?' he queried with a puzzled frown.

Lexi answered with a snort of disgust. Who was he kidding, pretending innocence? Certainly not her...

'Well, I suppose I can live with that. No Lorraine in my bed, and no Dante anywhere near you.' He smiled, a bleak twist of his hard mouth. 'Agreed.' And he held out his hand. 'Shake on it.'

Hardly knowing what she was doing, she put her hand in his. Lorraine, his mistress, or ex if Jake was to be believed, was near by, ready to take her job, the same way as she had taken Lexi's husband years ago. It was so evil her mind could not absorb it. He didn't even like her, and yet...

'You called me mercenary before, Jake; surely you don't want a gold-digger as the mother of your child?' she scorned in a last-ditch attempt to save herself.

'Let me worry about that, Lexi, you look tired. Get to bed, I have one or two more calls to make.' Jake's voice sounded almost gentle, but it could not mask the ruthless satisfaction she saw in his eyes.

'Yes, I'll go to bed,' Lexi agreed coldly. 'But first I want you to know I think you are utterly despicable, a man without conscience or morals, completely evil. I hate you and always will.' And the very softness of her tone was more convincing than any angry outburst could ever be.

CHAPTER FIVE

HEAD high, and stiff-backed Lexi marched into the bedroom. She would not give him the satisfaction of knowing he had frightened her into running away again. Anyway, hadn't he said himself that to touch her tonight would disgust him, she reassured herself as she undressed for bed. Hours later she plumped the pillow for the umpteenth time and, emotionally and mentally exhausted from trying to think of a way out of the disastrous situation she was in, she finally fell asleep, refusing to listen to the devilish imp inside her that traitorously wished Jake had joined her.

Lexi half opened her eyes, a distant ringing echoing in her head. Oh, God, the alarm—was 't seven already? she thought sleepily and, automatically stretching out her hand, she silenced the offending clock on the bedside table. She groaned and suddenly froze, aware of a hard weight around her waist and the pressure of strong fingers curved around the underside of her breast. The full horror of the previous evening swamped her sleep-hazed mind. Jake was back and, worse, in her bed...

Slowly, she turned her head; Jake was lying flat on his stomach, one long arm flung across her waist, the other dangling over the side of the bed. She couldn't see his face, only the back of his head, the dark hair rumpled, and his heavy breathing loud on the still air. Tense, she held her breath, the warmth of his fingers through the fabric of her nightshirt arousing an achingly familiar response. She bit her lip, fighting down the swift stab of desire, and, making sure he was sound asleep, with the utmost caution she carefully slid out from under his arm, her feet finding the floor. She stopped as he grunted and turned over on to his back. It was OK, his eyes were still closed, and she was standing on his pyjamas!

She stood up, pulling her plain cotton nightshirt down over her thighs, and glanced down at the sleeping man. Completely relaxed, he looked years younger, his hair fell casually over his broad forehead, his firm mouth gentle in sleep. She had to restrain the urge to reach out and smooth his hair from his brow. His muscular chest with its dark covering of body hair rose and fell in an even rhythm, the single cotton cover was wrapped around his thighs, barely covering the core of his masculinity. His long arms and legs were spreadeagled across the bed; he looked devastatingly male, open and somehow vulnerable, waiting to be touched.

God! What was she thinking of? She shook her head in self-disgust and stealthily moved across the room, her nose wrinkled in irritation; there was a strong smell of alcohol in the air. She cast one last glance at the sleeping man before slipping into the bathroom. Surely Jake hadn't turned into a drinker! That was all she needed, a drunken husband.

Ten minutes later, bathed and dressed in her usual uniform of dark skirt and crisp white blouse, she cast one last glance at the still sleeping figure, her lips quirked in the semblance of a smile; he was going to have a hell of a hangover when he finally surfaced. Serve the swine right, she told herself, as she strode into the living-room. An empty whisky bottle and glass on an occasional table beside the sofa caught her gaze. Jake had certainly made a night of it, and she couldn't help wondering why.

She had stormed off to bed last night, knowing Jake had won but refusing to give up entirely. She had lain for hours unable to sleep, trying to find an escape, until finally she had virtually passed out, still wondering and fearing what the outcome of the evening's events would be. One option she had never considered was Jake getting plastered! It was hardly flattering to her; he was a powerful, dynamic male, and the years had not affected his masculine virility one bit. There was something about him, the way he moved, an earthy maleness that attracted the female of the species like bees around a honeypot. She doubted if any woman had ever left his bed unsatisfied, until now...

Dear God! She was doing it again, fantasising about the man. Annoyed with herself, she caught her rambling thoughts before they sank into eroticism. She was trapped and supposed to be finding a way out of the mess, not dreaming about the man.

Closing the door of the suite quietly behind her she slung her shoulder bag over her arm and headed for the lift. Moments later, she walked into the hotel reception and stopped, her eyes widening at the sight that met her eyes. Franco was standing, his mouth hanging open like a goldfish, while a tall, elegant woman was telling him in a cold, clipped voice exactly what to do. It was Lorraine...

'Excuse me,' Lexi said firmly, striding across to the desk. 'Have we some problem here?'

Lorraine spun around to face her. The older woman was as stunning as ever, perhaps a few more lines around her perfectly made-up eyes, and a hint of more hardness in the glossy mouth, but the smart cream suit she wore screamed designer original, as did the matching hide bag and shoes.

'Not any more, Lexi,' Lorraine stated flatly, her dark eyes glittering oddly. 'As of now, I am the manager by order of the new owner, as you know. Now, where is Jake? I need to speak with him.'

'And hello to you too, Lorraine,' Lexi murmured sarcastically. 'Still as super-efficient as ever, I see.' It hurt her to see her husband's mistress; she hated herself for the weakness, and tried to hide it behind a cool control she was far from feeling.

'If this man is anything to go by you could do with some efficiency around here. I have been trying for the past ten minutes to discover which room is Jake's.'

It gave Lexi great satisfaction to say, 'Franco probably didn't realise Jake is sharing my suite; I left him asleep, he's worn out, poor man.' She deliberately dropped her tone suggestively. 'But if you insist on disturbing him...' And she held out the key. Lorraine snatched it from her hand and stalked off to the stairs without a word.

'Is it true, Lexi, you're leaving?' Franco burst into impassioned speech; it took Lexi five minutes to calm him down and her explanation was inept, to say the least. Finally, fed up with the whole affair, she did what she should have done the night before. She walked out of the hotel and to her car, started the motor and drove off. She wasn't running away, she told herself, but she needed time, time to think, time to plan, and she owed it to Dante to see him and tell him what had happened.

She drove down into Sorrento looking in her rear-view mirror every few seconds, afraid of being followed, although her rational mind told her it was highly unlikely. Jake, even if he was awake, was probably in no fit state to drive, and anyway Lorraine was with him... Jake had agreed last night to complete fidelity when or if they resumed their marriage, but technically they had not yet consummated their reunion. Did that mean Lorraine even now was occupying the space Lexi had so recently vacated. In bed with Jake...

Lexi brought the car to a screaming halt outside a small café that was open early in the morning. Dante's apartment was two blocks away. She sat down at the bar counter and ordered a cappuccino. She drank the first cup in seconds, grateful for the reviving brew, and ordered another, along with a handful of loose change.

Feeling once more in control, she picked up the counter-top telephone and dialled Signor Monicelli's number. She was not beaten yet, she swore silently. She needed to know for herself if Jake's story was correct. Five minutes later she had her answer; by a bit of judicious questioning, Signor Monicelli had confirmed her worst fear: there was no way he could or would want to delay the hotel sale. He was expecting the cheque to be paid into his bank that morning and he was leaving with Marco tomorrow for America.

'That's great…' Lexi heard herself murmur, her heart in her feet.

'*Si, si*. I'm praying nothing goes wrong, and I am depending on you, Lexi, to work as well for the new owner as you have done for me. It would be disastrous if he takes up his option of pulling out within twelve months, and I don't get the final payment.'

'Final payment?' Lexi queried.

'Yes, the finance is arranged in three instalments; I get the final one in eighteen months' time. So remember, be nice to the man.'

At the mention of eighteen months, Lexi's half-formed plan to disappear as soon as she got the opportunity bit the dust.

Lexi dropped the phone back in its cradle, his last comment echoing in her head. 'Let me know when you and Dante are to marry and I will return for the ceremony.' What a joke! But it solved one puzzle. Signor Monicelli had not betrayed her. He obviously did not know Jake was her wayward husband.

Reluctantly she picked up the receiver once again and dialled Dante's number. He had already left for work. She glanced at her wrist. Damn! She had forgotten her watch. She looked up at the clock behind the counter and was surprised to see it was nine. She finished her second cup of coffee and rang Dante's shop. She did not want to call round as that would be the first place Jake would look, she was sure. When she replaced the receiver for the last time, she had to brush the moisture from her eyes. It was so unfair—Dante was a good, kind man and he didn't deserve what she was going to do to him.

She walked out of the bar, her footsteps slow and weary. It was a hot, clear morning, the sun brilliant in a clear, blue sky and the temperature was already in the eighties. Slowly, she walked across to her car and, getting in, sat behind the wheel. She was meeting Dante at nine-thirty and she needed to work out what she would say to him.

Lexi closed her eyes, her head falling forward to rest on her arms crossed over the steering-wheel. She had nowhere to run to. Her life and everything she owned was back at the hotel. A tear escaped to roll down her soft cheek. She thought of Marco and his father; she couldn't possibly hurt them. Jake had done his work well, she was trapped and at his mercy. But the man she had seen last night didn't know the meaning of the word 'mercy'. She had seen it in his face, in his cold-blooded determination to have his own way. He was a ruthless bastard who would stop at nothing to get what he wanted.

She remembered the week before her marriage. She had assumed, because Jake had asked her to marry him and offered to pay her father's debt, that they would naturally keep Forest Manor, and he had quite coolly told her that nothing had changed in that respect, the house would still be converted to a hotel, though he promised her he would convert part of the building into an apartment for their own use. So she would not really be losing her home. With hindsight, she realised she should have known then that Jake was the type of man who never wavered in his resolve to get what he wanted. Instead it had taken her almost a year and the loss of her baby to discover just what a conniving swine he was.

She lifted her head, a deep sigh escaping her. She had no idea what she was going to tell Dante; she only knew she could not tell him the truth. He was the type of man who would insist on standing by her and fighting for what was right. But Jake was a vicious enemy and deep down she knew Dante would be no match for him. Jake would gobble him up and spit him out if Dante attempted to thwart his plan.

Lexi walked into the Piazza Tasso, the main square in Sorrento and the focal-point of the town. It must be almost nine-thirty, she was sure, and, having parked her car in another hotel car park—the manager was a friend—she dodged between the never-ending stream of vehicles to reach the Caffè Fauno, the most popular meeting place in the town. All Sorrento life passed by the place, but today she was not really noticing the people around her. She turned her worried gaze over the tables and found Dante. He caught her eye and smiled, rising to his feet; she hurried towards him.

'Not so fast, Lexi,' a deep voice drawled in her ear as a strong hand closed firmly around her upper arm.

'What?' With sinking heart she looked up into the hard face of the man holding her. 'Jake,' she choked, her startled gaze skimming over his tall form. This morning he was dressed in cream chinos and a blue short-sleeve cotton shirt with a button-down collar, open at the neck to reveal the strong line of his throat and the beginnings of dark, curling chest hair.

'Take your hand off my fiancée.' Dante appeared in front of her, his deep brown eyes narrowed angrily on Jake, before flicking to Lexi. 'Are you all right, *cara*?' he asked, reaching to plant a kiss on her cheek.

Brutally, she was jerked out of Dante's reach, as Jake's arm closed around her waist like a band of steel. His eyes flashed with fury, and a muscle jerked in his cheek. 'Keep your hands and your mouth off my wife,' he said dangerously.

'Wife?' Dante's brows rose in surprise as his gaze slid from one to the other then settled on Jake. 'Not for much longer,' he responded firmly, reading the situation at a glance and grasping Lexi's other arm. 'So, this is why you wanted to see me so urgently, *cara*. Is he trying to cause trouble?' His dark eyes sought hers, puzzled but caring.

She felt like a rag doll pulled between the two bristling males, and, before she could open her mouth to speak, Jake spoke for her.

'I'll cause you trouble if you don't get your hand off my wife. It's over, and if I ever see you anywhere near Lexi again I will break every bone in your body. Understand?' There was no mistaking the deadly intent in Jake's tone and everyone at the surrounding tables was aware of it, never mind that it was in English.

Jake stood towering over Lexi and Dante, his dark face hard as rock, the venom in his eyes there for all to see.

Dante's hand dropped from her arm. 'What has happened, Lexi? Yesterday you said your divorce was only weeks away. You agreed to marry me.'

She could have wept. Dante did not deserve to be humiliated in public by the arrogant Jake.

Jake's fingers bit into her waist. 'Yes, tell him, Lexi darling. Tell him how you spent the night in my arms.'

'You didn't!' Dante cried, his eyes dark with pain, and, breaking into his native language, he demanded to know if she had slept with Jake.

Haltingly she tried to explain, but she could see Dante did not believe her as he turned on her in a fury of Italian, demanding to know why, when she had refused him her bed, she could fall straight into bed with a man she had not seen in years.

She looked into his deep brown eyes, and could see the hurt and anger and she opened her mouth to try and explain, and closed it again. There was no explanation she could give. It was better that Dante thought the worst of her; he would get over her quicker that way. Sadly she realised she had never loved him, and he deserved better.

'Jake is right, Dante. I'm sorry,' she said in English for Jake's benefit, but it hurt to see the look of bleak disillusionment on Dante's friendly face, and turning angry eyes on Jake, she added, 'Jake and I are reconciled—that's what you want, isn't it, darling...?' she jeered, not bothering to hide her disgust with her so-called husband.

Dante, with a pride that did him credit, said, 'Congratulations; I hope you will be happy, but I doubt it.' And, swinging on his heel, his broad shoulders tense, he walked stiffly away.

Lexi watched him go with tears in her eyes...

'He isn't worth your sympathy. The man is even older than me; he could never have kept you satisfied.'

Jake's sneering remark fuelled her temper, and flashing him a bitter glance, she said, 'Did you have to be so brutal? I wanted to tell Dante myself. And anyway, how did you know where to find us?'

'Simple, I went to the man's shop and followed him when he left; I guessed you would run to him. But you're wasting time, Lexi. Monicelli told me you spoke to him this morning; you have nowhere to run to. So, unless you want a coffee, we will leave.'

He was right as usual but she could not resist getting a dig at him. 'I'm surprised you don't need a coffee, given the state you got into last night; the place reeked of whisky this morning.' She tilted her head back, the better to look at him. 'Is drinking another one of your vices?' she queried sarcastically.

It wasn't natural, she thought bitterly; his deep blue eyes were as clear and cold as ice, and if he had a hangover it certainly didn't show. He looked more vitally alive today than he had yesterday.

'Sorry to disappoint you, my dear, but my head is fine and I am in full control of my faculties. I didn't drink the whisky last night so much as spill it down my trousers. Jet-lag was responsible for my oversleeping; I flew in from America yesterday morning.' His dark head bent towards her. 'Sorry you were frustrated last night, Lexi, but have no fear, I'll make it up to you,' he promised silkily, 'now I've deprived you of your lover.'

Her mouth fell open in shock and colour rushed into her face as the implication of his words hit her. 'I was not...'

'This is hardly the place to discuss your sex life,' he said sneeringly. 'Come along, my car is parked around the corner.'

'Come along? Where to?' She was not going to be manhandled like a piece of spare baggage, but she had no choice but to go where he led, the arm around her waist gripped even tighter as they walked from the café and down the Via Cesareo. 'And what about my car? I've left it at the Continental Hotel car park...'

'That will be taken care of—get in.'

Seated in the low passenger seat of the gleaming Bugatti, she flinched as Jake reached across her, the back of his knuckles brushing the tip of her breast as he fastened the seatbelt.

His deep blue eyes captured hers, and he was amused by her reaction; his hand dropped to cover her breast through the fine cotton of her shirt. 'So sensitive,' Jake prompted cynically. 'I did you a favour getting rid of Dante, he was no match for your fiery passion.'

She searched frantically for a scathing response, but Jake simply settled behind the wheel and started the car while she was still seething with anger. With a defiant toss of her head she looked out of the side window. She was not going to argue with the man, she wouldn't give him the satisfaction, and with hard-won control she of-

fered, 'If you take the next left, it is the quickest way
back to the hotel.'

Jake glanced sideways at her stiff face and then returned his attention to the road. 'We are not going to
the hotel, but to my villa in Positano.'

Her head swung back, her glance going to his stern
profile. 'But I can't; all my clothes, everything I own is
at the hotel.'

'That's all taken care of. I'm taking no chances on
your running off again,' he told her bluntly. 'I want you
where I know you can't escape.'

Escape. It was an emotive word, but did one truly
ever escape from one's past by running away? With ma-
turity and hindsight, she recognised that her biggest
mistake had been running away from Jake and his mistress in the first place. If she had stayed, and immediately applied for a divorce on the ground of Jake's
adultery with Lorraine, she would certainly have won
the case, the poor wife having just lost her child. Her
solicitor had told her as much a couple of mornings ago.
Not that it did her much good, as he also explained that,
having been living apart for so long, to claim adultery
now was a bit of a non-starter; it was best to wait the
five years...

So near and yet so far, she thought, her violet eyes
resentfully skimming Jake's harsh profile. She had
almost won, a few short weeks to freedom. But almost
was not good enough, she sighed resignedly; Jake always
won... Her eyes fell on his hands lightly flexed around
the wheel. He drove the powerful car with the same easy
expertise he did everything. It was frightening to think
she was completely at his mercy.

But five minutes later she was glad of his dynamic
skills, as the powerful car picked up speed and flew along
the notorious Amalfi Drive. She glanced out of the
window and caught her breath: on one side were steeply
rising cliffs, and on the other an almost sheer drop into

the sea. It was noted as one of the most spectacular views in the Mediterranean, and many a film-maker used the scenic drive as a backdrop for famous car chases. But it took a skilful and courageous driver to navigate the dark tunnels and cliff-hanging bends. She didn't speak, didn't dare. Instead she drank in the sight of the isle of Capri, and the smaller islands near the coastline, the luxury yachts moving through the azure waters as smooth as swans on a lake.

Jake must have amassed an enormous amount of money to have a villa in Positano; she had visited the village once. A very sophisticated centre, the famous names in fashion owned the boutiques—Armani, Valentino and the like. Their customers the seriously rich people who holidayed in the villas dotted around the hillside. Roger Moore, the famous James Bond actor, and many more.

She gasped as the car swung violently to the right, and they were driving up a narrow road, and then, just when she thought they would surely crash into the tall iron gates ahead of them, Jake flicked a switch on the dash, and the gates swung open. A short, steep drive lined with trees ended in a huge stone arch and a large courtyard.

'My home—do you like it?' Jake was out of the car and holding the passenger door open for her.

Lexi, to put it crudely, was gobsmacked. She stepped out on to the paved yard, her violet eyes widened to their fullest extent. She gazed around her in awe. Gleaming white stucco with rough stone corners and arches—the villa was a work of art. Set into the hillside, long circular terraces curved around all three floors, a multitude of flowers and vines, hibiscus, and seemingly thousands of geraniums of every hue in huge ornate containers. It was how she imagined the hanging gardens of Babylon must have looked. She said nothing as Jake took her arm and led her up a wide stone staircase to the massive arched entrance door. The door was flung open and a small, dark-haired lady dressed completely in black burst into a voluble welcome in Italian.

Her footsteps halted in surprised astonishment as Jake returned the woman's greeting. 'I didn't know you spoke Italian.' She looked up into his smiling face, and was stunned by the obvious pleasure in his eyes at the sight of the old lady. Once Jake had looked at her like that. The thought stung, as the smile left his eyes when he turned his attention to her.

'There's a lot you don't know about me; you were never that interested.' Jake shrugged lazily, his broad shoulders flexing beneath his fine shirt.

He was right; when they were first married she had been too young, too much in awe of him to question him about anything, plus when they had been alone together they had spent most of their time in bed...

'Lexi, my housekeeper, Maria.'

Lexi with a start realised Jake was speaking, and, glad to banish the memories of the past, she took the older lady's outstretched hand in a brief handshake, but she got the distinct impression Maria was somewhat reluctant to accept her. She listened as Jake issued instruction for lunch to be served at one, and watched as Maria scuttled off to the back of the house, and Jake strode across the ornate marble mosaic floor to the foot of a large white marble staircase.

'Come along, Lexi.' A cool smile curved his hard mouth. 'I'm sure you want to get out of those clothes.' His dark eyes slid slowly over her face and throat, taking in the thrust of her breasts against the simple cotton shirt, the narrow waist and conservative straight skirt, and back up again to her face.

She felt as though he could see through to her flesh and she shivered, a sharp *frisson* of fear running down her spine, and stared at him in silence, incapable of responding.

Jake walked over to her. 'Your uniform is unnecessary here, Lexi; we are here to relax,' he said, and his long fingers closed over her chin and his thumb brushed along her bottom lip. 'And I am going to make you forget every man you ever looked at, except me.'

Lexi flushed, but there was no heat in Jake's eyes, she noted. She was looking at a stranger. His face was blank, hostile as he watched her; she felt the pressure of his fingers, the warmth of his body, and felt her throat tighten in fear.

'After you,' Jake drawled, and she heard the mockery in his tone as his hand dropped to curve around her back, propelling her forward.

Stiffly she moved towards the grand staircase. They climbed the stairs and walked down a wide corridor, their heels clicking like a death knell, Lexi thought fancifully, on the marble floors. Jake stopped at a door, opened it and urged her in. The room was bright and airy, flooded with the morning sun; the king-sized bed dominating it was covered with an intricate white lace bedspread.

'The master bedroom,' Jake drawled, and, going over to a door set in one plain white wall, he flung it open. 'Through here, the bathroom. The rest of this floor is taken up with another bedroom and the nursery suite. The top floor houses three more bedrooms and the service flat. The layout for the ground floor you can see for yourself later.'

'It's very nice,' she said politely. The room was obviously on the corner of the house, as two large windows were set in the wall to the right of her along with two long ceiling-to-floor windows that framed the huge bed. She walked across to the window directly in front of her and gasped.

The view was too beautiful for words. The tree-lined drive had disguised the exquisitely terraced gardens that marched down in row after row to end at what must be the edge of a cliff, and then the sea, glistening brilliant blue, the faint outline of Capri visible in the far distance. She let her gaze swing around in a shallow arc; to one side was visible the tiny port of Positano, the luxury yachts lying at anchor in the marina. It was picture-postcard-perfect. She clasped her hands together, suddenly nervous, as she felt Jake's presence behind her. She could sense the undercurrent of sexual tension in the air around them. A bedroom was far too intimate a place to be with Jake.

'How long have you owned this place?' She turned to look at him, hoping by her simple question to break the tension sizzling in the air.

He stared down at her, his dark eyes brooding. 'About a year.'

'Why buy here?' Had he wanted to be near her? the errant thought entered her mind.

'It was left to me by my father.'

She raised her brows. 'Your father? But I thought he died years ago.'

'Well, you thought wrong.' His blue eyes avoided hers, and for a second Lexi felt sympathy, until he added dismissively, 'And I have no wish to discuss it with you.'

She should have known better than to waste her sympathy on him, and, straightening her shoulders, she said, 'Yes, well . . . If you will excuse me.' She made to walk past him but was stopped as one long arm snaked out and curved around her waist, hauling her in hard against his body.

'Not so fast, Lexi.' His eyes darkened as he looked down at her. 'You owe me for this morning,' he said under his breath. 'No woman leaves my bed without my say-so.' She felt herself sway against him. 'And certainly not to run to another man.'

Lexi stared at him, and swallowed hard on the lump of fear that lodged in her throat. His blue-black eyes captured hers, and there was no mistaking the predatory animal look she saw in his dark face. 'I wasn't running away...'

'No...' he drawled mockingly. 'Then convince me...'

CHAPTER SIX

'No.' LEXI lifted her hands, intending to push him away, but his strong arm wrapped tighter around her small waist, his fingers biting into her side as he turned her fully in front of him, his long legs pressing against her slender limbs. Her hands came up against the hard wall of his chest; she could feel the steady beat of his heart beneath her fingers. The heat of his body, through the fine fabric of his shirt, burnt the palms of her hands, sending electric sensations shooting through her entire body.

'You want to, you know you do, Lexi. I saw it in those huge pansy eyes of yours last night when I kissed you. I could have taken you there and then,' Jake's deep voice husked beguilingly. 'Why deny yourself the pleasure?'

The horrible truth was she did want him. Held close against him, she could feel his rising awareness taut against her belly. But the mention of last night reminded her of her humiliation. She had come apart in his arms, only to hear him say she disgusted him ... She strained away from him but the action pulled her shirt taut across her firm breasts, without giving her the freedom she wanted. She could feel her pulse beat faster, the blood flowing thickly through her veins. She tilted her head back to look up into his darkly brooding face. 'I disgust you. You told me so. Why the change?' she queried, fighting to still the tremors curling her insides.

'I wasn't telling the whole truth; your mercenary nature I can do without,' he said with casual insolence as his indigo eyes slid from her upturned face to her breasts. 'But your body I want.'

She saw the darkening gleam in his gaze, and felt the subtle increase of pressure in his thighs. 'Well, I don't want you,' she croaked, her throat closing on the lie.

'Liar, you don't mean that.' And, holding her fast, he lifted his free hand to the buttons of her blouse and slowly unfastened them one by one, adding silkily, 'But perhaps you need *me* to convince you...'

Her violet eyes were trapped by the sensuous deepening gleam in Jake's, she knew she should stop him, but was paralysed by the hypnotic magnetism of the man. She felt boneless in the circle of his arm, her senses coming alive with every touch, every brush of his hard body.

His fingers quickly dealt with the front fastening of her bra, and her lush breasts broke free from their confinement as if leaping for his touch. 'You have developed into a very luscious lady, Lexi.'

She breathed a jagged breath, and tried again to push at his broad chest. 'Wasn't Lorraine enough for you this mor——?' she tried to strike back, but his strong hand closed over one naked breast, cupping the fullness, and words failed her.

'Forget about Lorraine; we have an agreement, you and I. Fidelity for the duration,' he drawled huskily as his thumb delicately grazed over the soft pink tip. 'And it won't be any hardship for either of us, if this is anything to go by, my darling *wife*.'

Lexi shuddered. He was seducing her with words and actions, and she had no defence against him.

'Look, Lexi, you do want me. See how this tempting pink bud aches for my touch,' his deep voice murmured sexily, as his fingers teased the rosy nub into pulsating rigidity.

She closed her eyes in shame, unable to bear the humiliation of knowing she had no control over her own body, as arrows of heat darted from her breast to her groin. She knew she should protest, but instead a soft moan escaped her.

'Don't close your eyes, Lexi. Look at me,' Jake commanded, his fingers nipping on the rigid tip of her breast.

She opened her eyes as liquid fire swirled through her, and glanced down. She saw his long, tanned fingers contrasting sharply with her soft, pale flesh, caressing, cajoling. It was madness, she hated Jake for what he had done to her, but it was a madness she could not resist. It had been too long...

'Tell me what you want, Lexi.' His hand stroked softly to the valley between her breasts then gently cupped the other one in his large palm, his forefinger tracing circles on her hardening flesh, but stopping well short of the hungry peak. 'Is this one feeling left out?' he teased sensuously as his dark head bent lower and his mouth closed over hers in the lightest brush of a kiss.

'Ask me nicely, Lexi, and I'll ease the ache for you...' he murmured, smiling wickedly as he watched her body arch instinctively towards him in helpless response.

Then his mouth once more closed over hers, his tongue slipping between her softly parted lips, and desire as sharp and piercing as a knife sliced through her. Her tongue touched his in thrusting response. She moaned as his fingers finally captured the taut nipple, tugging, rolling her between his sensitive fingertips; she raked her hands down his broad back, her lower body moving into him, pressing against him in a urgent need.

Jake raised his head, his dark eyes glittering triumphantly down into hers. 'You want me,' he grated 'Your body doesn't lie.' And his dark head swooped down to her aching breast and, as one hand caressed and teased her aching flesh, his mouth curved over its partner, nibbling, kissing then suckling long and slow until she thought she would go mad with pleasure.

'You're so responsive there, so ready for my mouth,' he rasped throatily as his dark head moved to her other breast. 'But we must make them both the same,' he chuckled, his mouth replacing his fingers, as he treated the rigid nipple to the same ecstasy as its partner.

Hardly aware of what she was doing, Lexi's hands crept up his spine to the nape of his neck, her fingers tangling in the dark hair of his head, holding him against her. She never noticed as he swept her up in his arms and carried her to the bed, because his mouth covered hers in an all-consuming kiss of passionate intent, his tongue plunging into her mouth, seeking to devour all the hot, sweet taste of her.

She felt the mattress at her back as Jake eased his mouth from hers, and, sliding on to the bed at her side, he deftly removed her blouse and bra, his hand stroking from her throat, his palm caressing over her full breasts, first one and then the other.

'Jake...' she murmured his name. Her tongue licking out over her swollen lips, she stared up into his handsome face; his mouth was a taut line in a face flushed dark with desire.

'Yes, Lexi...' he rasped, one hand sliding her skirt down over her slender hips. 'I'm going to make it so good for you.'

Jake's mouth brushed a soft kiss from the hollow in her throat down the valley of her breast. He lifted his dark head and looked slowly from her beautiful passion-flushed face to the wild mass of red hair spread across the pillow, like molten gold gleaming in the rays of morning sun cutting across the huge bed. His sensuous gaze slowly traced the thrust of her naked breasts, hard and pouting for his touch, the soft curve of her waist and gentle flare of her hips. His hand slid beneath the fine lace of her briefs and eased them down her shapely legs.

Lexi shivered uncontrollably, aching to feel his naked flesh. Her rational mind knew he was deliberately seducing her in broad daylight, but it had been so long... She reached up to his chest, her fingers fumbling with the fastening of his shirt.

'Let me,' Jake grated and, pushing her hands away, quickly shrugged out of his clothes.

Lexi's violet eyes skimmed his golden body, gloriously naked stretched alongside her, the dark swirls of chest hair arrowing down past his flat stomach, the curve of his buttock, the long, muscular legs. Five years had only enhanced his male perfection, she thought wonderingly. She reached her small hands up to his chest, her slender fingers weaving in his body hair, finding the hard male nipples. She smiled, a slow, sensual curve of her mouth, as she tweaked the rigid little nubs.

Jake groaned deep in his throat and pushed her hands away yet again. Leaning over her, he spread her arms either side of her head, and his dark eyes burned down into hers—passion, desire, she saw them all, and something else besides that slowed her rapidly beating heart.

'I've waited five long years for this moment,' he growled huskily.

He was lying; five years ago he hadn't wanted her, couldn't get rid of her fast enough. The errant thought flickered in Lexi's head, but vanished as his lips brushed against her brow in the lightest caress.

'I've dreamed of having your exquisite body pinned beneath me, of making you cry out my name once more, begging me to take you, and I will not be hurried, my darling Lexi.'

The drawled endearment should have enthralled her, but instead a quiver of fear pierced the sensual haze swamping her mind. Jake flung one long leg over her trembling limbs, holding her fast, his soft body hair, the hard heat of his arousal pushed against her thigh and she half closed her eyes, fear forgotten, at the lightning speed at which her body shook with want and need.

Through the thick fringe of her lashes she saw Jake's harsh face lower to within inches of her own. Her lips parted for his kiss.

'I am going to make love to you——' his lips moved against her mouth and away again '—until every other man who ever had you is banished from your mind. Until the only name you ever cry is mine. My magnificent, mercenary little wife.'

'Mercenary...?' she murmured. He had called her that before...

'That and more, but I can forget it all when I have sated myself in you.'

Lexi's eyes widened to their fullest extent as she gazed up into his taut features and she trembled at what she saw there, in the stark, bright morning light. It wasn't love, not even lust, but something more sinister...

Dazed with passion, she tried to think. Mercenary...he kept harping on that and yet she had never taken a penny from him. Then, with a flash of insight, she remembered their parting in London; she had pretended, to save her pride in the face of his infidelity, that she would rather have half his wealth than him. She smiled, and opened her mouth to reassure him.

'Jake...' She stopped herself just in time. If she explained why she had acted mercenary, he would realise just how much he had hurt her, how much she had loved him! It was the last coherent thought she had for a long time...

'Yes, Lexi; I know.' And releasing her hands, he stroked the length of her arms, the curve of her breast and her flat stomach; his strong hands curved over her hips, his long fingers trailing towards her inner thighs, but not lingering as they stroked right down to her feet and back up again.

Her heartbeat accelerated like a rocket. She felt how a cat must feel being stroked; she wanted to purr, and rub herself against the source of the pleasure. She clasped her hands around his broad shoulders, her body arching, writhing against his in wanton invitation.

'Easy,' Jake said, his voice ragged. He looked down at her sensuously flushed face, the softly parted lips. 'I'll give you what you want.' His dark head lowered and he was kissing her swiftly, repeatedly, on her mouth, her eyes, the slender line of her throat. 'I'm glad you haven't lost all modesty,' Jake murmured lifting his head. His dark eyes gleamed down into hers. 'There are a few interesting white triangles here.' One long finger traced the soft curve of her breast. 'A mathematician could have a field-day working out the angles,' he husked as he bent his head, his tongue tracing the slight outline in her flesh where her bikini top had left its mark, then, cutting across, his tongue laved the burgeoning tips of her breasts.

Lexi moaned her need, her mouth sought him, she kissed the back of his hand, biting on his forearm that lay across her breast-bone, holding her down. The taste of him was in her mouth, the male scent of him filled her nostrils; she was lost in a sea of tempestuous emotions she had thought never to experience again. Her hands grasped his hard flesh, clinging to his broad shoulders; her nails dug into his satin-smooth skin as he licked and kissed his way down her body.

She was aflame; everywhere he touched was transformed into million points of pleasure. His long fingers found the third curling red triangle, and she cried out his name, 'Jake...'

He looked into her face as one strong hand gently urged her legs apart, opening her to his final possession, while his fingers stroked erotically. She watched his eyes darken to black pools, and he was shaking with the same wild desire that consumed her.

It was as if her body had been in prison for five years and was suddenly given its freedom. She was free to experience everything, to relish once more Jake claiming her, but he didn't. His dark head bent and she quivered from head to toe as his touch, his tongue, became so intimate she thought she would die. She felt the tremors start in the heart of her womb, the tendrils reaching in ever widening circles.

Jake slid up her body, his mouth finding hers, his teeth and tongue biting and tasting her full pouting lips. 'You're hot, so hot,' he murmured, as his hand slid between her thighs, tangling in the soft, red curls and finding the soft, feminine folds again.

She trembled wildly on the brink while Jake looked down at her, his smile a mixture of savage triumph and fiercely held control.

'Tell me what you want, Lexi.' His fingers stroked.

She reached for him, needing his weight, his body over her, in her, as red-hot need scorched her innermost being.

'Say it, Lexi,' he growled, his deep voice shaking as he lifted himself into the cradle of her thighs.

He wanted it all; Jake wanted her to beg. She hated him, but desire overwhelmed her. The brush of the hard hot length of him against her was too much. 'Jake, I want you.' Her voice broke as her love-starved body quivered like a bow. She arched up to him, her shapely legs curving around his thighs. 'Please, Jake...'

Jake rubbed against her again but stopped just at the edge of taking her. 'You do it, Lexi. Convince me, lover...'

Her deep purple eyes clashed with Jake's. His skin was pulled taut over his high cheekbones; his dark eyes glittered with a violent light as he fought to control his own need. He brushed lightly against her once more, teasing, almost penetrating and with a sigh of surrender she gave him the triumph he demanded. Her hand slid eagerly between their sweat-slicked bodies, her fingers crawling over his flat belly and lower, finding the satin-sheathed steel of him. He jerked reflexively, and there was no need for guidance as he drove deeply into her.

Lexi's hands curved around his back, clinging as he drove deep and deeper; their bodies, hot, wet and wanting, moved in frenzied rhythm. Lexi felt the widening circles flinging her out into infinity, breaking in wave after wave of tumultuous relief. She sobbed his name, then his mouth ground down on hers, as, with one final thrust of body and tongue, Jake shuddered over the edge into oblivion with her.

'I'm too heavy for you,' Jake's rasping voice declared prosaically, and, rolling off her, he lay flat on his back, an arm flung across his eyes, as if shutting out the light.

Lexi glanced at him, his great chest heaving in the aftermath of passion, but the space he had put between them was more eloquent than words. 'Jake?' she queried, reaching out to him.

'No inquest, Lexi. You enjoyed it as much as me,' he drawled callously, not even bothering to look at her.

She briefly closed her eyes against the shame while admitting that Jake was right as usual. They had made love countless times in the past; it was nothing new, she told herself. But never had she felt so totally possessed. She tried to convince herself it was just good sex. She was more mature and could accept it as such, after all, he was her husband! Why not? That excuse was the most pathetic of all, and she knew it.

Jake sat up, and, glancing sideways at her naked sprawled body, his gaze finally rested on her face. 'You wanted me, Lexi! Thanks! You convinced me most satisfactorily.' His lips quirked in a mocking smile. 'I think we will get along just fine.' And, swinging his long legs off the bed, totally happy with his nudity, he walked around the room collecting his clothes.

Lexi flinched as though he had struck her, unable to respond. Five years' abstinence had been ended by Jake's sophisticated expertise in the art of making love. He had done it quite deliberately, reduced her to a mindless wanton in his arms. Before, she had believed Jake's lovemaking was the ultimate expression of his love for her, until she had caught him with Lorraine... Now he had demonstrated graphically that his lovemaking had nothing whatsoever to do with love, but everything to do with possession, ownership. Jake decided he wanted her back, for whatever devious reason, and dismissed the past five years of her life as though they had never existed. Bed the woman! Back to the status quo! Reconciled! Jake was right, she had wanted him, but now, looking at him strolling around the bedroom all arrogant, smug, self-satisfied male, she wished she'd castrated the swine.

'I need a shower, and then I have some work to take care of in the study.' Jake stopped with his hand on the bathroom door and glanced to where she lay as he had left her, naked on the bed.

Lexi met his gaze. 'I really do hate you,' she said bleakly, and she hated herself, she recognised sadly. The bright morning sun filled the room, exposing every minute detail; it was barely noon and she had... She couldn't bear to think of it! Grabbing the edge of the lace bedspread, she pulled it up over her naked body.

'Bit late for that, sweetheart, I've seen it all and more.' His masculine chuckle only added to her humiliation. 'I can have you any time I want and after this morning's little romp we both know it.'

His arrogant assumption was all it took to ignite Lexi's anger and, hauling herself upright on the bed with the cover firmly clasped above her breast, she recalled his words of the previous night. 'So much for waiting to make sure any offspring were definitely yours,' she lashed back defiantly.

For a moment she watched his eyes narrow assessingly on her small face, and then a cynical smile twisted his firm mouth. 'I don't need to, Lexi; your boyfriend was most forthcoming this morning. You forget, I speak Italian.'

She groaned inwardly as she realised Jake must have understood every word of Dante's angry speech earlier. Jake knew Dante had never been her lover. But still, she snapped back mutinously, 'You don't know everything.'

An expression of cold derision tautened his handsome face. 'I don't want to; your body in my bed when I say so is enough.' And opening the bathroom door he added as an afterthought, 'Your luggage arrived earlier from the hotel. Maria has put it in the room next door. Don't forget, lunch at one on the patio. Maria doesn't like to be kept waiting.'

Lexi bent her head, her hands curling into fists. Her fingers bit painfully into her soft palms, but it was nothing to the pain she felt inside. Silently she raged at Jake, at the circumstances that had put her here in his bed, and most of all at herself. You're a fool, a weak-willed sex-starved idiot! she told herself bitterly, and, worse, she had the sinking feeling she had let herself in for a world, possibly a lifetime, of pain.

Abruptly rolling off the bed, Lexi stood up, letting the coverlet fall back behind her; action might dispel her unwelcome thoughts. Quickly she searched for her clothes and, picking them up, she slipped on her briefs then winced as she fastened her bra; her breasts were still tender from Jake's ministrations.

Jake! Her nemesis! He couldn't have made it plainer. He would use her when and where he wanted to, and she had to jump to his order. She tried to tell herself she was glad that at least Jake was allowing her to have her own bedroom, but, as she wriggled into her skirt and blouse, and walked across the room to the door, deep in the secret part of her heart, that hurt most of all...

She walked along the corridor, and pushed open the partially opened door of what she presumed was the next room and looked in. Her eyes fell on her battered suit-cases standing just inside the door; she heaved a sigh of relief and walked in, closing the door behind her.

Lexi found herself standing in a small, arched alcove. She stepped forward and for the first time in ages her generous mouth curved in the beginnings of a smile as she looked around. The room was a delight; a symphony in gold, cream and the palest lavender.

The walls either side of her were a bank of mirrored wardrobes, which accounted for the small arched entrance-hall. On the wall to the left was a four-poster bed draped in yards of cream eyelet lace lined with lavender silk; a matching cover lay over the bed. Opposite her, two long windows were hung with complementary curtains, caught back at the sides by models of Eros in gold to reveal the terrace and breathtaking view beyond. Between the windows was a huge mirror in an amethyst frame, and in front of that, a deliciously feminine chaise-longue and matching button-backed chair, plus a circular glass and gold occasional table. On the right-hand side wall was a long kneehole dressing-table, draped in the same fabric, with a three-way mirror on top, and next to that was another door.

It was the most totally feminine room Lexi had ever seen, and it all looked new. A variety of pictures dotted the walls, from old-fashioned landscapes to a Gainsborough lady in a velvet frame, and they were all fixed with satin bows and suspended on ribbons. A couple of Aubusson rugs were placed at strategic points on the marble tiled floor.

She crossed the room, her handbag catching her attention; she hadn't realised she had left it in the car. It rested, along with a small leather box, on the dressing-table. Maria had been thorough. It was Lexi's jewel-box, not that she had much jewellery, but flicking it open she drew out her wristwatch and slipped it on; she had forgotten it in her haste to get away from Jake that morning. Not that it had done her any good, she sighed wearily. Her hand hovered over the box and slowly, reluctantly, she moved aside a few pieces of jewellery to reveal a plain gold ring. She hadn't looked at it in years, but she had never quite got around to throwing it away.

Lexi picked up the gold band and held it in the palm of her hand, such a simple piece of jewellery that had once meant the world to her. In her mind's eye she saw herself as a young girl walking into the register office on the arm of Meg's husband Tom. She had been nervous, but it had been a trembly, exciting kind of nerves. Her wedding-dress had been a delicate white *broderie anglaise* affair. Jake had insisted she must wear white, the same way after only a couple of dates he had discovered she was a virgin and insisted she marry him. At the time she had thought it was because he loved her and had too much respect for her to indulge in an affair.

With hindsight, she realised grimly, it had simply been a very smart move on his part to acquire Forest Manor and turn it into a hotel. True, he had paid her father's debts and made her a sleeping partner in his business, in fact he had insisted on it. She smiled drily; for all she knew she might be a very wealthy woman in her own right by now. She had had no contact with the London merchant bank where Jake had opened her account since the day he had taken her there to sign the necessary documents.

'You kept it. That does surprise me.'

Lexi jumped as if she had been stung, and whirling round her startled eyes clashed with cold blue. 'Do you have to creep up on people like that?' she burst out; she had not heard him approach, and she blushed scarlet, embarrassed and angry with herself.

'I did not creep, as you put it.' His cool eyes looked mockingly down at her. 'But you were so lost in thought that you didn't hear me. Pleasant memories, were they?' he probed, his hand reaching out and curving around her closed palm, forcing her fingers to open.

Lexi was incapable of responding with his unexpected presence only a few inches in front of her. The touch of his hand had set her heart racing and the image of what had happened earlier in his bedroom leapt to the forefront of her mind.

'Too simple for your taste. I imagined you had consigned it to the rubbish bin years ago.'

'Wh-what..?' Wide-eyed, she stared at him, her thoughts in chaos. His lips parted over even white teeth in a grin of genuine amusement at her obvious confusion.

'Never mind. It'll do until I get you a diamond one.' And with casual arrogance he took the gold band and slipped it on her ring finger, and she let him, too surprised to do anything else.

'Still a perfect fit. Just like you and I, Lexi.'

She stared at him, the colour flooding her face at his words. 'So you say,' she tried to jeer, but it was right, he had proved it very thoroughly not half an hour ago. She glanced down at their joined hands, anything to avoid Jake's too knowing expression, but the gold ring glittering on her finger only served to remind her of the hopelessness of her position, and swiftly she pulled her hand free.

Jake lifted her chin with one long finger. 'Don't look so shocked,' he chuckled. 'We are married.' And, trailing his finger up to her lips, he added softly but with deadly intent, 'And this time you will not escape. Which brings me to why I'm here.'

'I thought you had work to do,' Lexi said, finally finding the control to string a sentence together.

'True, but first your passport.'

'My passport...'

'Yes, it wasn't at the hotel and I want it.'

She glanced sideways at where her bag lay on the dressing-table, and Jake, intercepting her glance, swiftly picked up the bag and opened it.

Seeing Jake rummaging around in her bag was the incentive Lexi needed to find her pride and her temper. 'Put that down, damn you,' she demanded and, stepping forward, reached up to grab it. 'You have no right to go through my personal belongings.' She jumped up, trying to catch Jake's hand holding her bag, but only succeeded in losing her balance and falling hard against his broad chest. A long arm snaked around her waist pinning her to his side while the bag dropped to the floor, but she saw her precious passport firmly clenched in his fist, way out of her reach.

'Now, now, Lexi, don't get excited.' She heard his chuckle and saw red.

'Give me that.' She kicked out at his shin and futilely tried to reach his outstretched arm.

She almost fell over as Jake abruptly released her, his dark eyes turned from her open passport to her furious face.

'So that's how you did it. I should have guessed,' he said harshly, all amusement gone. 'Miss Alexandra Laughton.' He read her name as if it was a dirty word. 'You never did get this changed.'

She stared up at him, her violet eyes simmering with anger. But his embittered gaze made her bite back her angry demand. He looked ready to do violence and she didn't understand why, but a fine-honed sense of self-protection had her stepping backwards until she could go no further, the wall at her back.

Jake followed her, his large body tense like a coiled spring, his rugged features taut with barely controlled anger. His strong hands shot out and rested heavily on her slender shoulders. He pushed his dark face to within inches of her own.

'My God, you had it planned all along,' he hissed, his breath grazing her face. His dark eyes studied her, taking in the smooth forehead, the delicately arched eyebrows, the soft curve of her cheek.

Lexi's tongue snaked out over her dry lips in a nervous gesture, her heart thudding in her breast; a violent tension hung in the air between them, and she didn't know how it had happened.

'Such a beautiful, innocent face disguising a viciously devious mind.' Jake shook his dark head, his hands falling from her shoulders.

'That's rich...' Lexi stopped as her wary gaze clashed with Jake's, and what she saw in the black depths froze the blood in her veins.

'You have a good right to look afraid, Lexi, but right at this moment I don't think I could bear to touch you, or if I did I would strangle you.' And spinning around he stormed out of the room.

Long after he left Lexi was still leaning against the wall; she did not trust her legs to carry her one step. She had never seen Jake so furious or such hatred in another human being's face in her life. Slowly recovering her self-control, she pushed herself away from the wall and crossed the short space to the chaise-longue and collapsed upon it.

What did Jake mean, she had planned? Instead of ranting simply because she had never got around to changing her passport, he should have been thanking her. Five years ago it had enabled Lexi to walk away, leaving Jake and his mistress with her old home and a clear field... The man was obviously unbalanced...

As for a devious plan, that was laughable. Lexi had rarely planned anything in her life. It was one of her failings, she freely admitted. She tended to be a creature of impulse; she had married Jake on little more than an impulse. She had left England in the same impulsive manner, when, if she had stayed and fought, she could have been a free woman now. Instead of which, she was caught in a nightmare of a marriage where both parties hated each other's guts.

Jake had accused her of being devious. What a joke— if any one was devious it was Jake. He had married her for the manor; true, he had paid her father's debt, but she was sure it could not have been anything like the amount of money Jake intended making with the hotel. He had got her pregnant by mistake; he had not wanted a child. A tear slid down her cheek. Five years ago this very day Lexi had lain in the hospital bed having miscarried their child, and Jake had turned up hours after the event with a few lame excuses about business for neglecting Lexi. Now he turned up again, this time demanding a child, and with Lorraine, his mistress, in tow to take care of Lexi's job, while presumably Lexi obliged her husband. The black irony of the situation was too much to bear.

Collapsing on the chaise-longue, she gave way to her shattered emotions, tears of self-pity gushing down her cheeks.

CHAPTER SEVEN

LEXI rolled over and fell with a thump on the floor. Her eyes flew open and for a second she wondered where she was. Struggling out of what felt like a strait jacket but was in reality a light cotton sheet, she sat up cross-legged on the floor and gazed around her as the events of the morning filled her mind. She sighed, rubbing her elbow where it had caught the carved-wood frame of the front of the chaise-longue; it was an elegant piece of furniture but not the best place to fall asleep, she thought ruefully, her eyes widening as she realised someone must have come in her room and put the sheet over her. Not that it was necessary; she felt hot and sweaty and longed for a bath. She glanced at her wristwatch and jumped to her feet in shock. It was almost four. Jake had said lunch at one...

With a toss of her head she stalked across to the door set in the wall by the dressing-table. She had missed lunch, but what the hell! Jake could hardly kill her for it, and she badly needed to find the bathroom. Opening the door, her lips parted in a smile of pleasure, as she looked around the exquisitely appointed bathroom. Her smile vanished when she caught sight of herself in the length of one mirrored wall. God, what a mess! Her hair was sticking out like a bush, her eyes were red-rimmed and her clothes were wrinkled beyond belief.

Five minutes later, stripped naked, she stood in the huge double shower; her muscles ached in places she had forgotten she possessed and dark smudges marred her smooth flesh, telling their own story, but under the relaxing influence of the warm soothing spray she slowly

felt the ache and tension drain out of her. She washed
her hair with a sweet-scented jasmine shampoo, one she
had chosen from a good selection displayed on the
vanity-unit alongside the circular bath. She had toyed
with the idea of having a bath but after seeing the size
of it decided it would probably take half an hour to fill,
and, much as she told herself she didn't care about
missing lunch, she could not ignore the pangs of hunger
rumbling in her stomach for much longer.

Stepping out of the shower, blinking the water from
her eyes, she stretched out a hand to where she thought
the towel might be and was relieved to find it. With her
head bent she dried the water from her eyes then swept
the towel up around her hair in a turban. Throwing her
head back, she straightened and froze with her hands at
the knot in the towel.

Jake was standing in front of her, his blue eyes dancing
with amusement as he took in her shocked expression,
and quite a lot more besides.

'Very nice.' His gaze slid slowly down her naked body,
lingering on her full breasts, and before she realised what
he was doing he leant forward, his mouth catching the
tip of her breast.

She lashed out at his dark head, stepping back, trying
to ignore the flash of tingling awareness lancing through
her body. 'Get out,' she cried and, swinging round, she
grabbed a large white bath sheet from a nearby towel-
rail and wrapped it hastily around her heated body.

'I couldn't resist catching the drop of water from your
breast, Lexi, there's no need to throw a fit,' he drawled
with mocking amusement.

Lexi did not share his amusement; she was flustered
and furious, and the last thing she needed was his intimidating presence looming over her in the bathroom.
She glared at him; it was positively wicked how attractive Jake looked, she thought bitterly. Some time in
the past few hours he had changed into a pair of brief

white shorts, and sleeveless white T-shirt. His long, muscular limbs, bronzed by the sun, were enough to make her heart flutter. 'I expect privacy in the bathroom. Surely that isn't too much to ask?' she demanded furiously.

'You're obviously feeling better. You have your temper back.'

'I wasn't ill, I fell asleep.' She tried to explain her absence from lunch before he could ask.

'I know; I called in earlier and you looked so peaceful that I put a cover over you and left. See how kind I can be when you please me,' Jake prompted with a knowing reminiscent curve to his hard mouth.

So it had been Jake! Somehow it did not fit her image of the ruthless man who had burst back into her life so suddenly. 'Thank you...' she muttered reluctantly. 'But if you don't mind I'd like to get dressed.'

'Don't let me stop you.' And in an exaggerated gesture he flung open the bathroom door. 'After you.'

It was hard to look dignified wrapped in a bath sheet with a towel round one's hair, but Lexi gave it her best shot and marched past him with her head held high, while silently mumbling, 'Arrogant swine' under her breath.

'I thought you might be hungry, so I had Maria prepare a tray, a few sandwiches and a pot of coffee.'

Lexi didn't want to acknowledge his thoughtfulness. 'You needn't have bothered; I'm not hungry,' she denied and, walking across the room, she sat down on the button-backed chair, casually eyeing the food set before her on the occasional table. 'You're enough to make any woman lose her appetite,' she added for good measure, but just at that moment her tummy gave a very loud rumble.

Jake tossed back his dark head and burst out laughing, and Lexi's lips began to twitch and, before she could help it, a chuckle escaped her. She looked up at Jake standing a few feet away and, as blue eyes caught violet in shared humour, the laughter stopped. Lexi could not break the contact, and for a long moment something precious seemed to simmer in the air between them.

Jake looked away first. 'Eat, Lexi, and meet me downstairs in half an hour,' he commanded gruffly and, turning on his heel, walked out.

Twenty minutes later, the food long gone, Lexi's lips pursed thoughtfully as she surveyed her reflection. She looked slightly better, she thought; her eyes were no longer red-rimmed but the dark circles beneath betrayed the stress of the last twenty-four hours. She had chosen a soft cotton sleeveless shirtwaister in mint-green from her limited but classic wardrobe, surprised to find everything she possessed had been neatly put away, probably by Maria, including her shoes, neatly lined up in the rack at the bottom of the wardrobe. She had picked a pair of comfortable espadrilles in matching green; a trip to the chest of drawers alongside the dressing-table and she had found her underwear. Now, as she brushed her hair back into a neat ponytail, fastening it with a plain green slide, she knew she could not put off much longer going downstairs, and Jake...

She need not have worried... Lexi carried the tray that had held her snack down the grand staircase and, presuming the kitchen was at the back of the house, made her way through the hall to the door at the rear. Opening it, she walked into a huge light and airy room. A large antique pine dresser on one wall, stacked with blue delft china, caught her eye; in the centre of the room was a solid square pine table surrounded with ladder-backed chairs, and beyond the table a dividing bench to the kitchen proper. Maria, hearing Lexi enter, dashed across to meet her and take the tray from her.

'*Signora*, please you should not have bothered. It is my job to collect the tray, cook everything... What will Signor Taylor say?'

Lexi smiled at the older woman's worried frown. 'Don't worry, Maria; I am quite capable of looking after myself.'

'But it is my job,' Maria said firmly, and she placed the tray on the bench.

Lexi caught the housekeeper's disapproving look and sighed inwardly. Not a very good start, she thought hopelessly, missing lunch and upsetting the housekeeper. 'Sorry,' she apologised. 'But if you tell me where I can find Mr Taylor, I'll get out of your way.'

'Signor Taylor left fifteen minutes ago. He will be back for dinner at eight. Do you wish to eat in the dining-room or outside, *signora*?'

So much for his instruction to meet him in thirty minutes; obviously something more important had caught his attention—probably Lorraine. Lexi sighed and glanced out of the window, the fierce heat of the sun did not seem to have diminished since the morning. 'Outside, thank you, Maria.' Anyway, it would be less intimate to eat outside, she told herself and, turning, left the room.

She spent the next half-hour exploring her new home. In any other circumstances she would have found the place delightful. An elegant dining-room opened out on to a sunny patio, and the kitchen at one side of the house. A morning-room and what she presumed was Jake's study led out to the terrace at the front of the house, as did the extravagantly furnished salon, the imposing entrance-hall bracketed between them. The salon opened on two sides to the terraces. Strolling through the tall French windows, she found herself at the other side of the house. She walked on the edge of the terrace and, looking over, gasped. On the next level down was a free-shaped swimming-pool, the clear water sparkling in the late afternoon sun. She toyed with the idea of going for a swim, but she had no intention of allowing Jake to catch her in her bikini; she was far too vulnerable to his masculine charms, though it infuriated her to have to admit it.

Instead she wandered down the stone steps to the pool, and on down through half a dozen progressively narrower terraces cascading with flowers and vines, the warm, sweet smell of a variety of plants filling the air, and beyond the boundary wall the magnificent backdrop of the sea, and islands. It was a little bit of paradise, Lexi mused, casually leaning against the wall, her eyes skimming the perfect view. But to her, short of diving off the cliff, it was a prison...

Restlessly she turned and slowly began walking back up towards the house. How long did Jake intend to keep her here? He was a businessman based in the city of London, it didn't make sense, but ruefully she admitted that nothing in the past twenty-four hours had made much sense. His demanding she return to him and his desire for a child were a puzzle she could not fathom. Jake had hardly been ecstatic the one time she had been pregnant; only weeks after her pregnancy had been confirmed, suddenly he had needed to work in London— pressure of business, he had told Lexi. That was a laugh. Pressure from his mistress, more like, as Lexi had so suddenly and painfully discovered.

Lexi would never forget the first meal she had shared with Jake and Lorraine after losing her baby, and the other woman's callous comment, 'You wouldn't have much time for a child just now...it might be a blessing in disguise.' With hindsight Lexi realised what Lorraine had been getting at. Jake must have already decided to end their marriage, and was just waiting for a convenient time to tell his poor little wife. A child would have been a complication Jake didn't need. It made Lexi's blood boil to think of the pair of them still together five years later almost to the day, and once more wrecking her life.

She stopped as she reached the edge of the swimming-pool, and closed her eyes, clasping her hands in front of her as though in prayer. Why, why, why hadn't Jake gone ahead with the divorce she had heard him and Lorraine plotting all those years ago? Her violet eyes fluttered open and she stared down into the sparkling blue water as if it would give her the answer she sought... It could only be money...

Lexi, as far as she knew, was still a silent partner in his business. Maybe he was frightened that if she divorced him he would lose half his business, yet she had tried to reassure him on that point last night. But he insisted on believing she was mercenary. Lorraine had once tried to convince Jake Lexi was a gold-digger before they were married, and obviously now Jake believed her. It appeared the other woman had overplayed her hand. The very reason Lorraine had given for Jake not marrying Lexi in the first place was now preventing Jake from divorcing Lexi... It would be laughable if it wasn't so tragic. God, her heart cried, wasn't it enough that she had lost her beloved baby, given Jake and Lorraine a clear field; what had she done to deserve their continued persecution?

Bending down at the edge of the pool, she ran her hand through the cool water and brushed it over her hot forehead. It must be financial, it was the only motive that made sense. But there was something else, she was sure of it. Male ego. Pride maybe. Jake didn't like the idea of Lexi finding someone else.

But was it that simple? She didn't know. The Jake who had stormed back into her life was vastly different from the man she had married. She could see it in his eyes, hear it in the scathing comments he voiced, and feel it in the almost palpable hatred that flared between them. Sadly for her, passion flared between them with the same if not greater force and to her constant shame she was incapable of withstanding the force of Jake's desire. No, not desire! Lust... and that self-knowledge was the most shaming of all.

Straightening, she glanced at the ring on her finger, once a symbol of eternal love, or so she had thought, now a cold band of possession, nothing more. Sadly she took the last few steps to the house.

She walked back into the salon and, collapsing on an over-stuffed sofa, she glanced around. Very elegant, the furniture, a mixture of antique and modern Italian, was complemented by a selection of exquisite porcelain and bronze statuettes, a huge ornate marble fireplace with a magnificently carved over-mirror, everything in the best taste.

She sighed. Her job had been her life for years; she was not used to being idle. She had gone to college with no great career ambition, but had assumed she would end up as a translator in the foreign office. Marrying Jake and getting pregnant had changed all that. She supposed in a way she had Jake to thank for her career in hotel management. It was an occupation she loved. She had discovered that she had a flair for adminis-tration and she enjoyed meeting a wide variety of people, but it looked very much as if the career Jake had given her he had ruthlessly taken away from her again.

Restless and ill at ease in the quiet splendour of the salon, she let her glance settle on the telephone on a small table by the fireplace. Leaping to her feet she crossed and picked it up dialling the number of the Piccolo Paradiso. She had every right to check up on her job, never mind that Lorraine was now in charge. Plus she felt guilty disappearing the way she had, even though it wasn't her fault. She should have rung earlier to make sure everything was running smoothly, and she would have done if Jake had not swept her into his bed. She squashed the quick flush of remembered pleasure, as Anna's voice echoed down the line.

'*Pronto. Le Piccolo Paradiso.*'

It was great to hear a familiar voice. 'Anna, it's me, Lexi—I——' Before she could finish her sentence Anna cut in, her voice bubbling with excitement.

'Aren't you the dark horse? All this time you had a husband, and what a husband! He's gorgeous. I can't think why you ever left him. But it's so romantic him finding you again, it made me cry——'

'You've met Jake...?' Lexi cut in, not in the least interested in the younger girl's romantic fairy-tale image of him.

'Of course, he was here this afternoon for a staff briefing. There are going to be a few changes, but he congratulated us all on our hard work for Mr Monicelli and hoped we would work as well for him. Wasn't that nice? And guess what? I'm the new senior receptionist, and Franco, after two weeks' training with the new computer Mr Taylor is having installed, is going to take over from Miss Lorraine as the manager.'

'Yes, very nice,' Lexi managed to get out, silently seething; obviously she was not indispensable, quite the reverse if Anna was to be believed, and that hurt... 'So, everything is going smoothly, no problems?' she couldn't help asking.

'You're not to worry about anything, Lexi, just relax and enjoy your gorgeous husband. I know I would if I were you. In fact, he's here again now, I've just sent coffee into the office for him and Miss Lorraine. Do you want me to put you through?'

'No,' Lexi snapped, 'it doesn't matter. I'll be in touch.' And she dropped the receiver into the cradle.

She wished she had never telephoned. Her pale lips tightened at the way Jake had so quickly organised her life, cutting her off from her career and her friends with ruthless efficiency. She stood up and walked slowly back out on to the terrace. She thrust her hands into the pockets of her dress, and strolled around the terrace, her head bent, lost in her own thoughts; she didn't notice the magnificent sunset. Jake was playing havoc with her life, her emotions, and she could see no way out. The fact that he had dashed straight back to Lorraine she tried to dismiss from her mind but it was there like a gnawing cancer eating at her self-esteem, her pride. Jake had destroyed her trust years ago and agreement or not, she did not trust him to be faithful to her. Had he found time to bed his mistress this afternoon? she wondered. Or maybe that was what he was doing now.

Suddenly a flash of light startled her and she jumped, her heart thudding. She sighed and looked around, surprised to notice that she had walked right around the house, and it was dark. The outside lanterns had switched on. For a long moment she gazed around. Lights glowed in the trees, illuminating the flowers and shrubs. She turned her head towards the house and outside the kitchen was a white wrought-iron dining-table surrounded by half a dozen chairs. Soft cushions in pink and blue picked up the colour of a huge parasol with an exquisite Chinese lantern suspended from its centre. A few comfortable loungers were spread around in front of the dining-room window along with a low table. As she watched, Maria bustled out on to the terrace, a loaded tray in her hand.

'Can I help?' Lexi asked.

'No, *signora*,' Maria declared disappearing back through the patio door into the kitchen.'

Lexi sighed and sat down on the nearest lounger. Lying back against the soft cushions, she stared up into the night sky; it was so peaceful, but the turmoil in her heart would not be stilled.

'Did you miss me?' A drawling voice made her heart leap, her eyes widen in shock.

'Jake...' She sat up, swinging her legs to the floor, and stared up into his shadowed face.

'Well, did you?' he asked, his hand reaching out to catch a tendril of her hair and twist it lightly around his finger, before curving it gently around her small ear, his finger lingering on the soft lobe and pulling gently.

He was still wearing the shorts and shirt, his hair somewhat rumpled and a day's stubble darkening his hard jaw. He looked incredibly sexy and his teasing smile promised everything. Lexi shook her head away from his hand. She was confused and angry. How did he manage to affect her like this? Every time he came near her, touched her, his masculinity hit her like a blow to the heart.

'Some half-hour,' she snapped, angry anew at his casual disregard for her feelings. She had come down earlier at his instigation only to find him gone, and gone to the lovely Lorraine. He had a damn cheek asking if she had missed him.

'You did miss me, Lexi, though getting you to admit it is probably impossible. Sorry about before, but I had an urgent call and had to leave.'

'Says you,' she scorned, knowing full well where he had been.

'At least I was only gone a couple of hours, Lexi darling.' Jake gave her a derisive smile. 'Unlike you, who vanished for years without a word.'

Lexi felt her temper flare, and getting to her feet she looked straight up into his hard face. 'And I'm sure you missed me,' she drawled scathingly, knowing very well that he had been desperate to get rid of her.

'Yes. Yes, I did.' His soft-voiced confession had Lexi's eyes flashing wide open in disbelief.

'Tell it to the marines,' she snorted inelegantly, and would have walked past him, but Jake caught her arm.

'That's your answer to everything, Lexi. Run away. I had hoped you might have matured in the last few years but it seems I was wrong, you're the same selfish child you always were.' His fingers bit into the flesh of her bare arm and she flinched at the pain. 'It doesn't matter to you who gets hurt—not your husband, your friends,

Meg and Tom.' His upper lip curled in a cynical sneer. 'Just as long as little Lexi has what she wants.'

He had some nerve calling her immature and selfish, but his mention of Meg did hit a nerve. 'I wrote to Meg,' she defended, ignoring the way her heart-beat accelerated as she stood next to Jake.

'Once, posted in Bahrain; the poor woman thought the white slavers had captured you.' One dark brow arched with sardonic amusement. 'You might fetch a good price, at that.'

His gaze roved over her in insolent appraisal. Much as she imagined a white slaver would look. Realising the idiocy of her thoughts—Jake might be a lot of things but a white slaver he was not—Lexi said, 'No,' her lips twitching with amusement. Knowing Meg, she should have realised the old woman would think of something like that. But Lexi had given the letter to a visiting Arab guest to post when he left, not wanting to reveal her whereabouts, too hurt. It was her one regret that she had not kept in touch with the old couple, but she hadn't wanted to be reminded of her old life at Forest Manor; it was too painful.

'So, you think it's amusing?' Jake's smile was chilling. 'Did it never occur to you we would worry, wonder for your safety? I was, and still am, your husband, responsible for you.'

'I'm sure you set Meg's mind at rest,' Lexi snapped and tried to jerk away from him as the full meaning of his words sank in. He had the cheek, the gall, to pretend their parting was her fault. 'You always had a way with words and women,' she said sarcastically as he pulled her violently back to him, anger flashing between them like lightning.

His dark eyes narrowed to mere slits as he looked down at her. 'God, but you're a bitch!' Rage darkened his rugged features, and Lexi gasped, her heart lurching in her breast. 'You don't care, you really don't care for anyone but yourself.'

'Isn't that the pot calling the kettle?' she spat back furiously.

'I know this,' Jake responded in a bitingly menacing voice. 'You strolled into our London apartment, agreed to our deal, and, before I could open the champagne, you were dashing out having informed me casually you were going on holiday and never wanted to see me again.' His free hand reached up and grasped a handful of her hair, pulling it loose from its slide and tangling in the red locks. 'You're a very beautiful woman, but you know how to put the knife in, Lexi; that was a master-touch, leaving the little wedding-anniversary present on the hall-table.'

'Sorry I couldn't do better,' she gritted, 'but I was short of cash at the time.' She was surprised he had even noticed the gift she had left, when he'd had his new love to occupy him.

'Oh, I got your message all right. Leave the poor sod a gift and he won't worry; after all, you were recovering from losing our child. Post-natal blues—naturally I would allow you a holiday, even though it was so hastily arranged. I called your precious Dr Bell and he was of course all in sympathy with the little wife. A holiday was the best cure; he had suggested it himself to you, and, as for your not wanting to see me, he assured me you didn't mean it—it was part of your depression, et cetera et cetera,' he drawled with icy cynicism. 'A week later, when I began looking for you, it was too late; you had vanished.'

'I'm amazed you bothered, in the circumstances,' Lexi said scathingly, while her mind absorbed the fact that Jake had looked for her. Why? She could not possibly have been wrong about what she saw and heard that day in their apartment. Could she? No. She shook her head.

'Foolishly, I was labouring under the impression that you were still depressed and might actually need me.' His strong features were harsh in the dim light. 'You thought you were clever, but not clever enough, Lexi. You will never make a fool of me or get away from me again, that I can promise.'

'That makes me quake in my shoes,' she snapped back defiantly. 'As I remember, you were never great on keeping a promise.' Thinking of his broken marriage vows, she felt an urge to hurt him as he had hurt her which compelled her to add, 'With your record I should be home free and wealthy in a few weeks.' He was a callous brute who had blackmailed her into his bed and she despised him for it. But the brush of his thigh against her, the warmth of his body ignited a trembling awareness.

Jake jerked her head back. 'You couldn't resist reminding me. But this time it will be different. I have enough money to last a hundred lifetimes, enough to satisfy even you, and, my God, I intend to make damn sure you satisfy me, Lexi,' he drawled cynically. 'And after this morning I don't think you will find our reconciliation so arduous.'

She stared at him. She had the strangest feeling she was missing something vital, but then their eyes met and fused, and her legs turned to jelly at the harsh intention she saw in his eyes. 'No.' Her neck hurt as he pulled her head further back. 'No, you can't do this to me,' she cried desperately.

'Yes,' Jake said thickly. He dragged her towards him, and she struggled, hitting out at him with her clenched fist, anywhere she could reach. 'I can do what I like with you, my less than loving wife.'

'I hate you...' His dark head descended. She tried to twist away, but his superior strength defeated her.

'Then I'd better give you reason,' he growled, his hard mouth grinding down on her, pushing her lips apart against her teeth. Her head swam, and she was sinking beneath the savage onslaught of his plundering possession. Jake's head lifted and she gasped for air.

'What the hell—Maria?' he snarled and Lexi staggered on trembling legs; she was free.

She sank down on to the lounger, breathing hard. She raised her hand to her mouth, a trembling finger tracing her swollen lips.

Jake looked down, his black brows jerking together as he saw her gesture. 'You will not wipe me out of your life as easily again, and don't you forget it,' he grated angrily, and, turning, walked towards where Maria was setting the table.

Lexi heard his brief instruction to the housekeeper. 'Hold the meal fifteen minutes, Maria.' And she watched with hurt, angry eyes as Jake strode into the house.

Dinner was a silent affair. Lexi tried to avoid looking at the man opposite her. Jake had walked back on to the terrace five minutes earlier and, with a curt instruction to Maria to serve the meal, had issued an equally curt command to Lexi.

'Sit down and eat.' He pulled out a chair for her as he did so.

Lexi did as he instructed, taking the chair he offered. He had changed into a pair of dark pleated slacks and a crisp white shirt, and looked cool and somehow remote, which suited Lexi perfectly as she had no desire to speak to him; she was still seething from their last encounter. She sipped at her glass of wine and pushed the pasta around on her plate, making little attempt to eat it.

'More wine?' Jake's cool voice broke the silence.

'No, thank you.'

His blue eyes narrowed for a second on her mutinous face. Then he topped up his glass and raising it to his mouth drained it, as much as to say she wasn't worth talking to.

Lexi shot him a look of loathing. Damn him! He was so controlled, so sure of his own diabolical power to make all obey him. Would nothing dent the overwhelming arrogance of the man? She took another sip of wine. 'Tell me, Jake, how long is your sojourn in Italy likely to last? I seem to remember you were a workaholic, not at all the type to sit around smelling the roses.'

Deliberately he forked some more pasta into his mouth and slowly chewed while his deep blue eyes, reflecting the lantern's glow in their depths, raked over her face and the hint of cleavage revealed by the open neck of her dress and then back to her face.

'A week, perhaps two.' His dark lashes lowered seductively over his gleaming eyes. 'Surely you're not in so much of a hurry to return to England that you would begrudge me my first holiday in years.' He smiled, a sinister twist of his lips, and added mockingly, 'A second honeymoon, if you like.'

'I don't like,' she spat back, and, lifting her glass to her mouth, drained the contents.

'Oh, come on, Lexi, stop this nonsense.' His voice had a sharp edge. 'We're both caught in the same trap. A savage passion we both hate but can't deny. Why lie, Lexi?' Jake demanded, an odd bitterness roughening his tone. 'You're my wife. We're here together in one of the loveliest places on earth.' He glanced around the floodlit gardens and the ocean beyond, his knowing gaze coming back to rest on Lexi. 'Forget your silly resentment and enjoy yourself.'

'Silly resentment?' She almost choked on the words. 'Is that what you call being blackmailed, having one's job, one's life taken over.'

'I'm your husband,' he said quietly with an edge of steel. 'Blackmail apart. I have the right to keep you, and, as for your job, look on it as a learning process. Now you are eminently suitable to take care of my various homes and play hostess to the cosmopolitan collection of business acquaintances I am obliged to entertain occasionally. As my social secretary and mother of my children you will have more than enough to keep you occupied.'

Various homes! And she just bet that included her old home. Social secretary? What a flaming nerve... 'Won't that be stepping on your so-faithful Lorraine's toes?' she queried derisively, hiding her pain at his mention of the word 'mother'.

'Jealous, Lexi?'

'In your dreams,' she jeered.

'Lorraine is a brilliant businesswoman, but does not suffer fools gladly; she is far too outspoken for the social niceties, and a homemaker she is not...' Jake's eyes gleamed with latent amusement. 'Whereas you are perfect for the role. Your upbringing as a diplomat's daughter has taught you how to mix with anyone. Your gift for languages, your experience looking after the wealthy clientele at the Piccolo Paradiso, all conspire to make you the ideal wife for a man in my position.'

'I wasn't aware blackmailers needed a social secretary.' She gazed at him with utter loathing. What he had said made a horrible kind of sense, and she believed him, but it hurt to finally hear the truth. Jake would carry on as he always had with the lovely Lorraine, while Lexi would be little more than a glorified housekeeper and mother of his children, wheeled out on social occasions as his polite, eminently suitable little wife.

'Enough.' Jake slapped his napkin on the table, and, reaching across, he grabbed her hand curving around the wine glass. 'Stop these foolish recriminations, Lexi. Accept you are my wife.'

'Do I have a choice?' she asked dully.

Jake regarded her with unwavering scrutiny, as if searching for something she had no knowledge of, then said with stark cynicism, 'No.'

'I didn't think so.' Bitterness laced her tone.

'Let me do the thinking for both of us. Life will be a lot easier.'

The touch of his long fingers, the intensity in his dark eyes stopped the scathing words she was about to utter. Instead, she could only gasp helplessly as he uncurled her fingers from the stem of the glass and raised her hand to his mouth, pressing a soft kiss into her palm before lacing her fingers with his own.

'Tomorrow we start our holiday.' Jake stood up, dragging her to her feet. He walked to the top of the table and she had to follow on her side. They met and his other hand grasped her shoulder. He stared down into the pale oval of her face, noting her defiant expression. 'Forget the past.'

'And enjoy a holiday?' Lexi sneered. 'I'm not that good an actress.'

'It doesn't make any difference. You don't have to act in bed,' Jake said tautly. 'I can easily seduce you, and we both know it.'

His confident assertion was true, and she hated him all the more for knowing it. 'No...' she muttered.

'Yes...' he asserted as his hand left her shoulder and gently touched her mouth, where the soft contours of her lips had swollen at the force of Jake's kiss. She shivered at his touch.

'I'm sorry if I hurt you earlier,' Jake murmured with a faintly sardonic smile, as he noted her involuntary response.

Lexi gasped as the soft pad of his thumb gently caressed her lip, sending tremors up and down her spine. She knew she should stop him, break away, but the deep husky voice, the romantic setting, all conspired against her common sense.

'You have lovely lips; let me kiss it better,' he murmured.

His thumb teased her lips and tongue. She trembled and saw no point in denying him; she couldn't. She was trapped as surely as Jake was by the physical desire that flared between them at the slightest glance. She hated it, and hated him, but she could not stop her body swaying towards him.

'I've eaten, but I'm hungry again for you,' Jake husked, and without further words he swept her up in his arms and carried her into the house...

CHAPTER EIGHT

'FOR heaven's sake, Lexi! Will you hurry up?'

She heard Jake shouting right through the house and, with one last glance at her reflection in the dressing-table mirror, she patted her loosely pinned chignon and flinging her bag over her shoulder dashed out of her room. Today they were going to Pompeii, and by the sound of it Jake was in a hurry to get started. It was his fault she was late, she thought mutinously. Instead of Maria delivering her coffee to her room this morning, it had been Jake and before she could drink it he had climbed into bed with her. Her lips were still swollen from his kisses, and the rest of her body still glowed from his loving, though it galled her to have to admit it...

She sighed as she walked down the stairs. Jake was an enigma; from the first night together in the villa when he had swept her up to bed and made passionate love to her and then got out of her bed and returned to his own, she had been trying to figure him out. But without much success. Though in all honesty she had nothing much to complain about. That was, if she discounted the fact that she had lost her job, and was being black-mailed, she told herself drily.

When she had first known Jake she had been young and naïve. Now she congratulated herself that she was mature and sophisticated enough to meet him on his own terms. There was no point in denying the sexual chemistry between them, and she knew Jake was as much a hostage to the passion that flared between them as she was herself. The hatred they felt for each other only lent

their passion an added edge, a dark desire, a battle of
body and wills that turned the lovemaking into a fight
for control, and the bed into a battlefield with Jake
always walking away victorious.

Inwardly Lexi sighed. 'Lovemaking'—that was a mis-
nomer. Love didn't enter into their relationship. A wry
smile twisted her full lips as she reached the bottom of
the stairs. Lust, yes, an indefinable animal attraction;
whatever label she put on it didn't really matter. At least
she was mature enough to accept it as just that, without
having to label it 'love'. But sometimes, in the afterglow
of passion, when Jake with almost indecent haste dis-
tanced himself from her, as though to touch her in anything other than passion disgusted him, she could not
help feeling, deep down in the darkest reaches of her
mind, his callous rejection, and grieving the loss of the
tactile, loving man she had first married.

'Lexi,' she heard the roar, and ran the short distance
through the hall and out of the front door.

Jake was standing holding open the door of the lethal
looking black Bugatti, a frown on his handsome face.
Her heart lurched in her breast; he was wearing stylish
Armani tailored shorts in a navy linen and a lighter blue
polo shirt. The Mediterranean sun had darkened his skin
to a deep, polished bronze, and he looked as lethal as
the car.

'At last, woman. Who was it told me we had to visit
Pompeii in the morning, before the sun got too hot?' he
queried mockingly, then grinned wickedly.

She knew what the grin was for. 'And who was it delayed a poor girl in her bed while he had his evil way
with her?' she teased back easily.

A slow, sexy smile lit his blue eyes. 'Touché. Now get
in the car.'

It was like a day out of time. Jake relaxed completely
from the cold, guarded man Lexi had become used to
the past few days and became a typical tourist for the

day. Lexi did not question the change. Her nerves were shot and she was glad of the respite from the constant tension that had fizzed like an unexploded bomb between them; the least spark and they were at each other's throats. With a sigh of contentment she settled back in the passenger seat of the monster car and, straightening the short skirt of her simple blue sundress over knees, she determined to enjoy herself.

Having parked the car in the area provided, Jake surprised her by taking her hand, and, laughing together at a middle-aged tourist buried under a mountain of cameras, hand in hand they made their way to the entrance of the ancient city. Hundreds of tourists spilled in an ever-increasing horde from the dozens of coaches arriving seemingly every minute, the jostling crowd and the multitude of different languages filling the hot morning air.

A small, thick-set old Neapolitan man grabbed Jake's arm. 'Guide, sir? I, Luigi, am the best.'

Jake glanced at the old man. 'I don't...'

'Yes, let's hire him,' Lexi urged. 'It is a huge place and I hate to admit it but, although I've been once before, I'm not that knowledgeable.'

It was a brilliant decision; Luigi, with speed and a bit of deft manoeuvring, ushered Jake and Lexi through the crowd, the entrance fee paid, and up to the Porta Marina, the ancient gate that the public had to use to enter the city, in a matter of minutes.

Jake's hand squeezed Lexi's, and she glanced questioningly up into his handsome face. 'You were right, Luigi is worth the money solely for getting us to the front of the queue and in.' He smiled.

'Stop.' Luigi's upraised hand and the fact that he had planted himself directly in their path meant they could do no other but obey, and for the next few hours the little man managed to fill their heads with more facts about the ancient city than any guidebook could possibly accomplish.

'First, I give you the background and then we proceed,' Luigi told them authoritatively. 'Pompeii was a settlement and first given its name in the eighth century BC. Built at the end of an ancient lava flow from what was considered the benign Mount Vesuvius, one hundred and thirty feet above sea-level at the mouth of the river Sarno, it was for centuries the trading place between the north and south Italian states, conquered by many and occupied by a few; it had a population of twenty-five thousand. Then Vesuvius, suddenly, on the twenty fourth of August, 79 AD, shortly after midday, violently erupted, blacking out the sun. Red-hot volcanic matter rained down on the hapless people, buildings crumbled and then, when the ash fell, all forms of life were extinguished. For centuries it was considered a place of evil and one thousand, six hundred years passed before excavations were begun and a further hundred and fifty years before it could be said the city was rediscovered.'

'He can certainly talk,' Jake murmured softly in Lexi's ear, 'but he knows his stuff.' And, following the little man, they strode up the steep paved ramp that led to the gate's two archways; the left hand arch had been designed for pedestrians and the other for horse-drawn carts, the ruts in the stone-paved road were deep and easily discernible, and the same gauge was still used on today's railways, Luigi informed them proudly.

'It's incredible!' Jake exclaimed, eyeing the streets and houses. 'Two thousand years on and one can see exactly how people lived.'

Lexi agreed and, walking beside him, watching the light in his eyes, the intensity with which he examined every aspect of the place, she was filled with a bittersweet memory. He had shown the same enthusiasm years ago when they had first wandered around Castle Howard.

The Temple of Venus, the mighty open space of the Forum, they wandered through them all, and gazed in awe at the remains of the Basilica dating back to pre-Roman times. The triumphal arches of the temple of Jupiter, and the Temple of Apollo caused Jake to comment, 'They certainly hedged their bets where their gods were concerned.'

'But it did no good,' Luigi piped up. 'Nature is all-powerful, always has been and always will be.'

'I think we have a homespun philosopher for a guide.' Jake bent his dark head and whispered in Lexi's ear, she glanced up at him, a smile curving her full lips.

'I think you may be right,' she murmured as Luigi led them into the Forum Baths.

'See: hot and cold baths; central heating; drainage; everything you would find in a modern city today. They had everything we have today. Nothing changes,' Luigi declared, and as they walked on he pointed out what had once been a dress shop, and two doors down a barber's shop.

Grinning at Jake, Luigi said, 'Then as now, the lady went to the boutique, and the man visited the barber and waited to pick up his lady and pay the bill. Nothing changes.' Jake and Luigi chuckled in masculine bonding, while Lexi gritted her teeth and grinned, thinking, Male chauvinists.

Further on they stared in awe at the brilliantly coloured wall-paintings in the Villa of the Mysteries. Outside again, they gazed sombrely through iron bars into a warehouse where dozens of common household items, bowls and jugs and figures, an arm, a torso lay, all coated in the pale grey stone.

In a glass case lay the body of a young woman, obviously pregnant, petrified in stone for all eternity. Lexi shivered and, freeing her hand from Jake's, walked away. She looked around at the high walls, the scrolled pillars, the streets and houses, her eyes misting with tears.

She felt an arm curve around her shoulder, strong fingers kneading the soft flesh. 'Are you OK, Lexi? The heat getting to you?' Jake's deep voice asked quietly. She glanced up through thick lashes, and noted the concern in his dark eyes.

'Yes, no. I don't know,' she murmured.

'Reminded you, did it? The pregnant woman.'

Her eyes widened. Could this be Jake, the ruthless entrepreneur? Since when had he become so sensitive? 'Yes, a little perhaps. I miscarried, but that woman lost everything, and it suddenly struck me, even with all these people around——' she gestured with a wave of her hand at the dozens of tourists as they strolled along '—there is something about this place, an aura of sadness, doom.' She unconsciously shook her head to dispel the feeling of melancholy.

'I wasn't much help when you lost the baby, was I, Lexi?'

His words stopped her in her tracks, and she could think of nothing to say. The pressure of his hand on her shoulder turned her around to face him. With his free hand he lifted her chin. 'I'm truly sorry, Lexi. I let you down, the very moment you needed me most.'

The sincerity in his tone, the deep regret in his indigo eyes convinced Lexi he was telling the truth as he saw it. 'Oh. I wouldn't say that.' She lowered her lashes, suddenly confused by Jake's confession. 'I was depressed, not really aware of anything very much.' If she had been more alert to her surroundings she might have realised sooner that he was having an affair with Lorraine, the thought hit her. And, shrugging his hand off her shoulder, she added, 'I'm sure you did your best,' and moved on.

'No, damn it!' Jake caught her arm. 'No, I didn't. I was so caught up in my business troubles, I didn't give you as much attention as you deserved.'

Lexi glanced up at him. Business troubles. Looking back, she realised he had hinted as much at the time, but she had been too wrapped in her own grief to take much notice. Was he telling the truth? She studied his handsome face; his expression was stern but serious, and she was stunned by the depths of emotion she glimpsed fleetingly in his dark eyes.

'I couldn't talk about the loss of our son, it was too painful. But I want you to know, Lexi. Whatever our differences, when and if we have another child, I will be there for you every step of the way.'

A lump formed in her throat and she blinked hard to vanquish the threatening tears. 'Thank you for that,' she said softly. She believed him, all of it. So where did that leave her? she wondered. Could it be that Jake had turned to Lorraine simply for sex, when she herself had lost interest in it? It would explain why he hadn't married Lorraine. But did it make his betrayal any less if that was the case? She didn't know... and, catching the side of Jake's shirt, she added, 'Come on. Poor Luigi is going to lose us if we don't hurry up.' She urged him forward.

'You OK?' Jake asked, slipping his arm around her shoulder, a rather wry smile twitching the corners of his hard mouth at her blunt changing of the subject.

'Of course.' Lexi smiled back. But his confession had jolted her more than she cared to admit.

Striding along after the tireless Luigi, they walked along streets with pavements and gutters, a bar with a classic painting on the wall of a group of men cheating at a game of cards with the aid of a mirror.

'See, nothing changes.' Luigi laughed, indicating the painting, but Lexi was barely listening.

For the past few days she had lived in a sexual daze. But Jake's words had reminded her exactly what she was committed to. He had said she owed him a child, but she had conveniently blocked the message from her mind. She had nursed a hazy idea: a few months of Jake and sex, till his desire for her was burnt out, and then freedom. Suddenly it wasn't so simple. What if she got pregnant and had his child? She knew after losing one child that if she was lucky enough to get a second chance she would never be able to walk away from her own baby. She cast a sidelong glance at Jake. His interest was captured by the lead piping at the side of yet another villa, and for a moment she studied his rugged features. Jake was not the sort of man to let her walk away with a child. What he owned, he kept. She shivered at the thought of a lifetime with Jake without love, never knowing if she could trust him. Worse: how would a child feel, brought up in that kind of atmosphere?

'Cold?' Jake's demand and husky laugh broke into her chaotic thoughts.

'No, no,' she reiterated and, pointing to the lead pipe, she said the first thing that came into her head, 'I suppose, with your being in construction, this is doubly interesting to you.'

He glanced down at her, his blue eyes narrowing, his dark face suddenly guarded. 'Not really, my business is much more diversified now. I have little to do with construction. After the collapse of the property market a few years back I concentrated my efforts on finance.'

'Finance...' But the Jake she remembered had been a builder, a self-made man, and mad keen on his Docklands development. He had told her once he had taken a business and finance course at night-school, but she thought he would have stuck with construction.

'Yes, with the help of our mutual friend Carl Bradshaw and his German connections, I made a killing in Deutchmarks, when the pound fell out of the ERM and was devalued. It's amazing how easy it is to make money when you have a beautiful mercenary woman as an incentive,' he drawled mockingly.

Lexi wished she had kept her mouth shut; his crack was aimed at her. At least she thought it was, and in a rush of honesty she told him, 'I never wanted your money, Jake; in fact I've never looked at the account you opened for me, not since I left England.'

'Do you know, I almost believe you.' Jake hugged her and pushed her in front of him. 'Come on, the guide is escaping.'

Inexplicably Lexi's heart felt lighter as Luigi led them into the House of Vetii, a villa restored almost completely intact, and perhaps the most notorious in Pompeii, known for its pornographic paintings and statue. Within minutes Lexi could see why as she followed behind Luigi. Lexi stopped and turned bright scarlet at the statue in front of her. She heard Jake's chuckle behind her, but didn't dare turn around as Luigi burst into speech.

'The poor man suffered from an uncommon disease, as you can see.' And Lexi could see all too clearly the exaggerated masculinity of the man. 'A state of permanent readiness, shall I say.' His old face split with a huge grin. 'Many male tourists ask me how to contract this disease.' And with an arch of his bushy eyebrows, and an open palmed salute he added, 'But unfortunately, I cannot say.' And cackled with laughter at his own joke.

Lexi felt Jake's arms curve around her waist to hold her firmly against him, the back of her legs through the fine fabric of her sundress brushing against his thighs; she could feel the warmth of his breath at her throat.

'I can,' Jake whispered teasingly in her ear. 'All a man has to do is stay around you, Lexi, darling. You keep me in that state permanently.'

Herself and how many other women? she wondered, a flash of pain—or was it jealousy—piercing her breast. 'Jake,' she admonished. She could feel the stirring of his masculine interest all too plainly against her. 'There are people around,' she hissed in embarrassment.

'Shame.' Jake gave an exaggerated sigh and Lexi, pulling free, dashed after Luigi.

For the rest of the tour through the house, Lexi hardly noticed the magnificent wall paintings or the lovely garden; she was too intensely aware of Jake. He had caught up with her and rested one arm possessively over her shoulders, his long stride slowed to match hers, the brush of his thigh against her leg, the warmth of his hard body, the musky male scent of him all conspired to make her pulse-rate rocket. She tried to tell herself it was all the walking, the stifling heat of the noonday sun, but she knew she was only fooling herself.

'You're very quiet,' Jake said softly as they walked once more down yet another paved street. 'Had enough for one day?'

'It is rather hot, and the crowds...' She trailed off as Luigi stopped once more, but she was flattered at Jake's evident concern.

'We now go to the great Amphitheatre; today we still build a sports stadium in much the same design. Nothing changes. The only new inventions since the wheel are the new power sources, new ways to kill each other——'

'Very true, Luigi,' Jake interrupted the old man. 'But my wife has had enough for one day—the heat.'

'I see, I see. It is lunch time.' Luigi smiled, his dark eyes sliding over Jake with his protective arm around Lexi. 'Also, I think you enjoy a siesta, no?' His black eyes sought Jake's and he started to laugh. 'As I say, nothing changes. You marry, you make love, you make babies.' Jake's responsive chuckle mingled with the older man's laughter as Luigi led them speedily to the exit.

Lexi looked at Luigi, and then sideways at Jake. His eyes were crinkled at the corners in amusement, his firm mouth relaxed in a singularly masculine grin; he looked carefree, happy and vitally male.

'A siesta sounds good to me, sweetheart,' Jake drawled turning his glittering blue eyes down to capture hers.

It was at that moment it hit her like a thunderbolt. She loved Jake. Luigi was right, 'you marry, you make love, you make babies', and she realised, staring at Jake, that that was exactly what she wanted, had probably always been what she wanted with this man. She blinked and tore her gaze away from his handsome face, unable to answer the sensual message in Jake's eyes, too afraid she would give herself away completely. 'Whatever you say,' she murmured, and didn't see the flash of anger darken his bright eyes at her dull response.

In the car, Lexi laid her head back against the head-rest and closed her eyes. Jake had paid Luigi hand-somely and promised they would return, and she had smilingly accepted the old man's congratulations on having such a handsome and generous husband. But now, in the close confines of the car with Jake's strong body only inches from her own, his attractive face set in a look of determined concentration as he urged the car along the treacherous winding coast-road, avoiding the wild antics of most of the Italian drivers, she was left to her own thoughts, and they were anything but pleasant.

She could not believe her own stupidity. When Jake had blackmailed his way back into her life, she had told herself she hated him, and burnt with resentment at the ease with which he could tumble her into his bed. But at the same time she congratulated herself on being more than a match for him. She was quite capable of meeting him on the same sophisticated sexual level as the rest of his friends, Lorraine in particular. Now she recognised the depths of her own self-deception.

Married or not, five years' celibacy should have told her something. She was not the type to sleep with a man without love—not that Jake *slept* with her, the hurtful thought flashed in her mind; he made a point of leaving her bed and returning to his own... She had pretended to herself she didn't care, when in reality she cared far too much. She had loved him as a teenager and she still did. For years she had deceived herself into believing she hated him when in fact it had simply been the only way she could get through life without him, a way of masking the deep pain his betrayal had caused her.

'Do you want to stop for lunch?' Jake's voice interrupted her reverie, her eyes flashed open and she looked at Jake, then just as quickly away again.

'No, thank you. I'm not hungry,' she said flatly. She just wanted to get back to the villa and lock herself in her bedroom. The thought of sitting in a restaurant making polite conversation with Jake was an added strain she could do without. It was bad enough realising she still loved him. She needed to be on her own for a while, time to sort out her emotions, decide where she went from here.

A growing sense of despair settled in her heart as, with a grinding of gears, the car speeded up. After Jake's revelation about the baby they had lost, they had seemed to reach a new understanding this morning. But now, with the fear of revealing her love for him uppermost in her mind, they had slid back into the familiar tension-packed atmosphere of the past few days. Lexi didn't know what she could do about it.

Without speaking they drove through Sorrento and along Amalfi Drive. She chanced a swift sidelong glance at Jake. He was frowning, his dark eyes narrowed against the sun, his mouth a grim straight line; her laughing companion of the morning had changed into a darkly brooding, dangerous man.

She looked down at her clasped hands folded neatly in her lap, and was lost again in her own painful thoughts. Jake wanted her but he didn't love her. How could she live the rest of her life with a man who did not love her and whom she did not trust? It was hopeless...

Jake, bringing the car to a screeching halt outside the front door of the villa, made her sit up and take notice. But, before Lexi had managed to unfasten her safety-belt, Jake was out of the car and had the passenger door open and was reaching in to help her; his hand closed firmly over her upper arm and he almost dragged her from the car.

'Move it,' he snapped and his voice sounded rough. He led her into the house and up the wide staircase, his anger a tangible force in the still air.

'Where's the fire?' she tried to joke but, as her eyes clashed with his, she had her answer—it was in the glistening depths of Jake's eyes. Her pulse raced, a sudden heat igniting in her lower stomach.

'You know...' One dark brow arched cynically as he pushed her before him into his bedroom, his fingers gripping the flesh of her arm. He shut the door behind him and leant back against it, roughly pulling her into the hard heat of his long body.

'Luigi was right, nothing changes,' he rasped savagely, and she caught her breath as his lips moved against hers. 'You're running away from me again, and I won't tolerate it.'

Lexi, running away! With his long arms like bands of steel around her waist, she knew she had to be hearing things. She leant back and raised puzzled eyes to his, taking in the hard planes of his ruggedly chiselled features. 'Unless I'm dreaming, I am very much here.' She quipped, trying to sound casual, to defuse the tension cracking around them.

'Physically, yes. But mentally you ran away ages ago, as we left Pompeii.' His eyes narrowed fractionally, and she sensed the anger lying beneath the surface of his control. 'You did it in London, listened and agreed with me, and then vanished. Those innocent eyes haze with purple and it's as if a curtain has drawn across your mind, shutting out anything and anyone.' His warm breath fanned her temple. 'I'm damned if I'm going to let you get away with it again.'

'Why?' she said simply. 'You told me days ago it was my body alone that interested you.'

'I've changed my mind; it's not solely a woman's prerogative.' Jake taunted and his hands pulled her close so that she was made all too conscious of his arousal. 'I want to know your every thought.'

'Taking me in anger is hardly likely to make me bare my soul to you——' Lexi drew an unsteady breath '—even if I wanted to.' And she did want to; she ached to tell him she loved him, let go of her emotions completely, but she dared not. He had hurt her too much in the past. Suddenly the thought sneaked into her head: surely it was a step in the right direction if Jake actually did want to know her better, deepen the relationship. She loved him, and if their marriage was to have any chance at all it was up to her to try and make it work, to try and win Jake's love. That was always supposing he was capable of such an emotion, she thought wryly.

'I sometimes doubt you have a soul,' Jake snarled. 'The only way to reach you is this,' he muttered with menacing softness against her lips, just before his mouth ground down on hers.

She sighed, her breath mingling with his. Their tongues touched, danced, writhed, and she felt herself falling, down, down, down once more into the depths of desire, a passionate flood of need only Jake could arouse.

Suddenly he moved, thrusting her away from him. 'Get undressed, Lexi,' he said deliberately, swiftly pulling his shirt over his head, his hands going to the fastening of his shorts. 'Come on...!' A hard dark gleam sprang alive in his eyes. 'I'm in no mood for patience...'

She stood transfixed, her eyes roaming over his naked chest, the dark whorls of body hair glistening in the hot afternoon sun. A strange languor hung in the air and, as if in a dream, Lexi did as he said, whisking her simple sundress over her head, but all the time she watched as he slid his bermudas down his thighs along with his briefs. Even when he stepped towards her, his fingers digging into the skin of her shoulders as he pulled her close, she could not tear her gaze away from his strongly muscled, virile frame. She knew she should be afraid, there was a menacing calculation about his movements, but oddly she wasn't. She loved him, and she wanted him...

Lexi sucked in her breath and raised her eyes to his, and when she met his darkly unyielding expression she trembled, but something gave her the courage to try and deflect his anger.

'Why hurry, Jake?' she asked flirtatiously. Lowering her long lashes half over her eyes, she reached out a finger and trailed it lightly down the hard column of his throat. 'We can take Luigi's advice, and have a siesta,' she declared huskily.

She had surprised him. His forbidding expression lightened perceptibly, his sensuous mouth tilted at the corners in the beginnings of a smile. 'Damn you, Lexi...you confuse me to hell.' A masculine chuckle escaped him, his anger waning. 'But I wouldn't have it any other way.' And, swinging her in his arms, he carried her to the bed, his body following her down; he shifted his weight until he was lying heavily across her chest, crushing the soft roundness of her breasts against his chest.

His mouth came down on hers in a hard, hot kiss. His hands slid down her body, along her thighs, pushing her legs apart. He kissed her again, a ruthless demand that contained the lingering traces of anger and masculine frustration. She felt a shiver of fear ripple down her spine, but somehow she knew he would not hurt her, and she opened her mouth to welcome him, surprising him yet again. He reared back, a question in his navy blue eyes.

Lexi smiled and deliberately lifted her small hand and stroked the firm skin of his stomach, and lower, entranced by the lightning response of his aroused body. Jake moved over her, his tongue driving into her mouth, and she had the feeling she was being seduced, physically dominated, as if he needed to show her he was in control.

'You want me, you can't help yourself. Whatever else you are, Lexi, in this you are mine and mine alone,' he husked, and lowered his head to suck on the rosy tips of her breasts, bringing them to throbbing peaks of desire; his fingers slid down between her parted thighs, and began moving in quick sensuous patterns that had Lexi trembling all over.

Lexi's eyes widened to their fullest extent, her body arched, the breath nearly crushed from her, but she was ready for him as Jake drove into her soft, moist centre with a fierce aggression that made her shudder on the pinnacle of delight. For a timeless space he did not move, making her aware of the full weight of his possession, while withholding the release she craved. She cried his name. The sound of his name on her lips shattered Jake's control. Their bodies, bathed in perspiration, slid together, rocking, moving in a shimmering white-hot culmination so closely entwined they spun as one into the fiery rapture of climax.

Ages later Lexi groaned, but still she clung to Jake, reluctant to move, if not incapable of movement, she thought fuzzily. Finally, she lifted heavy lashes to find Jake staring down at her. She smiled lovingly, her soft gaze roaming over his darkly flushed face.

Jake rolled on to his side, one large hand supporting his head; a smile curved his lips and sparkled in his eyes. His other hand deliberately stroked across her full breasts. 'I could easily get addicted to this siesta idea,' he offered lazily, rubbing his mouth lightly against hers. 'But right now, I need lunch.'

It was hardly the words of love she had been dreaming about, but it was a step in the right direction, she thought with hope in her heart.

CHAPTER NINE

LEXI, wearing a brief black bikini with a floaty black and pink silk patterned overblouse on top, and carrying a matching beach bag, the whole ensemble a present from Jake, strolled out on to the terrace and down the steps to the swimming-pool. Shrugging out of her shirt, she flopped listlessly on to a convenient sun-lounger, rummaged in her bag and found her sunglasses and pushed them on her nose. Sweeping her long hair round to one side of her neck, she lay back down on the lounger and tried to relax.

The heat was almost unbearable, in the nineties; she glanced around the colourful sweet-scented garden, the pool, and the view of the sea beyond. She had watched Jake leave after a shared informal lunch in the comfort of the air-conditioned kitchen. He had said he had business to attend to... Maybe he had... right at this moment she didn't give a damn!

Tomorrow it would be exactly two weeks since she had moved into the villa. This morning, as she had been idly looking through her diary, ruefully reflecting on the fact it had been chock-full of appointments up until Jake had stormed back into her life and cost her her job, it had suddenly hit her. She was a week overdue with her period. She tried telling herself it wasn't important. What was a week, for heaven's sake? But, for a girl who had never been so much as a day late except the one time she had been pregnant, the week was beginning to assume gigantic proportions.

Instinctively her hand stroked across her flat stomach, her feelings ambivalent. She had always longed for a

151

child after her tragic miscarriage, she freely admitted, but in the circumstances...

Restless, she jumped to her feet and dropping her glasses on the lounger she took a running dive head-first into the pool. The shock of the cool water was a balm to her overheated flesh. She swam a few quick lengths and then turned over on to her back and floated, her mind idly wandering over the past.

Yesterday Jake had taken her in his power-boat to Capri. They had strolled around the town and Jake had ushered her into a myriad designer boutiques, and insisted on buying her a host of clothes: the bikini she was wearing now, and an extravagant evening gown he told her she had to have for a special engagement tonight. Another of his secrets!

Sexually they were compatible, the chemistry between them explosive. Jake made love to her every day—sometimes he came to her bed at night, sometimes by this very pool. He just had to look at her a certain way, a touch of his hand; their passion for each other was insatiable.

Ever since their trip to Pompeii, when Jake had talked about the loss of their child, they seemed to have developed a kind of rapport. They had long, interesting, sometimes argumentative conversations about music, art, the state of Italian politics, which was a subject one could debate a lifetime without running out of steam, Lexi thought with a grin. She could almost convince herself that her plan to win his love was succeeding, except for the fact that they still never woke up in the morning sharing the same bed. Lexi had not the nerve to ask why. She wasn't sure she would like the answer.

Jake never shared his thoughts, his inner self, as he had when they were first married. Though, her own innate honesty forced her to admit, she was just as guilty in that respect. Her pride and fear of being hurt contrived to prevent her revealing her own feelings.

Things could be worse, Lexi conceded, though he had infuriated her about her car. Jake had arranged for it to be delivered back to the hotel, saying there was no way he would allow her to drive the 'old wreck' and, in any case, strictly speaking it belonged to the hotel. He might as well have said she could not go out without him, because that was what it boiled down to. But, to give Jake his due, he had taken her out every day. To Sorrento, Naples and some of the smaller islands, and they had had fun. Jake was a good companion when he wanted to be, she mused. But one major problem was the same as always—Lorraine. The woman was forever calling Jake, and he dashed off at the summons. Lexi knew it was business, and she didn't really think Jake was still having an affair with Lorraine, mainly because she doubted that even Jake had that much stamina, given how often he and Lexi made love. But a nagging suspicion about the relationship haunted Lexi. There was something...

'Aghhh...' she screamed, a second before her head slid under the water. A hand had caught her ankle, pulling her deeper and deeper beneath the water, and then a strong arm wrapped around her and she was shooting back to the surface. Choking and spluttering, trying to sweep her tangled mass of hair from her face and at the same time dry her eyes, she screeched, 'What the hell did you do that for?' And tossing back her head, she looked up into the wickedly laughing face of Jake.

Clasping her around the middle, he hauled her between his muscular thighs. His lips brushed hers and, grinning, he said, 'Sour grapes... You looked so relaxed floating around, while I've spent the last few hours hot and harassed driving into Naples. When I got back and saw you from the window I couldn't resist the temptation.'

'Pig,' she retaliated, whacking her hand through the water and splashing him in the face. He jumped back, his legs releasing her, and Lexi chuckled at his astonished expression.

'You wanna fight rough, babe?' Jake drawled in a mock American accent, before placing his hands on her shoulders and dunking her again.

Lexi stayed under the water and swam between his long legs. Surfacing behind him, she flung her arms around his neck and tried to pull him over backwards. But his superior strength showed as he put his hands behind him under her stomach and flipped her high in the air and she found herself swung up and over his head in a somersault to land flat on her back in the water.

'Had enough?' Jake taunted, hauling her up by the front clasp of her bikini top.

Treading water, she yelled, 'You beast!' It was all right for Jake, he was so much taller that he could stand on the bottom with no trouble, she fumed, and tried to splash him again. Their laughter echoed on the summer air, until Lexi let out a yelp as she realised Jake was waving the top of her bikini around his head. She folded her arms across her chest. 'Pervert, give me it back.'

'One down, one to go.' Jake let out a war cry and dived on top of Lexi. In a tangle of arms and legs they sank to the bottom of the pool.

When Lexi surfaced again, she was folded once more in Jake's strong thighs, one of his hands supported her back so she was almost lying on top of the water and in his other hand he was proudly holding aloft both parts of her bikini.

'To the winner, the spoils,' he crowed triumphantly.

Lexi's gaze slid over his broad shoulders up the strong line of his throat to his proud head; his hair was plastered to his skull and he looked like a young boy again. Her heart squeezed in her breast, she loved him so. He must have seen something of what she was feeling in her eyes because he said her name.

'Lexi.' Jake pulled her up, his dark head bent, blocking out the sun, all laughter gone, as his mouth brushed hers.

Naked in his arms, the water lapping softly around them, Lexi curved her slender arms around his neck, and, her lips parting, she kissed him back.

He groaned, his hands catching her legs and wrapping them around his waist, as his tongue darted into her mouth in quick, searching thrusts.

Lexi crossed her feet behind him and clung. His hands stroked round her waist and up to palm her breasts. She felt the force of his masculine aggression urgent between her thighs, only the flimsy fabric of his Spandex briefs and the tantalising brush of the water preventing his completing the act they both craved.

'Jake, we can't,' she whimpered as his teeth nipped the rigid peak of one breast.

'Lexi, we can.' He trailed the words up her breast and over her throat, to find her mouth. 'Trust me.'

'We'll drown,' she moaned.

'Only in each other.'

Lexi felt his hands under her thighs at the edge of his swimming-trunks, pushing them down. She gasped, and tightened her grip on his shoulders as he reared up and into her in one swift movement, his hands gripping her waist, he held her impaled by his masculine strength.

She had never felt anything so erotic in her life; the water gave a weightlessness to her limbs and the contrast of the cool water and the hot sun on her naked flesh, the driving force of Jake, her breasts buried in the soft, wet hair of his muscular chest, the muffled groans, the heady scent of flowers and sea air all combined to make it a tapestry of scent, sound, sight and sensational eroticism, culminating in a shuddering ecstasy.

'We didn't drown,' she whimpered, still clinging to Jake's neck as he half-swam and half-walked to the side of the pool and, lifting her up, he sat her on the edge, and then hauled himself up and proceeded to collapse flat on his back, his feet still dangling in the water.

'I promised myself we would try that before we have to leave,' Jake rasped breathlessly, and getting to his feet he added, 'It was even better than my fantasy.'

But Lexi had heard. She sat up, only then remembering she was naked, she bent her knees and clasped her hands defensively around them. 'Leave? When are you leaving?' she asked quietly.

Glancing up, her eyes lingered helplessly. Jake, with water still trickling down his glorious golden body, was beautifully made. Thick black hair shadowed down his bronzed body to a flat stomach, powerful long legs, and a blatant masculinity that made her shiver with remembered delight. She looked up into his eyes and was stunned by the flash of pain she thought she saw in their shadowed depths.

'*We——*' he accentuated the single word '——are leaving on Monday. I have to be in London for a meeting in the afternoon.' He glanced at the waterproof Rolex on his wrist. 'But for the moment I suggest you go and gild the lily; we have to go out in an hour.'

'Just like that, no discussion?' Lexi prompted. Rising to her feet, she walked to the lounger and picked up her shirt and slipped it on. Jake might be happy with his nudity, but she, stupidly maybe, found it difficult to behave naturally stark naked—a relic of her convent upbringing...

Jake watched her with cool, assessing eyes and, when she turned back to face him, his hand reached out and long fingers tipped up her chin. 'There's nothing to discuss; you're my wife, you go where I go. Don't try to make a battle out of it, Lexi.'

'I wasn't,' she told him steadily. 'But I would like to be kept informed. It is my life you're playing with,' she couldn't help sniping sarcastically. While in her heart she wondered how they could make love one minute and end up facing up like two strangers the next.

As if sensing her dilemma, Jake's hand slipped from her chin to her shoulder, his fingers squeezing her tender flesh. 'You worry too much.' His dark head bent and his lips brushed along her brow, rather like a father reassuring a child. 'And be assured, I'm not playing. I've never been more serious in my life. But we'll talk later, after the party.'

'Party?'

'Damn, it's supposed to be a secret. Your half-naked body never fails to scramble my brain,' he offered with a chuckle. 'Now, run along while I have a swim, there's a good girl.' And spinning her around he slapped a helping hand on her bottom. 'Later, we'll talk.'

Lexi fumed at his pat and chauvinistic attitude, and, without thinking, she spun back around and, catching Jake completely off guard, she planted both hands on his broad chest, stuck her foot behind him and pushed. He hit the water with a very satisfactory splash, and Lexi, arching one elegant eyebrow, stood smiling down at the spluttering, enraged male and drawled sarcastically, 'Have a nice swim, there's a good boy.' And, grinning, she ran back to the house.

Later, washed and dressed in the designer gown Jake had given her, a strapless creation with a deep jade-green bodice that lovingly traced the swell of her full breasts, nipped into her slender waist and fell to mid-calf in shimmering handkerchief layers of multi-shaded green chiffon, she walked into the salon, and she was not feeling quite so brave.

She stopped inside the door. Jake was leaning against the mantelshelf, his dark head bent over whatever it was he was turning over in his hand, and he looked dropdead gorgeous... There was no other way to describe him. His evening-jacket was cream and with it he wore a white silk dress-shirt and a rich blue bow-tie; the jacket was hanging open to reveal a matching blue cummerbund, and his other hand, in the pocket of his pants, pulled the fabric taut across his muscular thigh. She couldn't seem to drag her eyes away. Jake had always been a conservative dresser, but tonight he looked slightly flamboyant and all virile, powerful male.

Lexi swallowed with difficulty. 'I'm ready,' she managed to say steadily, and watched as Jake lifted his head from his contemplation of whatever he had in his hand.

His deep blue eyes blazed as he made no effort to hide his masculine appreciation, his gaze travelling with slow, sensual scrutiny from her mass of red hair clipped behind her small ears with matching pearl-studded combs, falling in a mass of curls over her shoulders, to her lovely, if rather wary face. She did not need much make-up, her softly tanned skin glowed with health, but she had paid special attention to her eyes, outlining their shape with a brown eyeliner, and a soft dusting of muted taupe shadow on her lids, finished off with a brown-black mascara to emphasise her long lashes.

Lexi had no idea how stunning and slightly exotic she looked, and Jake's continued silent survey was beginning to get to her. 'I said——'

'I heard.' Jake cut in, his brilliant eyes lifting from the soft curve of her breasts to her face. 'You really have grown up into the most seductive-looking woman it has ever been my pleasure to see,' he drawled softly and, straightening, laughed, a low, husky sound, as Lexi felt herself blush from head to toe.

'Surely you can't still be shy?' Jake grated softly, crossing the room in a few lithe strides. 'Though I must admit blushing becomes you.' And he reached out and caught her small hand in his.

The contact sent a shock of electrifying awareness through her slim body. She had only to look at him to recall the hard power of his male body in hers, the wet

satin skin beneath her seeking fingers. She raised her
eyes to his; his hair was still damp and fell in a slight
wave across his broad forehead. Her face burnt, her pulse
quickened. It wasn't fair that only one man should be
so fatally attractive to her, when she knew, sadly, there
must have been dozens of women in Jake's life over the
past few years. The thought rapidly cooled her fluttering
emotions.

'I want you to have this.' Jake's voice quivered along
her nerves, and she looked down to where her hand lay
in his in time to see him slip a diamond-encrusted gold
ring on to her wedding finger.

'What? Why?' she stammered, staring in amazement
at the glittering jewel, alongside the plain gold band. It
must have cost a fortune.

'Because it's necessary for the wife of a man in my
position.' His dark eyes sought and held hers, something
unfathomable in the indigo depths. 'And, as I quickly
discovered, a simple gold band was never really your
style, was it?'

Lexi stared back at him, speechless; he could hurt her
so easily with one unkind slur.

'Well! Do you like it, Lexi darling?' he demanded
hardly.

She masked the flicker of pain in her violet eyes by
quickly lifting her hand and admiring the diamond ring.
'It's lovely. Thank you,' she said politely, thinking that
if Jake had truly loved her a ring-pull from a beer can
would have done.

'So gracious, so polite. Oh, hell!' Jake suddenly swept
her into his arms, his mouth covering hers; she expected
an angry ravishment, instead his lips moved over hers
in an achingly tender kiss. 'Sorry, Lexi, I swore tonight
I would keep my cynical barbs to myself. Tonight
is yours.'

Lexi gazed into his serious face, her violet eyes wide and puzzled. Jake lifted her hand and kissed the glittering ring on her finger.

'Forget what I said before. I bought you the ring because I wanted you to have it. Five years ago, it wasn't your fault.' He grimaced wryly. 'You were so young and I swept you into marriage without giving you time to think. I didn't think much myself at the time. I was thirty, a lot older and should have known better, but I wanted you. I saw you, took you, and I never even bought you an engagement ring. Then to cap it all I broke my promise to you.'

'It doesn't matter,' Lexi murmured. He had finally admitted he was to blame for their separation, and somehow it gave her no joy.

'But it does. Do you realise these past two weeks are the nearest I have had to a holiday in my whole life? You were right...'

Startled, Lexi waited, sure she was about to hear something of vital importance to their relationship, but at that moment the doorbell rang, and the moment was gone...

'Damn, the limousine is here. We'll continue this later, Lexi,' Jake said softly and taking her arm ushered her out of the house to the waiting car.

'Why the chauffeur?' she asked as she settled in the back seat of the huge car and Jake slid in beside her.

'Because tonight, my sweet, we are celebrating, and I intend to drink champagne with my very lovely wife, and I don't fancy risking the Amalfi Drive after downing a few.'

The party was a total and utter surprise to Lexi, but a delightful one. Jake led her into the foyer of the Piccolo Paradiso, saying he had some papers to collect from Lorraine, and did she want to have a word with Anna on Reception while she waited for him? Lexi hid her dismay at the mention of the other woman and, totally unsuspecting, she crossed the marble foyer towards the reception desk, idly noticing the dining-room doors were closed, which was unusual. Still, it wasn't her problem any more, she thought with a tinge of regret.

Then suddenly the doors were flung open and a crowd of laughing, smiling faces swept into the foyer, all shouting, '*Augurio*!' Lexi felt Jake's familiar arm curve around her waist as she was swept into the dining-room. Moisture hazed her lovely eyes as she saw the banner over the small band-stand. 'Good Luck, Long Life and Happiness, Lexi.'

She was swamped with well-wishers. The whole staff of the hotel appeared to be present along with the guests; it made a huge glittering, laughing crowd. The champagne flowed like water and to her amazement she spotted Signor Monicelli.

'Is Marco all right?' she asked after hugging the old man.

'Doing very well, thanks to your good husband,' Signor Monicelli replied, adding, 'Marriage suits you, Lexi, you look radiant.'

Anna grabbed her arm and demanded to know if there were any more back in England like Jake. Franco, all the housemaids, the porters, even the kitchen staff insisted on congratulating her, and all the time Jake kept at her side.

Someone shoved a glass of champagne in her hand, and before she knew it she was up on the stage being presented with an exquisite bronze sculpture of a sea nymph. Signor Monicelli made a brilliant and flattering speech, extolling Lexi's virtues, until she was scarlet with embarrassment.

Lexi held the beautiful bronze in one hand and stroked it gently with the other... A lump formed in her throat and she could hardly speak, one tear escaped from her hazed eyes. She swallowed hard, and then Jake's hand clasped her waist, giving her his support, and she managed to make a rather tearful but heartfelt speech of thanks. 'Thank you all, and I will never forget you.'

Jake led her from the stage and she glanced up at him, a question in her lovely eyes. 'You did this for me, Jake?'

'Your friends insisted,' he said, non-committal.

'But what about the hotel guests.' Most she recognised as regular visitors, but a few were strangers to her.

'I simply told them the hotel dining-room was closed for the night, but they were welcome to join the party.'

'It must have cost you a fortune,' she murmured—the champagne was vintage, she noted, and dinner was a superb buffet, with lobster and caviar, the long table groaning with the weight of the food.

'You deserve it, Lexi, love.' His dark head bent, his mouth erotically nibbling her small ear. 'You're worth a thousand times more to me than a party, and later I intend to prove it to you once and for all. We have to put the past behind us, forgive and forget. No more secrets, no more separate beds. Trust me.'

Hope burst in her heart at Jake's muffled words, and, glancing sideways up at him through thick lashes, she was stunned to see a tender, caring light in his deep blue eyes. 'Jake...' She put her hand on his chest. Was it possible? Could they start afresh? Yes, her heart sang. She could forgive him everything if he loved her.

'Later.'

'Alexandra.' A deep voice rang out, silencing the crowd.

Lexi turned and gasped her pleasure at the man accosting her. 'Ali!' she exclaimed. He was dressed in the flowing white robes of the desert, and flanked on either side by two bodyguards. Sheik Ali al Kahim was an old friend from her childhood days when her father was consulate in his small middle Eastern country; they had played together as children and coincidentally met up again at the Piccolo Paradiso where Ali was an honoured guest once a year, but usually in the spring. 'What are you doing here?' she demanded as he swept her up in a bear hug then put her back on her feet.

'My yacht is in the port for a few hours. I rang the hotel to speak with you and heard you are married and leaving. How could you do this to me, little Alexandra? And who is the lucky man?'

Jake, with his arm reaching out to pull Lexi into his side, said curtly, 'I am.'

Lexi effected the introduction, her worried gaze swinging between the two men. Jake was attractive, but Ali, the same age as herself, was strikingly beautiful, as tall as Jake with huge brown eyes and the classic features of a Greek god. Jake took one look at him and seemed furious.

'You have my congratulations, Mr Taylor. You are a very fortunate man. But I have only myself to blame I delayed too long.'

Delayed what too long? Lexi wondered, and then was stunned as Ali presented her with a long velvet box.

'A wedding gift, my dear Alexandra. May you have a long and fruitful union, though I could have wished it were with me.'

'Ali, you fool.' He had always been a frightful tease, and she opened the box. Inside was a jewel-encrusted tiny dagger. 'It's beautiful, Ali. Thank you.' She beamed up at him. But Jake was not so happy; she felt his fingers dig into her waist.

'My wife does not take jewellery from any man except me.' His icy blue eyes clashed with the brown of Ali's.

'So it should be,' Ali responded coolly. 'But if you observe, it is a letter-knife to remind you both to keep in touch.'

Ali left moments later, sweeping out of the hotel with his bodyguard chasing after him. He had explained he was sailing within the hour for home.

Jake turned Lexi into his arms and, relieving her of the jewel box, slipped it in his pocket. 'That man wanted you,' he said flatly, his intent gaze searching her up-turned face. 'He is one of the wealthiest men in the world, and you could have married him.'

'Don't be ridiculous,' she giggled. 'Ali is sought after by the most gorgeous women in the world and delights in letting them catch him, while his father despairs of him ever settling down. He is just a boy and he likes to tease.' And, suddenly feeling bold, she added, 'Haven't you realised yet, Jake? There has only ever been you.'

'What!' He stared into her laughing eyes, and what he saw there must have convinced him. 'God! Lexi, you choose the damnedest place to make a confession like that. We really need to talk.' He hugged her tight.

But at that moment they were accosted by Signor Monicelli, and for the next few hours Lexi was floating on Cloud Nine. She danced with the chef, Franco and host of others but always after each dance Jake was there to claim her.

Finding herself alone for a moment Lexi glanced around the room. Poor Jake had been dragged by Anna on to the dance-floor and she was trying to teach him to cha-cha amid much laughter. Lexi smiled to herself and carefully eased her way through the crowd and into the foyer; she felt slightly dizzy, the heat and the noise finally getting to her.

'Enjoying the party?' Lorraine appeared from behind the Reception desk. 'I'm supposed to join in when Anna remembers to come and relieve me, but frankly a rave-up with all the staff isn't really good for business.'

Groaning inwardly, Lexi faced up to the other woman. 'It was Jake's idea,' she said swiftly. Whatever Lorraine had meant to Jake in the past, Lexi was hoping against hope it was over. Jake's insistence that they talk and the way he had behaved today all pointed to that fact, and she would not let Lorraine dampen her spirit.

'Yes, I know; he asked me to arrange it all. But per-sonally I think it's a waste of money. I told him he was a fool, but then all men are. Why should I worry? He pays me exceptionally well to do what he wants,' she taunted with a smile that did not reach her hard eyes.

'He is a very generous man,' Lexi said firmly. She did not like the assessing look in Lorraine's gaze as she moved to stand directly in front of her.

'What is it about you, Lexi?' Lorraine questioned almost to herself. 'You're beautiful. You and I could have been friends if you weren't a threat to my position in the company.' She put her long-nailed hand on Lexi's bare shoulder, her fingers biting into the flesh. 'You're intelligent, but you have one failing—you're the type of woman who needs a man. What a waste. Jake knows you are a gold-digger, and he'll drop you in the end, and I'll still be around, his right-hand man.'

Lexi stepped back. Lorraine as a friend! The woman must be mad. 'That's enough. I will not discuss my husband with you.' She refused to let the woman get to her. Tonight was Lexi's and Jake was hers, and, spinning on her heel, she flung over her shoulder, 'I'll send Anna out.' It was odd; Lexi realised that even before she knew about Jake and Lorraine, the woman had always made her uncomfortable, and she didn't think it was just jealousy. With a toss of her red hair she headed for the party but before she had gone three steps Jake was at her side.

'What was Lorraine saying?' Jake demanded curtly. 'Did she upset you?'

Sliding an arm around his neck and another around his waist, she pressed herself against him. 'No more than usual, in fact she wanted to be friends, would you believe?' she teased; she wanted nothing to spoil this night, and she wasn't going to let Lorraine's catty remarks hurt her.

'She touched you.' His dark eyes fell to the red mark on her naked shoulder. 'Did she hurt you?' The harsh demand in Jake's tone made Lexi lift her eyes to his.

'No, of course not. She didn't punch me out for being with you.' Lexi grinned, but Jake did not respond; instead his eyes narrowed with some undisclosed emotion.

'Look, I'm sorry if I upset your girlfriend——' She was not going to let anything spoil her party.

'She is not my girlfriend.' Jake cut her off, his handsome face harsh in the artificial light. 'She works for me, nothing more, though not for much longer, I think.' And, sliding an arm around Lexi's waist, he led her towards the dance-floor. 'I'm beginning to wonder...'

'Wonder what?' Lexi asked, secretly delighted at the suggestion that Jake and Lorraine might part company.

Jake, in a quick about-face, spun her around; his eyes, gleaming with devilish amusement, gazed down into hers as he swept her into his arms, and said, 'Wonder if I should serenade you.' And he burst into song.

She knew he had deliberately changed the subject, but she didn't care, and, entering into the mood, she began to giggle as he whirled her around and around. 'You're a terrible singer.'

'I know, but I do do something well...' he drawled sexily, one hand sliding down to her buttocks, he held her firmly against him. The band started to play a Latin love song, and slowly they circled the floor, touching from shoulder to knee, their bodies moving lazily as one. Jake nuzzled her ear and she melted in his arms.

CHAPTER TEN

AT LAST the crowd was thinning. Lexi breathed a sigh of contentment. It had been a lovely party, and, wriggling out of Jake's arms, she whispered, 'I need the powder-room.' But as she crossed the foyer Anna called out,

'Lexi, do you want to collect your tapes now?'

'Yes, sure.' Lexi had left her favourite tapes in Anna's room when she had been sharing it with her for a week. Quickly, she followed Anna around Reception and down the corridor to her room at the rear of the hotel.

Ten minutes later with the box of tapes tucked under her arm, Lexi slowly walked back to the foyer. She was sad at leaving her friends; she had had some good times at the Piccolo Paradiso she mused, but she nursed a secret feeling of hope that the best was yet to come. Jake wanted to talk, and she knew in her heart that this time it would be all right. She wasn't sure she was pregnant, but had taken care to drink only two glasses of champagne all evening. In any case, she hadn't needed the stimulus. An attractive, caring Jake was stimulus enough for her.

She stopped, her eyes widening in shocked disbelief; her hand went to her heart, pressing at her breast in a futile attempt to stop it breaking. At the end of the corridor, silhouetted by the stronger light of Reception, stood a couple wrapped in each others' arms; the man had his back to her but there was no mistaking it was Jake, and Lorraine. As she watched, his dark head bent. Lexi turned and ran back along the hall, her eyes blinded by tears.

She leaned against the wall and gulped in the warm night air, her heart pounding; the box of tapes fell unnoticed to the ground as she rubbed her knuckles in her eyes, trying to stem the tears. Taking a shaky breath she straightened, and gazed dazedly at her surroundings. She was in the staff car park at the back of the hotel.

She was shivering and yet it was a hot summer night. She looked up at the sky; a million stars glittered and sparkled in the midnight blue of the moonlit vastness. But the beauty of the scene was lost on her. It had happened again. Once more she had allowed herself to trust, to love, had wished for the moon! And for a while she had thought it was within her grasp. What a fool! Her hopes and dreams were shattered like a burst balloon.

Lexi had no notion how long she stood there; an icy chill pervaded the very marrow of her bones until finally she moved, stiffly like a robot, one foot in front of the other, but with no idea where she was going; she only knew she had to get away. Then she noticed it. Her little car was parked next to the car park exit. It looked abandoned, much the way she felt herself, she thought sadly. Automatically she tried the door and it opened; she slid into the driver's seat, her hand finding the ignition. The key had been left in place...

She turned on the engine, her foot pressing on the clutch and slipped it into first gear. But suddenly the door was wrenched open, a long hand reached over and cut off the ignition, another arm pressed across her chest as a strong hand hauled on the handbrake.

'No, you don't.' Lexi turned her tear-stained face at the harsh command, and saw Jake's towering form blocking the door. His eyes flashed with rage and a muscle jerked in his cheek. 'Get out of that car,' he snarled.

'Leave me alone,' she said, her voice breaking on a sob as she tried to prise his arm off her breast.

'Running to your Arab friend, were you?' Jake's face was murderous. 'You bitch.' His lips drew back from his teeth in a snarl of animal fury.

How like him to blame her! Lexi thought and, in a mercurial change of mood, anger overtaking her former despair, she beat at his arm, trying to break free. 'Let me go, don't touch me, I hate you...' she cried, all her hurt and anger bubbling to the surface; she thrashed around in the seat trying to dislodge his aggressive hold. 'You great brute. Let me go...' she screamed almost hysterically.

'Never,' he ground out through clenched teeth.

With a frightened animal's instinct for escape Lexi changed tactics and scrambled the other way. But with the speed of light Jake was in the car and flinging her back against the passenger seat.

His face was inches from her own, his eyes leaping with rage, his breathing harsh. 'You go anywhere near that Arab again,' he rasped menacingly, his strong hand sliding up her neck to encircle her throat, 'I'll kill you.' His rugged face was tight with demoniac anger, the muscle in his cheek jerking as he tried to control his fury and in that moment Lexi believed him.

'I wasn't running to Ali, I was running away from you,' she cried scathingly.

Jake stared down at her, his hand gradually relaxing its grip on her throat. 'So what's new?' he grated. She watched his massive chest heave as he took slow, deep gulps of air, fighting to regain his control until finally he moved back into the driving seat and, with one withering glance at Lexi's huddled form, he started the car.

She bit her lip. 'What do you think you're doing? This is my car. Your limousine will be waiting for you out front,' she snapped sarcastically.

'And take the chance of you disappearing again? No way, Lexi.'

She cast a venomous glance at his harsh profile; his face was taut, his hands gripping the steering-wheel as if his life depended on it. She opened her mouth to speak but the car squealed on two wheels out of the car park and Lexi was flung against Jake.

She straightened back in her seat, she had felt the rigid tension in his arm in his whole body as they had touched, and the same tension filled the intimate confines of the tiny car. She turned her head and looked out of the side window and realised they were bombing along Amalfi Drive at a speed she was sure the car had never been built to achieve. Her heart in her mouth, she stayed silent, frozen with fear.

He was taking her back to the villa, that much was obvious. Jake could make her stay, he could make her love him. She already did, and that would never change, she accepted the fact sadly; and up until tonight she had thought maybe they could make their marriage work. But now she knew categorically that she had been fooling herself; it was an impossibility.

Jake had broken her heart not once but twice. She might just be able to stick the pieces back and continue to function; she could try. But, if she stayed, his infidelities, especially with Lorraine, would chip away at her self-respect, her pride, and little by little chisel away at her bruised heart until there was nothing left but dust, nothing to mend. She couldn't allow it to happen. She wouldn't.

She glanced at Jake. His profile looked as though it was carved out of stone; she despised the sudden lurch in her pulse while recognising that he was a formidable man in every way. But surely even Jake could not watch her all the time. She would get her chance and run as far and as fast as she could. She had done it once and she could again. She had no other alternative...

The huge gates of the villa swung open in front of them and Lexi gave a sigh of relief; she could breathe again, the harrowing drive was over. But her relief was short-lived, as the car ground to a jarring halt at the front door, and Jake was around the car, the passenger door open, and his hand curving around her bare arm like a vice as he dragged her out.

'I can manage,' she said, jerking her arm free, and blindly she turned and dashed for the house and the safety of her room, but she had barely taken two steps into the hall before Jake caught her.

'What the hell are you trying to do to me, Lexi?' he grated, and with a savage movement swung her around to face him.

Lexi stared up at him. 'Me, Jake?' she screeched. She couldn't believe his outrageous accusation—to her mind it was the other way around—but she was astounded to note the stain of red running along his high cheekbones, the taut fury in his handsome face.

'Yes, you. Who the hell else is there?'

Lorraine for one! she almost cried, but Jake, without waiting for an answer, swept her up in his arms, and carried her straight into the salon. She lashed out at him, her hands connecting with his head and his broad back. 'Put me down,' she yelled furiously and he did, dropping her unceremoniously down on the velvet-covered sofa.

He towered over her, huge and menacing; she had never seen him so consumed with rage. His glittering eyes raked over her with a ruthless savagery that made her feel as if he could see through to her bones. She fumbled with the skirt of her dress that had ridden high over her thighs, exposing her shapely legs, and tried to get up.

'Don't bother.' Jake lowered his body on to the sofa beside her and her attempt to sit up was blocked by his hand roughly pushing her back. His eyes flared like blue flame with rage. 'I'll have it off you in a minute.' His hard body pinned her beneath him. 'If this is the only way I can have you, so be it...' he snarled, as his dark head bent and his mouth covered hers in a ravaging travesty of a kiss. His hand wrenched the bodice of her dress to her waist while his other hand entangled brutally in the back of her hair, insensitive to the hurt he was inflicting.

Lexi twisted and turned, her slender body bucking against him, trying to break free from his crazed assault on her susceptible senses. She reeled from the force of his kiss, then gasped as his mouth found the rosy peak of her breast. She rained blows down on his broad back, but, to her horror, long shudders rippled through her body as she felt herself succumbing to his persuasive mouth and hands.

'No, no.' And with one last frantic effort she grasped his head between her hands and tried to push him way. 'I will not let you do this to me. I won't, I swear I won't,' she repeated over and over again, like a sacred mantra. Tossing her head from side to side, her eyes closed tight, she screamed, 'No! No...'

'Stop it, stop it, Lexi.' Jake's voice penetrated her distraught mind and she realised she was virtually free. Jake was sitting on the side of the sofa, his face as black as thunder, but his blue eyes were strangely blank. 'You can relax. I'm not about to assault you, though you are the most maddening, complex female it has ever been my misfortune to meet. I want some answers, and I want them now...' The cold implacability in his tone was in direct contrast to the fierce tension she could sense in his hard body hovering over her. He had rested one arm on the back of the sofa, while with his other hand he deftly pulled her up to a sitting position and adjusted the bodice of her dress up over her breasts. 'With no distractions,' he murmured almost under his breath.

Lexi drew a deep, shuddering breath, her eyes clashing with Jake's, and she knew the moment of truth had come. She had been on the very edge of hysteria, and there was nothing left in her emotional bank.

'I thought you and I had reached some kind of understanding, a level of commitment since Pompeii, and tonight I was sure. Was I mistaken?' Jake demanded tautly.

'No,' she murmured with a weary shake of her head.

'So why the devil did you run away again?' He sounded infuriated and almost unaware of what he was saying. 'My first thought was, mercenary little bitch, she's decided that flaming Arab was a better bet. But in the car coming home, when I had time to calm down, I realised I was wrong. Wasn't I?'

'Yes,' Lexi confirmed quietly.

'For five years I considered you a gold-digger of the worst kind. I told myself I was well rid of you, but it didn't stop me wanting you. Then, when I heard the hotel where you worked was on the market, I saw a perfect opportunity to get you back but on my terms, and I took it. I'd have you as my wife again in my bed and under my control,' he declared his eyes searching her face grimly. 'I told myself, to hell with your mercenary tendencies, I was wealthy enough to indulge them.'

'Gee, thanks. A girl could get a swelled head listening to you.' The sarcasm hid the hurt his words caused her.

His gaze narrowed speculatively on her stiff, resentful features. 'Hold your sarcasm, Lexi, I haven't finished,' he commanded bluntly. 'The past two weeks I have been forced to accept that I was wrong. I discovered you've never touched your account in London, and you actually worked to live, not just as an excuse to meet wealthy men, and yet you said you left me for money. I have seen with my own eyes Ali, one of the world's wealthiest bachelors, drool over you, but you were planning to marry Dante, a man I could buy and sell a million times over.' His hand closed over hers, his thumb rubbing the glittering ring on her finger. 'I don't like a mystery; I want some answers and fast.'

'Maybe I didn't leave you because I wanted money,' was as far as she was prepared to go in enlightening him. To reveal her real reason after seeing him with Lorraine again was not something she dared contemplate. She had her pride if nothing else...

'I know that years ago I let you down, Lexi, and broke my promise to you, but I thought you cared enough for me, were mature enough to understand.' Jake thrust a hand through his tumbled hair. 'I never expected you to take off then or now... Talk to me, Lexi, make me understand.'

Lexi stared at him. He had said as much before, and she had been unable to comprehend his reasoning. Perhaps because secretly, deep in her subconscious, she had not wanted to believe she could love a man so totally bereft of any morality. Looking away from his too penetrating eyes she said, in a voice devoid of all emotion, 'I understand I shouldn't have run away.' She tried to stand but Jake, with a brief tug on her hand, forced her back down beside him.

'You're not going anywhere until we have talked this through.' His dark eyes held hers, an intensely speculative look in their indigo depths. 'So, why did you run away, not once but twice?' he prompted.

'If I had stayed in England I could have been divorced and free within weeks. It's my one big regret in life, apart from meeting you in the first place,' she said curtly, an icy calm possessing her. She stared up into his harsh face. He still had her hand in his, but his other arm was curved over the back of the sofa, not touching her but effectively encircling her.

'I very much doubt that,' he drawled cynically. 'But do carry on, this is beginning to get interesting.'

Interesting. He had ruined her life, and had the audacity... Suddenly all her hurt, all her anger came streaming out.

'I was a naïve fool when I married you. I knew you wanted Forest Manor, but my mistake was in thinking you wanted me more. I discovered the truth that night at the London apartment. It was ironic really; for weeks I had suffered from hormonal depression after the miscarriage but that morning Dr Bell had convinced me to snap out of it.' She looked at Jake, not really seeing him. 'I caught the train to London, happy for the first time in ages, my passport in my purse, and dreaming of a wedding anniversary in Paris.'

Jake's only reaction was to tighten his grip on her hand.

'Instead, I found you and your mistress, virtually naked, calmly discussing how you could tell your poor little wife you had broken your marriage vow, and wanted your freedom, and would I settle for cash...?'

Jake's head snapped back. 'You what?' The words were rasped out hoarsely, but Lexi ignored his aghast query.

'Of course I said I'd take the money. I had some pride left, though not enough to drink champagne to your future happiness. But you know the real irony, Jake?' she asked with a harsh laugh. 'I would have sold you the house for the price of my father's debts without a qualm. Contrary to your opinion of my mercenary characteristics, I have never had any great desire for material things. So you see, our marriage was totally unnecessary.'

There was a silence, and she could hear the ticking of the ornate ormolu clock on the mantelpiece. She glanced at it. Almost two, her mind registered, as her gaze swung back to Jake. The expression on his ruggedly handsome face would have been laughable if the moment had not been so tense. His face was grey beneath its tan, his wide mouth parted in an incredulous gasp; he looked absolutely stupefied.

Well, why shouldn't he hear some home-truths? Lexi thought with bitter resentment. He had been the one calling the tune for far too long. 'As for your latest attempt at a reconciliation, Luigi was right. Nothing changes. I saw you and Lorraine tonight in each other's arms, and realised, much as I value my friendship with Signor Monicelli, I am not prepared to give my life for it.'

Jake dropped her hand and grabbed her by the shoulders, pushing her against the back of the sofa. He stared down into her pale face as though he had never seen her before, and when he spoke it was as if each word was forced out of him. 'Am I to understand that you left me because you thought I only wanted your house, and I was having an affair with Lorraine? Have I got that right?'

'Not thought, knew,' Lexi said scathingly.

'Oh, my God. I knew we needed to talk but I never realised . . . what you imagined . . . What a low opinion you must have of me . . .' His rich voice deepened with a strange urgency. 'Lexi, you've got it all wrong.'

'I don't think so.' She tried to sit up but Jake wouldn't allow it. Instead he swung her up and across his thigh to hold her on his lap like a small child, a strong arm firmly around her waist.

'Let me go.' Held in his arms close to his hard warmth, his strong thighs beneath her, she was far too susceptible to him, and she tried to slide off his lap, but Jake was having none of it. 'Sit still and for once in your life listen,' he demanded hardily, but, with an oddly gentle gesture, he brushed the tangle of her red hair from the side of her face before curving his hand around her leg.

Lexi stopped struggling. She would hear what he had to say. She didn't have much choice, she was trapped, but she didn't have to believe him . . .

'Do you remember that night when you arrived at the apartment?'

'Yes,' she said curtly. She would never forget.

'I asked you if you had heard all our conversation and you agreed.'

'I heard enough.' Lexi glared up at him. His betrayal was an ache in her heart. 'And I saw: the woman was wearing my robe.'

'For the very simple reason, if you cast your mind back, that there was a hell of a storm that night and we were both soaked to the skin. There is no way on this earth I could ever have an affair with Lorraine; her preference is for other women, and always has been.'

'What?' Lexi gasped. Her violet eyes clashed with his. He wasn't joking, he was deadly serious. 'You expect me to believe that Lorraine...' As excuses went it was a classic, but could she believe it? He was right about the rain. A brief memory of when they were on honeymoon prompted her to ask, 'In Paris, when I asked if you and she had had an affair—was that why you laughed? And I never got the joke.'

'Exactly. I should have told you, but I thought Lorraine's sexual preference was her own affair.'

'But I heard you tell Lorraine you were breaking your wedding vows.' However Jake tried to colour his story, that fact was unmistakable.

'No, Lexi, you heard me say I was breaking my promise to you. But what you obviously didn't hear was the first part of the conversation.' His sober gaze held hers captive as he continued. 'It had nothing to do with our marriage, but none the less it doesn't reflect very well on me.'

Lexi tensed, fearing what was to follow.

'I promised you that, when Forest Manor was converted to a hotel, you would always have a home there. But unfortunately it wasn't possible.'

Inexplicably, a tiny glimmer of something very like hope ignited in Lexi's heart. She squirmed on his lap and, lifting one hand, placed it on his chest urging him to continue. 'And? Carry on.'

'Sit still and I will,' Jake commented with a very masculine groan. 'Yes, well, the bottom had dropped out of the property market and I had sunk all my cash into the Docklands venture. The only good news was the meeting with Mr Stewart, the American I was dining with the night we lost our baby.' He hugged her tighter for a moment. 'It hurt me more than you knew, Lexi.'

'I think I do know, after Pompeii,' she confessed.

'Anyway, that night Mr Stewart loved the hotel, but— and this is the hard part—he didn't want to lease the rooms, but made me an offer to buy the hotel outright. I resisted at first. I didn't dare discuss it with you, not when you were ill and so depressed. The night you burst in on Lorraine and me we were arguing over the sale of Forest Manor. I knew it made sound business sense to liquidate some of my assets, and the hotel was the simplest one to dispose of; the offer was lying on my desk. I couldn't refuse. But it meant breaking my promise to you. I felt a heel, but there was no other way out. It would save the construction firm and solve my cash-flow problem.'

Lexi's violet eyes widened in horror as the full extent of her mistake dawned on her. 'You...I...' She could not find the words to express her feelings. She believed Jake. It all made perfect sense. While she had convinced herself Jake had broken his sacred wedding vow and wanted a divorce, he had simply been afraid to tell her that his business was in trouble and Forest Manor had to be sold. Maybe if she had not been so depressed about the miscarriage she would have recognised the signs— looking back he had given plenty of hints that business was difficult—but in her pregnant state he had not wanted to worry her, and afterwards she had been so wrapped in her grief that she had not listened to him at all.

'When I thought you were discussing breaking your marriage vow,' Lexi reasoned slowly, 'you were actually talking about the promise you made to keep the house!' she exclaimed, the enormity of her mistake too much to take in. 'Five years...at cross purposes...' The hurt! If only she had waited, allowed him to explain... With a flash of insight she realised something else. 'My father's debt. How much did it finally come to?' She had never asked at the time, but she had heard the rumours since of Lloyds names going bankrupt trying to pay off the appalling losses after a string of disasters.

'You don't need to know,' Jake said firmly.

'Please.' Her hand moved agitatedly against his chest. 'If we are to make anything of our marriage we have to have truth between us.' A flush stained her cheeks as she realised what she had proposed.

His hand covered hers where it lay on his shirt, his long fingers lacing with hers. 'The truth.' His eyes flared darkly. 'I'd do anything in the world for our marriage, Lexi,' he said emphatically, and pressed a swift hard kiss on her parted lips. She felt herself relax against him, then immediately went rigid in his arms when he mentioned a sum that made her head spin.

'Oh, my God! That much.'

'Yes, but not to worry, I can easily afford it now, but at the time it was touch and go for a while. That's why, when you told me that night you had heard everything and agreed, I was so relieved and delighted you didn't mind losing the manor, I suggested the celebratory drink. I couldn't believe it when you said you would take your share of the money and never wanted to see me again. For a few seconds I believed you were the gold-digger Lorraine had tried to warn me about before we married, and I yelled at you. But it didn't last for long. I thought you would come back to me. I told myself, Be patient, she's still depressed, let her have a holiday. When it finally dawned on me that I had lost you for good, I decided Lorraine must have been right all along: you were only after money.'

She saw the pain in his dark eyes, and she lifted her hand to stroke his cheek. 'I never cared about money and not much about the house. It was only you I wanted, Jake; I loved you, you were my life. I would have lived in a tent if you'd asked me,' she blurted. Still reeling with the shock of his revelation, she didn't realise what she was confessing.

'Past tense, Lexi?' Jake queried softly, and, catching her chin between his finger and thumb, he tilted her face up to his. 'I love you, I always have; the last five years have been hell without you. Will you give me another chance to let me try and win your love? Please, Lexi.'

The flicker of hope in her heart burst into a glorious flame. Jake, her husband, vulnerable and pleading for her love, was like a dream come true, and she wanted to believe it. Curled on his lap, his strength and warmth enveloping her, she almost did, but still a niggling doubt persisted. 'Lorraine—she was in your arms tonight. I saw you, Jake; are you sure she...'

Jake's strong arm hugged her to his broad chest as he said urgently, 'Tonight, in Reception, seeing you and Lorraine together, her hand on you.' His dark brows drew together in a frown. 'She hurt you, and that I will not tolerate, and if I'm being brutally honest I saw something in her eyes when she looked at you that gave me the same gut-wrenching jealousy I got when I saw you and Dante together, and it made me wonder how I could have been so stupid.'

'You mean Lorraine fancies me?' And she laughed out loud at his outrageous suggestion.'

'I don't know, but I'm not taking the chance.'

'But you more or less admitted she was your mistress when you insisted we resume our marriage.' Yet Jake's explanation didn't shock her as much as it should have done. Lorraine had always made her flesh creep.

A rueful grin flashed across Jake's sensuous mouth. 'Self-defence! I'm not proud of myself, but, seeing you with Dante, I wasn't above letting you think I was having an affair. The truth is that you are the only woman I have made love to in five long years.'

Lexi stared into his dark eyes, her heart pounding like a drum, and what she saw in the glittering depths almost convinced her he was telling the truth. Jake celibate for five years was a stunning revelation. 'But I saw you kiss her, Jake...'

'No,' he denied. 'But let me tell you about Lorraine, so there can be no doubt left in your mind. Much as I value Lorraine's business ability, there is no way I can stand by and watch her hurt you.'

'Lorraine has never liked me, but she didn't hurt me,' Lexi said honestly.

'You're too soft-hearted.' Jake dropped a swift kiss on her forehead. 'And I let pity and stupid teenage guilt blind me to Lorraine's obsessive character.'

Lexi tensed at the word guilt. Had Jake been involved with Lorraine? She still did not quite credit his tale of Lorraine's sexuality. She was sure the woman fancied Jake whether he knew it or not. But then, she was prejudiced, she thought ruefully, sure the woman didn't live who couldn't fancy Jake.

'As sixteen-year-olds, Lorraine and I were in the same class at school. She wasn't a friend. In fact her only friend was a girl called Pat. They were both real lookers, but never went out with any boys, and, as teenage boys do, we teased them unmercifully about being gay, which I might add they freely admitted to. It was also common knowledge that Lorraine's father was a drunk who beat up both her and her mother. On more than one occasion she appeared in class with a black eye.'

'Oh, the poor girl.'

'Yes, well, years later, when Lorraine applied for a job with my company, I remembered her and my own insensitive teasing as a teenager. She told me her friend Pat had been killed in a car crash some months earlier and I felt sorry for her. Plus I had had an embarrassing experience with my last secretary imagining she was in love with me and leaving in tears. Lorraine's qualifications weren't great, but at least I could be sure she wouldn't spend all day making cow's eyes at me, so I gave her the job. She's worked hard for me ever since. But tonight I realised something I should have recognised six years ago, when she first tried to convince me you were only after a wealthy husband. She had become far too ambitious, or perhaps possessive is a better word, of her position in my company.'

Lexi allowed herself a wry smile at Jake's arrogant confession about his secretary falling in love with him, but listened intently as he went on.

'Later, when you lost our baby, I should have got rid of her then. But with typical masculine arrogance I thought I understood the poor woman. An abusive father! It was only natural she was the way she was. I know now I should have left the psychiatry to the professionals, but at the time I thought, for someone with her family background to forget the message from the hospital was excusable. Family life was of no interest to her. But tonight I wondered how I could have been such a fool. Anyone, male or female, whatever their sexual preference or family background, receiving such a life-and-death message would never have forgotten. I have to conclude she did it deliberately. I can't tell you how sorry I am, Lexi. I was an idiot.'

Lexi had thought at the time that Lorraine had forgotten the message simply to hurt her, but she had been too ill, too depressed to make an issue of it.

'What you saw earlier in the foyer, Lexi, was our parting. I had just told Lorraine I was transferring her to the New York branch, and she knew it was more a demotion than a promotion. I suggested if she didn't like it, she should consider looking for a job elsewhere, and she resigned. I realised that over the years her efficiency had blinded me to the fact she had become far too interfering in my private and personal life. Lorraine kissed me goodbye, but I swear it is the closest she has ever been to me in all the time I have known her, and it was just a kiss on the cheek.'

Lexi hadn't actually seen the kiss, and she wanted to believe Jake's version of events. ·

'You do believe me, Lexi?' Jake asked urgently.

'Yes. Yes, I believe you.' It was too incredible to be anything other than the truth, she thought dazedly, and reaching up she gently outlined Jake's wide, sensuous mouth with one finger, her eyes shining with relief and love . . . aching for his kiss.

But doggedly Jake caught her hand and held it firmly against his broad chest. 'Today in Naples I signed the contract to buy back Forest Manor. You can have your old home back, Lexi, anything you want. If you will stay with me, I can make you love me again, I know it, if you will give me the chance.'

Lexi, her eyes moist with tears, gazed into the wary blue depths of Jake's. 'That wasn't necessary, Jake. You don't have to make me. I do. Even when I thought I hated you . . . I loved you. You're more than enough for me.'

'Thank God.' His lips captured hers in a kiss like no other, soft and tender and promising everything. When he finally ended the kiss he grinned wickedly down into her flushed face. 'I might as well confess, I did have an ulterior motive. I thought, along with the Piccolo Paradiso, it has the makings of a successful hotel chain with you as the administrator. I figured if I couldn't win your love at least I would be assured of keeping your interest, keeping you by my side.'

Lexi chuckled in delight. Jake, whom she had thought the world's worse chauvinist, was offering her not only his love but a career as well. 'I love you, Jake Taylor, devious as you are.'

'Darling Lexi,' Jake muttered, his voice husky with passion. 'My wife. I love you and I'll never let you down again, I swear.' And for the next few moments he set about convincing her very thoroughly.

When Jake finally allowed her to draw breath again somehow she was lying on the sofa, with his large body covering hers, his elbows supporting his weight either side of her slender body and his dark gaze lingered, oddly serious, on the pale perfection of her face. 'You do believe me, Lexi? Trust me? I need that.'

She looked at him all her love plain to see in the deepening purple depths of her huge eyes. 'Yes, my love.' She cupped his hard jaw in the palm of her hand and added with a tinge of sadness, 'And I'm sorry. Jake, this has all been my fault; if I had trusted you more, if I had allowed you to explain, we would never have wasted five years.'

'So why are we wasting time?' Jake rasped, one long finger tracing the soft curve of her breasts. But this time Lexi called a halt.

Suddenly it seemed imperative he knew how she had felt at the time. 'I think because I had lost our child I felt guilty, a failure and not really entitled to be happy; I was confused, and finding you and Lorraine together was the last straw. For a long time after we parted I told myself I hated you, I even thought losing the baby was a sign that our marriage was not meant to be,' she confessed simply.

'No, Lexi. You must never think that, never blame yourself,' Jake said adamantly. 'If anyone was at fault it was me. After a couple of months I decided you were a gold-digger, and I was well rid of you. When Carl Bradshaw showed me your photograph it only confirmed my suspicion. Carl omitted to tell me you were working, and I thought you were a guest at an expensive hotel on the look-out for a wealthy partner. Even so, I couldn't resist ringing the hotel and asking for Mrs Taylor. When I was told there was no guest registered in that name I assumed you must have left the hotel shortly after Carl, probably still looking for a meal-ticket and so confirming, to my mind, your mercenary tendencies.'

Her hands fell from his face. 'A guest! But you said you knew where I was all the time.'

A wry smile curved his hard mouth. 'So I stretched the truth a bit—a weak attempt to show you I didn't care. In fact, I didn't dare question Carl about you, because I didn't want to remind him of you, in case he decided to try and win you himself. It was only ten months ago, when he was safely married that I had the nerve to ask him about you once more, and that was when I discovered my mistake and realised you had been working in the hotel ... I immediately checked, this time asking under both Taylor and Laughton, and discovered you were still at the Piccolo Paradiso. I flew straight out to Naples and bought the villa—— '

'You bought it?' she cut in. 'But you said your father left it to you.'

'So I lied.' Jake had the grace to look ashamed but not for long. 'I didn't want to admit that as soon as I knew you were still in Italy I went straight out and bought a house to be near you.'

'Oh, Jake.' She could not believe this vulnerable man was the ruthless Jake of the past few weeks.

'I kept telling myself I didn't love you, and you weren't worth my regard. But all the time in the back of my mind was the desire to get you back. You have no idea how many times I drove past the hotel hoping to see you, but at the same time telling myself I hated you. And I was determined to make you pay for all the pain you had caused me.'

'Hence the blackmail,' Lexi murmured, lifting her arms to encircle his neck, and linking her hands together she urged his head down. 'You would not really have pulled out of the deal with Signor Monicelli.' She kissed him softly, swiftly.

'No,' he breathed against her mouth. 'After all, he kept you safe for me. But I was desperate; I found out you had a boyfriend, Dante, and it looked like getting serious, time was running out. The final blow was when I was in America on business and got the fax from my solicitor saying you were asking for a divorce. I knew I had to act or lose you forever.'

'That isn't possible; I love you too much.' Lexi rushed to reassure him.

'Now I'm beginning to believe it, darling.' He bent to kiss her again.

'Wait a minute.' Lexi pulled back. 'You speak Italian, so was your father Italian?' If he had lied about the house...

Jake started to grin. 'I haven't the slightest idea. I took a crash course in the language. I told myself if you love Italy so much then so must I, and if it pleases you to think of me as half-Italian, then that is what I am.'

Lexi couldn't get angry with him; instead a beaming smile illuminated her small face at the thought of the lengths he had gone to for her. 'As long as you're mine I don't care.'

'I am.' Jake gathered her close, a shuddering sigh shaking his powerful body, and she thought she heard him say 'always' before his mouth possessed hers with a poignant hunger that left no room for doubt.

'I refuse to make love to you on the sofa,' Jake murmured throatily. 'This calls for a celebration—champagne and the master bedroom, at the very least.'

Lexi tilted her head to one side, and pretended to consider. 'Will you sleep with me, though, I ask myself.' A tiny smile traced her full lips, but she held her breath as she waited for his answer.

Jake growled huskily, 'I didn't dare before, in case I blurted out my love for you, but now I intend to sleep, eat, drink with you. The way I feel right now, I will never let you out of my bed again.'

Her last doubt resolved. 'Promises, promises,' she teased as he swung her up in his arms and carried her upstairs. Gently placing her in the centre of the huge bed, he lay down beside her and kissed her willing lips. 'I love you, Jake,' she whispered against his mouth.

He leant up on one elbow and, cupping her chin in his hand, a film of moisture glazing his deep blue eyes, he murmured huskily, 'I don't deserve you, Lexi, you're beautiful inside and out,' he groaned. 'But I swear, nothing and nobody will ever come between us again; you can trust me with your life in this world and the next.'

'You are my world,' Lexi whispered and emotion flared in her violet eyes, turning them to deep purple as his mouth covered hers, kissing her with a deep, possessive passion that had her clinging to him.

Carefully he slipped her clothes from her body, scattering kisses over her melting flesh as he stripped off his own. Then they reached for each other, laughing, teasing, loving, at last free to celebrate openly with love in the sensual exploration of every single inch of each other, all the sweet, secret erogenous zones, until finally they joined as one in a rapturous acclamation of their love.

On Monday morning, Jake, with his arm firmly around Lexi's shoulder, stood glowering at the customs official behind his desk at Naples Airport.

'You realise, Lexi, that we're hopelessly late? That guide at Pompeii wasn't wrong with his "nothing changes". I'm not surprised the people were petrified in stone. It probably took them all afternoon to even decide the volcano had erupted if this chap is anything to go by. He's been reading the passports for at least ten minutes.'

'Oh, Jake, that's a terrible thing to say.' But she could not stop the chuckle that escaped her. 'Especially from a man who has just spent the last thirty-six hours in bed,' she teased with an impish smile at his frowning countenance.

'I did have some help.' His frown lifted as he gazed adoringly down at her. 'And it's true that nothing could ever change my love for you.'

The customs official handed back Jake's passport, and then, turning to Lexi, his black eyes gleaming appreciatively, gave her her own passport with a broad grin and, 'Have a good journey, *signorina.*'

Lexi repayed him with a brilliant smile, just before Jake grabbed her passport from her hand and hustled her through the departure gate.

'Some things have to change, and your damn passport is one of them. I'm not having total strangers assuming you're single, and openly ogling my wife...'

'Yes, Jake,' she meekly agreed, a secretive gleam in her lovely eyes; and why not? She had it all: the man she loved, the hope of a baby, and a great career to look forward to, if she wanted it...

Elizabeth Oldfield's writing career started as a teenage hobby, when she had articles published. However, on her marriage the creative instinct was diverted into the production of a daughter and son. A decade later, when her husband's job took them to Singapore, she resumed writing and had her first romance accepted by Mills & Boon® in 1982.

Now hooked on the genre, Elizabeth had her fortieth book published last year. She and her family live in London, and Elizabeth travels widely to authenticate the background of her books.

RENDEZVOUS IN RIO
by
ELIZABETH OLDFIELD

CHAPTER ONE

MARCUS was missing!

The moment she rounded the bend and saw Sylvie hovering beside the distant garden gate, Christa *knew*. A mother's instinct told her. Dismay struck, sharp as a pain, and she quickened her pace. Oh, heavens, where had he disappeared to this time? In her experience, most children of nineteen months or so were content to mosey around at home, if not cling; never Marcus. He eternally craved adventure, new challenges, activity—which, she supposed, was hardly surprising when you considered his parentage. Impatience flickered in the sapphire-blue of her eyes. Sylvie was aware of his addiction to wandering, why hadn't she kept a closer surveillance? She reined in her annoyance. She was being unfair. On the last occasion he had gone walkabout, the pint-sized explorer had been out of sight for what seemed like seconds, yet had managed to squeeze through a gap in the fence and trot three-quarters of the way across the meadow before she had missed him. On being caught, Marcus had earnestly explained how he had been 'lookin' for Dobbin'. Who had he gone in search of today, the retired carthorse again—or his father?

Probably his father, Christa decided, waving an

5

assuring 'It's OK, I'm back' hand to her neighbour
and moving into a jog. Although she had deliberately
delayed telling the little boy about Jeff's visit, with
hindsight passing on the news at breakfast this
morning could have been a mistake. Tomorrow his
papa was arriving on a big plane from Brazil! A room
packed with balloons would not have created more
chuckles, greater whoops of delight. But Marcus
possessed a meagre sense of time, and now it seemed
likely he had plunged off in premature hopes of a
reunion. Frowning, Christa brushed a brown-blonde
curl from her brow. Jefferson Barssi was the kind of
man who made an *impact*. Ever since his visit had
been arranged, it had dominated her thoughts and her
activities, so was it any wonder if her son had
similarly been affected?

'Don't worry, he won't have got far,' she called,
coming within earshot of the well-rounded brunette in
her mustard-yellow velour top and pants.

The calmness of Christa's message concealed a
breath-robbing surge of fear. No matter how short a
distance Marcus had travelled, she was well aware
that all it needed was for his sturdy little legs to carry
him out on to one of the narrow lanes, a solitary car to
appear and . . .

'How long has he been gone?' she panted, drawing
to a halt. After the hundred-yard dash her cheeks were
pink, her forehead sheened with perspiration.

'Just under an hour.'

'An hour?' Christa shrilled, the surface calm
shattering into a thousand horrified pieces.

Her heart banged against her breastbone. The situation was far worse than she had imagined. Five minutes had been her presumed time-scale, whereas her small son had been absent for almost sixty! She flung her neighbour a critical and disbelieving look. Why was Sylvie standing here doing sweet nothing, when there was the road to be scoured, fields to be searched, his name to be shouted around?

'Your husband took Marcus down to the play park,' the older woman explained, as Christa opened her mouth in protest. 'I was under the impression they'd be away just a short while, but——'

Christa's darkly lashed eyes stretched wide. 'Marcus is with Jefferson?'

'Yes. I thought they'd be back by now.'

'Don't worry.' Christa smiled, relief at her son's safety washing down over her like a warm flood. 'Once Marcus gets on the swings, it's the devil's own job to prise him off.' Abruptly her brow furrowed and relief was replaced with curiosity, hotly pursued by suspicion. 'Jeff's arrived a day early—but why?'

Everything had been geared for tomorrow. By then Christa would have put the finishing touches to a series of wonderful meals—courtesy of the freezer—perfected her appearance and, most important, would have knocked what was proving to be an alarmingly shaky composure into shape. But now all that had been ruined, leaving Christa feeling wrong-footed and slightly rebellious.

Sylvie shrugged. 'He didn't say. My guess is that, by chance, he found himself with time to kill and was so desperate to see the two of you that he hopped on a plane and—hey presto!'

'Jefferson doesn't operate like that,' Christa objected, as they walked up the garden path and into the cottage. 'With him, nothing happens by chance, there's never time to kill. He controls every hour, every minute, and uses each one to its limit. When I wrote and asked him to come over, he rang with a definite date and a definite flight. If he's altered his plans there must be a reason—a good one.'

'I think it's because he couldn't wait to be with you both again,' Sylvie persisted. Tentatively she reached for her jacket which hung on a peg in the hall. 'I'll go now.'

'There's no need to rush off.' Christa smiled, and gestured towards the living-room. 'Please, come and sit down.'

Admittedly her first reaction on hearing that Jeff was here had been to send her neighbour packing, yet that would be not only discourteous but selfish. From the day she had moved into the cottage Sylvie and her husband, Alan, had gone out of their way to be friendly. If a tap dripped, if Marcus needed looked after, if a prescription had to be collected from the chemist's, they were there. Nothing was too much trouble. A casual remark about having no proper place to store her ever-increasing collection of cookery books had even resulted in Alan building shelves. No, she could not allow Sylvie to depart. The older woman loved to chat, and besides, Christa thought philosophically, apart from some frenetic tidying and straightening, what would she achieve by grabbing a few minutes alone?

'You should have seen how Marcus's face lit up when his father appeared at the door,' her friend said, dumping herself down in a chintz-covered armchair. 'And how your husband's eyes filled with tears when he hugged him.'

'Sylvie, you're romanticising again,' Christa chided. 'Jeff doesn't cry.'

'He did! He found the meeting very emotional.'

'*You're* the emotional one. You get choked up over anything,' Christa teased, not believing a word. The brunette's Latin-American blood meant her joys, her fears, her everyday conversation, tended to be exaggerated and dramatised—often to Christa's amusement. Yet although Jeff hailed from the same continent, the same country and, by an odd coincidence, even the same city, he played life cool. He was level-headed, self-contained, pragmatic. Apart from the occasional fiery argument with his father, the only time he allowed his feelings to run riot was when he made love, and then . . . She tucked her aquamarine sweatshirt more securely into her short, straight denim skirt. 'I bet you wasted no time informing him he was in the company of a fellow Carioca and began mushily reminiscing about dear old Rio. The drive up Corcovado—such splendour brings a lump to the throat! The view from Sugar Loaf Mountain——' Christa pressed a theatrical hand to her chest '—grabs you right there!'

'It was comforting to receive an update, Rio isn't

nicknamed the *cidade maravilhosa* for nothing. The men can be pretty marvellous too.' Sylvie slid her a glance. 'Forgive me if I step out of line, but as the decision to marry a hunk like that was inspired, so deciding to leave him has to be marked down as moronic. Six foot three of even teeth, sleek dark hair and bronzed muscle isn't a combination that grows on tress, even in Rio.'

'But I didn't decide either to marry Jeff or to leave him,' sighed Christa. 'At least, not in any informed way. Both events just *happened*. When I returned to England six months ago it wasn't a formal separation. It never has been. He's come over twice since then and——'

'And on each occasion I was on holiday and missed Brazil's answer to Richard Gere!' the older woman exclaimed.

Engrossed in her thoughts, Christa was unable to respond light-heartedly. 'I left on the spur of the moment because—because circumstances forced my hand, but basically because I was in desperate need of space and time.'

'And after space and time in plenty, now you're getting together again,' Sylvie said contentedly.

'I believe we can work something out,' Christa agreed. 'In the past we both made mistakes. However, if I give a bit and he gives a bit, then——'

A line appeared between her brows. She was making the resumption of their married live sound as straightforward as one, two, three, but it was far more complicated. All manner of things must be talked through. All manner of problems identified. All manner of adjustments made.

'Then you'll live happily ever after,' her friend finished for her.

'Yes. You and Jeff didn't——' Christa hesitated. 'You didn't talk about why I'd asked him to come?'

'We never mentioned your reconciliation,' Sylvie assured her, rolling the word so flamboyantly around her mouth that Christa smiled. 'I simply made him a cup of coffee and chatted about Brazil.'

'Thanks.'

Fearful of premature and sidetracking arguments, Christa had been purposely vague about the matters which needed to be 'sorted out between us'. Over the past weeks a dissertation had been prepared, one which started at the beginning, worked through the middle, and finished at the end. It was important she do things *her* way and explain her point of view calmly and sensibly. She wanted them to plan their future in peace, with no inferference and no distractions; which meant they must talk here, away from Jeff's family and business.

'Would you like a coffee now?' asked Christa, rising to her feet. 'I refused one at the salon and——'

'Your hair! In all the excitement, I'd forgotten about it. Turn round,' her friend ordered, and Christa pivoted obligingly. 'Looks fantastic. It's a big change, but it suits you.'

A hand was ruffled through cropped curls. Cut in a pertly feathered style, her hair fell in tawny strands across her brow, curled around her ears and ended in a point at the nape of her neck.

'Do you think it makes me look older?' she enquired hopefully. Christa knew the day must dawn when she would be grateful her appearance belied her years, but she had grown weary of being mistaken for Marcus's teenaged sister.

'Fifty, at least. Yes, maybe a little older,' Sylvie said, when she pulled a face, 'but certainly far more sophisticated. You look as if you should be stretched out on a tiger skin advertising some bank-breakingly expensive perfume.'

Christa laughed. 'Can I give you that coffee?'

'Please. What happened, was someone else having their hair cut and you decided to follow suit?'

'No. I've told you, my days of being impulsive are over. I saw this style in a magazine a month ago and I've been weighing it up ever since.'

'Your two men are taking a long time,' the other girl remarked, when Christa returned to the living-room with mugs of instant coffee. 'Your husband was driving a hire car, and he'd come straight off a ten-hour flight, and he did seem a bit strained. I hate to say this, but——' her brow puckered '—you don't imagine there might have been an accident?'

'Never.' Christa's disavowal was firm. 'This isn't Rio, where they have thirty-five vehicle pile-ups every second day, this is the Home Counties. People here are sensible, they don't try to do the samba in their cars. Besides, tired or not, Jeff's an excellent driver.'

'Didn't he have a bad crash once and smash up his shoulder?'

'That was on a Grand Prix circuit long before I

knew him, and it happened because a tyre exploded when he was travelling at a hundred and fifty miles an hour through a chicane. Look,' Christa went on, when Sylvie mumbled about Jeff needing to drive on an unfamiliar side of the road, 'the last time he was here we went to the children's zoo near Windsor. Perhaps Marcus remembered and asked to go again.'

'Perhaps,' the older woman agreed doubtfully. 'It's just that I have this feeling——'

'If anyone's a couple of minutes late, you always have feelings,' Christa rebuked with affection. 'Remember when Alan got snarled up in that twelve-mile queue on the motorway, and you were so convinced of disaster that by the time he arrived home you were the grieving widow with the funeral already planned?' She sipped her coffee. 'How is Alan, still selling houses like hot cakes?'

'Business is brisk,' Sylvie smiled, and launched into a saga of properties which her estate agent husband was currently handling. 'Incidentally,' she finished up, 'if your father's likely to offload the cottage once you're settled back in Brazil, Alan can put him in touch with several people who'd be interested.'

'I don't know whether Dad would want to sell or not, though I reckon he should. I reckon he should have disposed of it years ago. The cottage makes a lovely home,' Christa said, her eyes skimming across the natural stone walls, the exposed beams, the inglenook fireplace pinned with gleaming horse-brasses, 'and I've been lucky to have had it at my disposal, but Dad comes here so rarely it's a sin. His argument is that property's an excellent investment, so it doesn't matter how long the cottage stands empty—though if someone appeared tomorrow with a lucrative offer he'd bite off their hand. Yet it's not as though he's avaricious or has a lavish life-style. It's the simple act of making a profit which appeals.'

'He's very clever at it.'

'He is,' Christa agreed, thinking of the company which her father had built into an international giant and which bore his name.

Henley Electronics more than filled any gap left by the wife who had died ten years ago, she acknowledged with a pang of regret. And his daughter came a poor second where his enthusiasm was concerned. She existed on the periphery of his world and always had done. George Henley had little time to spare for family. Even his grandson, whose huge brown eyes and impudent smile melted hearts daily, had failed to spark much of an interest. Marcus would need to be able to discuss import tariffs and quality control and margin percentages before he would do that.

Wasn't there a theory about women marrying men similar to their fathers? Christa mused. Jeff was a dedicated businessman too, yet he *did* care about those close to him, and especially about Marcus. After their whirlwind courtship she had presumed they would spend time getting to know each other and leave children for later, but Jeff had objected to taking precautions. Her reaction on becoming pregnant two months after their wedding had been one of surprised

misgivings—misgivings which had intensified when
the so-called 'morning' sickness had lasted all
day—yet his had been pleasure, pure and immense.

When the little boy had been born, Jeff's pride was
fierce, and throughout Marcus's baby days he'd paid
heart-warming attention—like so many others. Too
many others, Christa thought ruefully. Over the past
months father and son had been deprived of each
other's company, yet Jeff had ensured that the
occasions when they had been together were special.
Christa's face clouded. It could be argued that she had
been cruel to separate them, but she refused to feel
guilty. Coming back to England might have been
done with helter-skelter speed, but it had been the
culmination of incessant emotional to-ing and fro-ing,
of long-bottled-up discontent. She sighed. Her
departure had been fraught, and in the months which
followed there had been troubles enough. Troubles
which had forced her to stand on her own two feet.
Troubles which had matured her.

A gust of wind whining down the chimney broke
into her thoughts. The spring afternoon had been
sunny but, as evening approached, the blue sky was
turning a chilly shade of grey. Soon she would need to
put a match to the logs already laid in the wood-
burning stove.

'Was Marcus wearing his anorak when they went
out?' she enquired.

'With bobble hat and mittens, plus his sweater. And
he took his teddy.'

'He wanted his teddy? He usually only has it when

he goes to sleep,' said Christa, surprised.

'It wasn't Marcus who asked to take it along. It was your husband who insisted.'

'I wonder why?' She drew back her sleeve and examined her watch. It was almost five o'clock. If Jefferson had taken their son to the zoo, it seemed strange he had not rung to explain. 'Fancy another coffee?' she asked, suddenly feeling restless.

When the sun had been shining, Sylvie's talk of accidents had appeared alarmist and extreme. Now, with clouds filling the heavens and casting gloom, it was beginning to make a reluctant kind of sense.

'No, thanks, I'd better be getting home. Alan and I are dining out tonight, so I must go and bathe and decide what to wear. I wish I were tall and slender like you,' the brunette sighed, talking up a well-worn theme. 'On you, anything looks like Paris fashions. On me——' she raised despairing eyes to the ceiling, '—it's the *castanhas de caju* that do it.'

'The what?' asked Christa, distracted.

The minutes had begun to drag. Where *was* Jefferson? The more she thought about it, the more the idea of him taking off for the zoo seemed unlikely. After a long flight, he would not want to go gawking at goats and hamsters, for heaven's sake!

'Cashews. Remember I told you the Portuguese name when we were going through the shelves at the supermarket, and you wrote it in your notebook?'

'Oh. Yes.'

'Well, every evening when Alan comes home from work we enjoy a sherry or two and I wolf down a big bowl of nuts. Is it any wonder I need to squeeze myself into skirts and trousers with a shoehorn?' The telephone on the bureau burbled. 'This'll be your husband!' said Sylvie, in joyous relief.

Christa hurried to lift the receiver. 'Jeff?'

'Hi,' replied a familiarly deep voice.

'Is everything OK?'

'Everything's fine.'

She frowned. Time spent in the States as a student meant her husband's English came with an American accent. Add a residual lilt derived from his mother tongue of Brazilian-Portuguese and his voice was usually a relaxed drawl with its own intriguing cadence. But his tone sounded clipped and formal.

'You haven't had an accident?' she questioned, an anticipatory tremor running down her spine. After two and a half years of marriage she was alert to his vibrations, even over the telephone, and now she was convinced he must be keeping something from her. 'Marcus is——'

'He's fine too. Here he is. Say hello,' Jeff instructed.

''Lo Mummy,' trebled a little voice.

Feeling happier, Christa greeted her son.

'I told you he was all right. There's no need to worry,' Jeff said, taking over again.

'Where are you?'

'Heathrow.'

'Heathrow? The airport?' she queried, aware of Sylvie's brows shooting towards her hairline. 'Why go there?'

'Because this is where the jets leave for Rio.'

'You're confirming your return flight?' Christa said, puzzled. 'But I assumed you'd be here for a couple of weeks, so why——'

'You assumed wrong. I'm flying back tonight.' There was a pause. 'With Marcus.'

A muddle of thoughts shrieked and swirled in her head, but nothing made sense. 'You're taking Marcus to Brazil?' she gulped, choking in her bewilderment.

'I am.'

Christa cleared her throat, coughed. 'Now? This evening? You mustn't!' Her voice gathered an urgency. 'You say not to worry, then you spring something like this on me? It's ridiculous—I don't believe it. What are you playing at? Jeff, you *can't!*'

'I can. And if you intend to attack me for irresponsibility, don't bother. You flew off with him last year——'

She stopped him right there. 'That was different, totally different. I didn't spirit him away to the airport on the sly.'

'You told me the night before,' Jeff retorted, 'when your cases were all ready packed and you were so close to hysteria there wasn't a chance of me stopping you, short of using brute force and a strait-jacket.' An irritated sigh came over the wire. 'This is nether the time nor the place for raking over the past. My flight's already been called and I'm in an open phone booth.'

Christa ran a shaky hand through her hair. 'Be reasonable,' she pleaded.

'Were you?'

She could not answer that. 'Jeff, I want us to talk.

We *must!*'

'Not now.'

'Yes!' she insisted, then added a belated, 'Please. Come back to the cottage and——'

'You'll tell me your terms?' he enquired, in the supercilious tone he used if someone dared to cross him. Like most males of Italian descent, Jefferson Barssi possessed a degree of in-built arrogance. He did not take kindly to being messed around, though few were foolish enough to try. 'But suppose I don't have time to listen?'

'No time? Not listen?' she echoed idiotically.

'Has it never struck you that while your days are more or less your own—apart from wiping the odd runny nose—I have heavy business commitments? Well, that's typical of the Christa we all know and love. In she bowls and decides on a meeting, without thinking the damn thing through. However, what may have seemed credible to you is quite impracticable for me.'

'I did think it through and, impracticable or not, you did agree,' she protested. 'Why change your mind now? I'm sure Barssi & Company can manage without you for a few days. Vittorio and Tony are there to——'

'Right now my father and my brother need me,' Jeff came back at her. 'This is my third trip to Europe in six months, which——'

'They get shorter and shorter,' Christa interrupted. 'Last time you were supposed to be here for a fortnight but rushed off after a few days, and now—huh! I don't understand why you came all this way, just to turn round and go straight back again. Yes, I do,' she added, aware of a tight, coiling sensation inside her. She had been abysmally slow on the uptake, but all of a sudden phrases like 'tug-of-love' and 'child used as a pawn' flashed like sinister neon signs in her head. 'You came to kidnap Marcus!' she accused, a hand flying to her throat in panic.

'You're talking nonsense,' Jeff replied curtly. 'However, I wish to state here and now that I'm sick to death of him living in one country and me in another. I intend to see far more of my son in the future than I've seen of him in the past. Get that straight.'

'You *are* kidnapping him,' Christa insisted. 'But he's only a little boy, not much more than a baby. He'll miss me—he'll want me. He'll cry.' Her despair switched to the anger of defiance. 'Jefferson, you can't do this. I won't let you!'

'How do you propose to stop me?'

For a moment she floundered, like a squid lost in its own ink. 'You don't have Marcus's passport!' she announced in triumph.

'Open the bureau.'

'You do have his passport,' she said flatly, looking at the depleted pigeonhole. She should have known as much. 'I'll get a lawyer. I'll——'

'What you will do is catch a plane,' he cut in. 'The reason I rang was, one, to assure you that Marcus is safe, and two, to advise you that I've left a ticket at the Varig desk. You're booked on a flight to Rio the day after tomorrow. I'll meet you.'

Christa's fist clenched around the receiver. 'I don't want to come to damned Rio!' she flared.

'Hard luck, but if you want to be with your son, I'm afraid you'll have to.'

The telephone went dead.

On unsteady legs, she made it to the nearest chair and collapsed.

'Christa, I'm so sorry,' said Sylvie, placing a sympathetic hand on her shoulder. 'All along I had a premonition something was wrong. I said your husband seemed strained.'

'Strained? Preoccupied, more like! His mind must have been working overtime. Locate passport, make sure Marcus has warm clothes, don't forget teddy!' Christa blazed, her eyes glittering with hurt and resentment. She gave her friend a rapid résumé of the call. 'Do you think if I rang the police and explained, there'd be enough time for them to——'

'Explained what?' came the gentle intrusion. 'I don't see how a father can be prevented from taking his own son out of the country.'

'I suppose not,' she admitted grudgingly. 'Heavens, but he's a high-handed, low-down shark!' Name-calling was not her style, yet frustration gave no other choice. 'When I left with Marcus, I didn't do it cold-bloodedly. I didn't plan a retreat in advance, like a general planning battle strategy.'

'But did he? Don't you think it was more a case of him seeing Marcus and——'

'Snatching him on the spur of the moment? No, not Jefferson. He never does anything—*anything*,'

Christa insisted, 'without first making a meticulous assessment of the pros and cons. He's the most organised person I've ever met.' Without warning her eyes were dewy, and she brushed away a tear. 'This abduction must have been planned for ages.'

Sylvie was less than convinced. 'Christa, your husband didn't know I'd be babysitting, and if you'd been here how could he have whisked Marcus off? No, I think he just saw a chance and——'

'Taking Marcus was a premeditated and deliberate act. If Jeff hadn't managed it this way, he'd have done it another.' Christa's lips compressed. 'It's three months since I last saw him and six since we lived together, and it's clear to me now that I'd forgotten what he's really like. I'd even persuaded myself that my leaving had made him stop and think. How wrong can anyone be?' she added bitterly. 'Jeff was, and is, a domineering tyrant, just like his father. When Vittorio snapped his fingers, you should have seen how Isabel scuttled around!'

'I understood you liked your in-laws?' Sylvie said, perplexed.

'I did—I do. But Vittorio regarded himself as the Supreme Being, the King of Kings, and expected to be treated as such. A marriage of equals it was not.' Christa glowered. 'Jeff's a genuine chip off the old block.'

'Christa, his basic message was that he didn't have time to talk now,' her friend pointed out. 'And, as I understand it, he's taken Marcus to ensure that you do, though later. You were going to meet up anyway.

The difference is your rendezvous will take place in Rio, that's all.'

'All?' Christa queried, her voice frigid.

'I agree Jefferson's been over-hasty, but aren't you also being hasty in condemning him like this?' the older woman soothed. 'Maybe he was wrong to uproot Marcus, but it's hardly kidnap.'

Christa looked down at her hands. 'I suppose not,' she muttered.

Sylvie smiled. Progress had been made. 'As far as your reconciliation is concerned, surely it doesn't matter where——'

Christa leapt to her feet. Even if Jeff were not guilty of abduction, the way he had ridden roughshod over what *she* wanted was symbolic of his behaviour in the past. It was behaviour which had driven a wedge between them, behaviour she abhorred, behaviour she had sworn she would never accept again.

'Reconciliation? What reconciliation?' she demanded. 'As far as any getting back together with a manipulating bastard like Jefferson Barssi goes—you can forget it!'

CHAPTER TWO

IT WAS six a.m. and still dark when the jumbo jet touched down in Rio de Janeiro, yet even at that early hour the city worked its magic. Christa might deeply resent the arbitrary way in which she had been compelled to make the journey, but a glimpse of the illuminated hundred-and-thirty foot statue of Christ the Redeemer, seemingly suspended in mid-air with arms spread wide while the city lights sparkled beneath His feet, brought a catch to her throat. Poignant memories were revived. Here, although in the latter days there had been anguish and an increasing sense of isolation, she had known great happiness. Rio, with its unique symphony of sea and skyscrapers, spectacular beaches and mountains, had been a wonderful place to fall in love.

During the lengthy delay while everyone waited for their luggage, the night paled and translucent dawn colours of pale gold and grey streaked the sky. As the Brazilian airline steward beside her gamely attempted to make interesting conversation, Christa peered beyond the glass screen into the public domain of the arrivals hall. All she could see were a few yawning porters and the ever-hopeful band of raggle-taggle taxi drivers. There was no sign of Jefferson. He had said

he would meet her, but after so much travelling
maybe he had slept through the alarm. Or could it be
a case of him deliberately not turning up in order to
teach her some kind of lesson? Such mean-spiritedness
seemed out of character, but then, she thought grimly,
tearing Marcus from her was not the action of Mr
Nice Guy. Christa tapped the irritated toe of a soft
white suede boot. If she had been left to make her own
way to Casa Libra, the Barssi family home, so be it!

At long last the carousel yielded up suitcases and the
steward insisted on heaving her two on to a trolley.

'Thanks,' she smiled.

'My pleasure,' he assured her. Just to breathe the
same air was a pleasure, he thought. He had noticed
her the minute she had set foot in the cabin, attracted
by her English rose complexion, her heart-shaped
face, her beautiful blue eyes. They were eyes full of
laughter, full of tears, full of emotion. Add one of the
best figures he'd seen in ages and he had instantly
labelled her *'magnifica'*. Pity about the wedding ring.
'Will you be able to manage on your own?' he asked,
reluctant to let her go.

Christa flexed an arm. 'I'm stronger than you
think,' she grinned and, gripping the pushbar,
trundled off towards the doors.

'Isn't it rather early to be flirting with flat-footed
Romeos?' someone drawled as she emerged.

Her heart missed a beat. The dark-haired, golden-
skinned man who had spoken might have undertaken
two long-haul flights in as many days—the second in
the company of a toddler who rarely stayed still for a

minute—yet in open-throated shirt and dark trousers he looked vibrantly alive. Christa's heart broke into an unsteady rhythm. If she had forgotten how devastating her husband's behaviour could be, so absence had also blurred her memory of his devastating looks. A broad brow, high cheekbones and nose with a Roman curve gave him the air of an aristocrat—if a macho one. Add brown eyes which could make love without the necessity for words, or undertake an astute assessment, or flash with brilliant yellow flecks according to his mood, and next to him other men looked wishy-washy. Next to Jefferson Barssi, other men looked *safe*.

'You mean I should wait until after breakfast?' she enquired, assuming a brittle flippancy.

'Lunchtime would be preferable,' he said, and wrapped a tanned arm around her and kissed her.

Doubtless the impetus for his kiss came from a masculine need to stake claim—it could not be coincidence that the steward had appeared at that moment—yet Jeff's mouth was remarkably hard and hungry. Taken by surprise, Christa parted her lips beneath his. There was a moment when she submitted to the roughly persuasive stroke of his tongue, then she pushed back. Her pulse raced, her breath was shallow. What was she doing? she wondered in alarm. What was she allowing him to do? She could not afford to start wanting Jefferson now. She could not permit herself to be seduced. No, thanks. No way. Out of the question.

'How's Marcus?' she demanded, feeling hot

and disorientated.

'Fighting fit.' His mouth lifted at the corners. 'I'm amazed how different he is from the kid I saw in England. OK, prior to my first visit he'd had a cold and on the second he was going down with the measles, but he seemed so weak and pale and subdued.'

'An icy winter followed by a damp spring meant all he had to do was stick his head out of the door and he caught some virus or other,' Christa defended, with haste.

She received a look of reproof. 'I did suggest you bring him back to Rio and the warmth.'

'He couldn't have coped with the journey.'

Jeff's shrug indicated that he did not believe her. That could not be helped. She was not about to launch into the true confessions which would justify her claim, not now.

'Did Marcus sleep on the plane?' she asked, peeling off the navy blazer she wore with white tank top and trousers.

'Not much. He developed a fascination for the loo, so we spent most of our time tramping back and forth to that. The only benefit was he didn't wet himself,' Jeff said sardonically.

'So Marcus is all righ?' Christa persisted.

He gave an irritated sigh. 'Marcus is tired, but happy.' He prowled towards the exit. 'You'll be able to see for yourself in a minute. He's asleep in the car.'

'You've brought him to the airport and left him

outside?' she exclaimed in horror.

'I thought you'd want to check your son over at the first possible moment.'

'I do, but goodness, how many times have you warned me that Rio can be a mad, bad city?' she protested. 'Be careful if you wear jewellery, watch out for your bag, you used to insist; yet you leave a small boy unattended!'

'I didn't,' Jeff hissed through clenched teeth. 'I stood just inside the arrivals hall with one eye trained on the car, while the other watched for you.' Long strides took him out through the doors. 'Look,' he ordered, pointing to a silver Alfa Romeo where a child in dungarees lay sprawled on the back seat, his teddy beside him. Thumb fallen from his mouth, he was fast asleep. 'Marcus is still there—all in one piece.'

'By the grace of God,' Christa retorted, but the gibe went unnoticed, for a bearded man with a bow-tie and a briefcase had pounced, slapping Jefferson on the back and gabbling away in Portuguese. He was, she learned from the conversation which followed, a fan from his motor-racing days and was eager to know what had been happening to him since then.

'Sorry about the delay,' said Jeff, when the fan finally took his leave. He unlocked the boot and began fitting her suitcases inside. 'It's rare that anyone recognises me now, and when you think that it's six years since I last lined up on a Grand Prix grid, it's surprising anyone does.' As he closed the lid, his eyes sped over her. 'Are you dead on your feet?'

Christa straightened like a soldier ready for inspection. 'I don't feel tired at all,' she announced defiantly.

Oddly enough, she didn't, despite managing only an hour or two of shallow sleep. Indeed, her metabolism appeared to have speeded up, though whether this was due to time-change or to being with her husband again, she preferred not to debate.

Marcus awoke as they climbed into the car.

'Mummy?' he enquired, grinding small fists into his eyes.

'I'm here, *querido*,' she smiled, reaching over to caress his flushed cheek. She held out her arms. 'Want a cuddle?'

'Not now,' the toddler muttered, and his lids fell. A moment later he had dozed off again.

Christa slumped, feeling bereft. So much for imagining her son would pine! So much for thinking she would be missed! So much for *her* needing the comfort of an embrace!

'What's with the *querido*?' Jeff questioned, as they drew away from the airport. 'In fact, what's with the other Portuguese Marcus knows? He appears to understand quite a few words.'

'Oh, Sylvie's been teaching him—me,' she replied, the glib tone giving no hint that her 'teaching' had consisted of months of head-in-a-book study, weeks listening to tapes, the daily committing to memory of nouns, verbs and adjectives.

'Why?'

She frowned. What kind of a question was that? Jeff knew as well as she did that when she had lived in Rio her Portuguese had never got off the ground; so wasn't it obvious she had been brushing up the language in anticipation of her return? But if he expected her to spell out her linguistic failure he would need to wait a long time. Christa was damned if she would admit to inadequacies. And she was equally damned if she would garrulously admit to having— once—planned to come back.

'As Marcus is half-Brazilian, I considered it right and proper he should have a knowledge of the language,' she declared, all schoolmistressy.

Jeff subjected her to a piercing look. 'Thanks.' The Alfa Romeo sped on to one of the concrete flyovers which led towards the city. 'That new haircut of yours reminds me of a painting I once saw of Adonis, the beautiful youth,' Jeff remarked.

'Strange, when I happen to be twenty-five years old and female!'

'Your gender's obvious,' he said, his dark eyes dropping to divest her of her clothes in a studied, sensuous way which did nothing for Christa's equilibrium. 'The boyish head allied with the rapantly female body is a sexy combination, a real turn-on. It's making me feel exceptionally——'

Jeff stamped on the brake. A pick-up truck had jumped lanes and landed up inches in front of his bumper. As he gesticulated fervid annoyance, Christa gave thanks for his distraction. Whatever defects their marriage had suffered, physically they had always been in tune. But the last thing she wanted was to be reminded of how *good* they had been at arousing each other, at exciting each other, at creating that wonderful delirium.

'I notice the traffic doesn't improve,' she commented, checking behind her to find Marcus sleeping undisturbed.

Jeff's shoulders moved in dismissal. 'All you need is the will to survive.'

'Or a death wish,' she said succinctly.

Although she drove back in England, Christa had had a few tries in Rio and given up. Her husband might switch between mannered Anglo-Saxon style and dodgem-driving with fluent ease, but she had been disinclined to throw in her lot with a nation which passed on both sides, which regarded 'stop' lights as more of a suggestion than a command, which blithely parked its cars any old place and strolled away.

'I would like to put it on record that I strongly object to you removing Marcus,' she announced, as a chaotic mix of old ornate churches, orange-roofed houses and glass and chrome tower blocks signalled the start of the city.

'Long live the revolution,' he said, with an air of accepting the inevitable.

Christa's eyes emitted blue fire. 'I also resent being railroaded into coming here. However, it's the last time you manoeuvre me. It may have worked in the past, but I'm older and wiser now, and fully capable of making my own decisions.'

'I wasn't aware I had manoeuvred, but there's no need to come on like a Sherman tank.'

'I'm not!'

'You're being hostile,' Jeff said sharply.

'I'm being assertive, and not before time! Forcing me to come to Rio was quite unnecessary. If you'd telephoned and explained how a visit wasn't convenient at this point in time—that business took precedence *again*,' Christa slid in astringently, 'I would have been willing to fly out here.'

He gave her a steely-eyed glance. 'That wasn't the impression I had from the letter you wrote insisting *I* come to England, nor when I rang from Heathrow. You didn't sound so keen then.'

'I didn't say I was keen, I said I would have been willing. There was no need for your gangster tactics. I'm a civilised human being. I would have co-operated.'

Jeff's mouth twisted. 'Yeah?'

'Yes. What happened to your shoulder?'

'My shoulder?'

'You were telling the man back there you'd had an accident and couldn't move it for a couple of weeks.'

'If you understood that much, your Portuguese has improved,' he remarked laconically.

'What did you do?' asked Christa, keeping her tone amiable.

'Being a member of the sexually deprived——' for an instant his gaze accosted hers '—I need an outlet for my frustrations and I've been playing the odd game of squash. One evening I erupted into a move too violently and slammed up against the wall. Apparently when I damaged my shoulder before a tiny piece of bone was left floating and I knocked it out of place.'

'It hurt?'

'Very much. The entire joint and most of my arm swelled up like a balloon.' Jeff rolled the shoulder in question. 'But the bone seems to have settled back. There's not been so much as a twinge when I've lifted Marcus.'

Christa cast another look at their sleeping son. 'Your parents must have been pleased to see him again.'

'Ecstatic would be a closer description. He seemed pretty delighted too.'

'He couldn't have recognised them, not after all this time?'

'I wouldn't have imagined so, and yet when we walked into the house——' Jeff frowned out of the side window '—he ran straight to my mother. After that it was hugs, kisses and tears in grand, emotional Latin-American style.'

Uncomfortable with thoughts of how Isabel and Vittorio Barssi adored Marcus, their one and only grandchild, Christa concentrated on the road ahead. It was all too easy to imagine her in-laws' elation—as it was all too easy to imagine their distress last year when he had suddenly disappeared from their lives.

'I presume Esther and Tony haven't decided to start a family?' she enquired conversationally. 'At least, not yet.'

'They won't. Not ever.'

Christa jammed her lips together. She did not appreciate having her suggestion shot down in such an autocratic manner.

'Esther's still fascinated by her career?' she said, biting back a retort.

'She is, though her figure comes a close second. Five days a week she's the super-efficient public relations executive, and on the remaining two it's down to the beach to parade her wares. I've never met anyone so obsessed with being top dog—top bitch,' Jeff adjusted, 'in everything they do.'

Although Christa could not imagine them ever being close friends, Esther had taken the trouble to write during her absence—and now she leapt to the defence.

'Perhaps if you'd been one of eight kids born in a shack in the poorest part of town, you'd——'

'Be pain-in-the-neck *driven*? I hope not!'

'Esther isn't driven, she's just a bit more . . . committed than most.'

'Committed like the Borgias,' he said darkly.

Jeff remained forever irked by his sister-in-law, something which, Christa knew, had much to do with her domination of his brother. Personally, she felt the meek and mild Tony cried out to be bossed, and if his wife overruled him it was his own fault. But Jeff reckoned the figure-conscious brunette had a pathological need to be Number One—and woe betide anyone who dared stand in her way.

'How old is Esther now?' she queried. 'Thirty-two?'

'Thirty-three.'

'Give her another couple of years and she'll hear the tick of her biological clock. Then, before you know it, she'll start producing offspring like rabbits.'

'You're wrong.'

The outright rejection stung. It was impossible to bite back a retort this time.

'Thanks,' Christa snapped. 'I'd forgotten how you always did value my opinion.'

'That was heavy-handed,' Jeff agreed, and his dark eyes met hers. 'Forgive me?'

For a moment she stared back at his smile, then she relented. 'Forgiven.' Determined not to be browbeaten, she added, 'But everyone is capable of changing their minds about what they want from life.'

His smile switched off. 'Yes,' he said.

Christa could recognise a reference to her hotheaded departure when she heard one, but refused to react. While she did not feel tired, she would admit to being a tiny bit uptight. If they embarked on a review of the past, then the conversation must lead to the future—a topic where calm detachment was essential. Right now, she felt neither calm nor detached. But there was no rush to talk. There would be plenty of time tomorrow, or the next day, or the one after that. Nothing was to be gained from rushing things. Indeed, the more time passed, the less certain she became about what she intended to say. Though it was not a question of second thoughts, oh dear, no.

'How did your parents like the last batch of photographs?' she enquired, as a turn beside a luxury hotel brought them on to the dual carriageway which ran the three-kilometre stretch of Copacabana beach.

'They thought they were wonderful. Half the

population of Rio must have seen Marcus building a snowman and sniffing daffodils by now.'

Like every one of the beaches which spread around the city, Copacabana had its own personality and its own admirers. To their right the broad mosaic pavement was patterned with umbrellaed tables, where later tourists would drink beer or small cups of *cafezinho*, the strong local coffee. To their left lay the sand where volleyball was played with a typically Brazilian blend of wild improvisation and flair. Christa was blind to right and left, to cafés and beach. Instead her mind's eye was fastened on her father, tepidly flicking through those same photographs. 'Nice,' he had managed, before putting them aside in favour of a report on software sales.

'How's George?' asked Jeff, as though he had guessed her thoughts. 'I spoke to him last week about a business matter, but briefly.'

'Then you're more up to date than me. I rang before I left, but he was visiting one of the factories and although his secretary promised he'd call back he never did.' Christa slid him a glance. 'The last time we made contact Dad was enthusing over how successful the joint venture between Barssi & Company and Henley Electronics is proving to be. I understand the computers are popular over here?'

'In just a few short months they've blown the market apart,' Jeff confirmed, pleasure glowing in his brown eyes.

'So you're making plenty of money?'

'Brazilians believe it's every man's right to get rich,

and quickly,' he grinned, deaf to the tension which had entered her tone. He sobered. 'We are, on both sides. And we're destined to make much, much more.'

Founded by Vittorio Barssi forty years ago, the family firm had assembled and sold office equipment in the capitals of South America. From their desks, filing cabinets and comprehensive range of sundry items, good profits had been earned. Then Jeff had insisted they make a move into modern technology—wholeheartedly and unsparingly. Yes, he knew such an expansion involved risks. Yes, he agreed, it demanded a hefty financial investment. But if Barssi & Company were to continue to prosper, they must keep pace with the times. His father had wavered, while Tony had plumped for leaving well alone. Long and hard, Jeff had argued the case—and he had won.

An affiliation with one of the international computer firms was what he had in mind, with Henley's already identified. At a speed which would have done credit to his racing days, overtures had been made, meetings arranged, negotiations for local manufacture started. Competition from other companies also eager to snare George Henley's Brazilian licences had been eliminated, and once again Jefferson Barrsi emerged the victor.

'Nice,' Christa remarked crisply.

'We're making plenty of money only because everyone's worked plenty,' he stressed.

'Especially you.'

'The link-up with your father is my particular

baby,' he said defensively, then he frowned. 'But the adage about there being no gain without pain is true.'

Christa's thoughts went to the transformation of green-field site to a fully operational factory and warehouse—a transformation which had obsessed Jeff from the early weeks of their marriage until her departure.

'Now that production's off and running, your workload will be easier?' she suggested, as they motored along the shopping street which connected Copacabana to Ipanema.

Jeff gave a wry smile. 'Some, though at times it seems all I've done is swap one load of problems for another. Introducing a new range of PC's has been no picnic. The five thousand mail shots we sent out brought in hundreds of enquiries—thank heavens!—but following them up has meant a multitude of visits and endless correspondence. My dictating machine's been red-hot. There was a long spell when Ruth and I never managed to get away from the office before eight.'

Christa lifted surprised brows. His secretary had put her boss before her husband and agreed to work late? Wonders would never cease! In the past, the middle-aged redhead had been happy to do whatever was required between eight-thirty a.m. and four-fifty-nine—and do it with the utmost efficiency—but five o'clock marked the cut-off point. After that, she was sorry but she must be home to welcome her Gilberto and cook his evening meal. Fifteen years married Ruth Mayor might be, yet she doted on her husband like a newly wed and nothing—neither work, tempest nor earthquake—was allowed to disrupt her loving routine.

On the point of asking the reason for the change, Christa realised they had passed the turn which led to the huge Barssi mansion.

'Where are we going?' she enquired.

'To my apartment.'

Her head jerked round. 'Your apartment? You have an apartment?'

'There's no need to look so incredulous,' rasped Jeff, as she stared at him wide-eyed. 'You knew Casa Libra was a temporary base.'

Christa switched her gaze to the esplanade where joggers, young and not so young, pounded along beneath a crystalline blue sky. He had bought an apartment *now*? One part of her felt like bursting into maniacal laughter, another part was tempted to sob. What abysmal timing! Last year she had been desperate for them to flee Casa Libra and he had been in full agreement; or so he had said. After a long and arduous search, she had been delighted when they had both fallen for the same airy duplex. The deal had been agreed and they had been all set to go when, on that fateful evening, Jeff had reneged. Out of the blue, he had claimed they were rushing things, denounced the accommodation as inadequate, said they must look for something better.

Christa twined a tawny strand of hair around her finger. If he had not backtracked, she would not have left Rio and she would not have separated him from his son. Yet, looked at realistically, although quitting the Barssi mansion would have solved some of their problems, it would not have banished each and every one. Maybe all moving into the duplex would have done was postpone her departure. She sighed. She would never know.

'You might call a year and a half temporary—I don't,' she told him.

'Christa, when we were asked to leave my bachelor flat and I suggested we move in with my family, you didn't object.'

'You didn't suggest, you told me it was going to happen. However,' she continued, before he could refute her claim, 'I was so madly in love, I wouldn't have objected if we'd moved to an igloo!'

A muscle tightened in his jaw. 'Casa Libra has plenty of space,' he defended. 'We had our own suite of rooms, Marcus had his own nursery. We weren't exactly tripping over my parents, or Tony and Esther.'

'Maybe not, yet did you never notice that whenever we raised our voices someone always seemed to be around? Always.' She took a breath. 'Let's not get into that right now. Where is your apartment?'

'Overlooking the sea on Barra da Tijuca.'

My first choice of beach, Christa thought wryly, recalling the mile upon mile of unspoiled sand.

In silence they drove on, and soon Ipanema was left behind and the shores of Leblon became a memory. A quarter of an hour later they arrived at their destination. Close to the sports club and not far from a flourishing shopping mall, Barra da Tijuca was rapidly becoming one of Rio's smartest residential districts. Some of the apartment blocks which ranged along the coast were already well-established, but many were not. The one they stopped outside, set amid sprouting green lawns and infant bushes of purple bougainvillaea, was newly built and only half occupied.

As Jeff cut the engine, a mumble sounded from the back seat, and Marcus appeared between them, bleary-eyed and yawning.

'Where this?' he wanted to know as he came awake.

Jeff shot Christa a look. 'It's your new house,' he said firmly. Climbing from the car, he lifted him up. 'Think you'll like it?' he asked, as the little boy tilted his head to gaze, mouth agape, at the stylish building with its tinted glass and white marble, its wide verandas and gracefully arched windows. 'Around the back there's a swimming pool and a playground. A slide and a sandpit have been installed, though the area isn't finished yet.'

'Swings?' the toddler asked hopefully.

Jeff tickled his tummy. 'Yes, hotshot, there are some swings. We'll have a look at where you're going to live first, then I'll take you down.'

If Marcus was delighted with the prospect of what the outdoors held, Christa could not help but be enchanted with indoors. The first-floor apartment had a spacious living-room, a study, dream kitchen, three good-sized bedrooms with walk-in closets and en suite bathrooms. In almost every room a glass door slid back, permitting them to step on to wrap-around balconies; all fitted with child-proof safety screens of scrolled wrought iron. Carpeted in a smart eau-de-Nil, the apartment was sparsely furnished. A desk, cream leather sofa and chairs, and a smart Swedish dining-suite had been moved in, but there were no pictures, no plants, none of the knick-knacks that change a house into a home. Christa noticed that the beds—a king-size in the master bedroom, and a double in each of the other rooms—had been made up. It was just as well there were three; she had no intention of accommodatingly snuggling up beside him!

'How long have you had the apartment?' she asked, as Jeff's tour ended and they returned to the living-room with its kaleidoscopic views of white sand and turquoise sea.

'I signed the papers four months ago, but at that time it was a shell. Since then I've been doing my best to get it habitable and the services fixed. I seemed to spend a good hour a day chasing up furniture, painters, the telephone company. You name it, I ring them!' He rumpled his dark hair. 'I never realised getting the place ready would involve so much hassle.'

Christa looked around her. 'Your efforts have been worth while. It's lovely.'

'Papá!' Marcus yanked at his trouser leg. 'Swings, Papá!' he demanded.

Jeff clicked his heels and saluted, making the little boy chuckle. 'Yessir.'

'Do you mind if I stay here and have another wander around?' Christa asked, as he hoisted the child into his arms.

'Carry on.'

Left alone, she slid her hands into the pockets of her white trousers and walked slowly from one room to the next. Her husband had bought an apartment on the beach she liked best, on a floor which suited her—she had never cared for heights—and begun furnishing it in a way which was very much to her taste. Could this have happened by chance? She didn't believe so. What she *did* believe was that Jeff was reaching out and apologising for the past. He was showing her how much he cared. Stricken by a sudden lump in her throat, a stinging at the back of her eyes, Christa swallowed. The meticulously planned apartment represented an olive branch, a peace-offering, a gift—for her.

So where did this leave her outburst of a couple of days ago? She swallowed again. No reconciliation, she had declared, but . . . After endless reappraisals and contemplation, she had felt overwhelmingly positive about their marriage until, in a split second, she had performed not so much a U-turn as a violent handbrake spin. Did it make any sense? Had she really meant it? The honest answer to both questions was a resounding *no*. Her reaction had been a throwback to the rash and precipitate days, days she had believed had gone for ever. But old habits die hard, it seemed.

Christa walked through the master bedroom and out on to the balcony, where a cooling breeze tempered the heat which had nudged into the mid-eighties. Olive branch, peace-offering or gift, to allow herself to be persuaded into a swift and unquestioning return would make no sense either. She could not agree to a resumption of their relationship—as it had been. Time altered everyone, and she was a far different person from the girl who had flown off into the wide blue yonder six months ago. Before they joined forces there were needs which must be recognised and met. Jeff must understand she was no longer willing to be 'bounced' along. He must realise she was an independent person who had rights. He must accept——

'Hi,' he said, strolling up behind her.

Startled, she spun round. She looked beyond him, but no dungaree imp tottered in his wake.

'What have you done with Marcus?'

'He's teamed up with a kid called Niero, and Niero's nanny is watching over them both. She's promised to bring him up in half an hour.'

Christa grinned. 'Making friends didn't take him long.'

Two large tanned hands were spread around her waist, and Jeff drew her from the balcony.

'I know something else which won't take long, either—not the way I'm feeling!'

Recognising the look in his eyes, a languorous gleam which concealed a fierce level of desire, she covered his hands with her own.

'Jeff, I've discovered that in this life you have to be tough, otherwise you tend to get sat upon,' she pronounced, having no wish to be enticed. Later, yes—please, yes. But not at this moment. 'So it's vital you realise——'

His lips twitched. 'Honey, the last thing I have in mind is to *sit* on you,' he said, then his face took on a serious slant. 'I'm in the prime of my life and for the past goodness knows how long I've slept alone. I don't like it. To be precise, I hate it!'

'I realise that, but first——' Before she knew what was happening, his mouth had covered hers and he was kissing her, his tongue probing with a knowing sensuality which made every nerve-end tingle. Christa pressed her hands against his shoulders and pulled back. 'I want to talk,' she finished unsteadily.

'And I want to——' Jeff paused, replacing the word he had chosen with something less earthy, more polite, 'make love.'

'Not now.'

'Yes!' His hips moved suggestively against hers, reminding her—as if she had ever forgotten—how he had always been strong on virility. 'Did you know a survey revealed that between the ages of thirty and thirty-nine, men think about sex on average four times an hour? I reckon that since you went away I've been thinking about it at least twice as often. Which means that every seven and a half minutes I'm stricken by this violent urge to——'

He clasped a hand on either side of her head and started to kiss her again. They were long, searching kisses deep inside her mouth, kisses which knocked her off balance and confused everything. Christa's head said she must push him away, yet her heart demanded she draw him near.

'No, Jeff,' she said when, without warning, he swept her up in his arms and laid her on the bed, but her protest had lacked decision.

Smiling down at her wide eyes and flushed face, he began to unbutton his shirt.

'What say you we strip off?' he grinned.

Reminding herself that there were far more important matters than making love, Christa sat up. 'Before we—we do anything we need to—to talk,' she said, speaking jerkily because the gleam of his bronzed skin and the coils of black hair on his chest were distracting.

'I find this obsession of yours with talking a pain in the ass,' he complained, and still wearing his trousers—mercifully—swung on to the bed and pulled her down again beside him. 'But I do like your ass,' he said, squeezing the roundness of her backside, 'and I do like your silky skin. No one else has skin like yours, Christa,' he murmured, sliding his hand beneath her tank top. 'I also like your breasts.' He cupped a burgeoning curve. I like their firmness and their——'

'I don't like us doing this,' she interrupted.

Jeff pushed aside her lacy bra to trail his fingers over her tightening nipples.

'You don't want to be the recipient of all my smouldering passion?'

'No.'

Christa attempted to sit up, but he held her down, and when she began to speak his kiss stopped her words. Masterfully, he captured the sweet moistness of her mouth and stroked her breasts, murmuring his need and what he intended to do to her. A powerlessness spilled into her limbs. The first time they had made love Jeff, with his lips and his hands and his words, had made her aware of her body in a way no other man had done before, and she had been lost. She was lost now.

'Liar,' he said, when at last he raised his head. He was smiling, the satisfaction of a man who knows he has aroused a woman shining from him.

Christa summoned up tatters of resistance. 'Jeff, the only time you took me seriously before was when I was horizontal!'

'Not true,' he objected, running a finger along the newly exposed groove at the nape of her neck.

'It iş! Which is why I want to be vertical now. We suffered a breakdown in communication, and——'

'It's communication I have in mind.'

'I mean *talking* communication.' His hand had returned to her breasts. She wished she could find the strength to remove it. 'Marcus'll be back soon,' she said, by way of a protest.

He gave an irritated sigh. 'Soon is a long way off.'

'It's three months since we were last together,' Christa said, trying another tack. 'Do you really want us to rush into a—a quick fumble?'

'A quick fumble?' Jeff's voice roughened and his caresses ceased. 'Surely you know me well enough to give me credit for a little more finesse?'

'I've come straight off the plane.'

'You assured me you weren't tired.'

'Yes, but——'

Yellow flecks glittered in the depths of his eyes. 'To quote the jargon, you were always user-friendly. I can't say I care for the way you've become user-repellent all of a sudden.'

'I'm not. I just don't like being forced,' Christa objected.

'I am *not* forcing you.'

'You are.'

His scowl warned that his patience was in grave danger of running out. 'Honey, I need you. Now.'

'Jeff——'

'You want me to go down on my hands and knees and beg for it?' he demanded.

She sighed. 'Of course not.'

His fingers went to her belt. 'Then, please, lay off the excuses.'

Christa hesitated. Suddenly she felt guilty. Her husband was a healthy and passionate man, and after so long apart it was only natural he should want to make love. Not only that, she wanted to make love too. She yearned to run her hands over his body, wrap herself around, feel him hard and thrusting within her. And why not? They could talk afterwards.

'If you'll tell me one thing,' she said.

Jeff gave a low growl of exasperation. 'Shoot.'

'I'd like to know what made it so important you get me out to Rio *now*. Fine, we're going to talk, but——' she grinned '—I suspect you could be guilty of an ulterior motive?'

'Yeah,' he agreed, engrossed in unfastening the button at her waistband.

Christa's mind winged joyfully around the apartment. 'And it is?'

'Later.'

'Now,' she pleaded, longing to hear him say he had chosen this dream house for her—because he loved her. Abruptly, she lifted her head and listened. In the distance was the march and accompanying skitter of footsteps. 'Someone's coming.'

'I said no excuses!'

'But they are.'

The footsteps grew louder, then ceased as someone rang the bell. Scattering expletives like machine-gun bullets, Jeff swept from the bed. His shirt was retrieved and flung on.

'Great, you got your way. I sure as hell hope you're satisfied, because I'm not!' Handfuls of shirt were thrust into his trousers. 'You asked why I wanted you to come to Rio. The answer is—my father.'

Christa pushed herself up. 'Your father?' she repeated, in bewilderment.

'He doesn't have much longer to live,' Jeff said brusquely.

'Vittorio's ill?'

'He's dying, and if you and I could present a united front it'd go a long way towards making his last days happy.'

She made a frantic attempt to grasp what he was talking about. 'A—a united front?' she faltered.

'I gather from your expression that you're less than thrilled with the idea. Well, I'm sorry if taking part in a masquerade doesn't appeal, but it will only be for a short time.' A man of passionate conviction, at times he possessed a glacial reserve—and Jeff was icy cold right now. 'If it's possible, I'd prefer my father to rest in peace, which means——' The bell rang again, summoning him to the door. At it he stopped, and flung the final words back over his shoulder. '—putting our differences aside and acting like our marriage is rock-solid.'

CHAPTER THREE

CHRISTA stared at the door which had slammed shut. She had been pressganged into coming to Rio in order to provide his father with some kind of comfort? That was Jeff's prime motivation? It couldn't be! What had happened to sorting matters out between them? she wondered wildly. What about making adjustments? Where had getting back together again disappeared to? Her head began to thud. All of a sudden, the interpretation of Barra da Tijuca as her future home became a doubtful assumption. It seemed possible that, once more, she had been guilty of making a snap decision—and a wrong one.

She refastened her belt, straightened her tank top. Her husband's references to their partnership had been indisputably negative, and if he saw it in terms of a masquerade, a sham, didn't it follow that he might also regard it as a . . . lost cause? Her throat closed convulsively. Never an individual to pussyfoot around, she knew how Jeff dealt with lost causes. He jettisoned them!

Their marraige could be over? All the clichés of panic—the dry mouth, the palpitations, the intestinal churning—struck. The idea seemed like an amazing discovery, for, despite their problems and despite her

rash denial of reconciliation, never in her heart of
hearts had Christa ever imagined their relationship
dwindling away to become just another failed statistic.
Yet why not? It carried no divine right clause, and in
the six months they had lived apart Jeff would have
had more than enough time to think, assess,
reconsider. The intensity with which he had agreed
with her comment about people changing their minds
came back to her. She had taken it personally, yet now
she realised he could well have been talking about
himself.

But why had he changed his mind? Was it a case of
him growing impatient or—Christa winced as the idea
slunk unbidden into her mind—had he decided that,
having served her purpose, she could be dumped? No.
Never. Jeff was not *that* cold-blooded. Could an
outside influence have been brought to bear? she
wondered, recalling the press cuttings his mother had
collected during his Grand Prix career. Some featured
his involvement with a 'Miss Piaggio', one of the
leggy and nubile groupies who haunt the motor-racing
tracks. He had always maintained that newspaper
reporters were addicted to turning the occasional
encounter into a procession of hot romances and that,
in truth, his love life had been inordinately dull,
but . . .

Jeffferson Barssi was the kind of male who, with his
long-limbed grace and direct gaze, made women
sexually aware of him. It was an unconscious trait, she
knew, but it was there. Had another woman wandered
on to the scene? Could the apartment be for *her*?

He had claimed to be sleeping alone, but husbands were seldom in the habit of informing their wives when they committed adultery! Christa wrapped her arms across her stomach and slowly shook her head. She was seeing spectres where they did not exist. Jeff's blistering work schedule would have prohibited the development of *any* kind of attraction, let alone a serious one.

On his visits to England he had given no hint that he wanted out, yet now she found herself wondering if her refusal to return with Marcus at the time he suggested could have been the turning point. Had her lack of co-operation decided him to cut loose? So many questions, so few answers. Christa's shoulders hunched. She accepted that in addition to the mileage which had separated them an emotional gap existed, but she had never believed it to be *this* wide.

A thought snapped her upright. Emotionally a chasm might yawn, yet physically there wasn't room to slide paper between them—or there wouldn't have been minutes ago if Jefferson had had his way. Her sapphire eyes darkened into a stormy blue. His lack of faith in their relationship had not prevented him from doing his damnedest to make love. Talk about arrogance! Talk about taking advantage! Talk about being a self-serving, chauvinistic trickster! Ferociously she tugged at a curl of hair. And to think she had been on the brink of submitting!

'Mummy?'

Christa looked up to find the door being opened and two little heads peeping round; the first mischievous and smiling, the second solemn. Putting her thoughts on hold, she rose from the bed. Marcus had brought his new friend to be introduced.

'*Bom dia*,' she said, shaking the hand presented by a formal, bespectacled child of about four. With dark hair severely combed, grey shorts well pressed and black leather shoes polished to glass, he reminded her of a miniature tax inspector. '*Como vai?*' she enquired.

Niero professed to being in excellent health, *obrigado*, but Marcus wasted no time in informing her that he had fallen and scraped his knee; hence the early return. His *papá*, however, had made everything better and now he was eager to resume play.

'Come, come,' the toddler gestured, and as he scampered back into the hall Niero and Christa followed.

Jeff had been talking to the nanny, a woman of indeterminate years clad in tidy navy blue, and when he turned Christa recognised the quick-change artist. The man who not so much earlier had been first seductively carnal, then icily angry, was now the amiable father—and husband.

'Thanks for attending to the wounded soldier,' Christa said, smiling back into the brown eyes which had smiled into hers. If he could be sweetness and light in the company of others, so could she. She had claimed to be civilised, after all!

'More swings,' demanded Marcus, hopping up and down.

Jeff shook his head. 'I told Grandma and Grandpa

we'd be with them mid-morning, and they'll be wondering where we are. But,' he added, as the pout of a lip threatened resistance, 'you can play with Niero another day.'

''Nother day,' the little boy told his uncomprehending companion.

When Jeff had translated, Niero nodded politely, and after another shaking of hands he and his nanny departed.

'What's the matter with your father?' Christa enquired, as the door was locked and they set off along the marble-floored corridor and down the staircase.

The question, she acknowledged, was evasion, if not downright cowardice. What she should be doing was demanding a clear-cut, shot-from-the-hip statement on the future—their *separate* futures!—but she was having difficulty getting used to the idea and could not talk about it . . . yet.

'Stomach cancer.'

'How awful!' Instant tears of sympathy welled in her eyes. 'Is he in much pain?'

'There was a time two or three months back when he went through hell.' Marcus stumbled and Jeff took a firmer hold of his hand. 'Watching him suffer wasn't much fun, either.'

'I'm sorry,' she said, the need to comfort sending her fingers flying to his arm. 'I know I've criticised Vittorio for acting as if he's omnipotent, but,' she sniffed inelegantly, 'I'm very fond of him.'

'And he has a soft spot for you, honey—a big one. But he has the conquistador attitude, even now,' Jeff said drily. 'His health might be failing, yet he'll still annihilate any pesky injun who gets in his way.' He stroked her hand. 'Thank you for your concern.'

Christa gave a tremulous smile. She wished she had not clung on to his arm, she wished he had not called her 'honey', and she wished he was not touching her. She knew it was only the trauma of the moment which had released this intimacy, yet felt uneasy with it, none the less. From now on, intimacy was out. She must be aloof, controlled and always circumspect. How else could she survive?

'How's your father now?' she asked, as they went across the lobby and out into the sunshine.

'Frail, but comfortable. The doctor has him on regular doses of pain-killers and, so far, the régime's working well.' Reaching the silver Alfa, Jeff lifted Marcus through to the back seat. 'There you go, hotshot.'

During their traipse down the stairs the little boy had begun sucking his thumb, a sure sign of tiredness, and now he propped himself up in the corner with his teddy clutched to his chest.

'How long has Vittorio been aware of the cancer?' Christa enquired, as Jeff started the car.

'It was diagnosed nine or ten months ago.'

She frowned. 'I presume you were told?' He nodded. 'Then you must have known when I was here?'

'Right.'

'Why didn't you say something?'

'Because Vittorio didn't want anyone to know.'

'I wasn't just *anyone*,' Christa protested. 'I was a member of the family. I lived in the same house. Good grief, I was your wife! I can understand your father not wanting the subject bandied around, even at home, but you could have told me—in confidence.'

Jeff swung the Alfa out on to the road. 'No.'

'Typical,' she muttered. 'You were happy enough to fraternise with me in bed, but as far as sharing anything else went——' In a bleak gesture, she threw up her hands. 'No, thanks!'

'At the beginning just Tony and I knew,' Jeff said heavily. 'One day my father called us into his office, extracted a promise that what he was about to reveal would go no further, then explained that he had a tumour.'

'Vittorio had already spoken to your mother?'

'She was not to be informed.'

'Wonderful! The woman who'd devoted herself to him for fifty years, run his household, borne his children, did not rate as a confidante? And here I was thinking *I'd* been hard done by!'

Jeff drummed tanned fingers on the steering wheel. 'Has it never occurred to you that my mother might enjoy the patron syndrome?' he demanded, veering off at a tangent. 'Might find it comfortable to have someone around to make the decisions for her? Might have been reared to obey her husband, to cosset him, and not be capable of acting any other way?'

'Yes, it has,' Christa admitted. There was a short silence. 'I still think she deserved to know.'

'My father's a proud man, a stubborn man, and in

many ways a very private man,' he said, starting into a thoughtful explanation. 'He believes in keeping his own counsel, and I figure one of the reasons why is that,' Jeff scowled, as though momentarily beset by inner demons, 'dependency frightens him. He regards it as a sign of weakness, which was the way he initially regarded the cancer.'

'But cancer can hit anyone,' Christa protested, 'and Vittorio is over seventy.'

'It didn't matter. All his life he's prided himself on being fit, vigorous, in fine physical shape. A strong body was an integral part of his persona, then it lets in cancer and lets him down. Overnight his view of himself as the master of any situation had been wrecked. Irrational maybe, but——' His shoulders moved. 'However, my mother *was* told. Tony felt she ought to be briefed.'

'You didn't?' she demanded.

He expelled a breath. 'I was torn. On the one hand, I felt we should respect my father's wishes. On the other, it seemed wrong to leave my mother in ignorance.'

'How did she take it?'

'How d'you think?' he said ruefully. 'When Tony told her he'd warned her not to say a word, but apparently the moment she and my father were alone that night she started to cry. Within seconds everything was out in the open. Vittorio hit the roof, and at the end of it all made her swear she wouldn't tell anyone else.'

'And your poor brother was put on the rack?'

Jeff gave a curt laugh. 'It was Armageddon at the office the next day!'

For a few minutes Christa sat quietly, thinking of how this trauma had taken place around her and how she had not had the least suspicion. At the time she had been wrapped up in her own problems, yet surely not so wrapped up as to have been insensitive to this? Her mind went to Isabel Barssi. A good-natured woman with not a mean bone in her body, her mother-in-law was notorious for her indiscretions. She always intended to be prudent, yet information which went in through her ears had a naïve habit of gushing out through her mouth.

'I'm amazed your mother managed to keep the secret.'

'It must have been the hardest thing she's ever done,' Jeff agreed. 'But when everything had calmed down, my father said he was glad she knew. He found it a great relief to be able to talk to her openly and honestly.'

'You could have been open and honest with me,' Christa demurred. 'I wouldn't have said anything.'

'I dared not take the risk.'

Her chin jutted. 'Risk?'

'Christa, you're warm and spontaneous and there's very little guile about you. Pretence cuts across guidelines which have been there from birth.'

'Isn't psychoanalysis outside your area of expertise?' she questioned tartly.

Jeff ignored her. 'In these days of people faking everything from the hair on their heads to their orgasms, it's refreshing. You've never faked an orgasm in your life, have you?' he said, in amused enquiry.

Her cheeks grew hot. 'No.'

'Never had the need?'

'Don't get smug. What we're talking about here is——'

'Is that you're capable of doing things without thinking of the consequences,' he told her, abruptly serious. 'And of saying things.'

'You imagine I'd have blurted it out about Vittorio having cancer?' Christa asked, insulted to the marrow of her bones.

'Not blurted, no, but in a highly charged moment there was a possibility you might not have been entirely discreet. Not with what you said, but—well, the expression on your face could have been too revealing. That's the way I saw it at the time.' Jeff hesitated, as though in retrospect he might have been over-cautious. 'You do have remarkably eloquent eyes,' he finished lamely.

'Thanks for that vote of no confidence. You make it sound as though you were married to someone,' she glanced back at Marcus, whose lids were drooping, 'with the wits of an infant!'

'There were times when I wondered if I was,' Jeff retaliated. 'When you sprinted away from Rio last year, you were acting just like a damn child!'

'Very much so,' Christa shot back.

'You—you agree?' he faltered.

'I do. And guess why I acted like a child? Because I

was being *treated* like one! I presume that as you've deigned to tell me, your father's illness is now out in the open?' she continued.

Jeff nodded. 'He's come to terms with people knowing and, surprising though it seems for someone who's always held life by the scruff of the neck, he's also come to terms with the idea of dying. He's genuinely accepting. My mother's relatively calm too—though she always does take his lead.' He shot a swift sideways look. 'With regard to us putting on a front; according to the doctor, although my father's on a plateau, his condition could deteriorate at any moment. Now if you and I were to be the man and wife very much in love, it would——'

Christa gave an all-purpose smile. 'Why not?'

Chaos might reign in her own head, but she could not be so heartless as to deny the dying Vittorio Barssi some peace of mind.

'You'll do it? Thanks,' he said grimly. 'I'd also be grateful if we could postpone any soul-bearing sessions. There could be bad vibes if we start discussing——' travelling at a steady fifty, he pulled out to overtake a car, '—our situation.'

Her pulse-rate quickened. She had been presented with an ideal opportunity to ask a question—*the* bottom line question—but her throat was parched and her tongue felt as though it had been glued to the roof of her mouth.

'Our situation?' she got out, and heard herself croak.

'A divorce, that's what you have in mind, isn't it?

My father's virtually house-bound now,' Jeff continued, not missing a beat, 'though still walking around. If he was confined to bed, I suspect he'd drive himself and everyone else crazy.'

Divorce, divorce, divorce—the word reverberated in her head and for a moment the world seemed to sway on its axis. A split was *her* brainchild? *She* had designs on severing their connection? Wowee! Fancy that. Give the gentleman top marks for male transference of responsibility! Top marks for avoiding the blame! Top marks for obliterating the truth!

'What does Vittorio do all day?' she enquired, regaining her balance.

'Harass,' Jeff said crypitcally. 'The office is forever receiving calls demanding to know whether such and such an order's been sent out, or has the price been fixed for this, that and the other? Despite being ill and at a distance, he isn't about to relinquish his authority, not if he can help it. In the past nine months there's only been one occasion when——' Jeff frowned. 'D'you remember how I cut short my last visit?'

Christa nodded. 'Tony rang to discuss a business matter and,' hurt tightened her mouth, 'the next morning, you were gone.

'He rang because Vittorio had woken up in agony. At the time his condition looked critical, but a day or two later an operation to remove a blockage eased matters considerably. Then my father did hand over the corporate reins, but only because he had no alternative.'

Christa slung him a very black look. 'And you never said a word about his illness, even then.'

'It was still under wraps. Look, how was I to know if you'd suddenly come back to Rio and——'

'Be spontaneous?' she inserted acidly.

Jeff made a gesture of agreement, then, as though his silence required greater justification, added solemnly, 'There are certain circumstances which demand a measured approach.'

Christa said nothing, but as they drove on she found herself thinking that divorce could be described as one of those circumstances. Where their separation was concerned her husband would, no doubt, have everything not only measured but cut and dried, she decided pithily. A breath was snatched up. Everything *was* cut and dried, she realised, in dragging, dawning horror. Listening to Sylvie back in England, she had dismissed the kidnap theory, but now . . . After telling her how tired he was of living in one country while Marcus lived in another, Jeff had smartly transferred the toddler to his territory; and wasn't possession nine points of the law? Certainly, without his passport, she could not remove her son from Brazil. But in addition to possession, Jeff also had a home prepared, plus a supportive group of grandparents, uncle and aunt, and lesser Barssi relatives waiting in the background.

Where did she stand? Christa's palms had grown damp, and she wiped them on the seams of her trousers. Her father's cottage could not be legitimately claimed as a settled residence and, as far as family went, she operated very much on her own.

In other words, she was a lone-handed mother of no fixed abode. Place that information before a judge, here or in England, and the likelihood of her gaining custody was a long way from automatic.

Marcus could be removed—permanently? Her child might grow up without her? Christa's blood ran cold. How naïve she had been, placing herself in a position where she could be so easily exploited. What a fool to ignore Jeff's ability to fight his own corner. His flair for knowing what he wanted and how to get it was nothing new. Hadn't she had first-hand experience of it in the past? She thought bitterly back to those days . . .

CHAPTER FOUR

HER FATHER'S suggestion that she join him for a month in Rio had rocked Christa back on her heels. A break from her duties as manageress of a small catering firm was long overdue, yet she was astonished he should have noticed how much she was wilting. And for him to request her company bordered on the incredible. She knew she would not be receiving his exclusive attention—for him it was a business trip—yet she wondered if, for the first time in his life, he had realised his neglect and felt guilty. Did the invitation come from a reformed character? Had he belatedly decided to be a proper parent? Her head full of images of them enjoying 'quality' time together, Christa had rushed to accompany him.

George Henley spent the flight checking page after page, column after column of figures. Briefcase in hand, he had exited after breakfast on the first day and arrived back at the hotel in time for a very late, very rushed dinner. On the second morning, the balding tycoon had downed a cup of coffee and departed, muttering about paperwork which might well involve his entire evening. Left to munch her croissant alone, Christa accepted the extravagance of her hopes. Nothing had changed. If notions of turning over a new leaf had once existed, they must have been fleeting.

That afternoon she had been stretched out on the sun-deck, studiously ignoring a trio of ageing Lotharios who were taking a lascivious interest in her physique, when a dark-haired young man in brown short-sleeved shirt and trousers had appeared beside her.

'Christa Henley?' he asked, grinning down.

Suspicious of a more audacious pick-up, she eyed him severely. Christa might have spent a mere thirty-six hours in the country, yet she had already learned that if a Brazilian male spots a woman he fancies he goes in pursuit—no holds barred—and her luncheon bill lay on the table, bearing her signature.

'Correct,' she replied, refusing to be cajoled by what was, undeniably, a most engaging smile.

He introduced himself as Jefferson Barssi. 'Your father said you'd be here,' he carried on, 'and it occured to me you might like to see more of Rio than a swimming pool?'

'I shall be doing. I've booked some excursions,' she explained, sitting up cross-legged on the lounger.

So this was the business associate George Henley had described as 'smart'? Spoken with a wary degree of respect, from her father the word was praise indeed; and after several meetings—the current round of talks was the third—he was in an ideal position to know.

'You enjoy being herded in and out of stuffy minibuses?' her visitor enquired.

Christa hesitated. One hand in a hip pocket, he was

leaning against the sun-deck's balustrade. Tall, lean and inherently relaxed within his own body, Jefferson Barssi gave new meaning to the phrase 'animal magnetism'.

"Pull a T-shirt over your bikini and let's go,' he said.

Her eyes widened in surprise. 'Now?'

'Now.'

For a moment they had exchanged look for smiling look, then came a crazy sweep of response.

'Why not?' she agreed, laughing.

Although Christa had boarded a minibus—however much the daughter appealed, business insisted the father came first—most of her sightseeing was done from the front seat of Jefferson Barssi's sports car. It was fun. Within hours her escort had shown himself to be intelligent, witty, good-humoured. Within days he had captivated her—and she him.

Three weeks later they had a conversation which contained a strong sense of *déjà vu*. It was late one evening and they had driven out to a deserted bay south of Rio. As they strolled among the palms, Jeff had drawn her into his arms and started to kiss her. They had kissed before, so often and so ravenously that keeping their hands off each other had become a problem. Now her shirt lay discarded on the sand and moonlight silvered her breasts.

'Do you really want to go back to England and start providing business executives with hot lunches again?' he had asked.

She had hesitated. 'Well——'

'Let's get married.'

'Just like that?'

'Just like that. Christa, I love you and I want to make love to you—every night. And afterwards I want to sleep with you and wake up with you—every morning. I want us to be together for the rest of our lives.' Jeff had taken a steadying breath. 'Please,' he had murmured.

How could she resist?

'Why not?' she had agreed, laughing.

Eight weeks later they were man and wife, and eight weeks after that Marcus had been conceived.

Although startled to find herself a mother-to-be—she had never imagined it would happen *that* quickly—Christa possessed the confidence of the ignorant. She was young and healthy, *ergo*, pregnancy would be a cinch. It wasn't. It turned out to be a full-time job. Her hair might shine like molten gold, her skin might glow, but marathon bouts of morning sickness dogged her days. Only in the evenings, when the nausea abruptly vanished, did she spring to life. For a few hours she could be bright and vivacious, then next morning—ugh!

After she had rushed from the classroom on one too many occasions, the Portuguese lessons she had so enthusiastically started had had to be abandoned. Likewise, the course in Brazilian cuisine. Mobility strangled, she pottered around their small flat, reading, resting, knitting for the baby, until the landlord had received an offer for the building he could not refuse. 'Do me a favour and go!' the man begged. Pressure of work allowed Jeff no time for househunting, but if she had been able she would have gone straight out and found them somewhere else to live. As it was, Christa had not argued when he had proposed they move into Casa Libra.

'It's a stop-gap solution,' he had said, 'but one benefit is that you won't be on your own.'

'I'm only being sick,' Christa had protested, seeing the concern in his eyes. 'I'm not about to miscarry.'

'Please, don't say that.' He had caressed her cheek. 'But the sickness will pass.'

Although she had hardly dared believe him, it had. One morning she had climbed out of bed, become vaguely aware of something missing, and realised she felt fine. Wary of a phony reprise, Christa had made herself wait five nausea-free days and then celebrated her return to normality—more or less.

'Next week I shall make a fresh start on my Portuguese and enrol for another cookery course,' she informed Jeff. 'I'll also do the rounds of the agencies and gather in details of apartments.'

'Atta girl,' he said, grinning at her earnestness, 'but don't overdo things.'

On Sunday, Christa had been tanning herself in Casa Libra's courtyard when Esther had strolled in from the beach. With chestnut-brown hair swept to one side, model-girl fashion, and her face made up to perfection, she looked as though she had just emerged from a beauty salon. Sunbathe she might, but not messily. And no matter how high the temperature soared, Esther never seemed to sweat. How did she do

that? Looking at her, Christa found it hard to imagine
that someone so impeccable could have started life as
a snotty-nosed urchin. The metamorphosis must have
required discipline, dedication, guts; she was full of
admiration. She was also a little bit in awe. Several
years older, Esther possessed a soignée confidence
which Christa doubted she would ever achieve. Cool
and calm, nothing fazed her. She seemed to have a
knack of controlling events rather than allowing them
to control her. One thing was for sure, had Esther
been pregnant, she would not have spent her time
dashing hot and flustered to the bathroom!

'Is Jefferson still at the site?' the new arrival
enquired, tying on a filmy beach-wrap.

''Fraid so. When the contractor rang asking for a
pow-wow he thought he'd only be away a short time,
but——' As Christa sighed, her eyes went from
Esther's willowy frame to her own thickening
waistline. All of a sudden, she felt fat and frumpy. 'I
wonder whether Jeff'll enjoy watching the 34-23-34 he
married swell to elephantine proportions?' she
speculated.

'He won't mind. Why should he? Whatever size you
are, you'll still be George Henley's daughter.'

Christa shot a wary glance sideways. If the
comment had been in Portuguese she would have
thought she had misunderstood, but Esther used
English with her. Although the girl insisted it was to
help her fluency, she was grateful. Jeff, Vittorio and
Tony might talk to her in her own language, but they
were a minority. Most people—particularly her

mother-in-law—would attempt a word or two, then cheerfully gabble away in Portuguese, and keeping up could be a strain. But there was no strain now, just a sense of something which boded ill.

'What's that got to do with anything?' she enquired.

Esther smiled. 'We all marry for reasons, y'know. You can't deny that Jefferson being good-looking and dynamic had much to do with you falling for him, and obviously you being——' the tasselled end of her sash was twirled '—the only daughter of a man who owns a multi-million-dollar company accounts, to a degree, for him falling for you.'

'My father may be wealthy, but most of his money's tied up in his business,' Christa protested. 'Added to which, he has yet to turn fifty and is in excellent health. The odds are I'll be fifty myself, or older, before I inherit a single bean.' Her voice had sharpened. Her cheeks burned an indignant pink. 'So if your idea is that Jeff married me in order to get his hands on some money which is dangling out of reach in the next century, I suggest you reconsider. For anyone to do that, they'd have to be a mega-watt mercenary, plus excessively patient!'

'Slow down! Take it easy,' laughed Esther. 'I never said Jefferson was mercenary.'

At a loss, Christa frowned. The smear had surprised her—Esther frequently put down her own husband, but she had never before criticised Jeff—so maybe she had misjudged and over-reacted?

'Then what are you saying?' she asked, feeling foolish.

'That he's ambitious. Is it a sin?'

'No, not unless——' Christa stopped and started again. 'How do you relate his ambitions to me?'

Her companion's sigh indicated she had been saddled with a slow-witted, though lovable, child. 'Before you and Jefferson met, several firms had been keen to combine with your father—and who wouldn't be when a joint venture with the Henley Group is like being given permission to print money? But by the time he sought you out they'd been whittled down to two. Barssis' and——' Peach-tipped fingers enscribed vague circles. 'I forget the other one.'

'UWC,' Christa provided, though the wisdom of contributing to such a conversation seemed in doubt.

'The two companies were neck and neck, until— pouf!—out of the blue and after you'd known each other mere weeks, Jefferson announces you're to be married. A day or two later your father and Vittorio sign the contract. There are,' Esther added lightly, 'many ways to skin a cat.'

Christa felt dizzy. 'You're saying Jeff married me to—to secure the deal?' she ventured.

'Have I struck a wrong note here? I do apologise.' The tassel was twirled again. 'You're young and starry-eyed, but if you examine the nuts and bolts of marriage you'll realise it's nothing more than a consolidation of resources. The man provides the woman with something she needs, like security, affection, a home—and vice versa.'

For a moment Christa floundered in a maelstrom of uncertainty. The sequence of events had been as stated, yet it had never occurred to her to link their high-speed romance so pertinently with the merger. Why not? she wondered, then answered her own question. Because, whereas Esther had been on the outside looking in, she had been where it mattered, on the inside looking out!

'My father's a hardline businessman. He wouldn't have chosen Barssis' unless he'd been positive they'd serve his needs best,' she said forcibly. 'Family considerations would never have swayed him. But secondly, and most importantly, Jeff was as crazy about me as I was about him. And he still is. I still am. What started out as a summer alliance became a full-blown love-affair within days. Sounds corny, I know, but for us time didn'tmatter. We clicked, and from the start we both knew this was IT, in capitals a foot high.'

Esther admired her frosted fingernails. 'You have an awful lot to learn,' she sighed. 'Isn't Jefferson also a hardline businessman?' she enquired, after a moment.

'I—I suppose so,' Christa had to concede.

'And a shrewd manipulator of situations?'

Energetically, Christa shook her head. 'I don't agree.'

'You would agree that he's smart?'

Bells rang. Her father had also called Jeff 'smart'. Then the word had seemed a straightforward compliment, now it contained unwelcome shades of hard-headedness, cunning, opportunism.

'Yes, but——'

'A cooling drink?' Isabel Barssi asked, arriving with a pitcher of iced lime.

The conversation had been abandoned, yet although Esther appeared to forget what had been said the effect on Christa was catatonic. Evidently the brunette saw little wrong in marrying for financial gain, but did all Brazilians feel the same? she wondered, feeling very much the alien. Did Jeff? Continually she learned new things about him—an unexpected taste in food, his preference in books, snippets concerning his past travels. Could this revelation be yet another fact in her ongoing education? Her heart lurched. Unlike Esther, she did not possess inviolate self-assurance. She was not worldly-wise. Her upbringing had not been Brazilian. If Jeff had married her for reasons other than love, albeit they were secondary reasons, it mattered very much—to her.

Christa tried telling herself to take no notice, that talk, even light-hearted, was one thing but evidence was another. And yet. And yet . . . It was difficult to escape the fact that there did seem to be evidence. Barssis' *had* been hellbent on joining up with her father. Their love-affair *had* advanced at breakneck speed. Jeff *had* proposed with expert timing. And the crunch—why would Esther say such things unless she believed them to be true?

When the new week dawned, improving her Portuguese did not seem so vital any more. Becoming a virtuoso at Brazilian cookery also lacked lustre. Her plans, hopes and dreams had been clamped, though she was not so much waiting for something to happen as essentially preoccupied. When Christa announced that she had decided to heed his warning and would be taking life easy, Jeff did not argue. All he wanted, he said, was for her to be happy.

At first, she was not. At first, she spent much of her time brooding. Swept along on the excitement of meeting, marrying, mating, she had never stopped to analyse, but now the past was painstakingly dissected. Christa accepted that she had jumped into marriage, yet her commitment had been total, with no strings attached. What about Jeff's? Most of the time she knew Esther was wrong, wrong, *wrong*. Yet there were moments when her reading of events possessed a sneaky potential. When Jeff failed to notice her restlessness, it did not help. These days most of his thoughts centred on the embryo factory, which seemed to emphasise the importance of business in his life.

Hither and thither her mind scuttled—did pregnancy reduce the ability to separate fact from fiction, did it encourage gloomy imaginings?—but as the baby began to move inside her gradually Esther's views were relegated to fantasy and Christa's doubts mothballed. What mattered was how Jeff treated her and, whatever his work involvement, he was unfailingly tender, protective, loving. Even though she waddled around like a duck, if not an elephant, he insisted she was gorgeous.

As if to compensate for the morning sickness, Marcus's arrival into the world was ridiculously easy.

Now Christa had a lusty son, an adoring husband, and life was wonderful. A marvellous sensation of well-being engulfed her. For a while caring for her child was enough, but in time her vision widened.

'The minute this guzzler can manage without me, I'm taking a course of intensive Portuguese,' she told Esther, who had wandered into the nursery one evening.

People were always wandering in—Jeff, Vittorio, Tony and the elderly housekeeper. As for the *wunderkind*'s grandmother, she clucked over him a hundred times a day.

'Why the urgency?' Esther enquired.

Christa smiled at the baby suckling at her breast. 'Jeff says there's no rush, but I know he'd like a daughter, and before that happens it's essential I become fluent.' Her smile dissolved. 'Isabel translates at the clinic and I'm grateful, but that's meant it's been her and not me who——'

'Jefferson would more than like a second child, he'd be delighted,' Esther interrupted. 'Then he'd have another link with your father.'

Once rejected, Esther's earlier insinuation had stayed rejected, yet instantly something quivered and sprang to the alert inside her.

'Marcus is a link with my father?' Christa echoed, aware of walking on eggshells.

'You must agree Jefferson's insistence on becoming a parent was a touch overdone? I know you would have preferred to delay matters, but no, he wanted a child and a child you had.' Her companion brushed a speck of lint from her skirt. 'I believe it's what's called, "hedging your bet".'

Christa had vowed that if any fantasies were aired again she would ignore them, but biology honours were not needed to know Marcus had been conceived because, having banned birth control, Jeff had proceeded to make love to her night and day. She raised the baby to her shoulder, finding solace in the warmth of his small fuzzy head. In retrospect, her wish to wait had not been granted a single minute's consideration.

'And what's this bet he's supposed to be hedging?' she enquired, gently rubbing Marcus's back.

'Isn't it obvious? If the joint venture should go wrong, your father'll think twice about pulling out when he has a daughter *and* a grandchild involved. Jefferson's having difficulties with the firm who are building the factory——'

'He's never mentioned any difficulties to me,' Christa said, as Marcus obliged with a loud and satisfactory burp.

Esther shrugged. 'He puts on a brave face. But if the thing should turn sour and the investment be lost, your father won't dance for joy. That's when family ties will come in useful. Jefferson doesn't intend Barssis' to be cut adrift, and so long as he's providing George Henley with grandchildren, he knows they won't be. See you later,' she smiled, and strolled away.

Christa required a few minutes to pick herself up and dust herself off, but then she gave herself a short, sharp lecture. Previously she had tiptoed around her anxieties—for some reason she had never plucked up the courage to tackle Jeff head-on—yet a problem was not solved by avoiding it. That grandchildren had the least influence on her father's business decisions seemed unlikely, but nevertheless it would be interesting to know what had made Marcus's birth so imperative.

Although she assured herself the encounter was not crucial, it did appear to merit a special mood and a special hour—but both proved elusive. Two days later Jeff had mentioned his difficulties; he told her the builders had gone bust! For a time everything did turn sour, but he searched, agitated, and finally found another contractor willing to take over. Unfortunately the transfer demanded he spent many evenings, as well as his days, at the site. When he did come home, he was tense and preoccupied, and the moment his head hit the pillow he fell fast asleep. On the rare occasions when Christa attempted to ease her way into the subject, either he had started to talk about something else or Marcus had cried.

'Why did we have a baby so soon?' she blurted out, one night as they climbed into bed.

Her question was far from the precisely phrased query she had rehearsed, but what Esther had implied had begun drip, drip, dripping away like acid rain.

Jeff slung his leg over hers. 'Because I like doing this to you,' he murmured.

'Don't joke,' she protested. 'I want to know why you were so keen on getting me pregnant.'

'Takes two,' he grinned, running a hand along her thigh.

With a ferocity which surprised them both, Christa wrenched herself from him.

'Tell me!'

'What is this?' he enquired. 'A dose of pre-menstrual tension?'

'No, it's not,' she blazed. 'It's——' She froze. Someone was creeping past their door and there was no need to see through walls to know it would be Isabel. Recently Marcus had begun to teethe, and no matter how often she emphasised that her son was *her* responsibility and she could manage very nicely, thank you, his grandmother persistently checked on his well-being. 'Never mind.'

They spent precious little time together these days, yet how could she ask what had become a pivotal question when her mother-in-law patrolled the corridor outside? Privacy to talk was essential, but there seemed no hope of achieving it, of achieving *anything*, so long as they remained at Casa Libra. Christa's priorities changed. First they must move back into a home of their own, then she would sort out just *why* her husband had been hellbent on fatherhood, and finally she would get to grips with her Portuguese.

'All right if I start house-hunting again?' she enquired, when the closing of a door told her Isabel had returned to her own room.

Jeff yawned. 'Please do.'

Christa embarked on a search which led from

agency to agency, but the market had hit the doldrums and there was a dearth of anything decent. She refused to fall apart. Even though they would not be relocating tomorrow, their name had been added to a hundred mailing lists and something good must surface soon. One month drifted into two. The market stayed in the doldrums. They stayed put. If she was to find somewhere, their requirements must be adjusted, Christa decided. Around Rio she travelled, desperately seeking charm in odd-shaped rooms, turn-of-the-century kitchens, remote neighbourhoods. Sometimes she found it—to be thwarted by Jeff. Weekends were the only time he could view, and several properties had been snapped up before he arrived.

'Don't be so disappointed,' he protested, when yet another hopeful had been grimly scored from her list. 'I know you reckon the place came straight out of *Homes and Gardens*, but the layout didn't look so good. We wouldn't have been happy there.'

Despite all insistence that they would have been ecstatic, Christa recognised he could be right, and when she set off again it was with her desire to move held firmly in check. Now her approach was more mature. Only a property which met *all* their agreed stipulations would do. Marcus had cut one tooth, another, then four more, before an attractive duplex came up for sale. To her relief, Jeff saw it, declared himself as enamoured as she, and a verbal offer was made and a verbal bargain speedily struck. Now at the paperwork stage, the transaction crawled at snail's pace. Six long, frustrating weeks went by.

'Progress at last!' Christa whispered, when Jeff joined her at the dinner-table one evening. The intention had been to break the news when they were on their own, but as usual he was late and she was bursting to tell him. 'The lawyer phoned to ask if we'd go to his office tomorrow and sign the documents,' she continued excitedly.

He nodded to the rest of the family and waited as Anna, the housekeeper, served his soup. 'I'm sorry, honey,' he said, frowning, 'but——'

'Jeff, when I agreed I knew tomorrow wouldn't be entirely convenient, but on current form neither will the next day or the one after that.'

'I'm a course behind, let me catch up,' he muttered. 'We'll talk about this later.'

Christa returned to her meal. 'Signing will take half an hour at most,' she coaxed.

'No.'

'I'll fix an appointment for Saturday,' Christa offered resignedly, but he shook his head. 'You have an aversion to putting your name on dotted lines?'

He shot her a furtive look along the table. 'Christa, I don't think the duplex is right for us.'

'You mean you don't intend to sign *ever*?' she exclaimed, in a squawk which ensured that everyone else sat up and took notice.

'Not for that particular property.' His grin would have drawn birds from trees. 'Honey, you must agree you've gone overboard for some pretty weird places and——'

'Extremely weird, from what I've heard,' Vittorio Barssi said, with a soothing smile.

Christa's eyes sparked. She was in no mood to be soothed. Not by her husband. Not by the high and mighty patriarch. Not by anybody.

'The duplex isn't weird!'

'That third bedroom's on the small side,' said Jeff, in the tone of someone announcing a disaster of major proportions.

'You've never mentioned it before.'

'Maybe not, but——'

'What's going on here?' Christa demanded suspiciously. 'You must have a better reason than that for changing your mind.'

His cheek muscle twitched. 'I just reckon we've moved too fast.'

'Too fast?' she echoed, in deep disgust. 'It seems to me, we shan't be moving at all!'

Appetite gone, she stared down at her plate. Why had she spent so many months searching? she wondered miserably. Why had she forced herself to be patient? Why had she ever imagined they would soon be installed in a home of their own?

When Jeff arrived back from work the next evening, she was busy in their bedroom.

'What the hell are you up to?' he asked, cannoning into the first in a line of suitcases.

'I'm leaving.' Christa ignored the flutters in her stomach. 'Tomorrow.'

'Isn't that a bit extreme? I realise you're bothered about the duplex——'

'Bothered? You have all the sensitivity of a dung beetle! This isn't *bother*. It's a matter of life and death.' A pair of shoes was jammed into a bag. 'Your father has a lot to answer for,' she said savagely.

Jeff raked at his shin. 'And what's that supposed to mean?' he demanded.

'The world according to Vittorio Barssi is how he runs things, and you're following in his footsteps.' Christa shone a smile which was a bit deranged. 'It wouldn't surprise me if when he's in his grave your father finds a way to give your mother her orders,' she said, deriving perverse comfort from hitting out at a Barssi male, even though it was the wrong one. 'He wouldn't let a little thing like *rigor mortis*——'

'Stop it!' thundered Jeff, then sank down on the bed. When he had walked in the door his face had been drawn—he maintained that the factory troubles were long gone, yet in recent days he had seemed increasingly perturbed—but now he looked haggard. 'You never throw a pebble when there's a brick handy, do you?' he said wearily. 'Honey, threatening to leave is overkill.'

'I'm not threatening, I'm telling. I've decided to do what *I* want for once!'

'And you want to leave me?'

'I want to leave Casa Libra!'

'You will. We'll move soon, I swear.'

'Soon won't do.'

'There's no need to go tomorrow. Hang on for a day or two, please, honey.'

Christa flung a sweater into a case. 'Don't call me

honey, you—you jerk!'

'Calm down,' he appealed, when voices on the landing indicated that Esther and Tony were going down for dinner.

'I am calm!' she snapped.

Jeff sighed. 'If you think about it, you'll realise you've got the whole thing out of proportion. All I'm asking for is forty-eight hours in which to——'

'All I'm asking is that you sign up the duplex,' Christa shot back, when he hesitated.

He rubbed at his brow. 'I can't.'

'Can't?' She marched into the bathroom, gathered up an armful of shower caps, cosmetics, a hairbrush, and marched out again. 'Don't you mean *won't*? You never had any intention of us moving. Your agreement was simply a token gesture meant to keep me happy,' she declared. 'The truth of the matter is *you're* happy living at Casa Libra—not that you're here so damn much—and I'm not supposed to mind if we stay for ever more. Well, I do mind. I mind! I mind!' she shrieked.

Jeff leapt up, and for a moment seemed undecided whether to clamp his hand across her mouth, or strike her. Instead, he took a breath.

'This isn't something we can resolve through emotion.'

She dumped her load. 'Oh, don't be so . . . patronising!'

'Twenty-four hours?' he asked.

'No!'

'Surely you can give me a chance to——'

'Watch my lips, Jefferson. *No.*'

'Go, then.'

'Go?' Christa repeated, taken aback by this abrupt submission.

'It's obvious nothing I can say is going to give me any leverage, and,' he scowled at his feet, 'maybe a break'll do you good. You haven't been back to England since our marriage, and I'm sure your friends would like to see Marcus. Your father might even welcome——'

'You're encouraging me to leave?' she demanded.

Jeff uttered a frustrated sound. 'Must you be so damned cussed?'

'Me, cussed?' Aware of shrieking again, she reduced her tone to a fevered hiss. 'It's you who's cussed!'

He walked to the door. 'I fail to see any point in pursuing this conversation,' he said, and went.

Left to finish her packing alone, Christa fizzed and fretted. She did not like his sudden agreement—the damn man was supposed to be in love with her—and neither did she trust it. Maybe she had instigated the exodus, yet with her out of the way there would be nothing to stop him devoting himself twenty-four hours a day to his stupid factory—and what could suit him better? Perhaps she was being irrational. Perhaps she was wrong. But, when she left Brazil the next morning, it was with the exasperating feeling that she might have played right into Jeff's hands.

CHAPTER FIVE

'ME OUT,' Marcus demanded, jolting Christa back to the present.

They had arrived at Casa Libra, yet although the little boy scrambled eagerly from the car, she hesitated. Embroiled in her thoughts as she was, no consideration had been given to meeting Isabel and Vittorio Barssi again, and now apprehension struck. How would she be greeted? she wondered, as she went with her husband and son across the narrow strip of pavement to the pillared portico. What did she say? Was she supposed to apologise for last year's hasty departure, for taking Marcus away? Her shoulders straightened. She had done nothing to be ashamed of, and if her in-laws expected her to beg forgiveness they would be disappointed. But how had Jeff told the tale? she wondered, realising that this was a question she ought to have asked earlier.

Mind abuzz with queries, she swung to him, but too late, for the brass-studded door had swung open to reveal a plump, grey-haired woman in a maroon dress. For a moment her brown eyes drank in the trio of the man, the young woman, the small boy, then she gave a smile a mile wide. Her jubilant peal of laughter startled several passers-by, and those who turned were treated to a display of unalloyed affection.

'Christa! Christa! My darling, *minha* sweetheart—at last you return!' Isabel Barssi cried, and hugged her so tightly and for so long, it seemed she would never let her go.

If her mother-in-law had not wept, she would not have done—after Jeff's censure Christa had no wish to provide further confirmation of her spontaneity—but, although she bit her lip, still the tears came. Whatever had happened in the past and whatever was destined to happen in the future—maybe she was crying about that, too?—the Barssis were kind, friendly and open-hearted people. As Jeff's bride, she had been welcomed into their family and later into their home. If they had had reservations about him marrying a girl from a different country, a different culture, none had ever surfaced. Isabel had claimed her as a daughter and, in many ways, had become a mother.

'It's good to see you again,' Christa said, in sobby Portuguese. She blinked, took a breath and carried on. 'You must have been surprised when I went away, but at the time it seemed the only thing I could do. I know how much you'll have missed Marcus——'

'Christa!' Her mother-in-law was staring with mouth open and eyes stretched wide. 'Christa, you speak in *my* language!'

'I've been taking a refresher course.'

'And learned well.' Happily Isabel reverted to her mother tongue. 'You sound like a true Carioca.'

'Don't speak too quickly,' Christa pleaded, as the older woman enthused over her expertise.

'I won't,' came the promise, but before they were half-way across the high-ceilinged hall Isabel was rattling away at top speed again. 'Father, here she is,' she announced, as they entered the study. 'And guess what—the clever girl speaks Portuguese as well as you and me!'

Christa's gaze sped around the room with its familiar book-lined walls, the heavy crimson curtains, the Persian carpet. In the past her father-in-law had invariably occupied the wing chair behind the leather-topped desk, but today it stood empty. Where was he?

'*Olá*,' said a voice scraped from a gravel pit, and her gaze swung to the depths of a red velvet armchair.

'*Olá*,' she replied.

Her smile masked her dismay. The Vittorio Barssi she remembered had walked tall as if in armour plating, but now she saw a shrunken old man. As she pressed her lips to the paper-dry cheek he offered, tears threatened to flow again, but this time Marcus came to the rescue. Striking a casual pose, the toddler leant against his grandfather's knee and began a long rigmarole about the swings at his new *apartamento*. As he spoke, Christa recovered, and when questions came about her journey she was able to answer cheerfully.

'I expect Jefferson's acquainted you with this trouble of mine?' Vittorio said, when Isabel took Marcus off to the kitchen.

Lunchtime was approaching and instructions needed to be given to the housekeeper. Anna might have worked for the Barssis for fifteen years, yet her mistress could never allow a meal to be served unless *she* had presided over its preparation.

Christa nodded and began to sympathise, but her halting words were swept aside.

'Don't feel sorry for me, my dear. I've enjoyed a full and interesting life with a faithful wife, and I leave behind me two fine sons. I've had my fair span, and nobody lives for ever.'

'No,' she agreed, 'but——'

'I have no buts,' Vittorio said serenely. 'Now, as you know about me, so Jefferson's explained all about you.'

Christa flashed Jeff a look. This was his cue to say something. This was his time to wade in. Yet all her help-me signals received was an enigmatic smile.

'He has?' she said carefully.

The old man nodded. 'I know about the homesickness.'

'Oh.'

Always interested in new people, new places, new experiences, Christa had not suffered from nostalgia or longing. There had been times before she left when she had felt lonely, but she had never actively pined for home. Indeed, she had relished the fun, the energy, the friendliness of Brazil.

'Covering it up was a mistake. Instead of rushing away without a word, you should have told us how you felt. We would have understood. We might have been able to help. But that's in the past,' Vittorio smiled, 'and now I'm delighted to hear that you and

Jefferson will be doing what comes naturally.'

Christa shot her husband a second glance, but he had roamed to the window which overlooked the courtyard and his back was towards her. On purpose, she had no doubt.

'What's that?' she enquired.

Her father-in-law chuckled as though she had cracked an enormous joke.

'Why, providing Marcus with a little companion.'

The homesickness tale had been a surprise, but this nugget of information left her staggering. Their marriage was not only fine and dandy, but they were going full speed ahead for a second child? Why had he said that? What was the point? Christa felt a stab of pain. When she had been mapping out their future, another baby had been a hoped-for addition, but how could he? She threw a look like a dagger at Jeff's broad back. He had shown a rare flair for innovation and, by his silence, made it clear he expected her to support him—the conniving, unfeeling goat!

'What do you think of your new apartment?' her father-in-law enquired.

At last Jeff spoke. 'She loves it,' he said, coming to curve a proprietorial arm around her waist and drew her against him. 'Barra da Tijuca has always been *o numero um* on her list of beaches.' He looked down and grinned. 'Yes?'

Trapped by his question and trapped in his embrace, Christa was sorely tempted to resist—why should she allow him to dictate everything she did, every damn word she said? But his closeness had a disastrously sapping effect.

'Yes,' she agreed; then, hearing how compliant she had sounded, she broke free. She might be aiding and abetting, but only because the alternative was flaying her in-laws with a blunt and stressful announcement.

'*Almoco*——' piped a voice. Marcus and his grandmother had appeared to announce lunch, and the little boy's tongue curled in concentration as he attempted the words she whispered, '—'*ta pronto.*'

'*Excelente,*' Isabel told him, while his grandfather applauded.

As Vittorio eased himself from his chair and joined them, Christa blocked Jeff's exit.

'I don't appreciate being made to play comic to your straight man,' she hissed. 'Why didn't you tell the truth about why I left?'

'The truth?'

She glared. 'That I was fed up with being treated like a second-class citizen! And why now produce this——' the painful stab came again '—this fatuous tale of us planning another child?'

'I thought it'd cheer everyone up.'

'That's all the excuse you need for dispensing a solid chunk of fiction?' she protested.

Jeff checked that the doorway remained empty. 'Run with it—please!'

'Run with flagrant deception?'

'It wouldn't hurt to pretend for a short time,' he coaxed, and his arm entwined around her.

Caught off balance, Christa fell against him. Pressed close to his chest, she could feel the thump of his heart. Or was it hers? Whichever, Jefferson was too close for comfort.

'I thought you reckoned I had very little guile?' she reminded him.

'I thought you reckoned to be older and wiser now?' he reparteed.

'Why should I do what *you* want?' she prevaricated, in a voice which emerged far too breathless.

He shrugged. 'Because some time, some day, there might be something I could do for you?'

'I doubt it,' Christa rejected, yet even as she spoke her mind went to the future. If they were to compete over Marcus—the thought made her shrivel—she would need as much of Jeff's good will as she could muster, which meant it would be foolish to antagonise him now. 'All right,' she sighed.

Jeff ran his thumb across the soft fullness of her lower lip. 'Thanks,' he murmured, and bent his head to brush his mouth gently against hers.

She raised her hands to his shoulders to push him away, but, when his kiss deepened into a subtle exploration, there they stayed. She had been starved of him for so long and now the flickering of his tongue worked a melting magic. Christa knew it made no sense, knew she must resist, yet with slow stealth her arms wound around his neck and her fingers crept into the thick, dark hair at the back of his head. She feasted on the feel of him, the taste of him, the male fragrance which was essentially Jefferson. When he raised his head, she gazed up, her lips parted, her breasts rising and falling—trapped helplessly beneath the spell of his brown eyes. He smiled, and proceeded to kiss her again.

It was a discreet cough from the doorway which broke her from him, and she swung round to find Isabel Barssi standing there.

'Sorry to keep you waiting, but I've been getting to know my wife again,' said Jeff, with a grin.

The older woman chuckled. 'So I saw.'

Face flushed, her spine a ramrod, Christa stalked to the door. One minute enchanted, now she was furious—with him and herself. For some inane reason she had attributed Jeff's embrace to genuine desire, but it had been for appearances' sake only. Aware that someone was bound to come looking, he had staged a show—and once again she had been manipulated!

In the dining-room the housekeeper's greetings were followed by praise being heaped on Christa's improved Portuguese. Anna would have chattered on, if a rap on the table from Vittorio had not reminded her that bowls of ice-cold *gazpacho* were waiting to be served.

'You sit on my knee to eat?' Isabel suggested, smiling across at Marcus.

Furnished baronial style, the wood-panelled room contained a refectory table and stiff-backed Jacobean chairs, and, perched as he was, the little boy's nose could barely be seen above the white linen cloth.

'*Não*,' said Christa, as he prepared to slide down.

'But he's so tiny,' his grandmother protested. 'Tomorrow, my darling, I shall shop for you a——'

For Marcus's sake she had been speaking in English, but now she reverted to Portuguese.

'High chair,' Vittorio translated.

'Thanks, but he doesn't require a high chair and he doesn't need to sit on anyone's knee,' Christa replied, pleasantly but firmly. 'He might be a little boy, but he isn't a baby.'

'Me not baby!' Marcus declared, picking up the phrase.

'He'll be fine on a cushion,' she carried on.

'A cushion?' Isabel looked doubtful. 'But he might fall. I think it is better if he sits on my knee.'

'*Não*,' Christa repeated, and a look passed between Isabel and Vittorio which said their previously biddable daughter-in-law must be travel-worn.

'You know best,' Vittorio agreed.

'Of course she does, she's his mother,' said Jeff, providing some much appreciated support. He held out a hand. 'Come along, hotshot, we'll find a couple of big soft cushions and you'll be able to sit on top like the king of the castle.'

The problem solved, the meal began with Marcus seated in state. After the *gazpacho* came the main course of fillet steak, salad and jacket potatoes, accompanied by glasses of a full-bodied red Brazilian wine. Everyone ate well and heartily, and the conversation flowed. When the plates had been cleared, Anna carried in a huge bowl of chocolate ice-cream.

'We remembered how much you enjoyed *sorvete* before,' Vittorio laughed, as Marcus wriggled in anticipation. 'And we thought you would enjoy it now.'

He did. The little boy wolfed down one helping, then demolished another.

'More?' his grandfather asked, raising comic eyebrows when his dish was empty a second time.

'He's had enough, thanks,' Christa intervened.

'Please,' Marcus appealed, and when she shook her head he turned to his grandfather. 'Please!' he entreated, with a winner of a smile.

Vittorio reached for the bowl. 'One spoonful,' he agreed.

'*Não*,' said Christa, and lobbed out a gracious smile.

'A small spoonful,' her father-in-law smashed back tersely.

Weak in the flesh he might be but, as Jeff had said, Vittorio Barssi's spirit remained as strong as ever. Worshipped and pampered by his wife, he took it for granted that every other female would bow to his will and, be they housekeeper or secretary or passing stranger, they did. Christa could not recall a single woman disagreeing with him. She never had. Her tongue moistened lips which had gone dry. She had no desire to cause trouble, but it was important, one, that she stand her ground and, two, that Marcus was not allowed to play one person off against another.

'*Não*,' she repeated.

Black eyes speared into hers and a tightrope tension built. The old man might have given in over the cushion, but his undeviating gaze made it clear that one amiable gesture was her quota for the day. Christa gasped in air. How long he remained mute and glaring, she did not know. It was probably no more than a minute or two, yet it seemed like years. But, tempting as it was to submit, she refused to be arrowed down like another pesky injun.

'Marcus, your mother is right,' Vittorio said at last, and she breathed again.

'Everyone seems to have finished, so shall we adjourn to the study for coffee?' Isabel suggested, twittery with nerves.

The silver-haired patriarch rose from his chair. 'Good idea,' he declared, and marched out.

'Congratulations,' said Jeff, as they went along the hall. 'When I quarrel with the old man, the shouting can be heard all over Rio, but you handled that beautifully.' He shot her a speculative glance. 'I never realised you could be so cool under fire.'

Christa gave a weak grin. 'Neither did I.'

The distribution of coffee enabled the tension to diminish, and by the time cups were drained normality had been restored.

'I don't want to desert you, but I need to call in at the office,' Jeff apologised.

Tiredly, she massaged her brow. 'That's OK. I don't know whether it's the wine or jet lag——' or the clash with your father, she added silently '—but all of a sudden I feel like I'm sleepwalking. Could you drop Marcus and me at the *apartamento* on your way?'

'You can't go there!' Isabel exclaimed.

Christa sighed. She did not want another battle, all she wanted to do was to lie down; but everyone seemed determined to subvert her authority today.

'I realise the place isn't fully equipped, but I'm sure we'll manage,' she protested.

Jeff shook his head. 'The electricity was working fine until last week, then for no apparent reason it packed in. The electricians have made several attempts to discover what's gone wrong, but so far,' he grimaced, 'no joy.'

'You're back in your own room here,' Isabel said, pleasure beaming from her, 'with Marcus in his old nursery. If Jefferson will bring in your luggage, you can——'

The remainder of the arrangements came from afar. They were to stay at Casa Libra? Christa thought sluggishly, but that meant she would be expected to sleep with Jeff. Was the electricity genuinely kaput, or could this be yet another manoeuvre? Her tired mind was having difficulty functioning, and she could not decide. She must sleep, and later, when he returned from the office, she would make her resistance excruciatingly plain.

'I'll go and lie down,' she said, and took hold of her son's hand. 'Marcus is coming with me.'

Nobody argued this time.

CHAPTER SIX

THE SUN shining behind golden brocade curtains seeped into her consciousness and slowly Christa awoke, becoming aware of daylight and a body warm against her. Opening her eyes, she performed a startled double-take. Marcus might have accompanied her to bed, but now Jeff lay alongside, one arm stretched protectively over her breasts. He was fast asleep. Turning her head on the pillow, she studied him. With long lashes spread against his cheeks and dark hair tousled, he looked younger, softer, vulnerable. She sighed soundlessly. Who was she kidding? Hadn't the events of the past few days proved that in the vulnerability stakes Jefferson Barssi was a non-runner?

He stirred, moving closer, and his leg draped itself across her thigh. As she felt the glide of his skin, the pressure of bone and flesh and muscle, Christa's heart began a fierce, mad throbbing. She had climbed beneath the sheets in a coffee-coloured satin teddy, but Jeff was naked—and aroused. When she had slept with him in this room before, sometimes in the night he had tried to make love to her in his sleep. Then she had giggled and pushed him away, and he had rolled over to his side of the bed; in the morning he had not remembered. Now as she edged from him inch by discreet inch, Jeff followed, murmuring an incoherent and drowsy complaint. His fingers closing on her hip transformed the careful retreat into a hasty withdrawal. Christa squirmed to escape from beneath his arm, but her movements disturbed him and as he awoke the golden-skinned limb wound around her like a hoop of steel.

'*Bom dia*,' he smiled.

'Morning?' She shot a disbelieving look at the sunlight which was peeping in. 'This is morning?' she said, realising it had to be. 'You mean I've slept——'

'—around the clock and much more.' He raised his free arm and squinted at the watch strapped to his wrist. 'I should have been at work an hour ago, but what the hell!' He nuzzled his face into her hair. 'How do you feel?'

Astonished was the answer. Astonished that she had slept so deeply and for so long, yet even more astonished that he should find no ambiguity in continuing a physical rapport at the same time as he intended them to split.

'If you would release me, I'll tell you,' Christa said primly.

He laughed. 'In that case, I don't want to know.'

'And you call me childish!' She lay stiff as a board. 'Where's Marcus?'

'Next door. He surfaced mid-evening and had a bite of dinner, then I bedded him down in the nursery.'

'You could have woken *me* for dinner.'

'You were flat out and I didn't see the point in

disturbing you—though Esther and Tony were sorry you didn't make an appearance.'

'So am I,' Christa retorted. 'I'm also sorry I was in no fit state to protest when you decided to get into my bed!'

'Your bed? For the past six months it's been *mine*, and where else was I supposed to go?'

'There are several other bedrooms, and even though we are supposed to be . . . cohabiting, you could have said you didn't want to disturb me and slept in one of them.'

'Have I disturbed you?' Jeff enquired silkily.

She scowled. 'Well—no.'

'You don't sound too sure.' A grin blossomed in the corner of his mouth. 'Don't tell me I attempted to indulge in a spot of nocturnal rape?' She shook her head. 'Then what's your gripe?'

'I don't appreciate being used!'

The grin flowered. 'But you've assured me I've neglected to use you.'

'I don't mean like that. Yes, I do!' Christa declared, undertaking a swift slalom. 'You reckon I'm in Rio for your father's sake, but it seems to me you intend to benefit.'

His grin died and grave brown eyes locked into hers. 'How?' he asked quietly.

'You said you hated sleeping alone and you appear to imagine that all it takes is a smile and a kiss, and——' facing him had become impossible, so she stared at the ceiling. '—and I'm panting for you to make love to me. You always did suffer from gigantic blind spots,' she continued scathingly, 'and you still do. But I fought you off yesterday,' she proclaimed, with more vehemence than accuracy, 'and I shall fight you off again.'

An angry flush had crept up Jeff's neck. 'There won't be any need,' he rapped, and was out from between the sheets and wrenching a black towelling robe around him. 'Don't worry, I have no intention of——' a vicious knot was tied '—*forcing* you a second time.' Spinning on his heel, he powered towards the en suite bathroom. 'I'll have a quick shower and——'

'I should make it a cold one,' Christa inserted.

'—go to work.'

She gave a saccharine smile. 'Have a nice day.'

All things considered, Christa's own day turned out to be surprisingly pleasant. Having trounced Jeff, she was in the perfect mood to stand up to his father; though, in the event, her resilience remained untested, for when Vittorio Barssi greeted her he was all conviviality. Whatever his faults, bearing a grudge was not among them and he was friendly, relaxed, charming.

Initially Christa decided they were back to their previous relationship, yet as the morning progressed she began to notice small but significant differences in the way her father-in-law treated her. He continued to dominate Isabel—his wife was *not* to dust his desk without permission, she was *not* to gossip while he telephoned, she was *not* to keep pestering him to rest—but the cutting edge of his superiority towards her had been blunted. She had, it seemed, ceased to be a minion and become a person whose views warranted consideration.

This shift ın attitude had a knock-on effect, for whereas Christa had tended to keep a respectful distance, now she felt more at ease. So much so that after lunch she took the initiative and suggested an outing, something she would have hesitated to do in the past.

'I'm taking Marcus to the beach,' she smiled. 'How about coming along with us?'

'Good idea,' Vittorio replied promptly. 'It's time I had a change of scenery and some fresh air.'

'And you, Isabel?' she asked.

Her mother-in-law shook her head. 'It's Anna's day off and I have things which need attention. But do you think you should, Father? The beach isn't far, yet even so——'

'It's a hop, skip and a jump,' Vittorio rebuffed.

'Suppose you feel tired?'

'We can take a folding chair. Christa will carry it.' Black eyes twinkled. 'If she doesn't mind?'

She grinned. 'I'd be happy to.'

At first, spending time alone with her father-in-law was a novelty, but when one hour drifted into two, and still they chatted, Christa recognised the beginnings of a genuine affinity.

'It's such a comfort to know you and Jefferson are back together again,' Vittorio remarked, fondly watching the little boy who built sandcastles at his feet. 'Even though there was far more involved than a spell of homesickness.'

Christa shot him a glance. 'More?' she said warily.

'Isabel took the excuse at face value, however I can tell when my son is—how do you say in English—glossing over things? But whatever the problem I knew you two weren't like those muddle-headed young couples who give up at the first quarrel. This notion that you solve your difficulties by filing for a divorce is abhorrent to me. Indeed, I firmly believe that anyone who can make a solemn vow one year and break it a couple of years later has a serious flaw in their character.' From rank disapproval, the old man suddenly grinned. 'Mind you, marriage was once described as a glorious struggle, and oh boy, do I agree!'

Light-hearted again, his mood continued and he was still joking when they returned to Casa Libra. Even Isabel, who had been on tenterhooks throughout their absence, was forced to agree that the excursion had done him good. She scuttled around providing tea and biscuits, then insisted he must go and lie down.

'I don't care if you do normally take your nap at two, and now it's almost five, you need to recuperate.'

Vittorio gave a loud tush of impatience. 'See what I have to put up with?' he complained, but the smile he shone on his wife was sweet.

Christa looked down at Marcus, who had come to sit on her lap. Eyes half closed, he was sucking his thumb.

'And here's someone else who needs a siesta,' she said, and as the old man went upstairs to his room she followed behind with his grandson. In two minutes the little boy was fast asleep.

'What can I do?' she asked, returning to the kitchen where Isabel was busy preparing the evening meal.

'Nothing. Why don't you rest as well?'

'No, thanks, that mammoth sleep's left me feeling——' Christa was speaking Portuguese, and as she did not know the words for 'bright-eyed and bushy-tailed' she settled for '—*alerta*. I must be able to do something,' she appealed, as the older woman assembled ingredients for a local dish of chicken cooked in a sauce of dried shrimp, peanuts and parsley.

'Run along and read a book.'

'I'm not running anywhere,' Christa persisted. 'I want to help.'

Isabel laughed. 'I give up! You win. Would you peel the carrots?'

After the vegetables, Christa boned the chickens, and later, when she suggested she make dessert, a pumpkin-paste cake with coconut, her offer was accepted. As the two of them worked they talked, until suddenly her mother-in-law grinned.

'It's good to speak to you in Portuguese. I used to think we managed fine, but now I realise our conversations were very basic.'

Christa agreed, and sighed. 'I should have tried harder when I was here before.'

'Tried harder with what?' someone questioned, and she swivelled to find Esther in the doorway.

Hands on hips and fine-plucked brows lifted in

query, the brunette had arrived back from her desk at the prestigious Romano Palace Hotel. In a French designer uniform of black and white herringbone jacket and pencil-slim skirt, crisp white blouse with pussy-cat bow, she combined high fashion with a look of sharp efficiency. This is power dressing, Christa thought.

'Portuguese,' she said, ditching the coconut she had been grating to greet the new arrival with kisses on both cheeks. 'How are you?'

The swathe of straight shoulder-length hair was patted into place. 'I'm well.'

'She's dieting too much,' Isabel tut-tutted. 'Just look at her—no bosom, no hips!'

In pursuit of the body beautiful, violent war had been waged on any extra ounce which had dared attach itself to Esther's reed-slim frame, yet Jeff's sister-in-law had always been slim but shapely. Now that slimness edged dangerously close to skinny.

Esther gave a high-pitched laugh. 'You think *I* want to be fat?' she sniggered, in a noticeable reference to the older woman's bulky frame. She swung to Christa. 'I understand you've been arguing with our esteemed father-in-law?'

'I stuck to my point of view, that's all,' Christa said briefly, for although Esther was smiling her dark eyes showed something different. Something mettlesome and obstructive. Had her voice always sounded so brittle? Christa wondered. Had she always looked so hard? Weight loss accounted for the unflattering sharpening of her features, yet it could never have bestowed this air of . . . malice.

'But he backed down,' the brunette persisted, clearly relishing a derisory post-mortem.

'We reached an amicable agreement,' Christa dismissed.

With a pout, Esther turned to Isabel again.

'Now it's been proved it's possible to fight Vittorio and win, shouldn't you try it some time?' she challenged.

Her victim reddened. 'Oh, I don't think——' The front door was opened and shut with a bang. 'Sounds like someone's home,' she said with a grateful smile, and seconds later Jeff walked in carrying a newly awakened Marcus.

'Where's Tony?' Esther demanded, as the doting grandmother rushed over.

Jeff fixed her with cool brown eyes. 'Don't worry, I haven't taken him off to a dark alley and strung him up. Your ever-lovin' husband's still at the office. He'll be another half-hour.'

'Huh!' she snorted, and flounced off.

'Wanna kiss from my mummy,' said Marcus, when Isabel had finished paying homage. He bent from his father's arms towards Christa. 'Pleeeease!'

'Now me,' said Jeff, when she had pressed a noisy peck to the little boy's cheek.

Christa stood very still. She had taken this morning's furious withdrawal to mean an end to physical contact, but devilment danced in his eyes. A code of behaviour needed to be drawn up, she realised—and soon.

'Kiss you?' she said.

'If I ask nicely? Pleeeease!' he mimicked.

This was not force, she could not help thinking, this was a request—and they were supposed to be in love. What did she do? Isabel, laughing beside the cooker, took the decision out of her hands.

'How can you turn away a request like that?' she appealed.

Christa's lips were aimed for Jeff's cheek, but at the last moment he turned and their mouths met. The kiss, which by Jefferson Barssi's standards was tame, sent a warmth tingling through her body. She clenched her fists. Two thirds of her objected to being outsmarted, but the other third traitorously applauded. He always had attracted her with flypaper ease and, unfortunately, he still did.

Marcus grabbed Jeff's ear to get his attention. 'Me go beach. Me build big, big sandcastle.' His chest puffed out. 'As big as *apartamento*.'

'You didn't!'

'Me did!' the little boy protested, knowing he was not quite believed. 'Me show you.'

Jeff looked at the clock. 'I guess there's time.'

'Yes! Yes!' shrilled Marcus.

'Leave the cake, Christa,' shooed Isabel, 'and go.'

'No, thanks. When I've finished I'd like to grab a catnap. Earlier I reckoned to be alert, but now——'

'Jet lag's hit?' Jeff sympathised, as she portrayed hand-to-brow exhaustion. 'That's the way it goes. One minute you're fine, the next—pow!'

'Pow!' shouted Marcus. 'Pow! Pow! Pow!'

'I'll take this noisy kid down to the beach,' said Jeff, giving him a shake which transformed the shouts to giggles, 'and leave you in peace.'

When the pumpkin-paste cake had been made, Christa excused herself and went upstairs. Kicking off her sandals, she lay down on the bed. She intended to take a short rest and then return to help Isabel but, as before, she slept on, and it was only when Jeff and Marcus came in from the beach that she awoke.

'Had a good time?' she enquired, stretching.

'Busy.' Jeff was droll. 'I retract what I said about your time being your own apart from wiping the odd runny nose. Marcus is about ten times more trouble now than he ever was six months ago,' he said, pulling a face at the child, who had clambered on to the bed. 'At one point I lost him. He was beside me one second, and the next he'd vanished. In the minutes before I found him I'd had him drowned, run over, up to the chin in quicksands.'

'Join the club,' said Christa, as small arms wound around her neck and she was almost throttled. 'Yuck, Marcus, you're all sandy!' she protested, holding him off.

'I'll take him into the nursery shower with me,' Jeff said, catching hold of the wriggling culprit, 'then get him ready for dinner.'

'That's good of you.'

He bent to kiss her on the mouth, swiftly and completely. 'I'm not *all* bad,' he said.

A victim of surprise, Christa just looked at him.

For someone who had resolved to be aloof, controlled,

always circumspect, she was giving a fine imitation of an endlessly pliable dimwit, Christa thought, as trousers and T-shirt were shed in favour of a black scooped-neck dress with just a hint of silver. Always, always, she must remember that Jeff's tactical brain was at work, and that the only reason he kissed her in private was to keep her sweetly acting the loving wife in public. It was all part of an act. So—whatever he said, or did, in future, she would remain calm. If he touched her, she would respond with a merry quip and swiftly remove his hand. And if she suspected a kiss was in the vicinity, instead of sitting there like a stuffed prune, she would duck!

Satisfied her mental attitude could meet any challenge, Christa turned her attention to her appearance. Shimmering blue shadow was fingertipped on to her eyelids, a line of kohl drawn, mascara brushed on to her lashes. A touch of blusher to her cheekbones and an application of rose-pink lip-gloss came next. She fastened silver filigree hoops into her ears and slid her feet into black mules. Finally she brushed her hair, taming the tawny wisps which curled around her face, and sprayed a mist of *Ysatis* on to pulse-points. An inspection in the mirror confirmed that, as Sylvie had said—was it only three days ago?—she looked sophisticated.

'Sophisticated and ready for anything,' she muttered, as she went downstairs.

Casa Libra's living-room was stately, but the marble fireplace, the stiffly arranged occasional tables, the polished parquet floor, ensured that it would never be comfortable. When Christa walked in, she found everyone else had assembled. Jeff and Tony were chatting beside the long sash windows, Vittorio and Isabel occupied the couch with Marcus, while Esther sat apart, leafing through a magazine. All the men wore lounge suits and the women were in cocktail dresses. Dinner on Friday evenings, so Vittorio had long ago decreed, was a formal affair.

Marcus greeted her first, scampering across to grab hold of her hand and receive a cuddle before returning to his grandparents.

'You look beautiful,' murmured Jeff, as he and Tony joined her.

Christa cursed her pulse for its abrupt acceleration. 'Thank you.'

'Great to see you, kid,' her brother-in-law said, opening his arms wide.

'And you,' she grinned, as he enveloped her in an enthusiastic bear-hug.

Christa's pleasure was real. She had always liked Tony. He might be a touch weak-kneed, but he was also easy-going, uncomplicated and undemanding—in other words, as different from Jeff as any man could be! Even physically they bore no resemblance; Tony being shorter, round-faced and chunky. He was, however, as dedicated to the family business, and one day—a day not too distant, Christa realised with a swift, distressed glance at Vittorio—would take control.

For a moment Tony studied her, then he grinned. 'Ten out of ten for the hairstyle.'

Esther glanced up from her glossy magazine. 'Ten

out of ten for the dress, too. It looks expensive. Who bought it for you?' One of the *Dynasty*-style shoulders of her ruby-red tunic received a minuscule adjustment. 'A man?'

Christa had been prepared for anything Jeff could throw, but this question took her aback.

'Sorry?' she said in bewilderment.

'Joke, dear, joke.'

'What would you like to drink?' Jeff demanded curtly.

She dragged her gaze from Esther. 'Er—*caipirinha, por favor.*'

'Remember the first one you ever had?' he enquired, shepherding her across to the corner bar.

She nodded. 'On Paqueta.'

'Such a restful place,' Vittorio smiled, and, as Jeff mixed the delicious blend of lime juice, *cachaça*, sugar and ice, the old man started to reminisce about happy times he and Isabel had spent on the islands which lay a short sail away from the city.

'I prefer the mainland beaches myself,' Esther declared, when a general discussion broke out about the best places for sunning and swimming. 'You can't beat Ipanema. Tony and I will be there first thing tomorrow, soaking up the sunshine.'

'I'm afraid you'll have to count me out,' her husband said, with a awkward smile of apology. 'I need to go into the office.'

Pettishly, the magazine was cast aside. 'You know what they say?' came the demand. 'All work and no play makes for a very dull——'

'I asked him to go,' Vittorio announced. 'Any objections?'

Esther's mouth etched the thinnest of lines. 'None,' she said, after an infinitesimal pause.

Isabel caught Christa's eye and smiled.

'Me build big sandcastle,' Marcus reminded everyone, and the conversation started up again.

Esther spent the evening talking too quickly, laughing too loudly, and being generally tense. Her mood put a dampener on the proceedings, and Christa was not surprised when the gathering broke up far earlier than usual.

'The air was thin tonight,' Jeff remarked drily, as he closed the bedroom door behind them.

'What's the matter with Esther?'

'Jeez, you're not admitting the woman has faults?'

Christa shrugged. 'I thought her gaiety seemed a bit forced.' It had been a relief to escape from downstairs, but now she noticed an acute lack of oxygen on the upper level of Casa Libra too. Jeff was unbuttoning his shirt, and without his clothes he would be dangerous. How did she handle a night in close proximity? 'I noticed she only picked at her food,' she continued, 'but dieting can't be wholly responsible for her mood.'

'It isn't.' His shirt was tossed on to a chair. 'She and Tony are going through a bad patch.'

Us and now them, Christa thought bleakly, as Jeff disappeared into the bathroom. She sat down at the dressing-table to unscrew her ear-rings. If Isabel and Vittorio were faced with both their sons' marriages going wrong, it would crucify them. Lost in her thoughts, she was only vaguely aware of water running and Jeff washing and brushing his teeth.

'Want me to check on Marcus?' he asked, joining her again.

'Please.' As she swivelled, Christa's eyes opened wide. 'I wasn't aware you went in for that kind of thing,' she said, unable to stop a smile.

'I didn't think you'd want me in *your* bed naked,' he muttered, tugging irritably at the waist of black silk pyjama bottoms. 'Don't you like them?'

'They're fine.'

'You want me to wear the jacket as well?' Jeff demanded.

Embarrassed at having been caught staring, she felt hot colour rush up her cheeks. 'No, no,' she assured him. 'Go and see Marcus.'

As he stepped on to the landing, Christa fled to the bathroom. Her clothes were ripped off and the coffee-coloured satin and lace flung on. If only she had brought a nightdress, preferably one in heavy-duty sacking which buttoned up to the neck and came equipped with padlocks at the hem! A lightning cream of her face, a hasty clean of her teeth, and as the door opened she was leaping into bed, pulling the sheets up to her chin.

'He's fine,' Jeff reported.

'Who? Oh, yes. Good.'

'Broken the four-minute mile?' he drawled, surveying her flushed face. 'You needn't have bothered. When I said I wouldn't *force* you, I meant it!'

Christa gave a weak smile. 'I know.'

'Then if it's not my lust you're afraid of, what is it?' he asked, as he climbed in beside her. He switched off the bedside lamp. 'Your own?'

'No!' She knew she had rejected the suggestion too quickly. 'Of course not,' she said, with a reflex trill of laughter.

'Are you sure?' he taunted.

She had positioned herself to one side of the mattress, but now she withdrew even further. 'I'm sure. It's just that—that I think we need to lay down a few ground rules.'

'Such as?'

Christa swallowed. 'I'd—I'd be obliged if you wouldn't kiss me.'

Jeff had moved as he settled himself, making the bed dip, and she needed to cling on to the edge to remain in place.

'Carry on,' he said.

Her mind had gone blank. She could not frame a single sentence. All she could focus on was his nearness.

'Not kiss you, that's it?' he demanded, impatient of her silence.

'Er—yes.'

'Fine. Goodnight.'

'Goodnight,' she said.

She felt him turn on his side away from her, dragging the sheet with him. She lay there, eyes wide open and staring into the darkness. She wanted to sleep, but her awareness of him—male and lithe and muscular—revived memories she would rather forget. She plumped up her pillow.

'For heaven's sake keep still!' Jeff complained.

She lay like a statue. 'I'm cold,' she said, after a few minutes.

'Cold?' he rasped, and the mattress depressed as he flung himself over to face her.

'Just a bit. You see, the air-conditioning's on and you have the sheet.'

'Take it. Take it.' What seemed to be acres of cotton were flung over her. 'Happy now?' he enquired, and she could see him glaring in the gloom.

'Yes.'

Jeff turned away, and when his breathing became a steady rhythm Christa decided he must be asleep. She did her best to settle down too. She counted sheep. She laboured her way backwards through the alphabet. She tried to pretend she was at the cottage and he wasn't there, but every nerve, every cell, every fibre of her body clamoured that he was. He was. He was. She lay on her stomach. She lay on her side. She lay on her back.

'You really are a piece of work, aren't you?'

She jumped. 'I beg your pardon?'

Jeff swore and rolled over to face her. 'You get into bed wearing the nearest thing to zilch and looking like a sex kitten. You squirm around, you positively throb with desire, yet——'

'Desire? Huh!'

He shrugged. 'I guess it's time for another cold shower!'

'No,' she said, as he swung his feet to the floor and stood up. She reached across to catch hold of his wrist. 'Don't go. Please!'

If he was as excited by her as she was by him, then perhaps a divorce was not automatic? Maybe. Maybe not. All of a sudden, it did not matter. What mattered was that he hold her close. Very close. So close that she would feel him all around her.

Jeff gazed down. 'I never intended to force you into anything yesterday,' he said. His mouth tightened. 'I—I just needed you so much. I admit I was thinking more of what I wanted than of you, but—hell, I'm not one of your stiff-upper-lip Englishmen. My temperament is Latin and——'

'Kiss me,' Christa said softly.

'I thought kissing was out?' He made a husky attempt at a laugh. 'Or have you granted a special dispensation?'

'I have—with privileges.' Slowly and sinuously, she slid the narrow straps from her shoulders and eased down the coffee-coloured satin. A lift of the hips, a kick of an ankle, and she was naked. 'How about removing these fancy pyjamas of yours?' she murmured.

His dark eyes locked with hers. 'I'd rather you removed them for me.' She knelt. There was just one button, yet her fingers were all thumbs. 'Shall I?' Jeff asked.

As the black trousers slid to the floor, he drew her close and she sighed, feeling the heat of him against her breasts.

'Christa!' he groaned when she began to move, dragging her nipples across his skin again and again and again. He shuddered and lowered her on to the bed to kiss and stroke and caress with fingers and mouth, until she felt as if she was drowning in a sea of molten pleasure.

'This isn't a fumble—at least, I hope not,' Jeff muttered, his lips against hers, 'but I'm afraid it'll need to be quick.' In an effort to control the ragged tempo of his breathing, he gulped in one breath and then another. 'Honey, I'm sorry, but if I don't take you now I'm going to——'

'I want you quickly,' she assured him. 'I want you now.'

With a moan of pleasure, he slid inside her, filling her, possessing her. A jolt of sexual electricity shot through her body and her fingers bit deep into his back. As he moved, Christa abandoned herself to the spiralling passion. The only thing in the world was Jeff's body on hers, the thrust of him, the blood which thundered in her head. Higher and higher he took her until, in a racking, shuddering, wonderful explosion, she called out his name.

CHAPTER SEVEN

JEFF rinsed away traces of foam and patted dry his freshly shaven cheeks.

'That's better,' he said, as Christa walked into the bathroom.

It was morning, and after a night lavish with lovemaking the shrill of the alarm had been a crime against humanity. Jeff had surfaced rapidly enough, but vast reserves of will-power had needed to be plumbed before she could stagger out of bed.

'Mmm,' she yawned.

'Only mmm? So I've failed to dazzle you with the smoothness of my jaw, the regularity of my features, the blinding white of my smile?' He glanced down. 'And other things?'

Christa frowned. Presumably he was joking, yet his comments contained precious little humour. Jeff's voice had been clipped and the rigidity of his stance betrayed an inner agitation. With daylight, it appeared, had come a different mood.

'You've blown my mind,' she declared, flinging a brilliant grin into the mirror. His reflection remained straight-faced. 'Especially with the other things.'

Jeff flexed his shoulders, like a boxer bracing, himself to despatch a left hook. 'You know how you were keen for us to talk?' he said.

Involuntarily, her stomach muscles tightened. For eight hours the backlog of problems, their current circumstances and the future, had been irrelevant, now they were of climactic importance. Had the sharing of their passion changed anything? she wondered. Had it shown him he still cared? Jeff had to care. After making love with such tenderness, such generosity of body and spirit, he *must*. But . . . But . . . But . . . Everyone knew men and women approached sex from different angles, so maybe all he cared about was . . . her body? Christa gulped down air. Did his mood indicate that last night had changed nothing—and a divorce continued to feature on his agenda?

'Talk?' she bleated, in a voice which bore no resemblance to her own.

'Yeah.' He swung to face her. 'Now.'

Now? With his next breath he could announce that it was exit time, *fim*, the end? In another second he might demand that they buckle down to the dismantling process. The wary part of her reared its head. A man who, whether it was in a racing car, or business, or in seduction, could zoom from zero to sixty with the greatest of ease, Jeff would have already defined what he required in any settlement and how much he was prepared to concede. For her, however, the concept of divorce was a whole new ballgame, frightening and serious. Decisions made now would affect what happened in the rest of Marcus's life, and in her own. She could not afford to ad lib her strategy.

Indeed, until every aspect had been examined, until each complexity had been worked through, she would be foolish to say a single word.

'You can't mean us to talk right this minute?' she protested.

'Why not?'

Christa searched desperately around for a reason. 'I—I thought you didn't want any bad vibes. And I've only just woken up,' she gabbled. 'And I'm not dressed. And we haven't had breakfast. And——'

Jeff scowled. 'OK, we'll leave it until later.'

In the bedroom Christa pulled on a coffee-on-white spotted halter-neck, while he dressed more formally in button-down shirt and dark trousers. The silence was hanging heavily between them when a knock came at the door.

'I was wondering whether you'd join me at the office this morning?' Tony asked, looking in. He gave Jeff a hopeful smile. 'There's a meeting fixed with that guy from Sao Paulo, and Vittorio insists I don't allow him to leave until he's paid off the money he owes. I know this isn't in your area, but the guy's as devious as they come and I'd be grateful for some support.'

'No problem,' Jeff assured him.

'Thanks, you're a pal. Sorry to take lover boy away on your first Saturday back,' her brother-in-law apologised to Christa.

'As the man said, no problem,' she replied, privately welcoming the chance to be on her own.

'However, I'm not leaving you at a loose end,' he continued cheerfully, 'because you're going on the beach with Esther. She insists.'

Her heart sank. Whether Esther insisted or not, she guessed it was Tony who had organised the outing, and she did not want to hurt his feelings—but, in addition to doubts about his wife's company, she badly needed time to think. She was trying to find a polite excuse when a small bundle of energy in a space-rocket-patterned sleepsuit hurtled into the room.

'Fancy building more sandcastles this morning?' Tony enquired, ruffling his nephew's hair.

'Yes!' Marcus yelled excitedly.

Christa looked from her hop-skipping son to her expectant brother-in-law, and sighed. 'Good idea,' she said.

When they joined her at breakfast, Esther was in a more relaxed state of mind. To Christa's relief, yesterday's brittleness had been replaced by amiability and she smiled, chatted, and professed real pleasure at the prospect of company. As she spoke, Christa's gaze went to Vittorio. Would he like to join them? she wondered. She felt tempted to invite him, but hesitated—the outing *was* Esther's show.

'Maybe I'll tag along the next time,' the old man smiled, demonstrating a bent for telepathy, 'but not today. Today I intend to take life quietly.'

'You are feeling well?' Isabel asked, her round face flushed with sudden anxiety.

'As well as can be expected.'

'You've taken your pills?'

Vittorio's tongue clicked. 'You put them out for me. You poured the glass of water. You saw me swallow them!'

'I only saw you swallow the little blue ones. If you remember, I went out of the room to——'

'Don't nag, woman!'

Isabel switched her attention to Christa. 'You will make certain Marcus doesn't have too much sun? Coming from a cooler climate, his skin could easily burn.'

'Christa knows the dangers,' Vittorio snapped. 'She'll do what's necessary.'

The digital temperature/time signboards had yet to display eighty degrees and ten a.m, yet already the beach was beginning to fill. Esther's ritual sunbath took place in a specially selected spot, and she led the way towards it like Boadicea leading her troops. Christa had tied a carnation-printed kanga over her bikini, but the Brazilian woman strutted along the promenade in a meagre two-piece known as *fio dental*—dental floss. The upper latticework was respectable anough—her reduced curves did not require too much concealing—but the bottom half consisted of a fragile strand which went down from the waist to dive out of sight in a way which left little to the imagination and even less room for error. Why breasts should be bared on European sands, yet in Latin-America buttocks formed the major erogenous zone, Christa had never discovered.

As she followed Esther past couples flirting beneath

striped umbrellas, old women gossiping, children playing *frescobol*, she smiled. In Rio the beaches served as town square, club house and sports field. Everyone gathered there. Everyone watched everyone else. Everyone knew everyone else watched *them*. It was a poseur's paradise. Brazil, some visiting VIP had once remarked, was not a serious country, and Christa tended to agree. Yet who wanted to be serious when wherever you went you heard the pulsating beat of the bossa nova, the *frevo*, the *coco* and a million and one other different rhythms, when the people sang and danced on a whim, when the very air was intoxicating?

As they reached the appointed place and Christa removed her kanga, her grin spread. Back in England her pink thong bikini had seemed the ultimate in risqué, but now—she glanced at the bathing beauties laid out in all directions—it had taken on the dimensions of a boiler suit!

'If I was ratty yesterday, you must blame Tony,' Esther declared, as Christa positioned Marcus before her and began to apply lotion. 'He's so immersed in what's happening to his father and with business, my needs are totally neglected. What's the situation like between you and Jefferson?'

'Everything's fine,' Christa said casually.

Eyes heavy with mascara swung her way. 'No kidding?'

Christa concentrated on oiling her son. She did not welcome an assault on her private life, and if this conversation continued an assault it seemed destined to be. After all, whenever matters had taken a personal turn in the past, hadn't Esther always managed to air some disturbing insinuation?

Sun protection complete, she handed Marcus his bucket and spade. 'Get to it, *querido*,' she smiled.

'So it's happy families again?' her companion persisted, as the little boy capered off to begin his digging.

Christa kept her voice nonchalant. 'It is.'

'If that's the case, then tell me, why did Jefferson go to England and fly back the very same day?' Esther demanded, leaning forward like an inquisitive weasel. 'And why did you arrive forty-eight hours later? He spouted some tale about a last-minute change of plans and trouble getting a seat, but if that was true why did he bring Marcus and not you? It seems most odd.'

'What is this, Twenty Questions?' queried Christa, but the quip was ignored.

'My guess is you had no intention of coming to Rio, and Jefferson engineered the entire thing!' Esther paused, deliberating creating tension. 'Am I right?'

Christa pushed her feet into the sand, feeling the grains between her toes. She could lie and say no, but what would that achieve? Far from persuading the other woman to transfer her interest to the weather, a negative would guarantee that she continued to probe and pry.

'You are,' she began, thinking that, somehow, she must assemble an ultra-bland, ultra-discreet, minimal explanation. 'But——'

'We both know why he wanted you here, don't we?'

Esther enquired, arching disdainful brows. 'In order to convince everyone that your marriage is of the "till death us do part" variety!'

Christa searched in her bag for her sunglasses. Such an accurate reading could only be the result of keen analysis, which meant their relationship had languished long beneath the microscope. She slid the glasses on her nose. She had no idea why Esther should be so fascinated with their affairs, but she did not like it.

'This is a difficult time, and naturally Jeff's anxious to help his parents in any way he can,' she said, aware of the irony of defending an action, aspects of which she had so recently railed against.

'He's anxious to help himself!'

Christa's eyes flew to Marcus. The little boy was engrossed in play, but she needed to confirm that he was also too far away to hear the conversation. Her companion did not seem to care, but who knew what a child could pick up and repeat, or worry about?

'How?' Christa asked quietly.

'Vittorio's so anti divorce that if he suspected Jefferson was heading for the courts there's a strong chance he'd expel him from Barssi & Company and cut him off without a penny. From director to street cleaner in one fell swoop—your husband wouldn't like that! You don't consider Jefferson has the capacity to gauge which actions get the results he desires and which do not?' Esther jeered.

Christa was convinced he not only possessed the capacity to gauge actions, but could move entire mountains—and small boys, she thought unhappily—should he so wish; but in the face of such hostility she was not about to admit it.

'As for Jeff plotting and planning to make sure he stays in Vittorio's good books, you're as off the wall about that as—as you were about why he married me,' she said recklessly.

'Pouf! You can't *still* insist that the timing of his proposal and the signing of the merger were mere coincidence?' Esther demanded.

A shadow darkened Christa's blue eyes. 'I do.'

'And I suppose the fickle finger of fate was responsible for Marcus's conception?' came the sly query. Straps at shoulder and waist were repositioned to ensure immaculate tanning. 'Has Jefferson said anything about Ruth?'

The subject had been changed? She was being let off the hook? Christa only just managed to disguise her relief. Allowing herself to be drawn into a discussion had been madness—no matter what Esther had said, she should have ignored her—but to raise the marriage skeleton was a most peculiar masochism. For an age Jeff's whys and wherefores had been left to moulder undisturbed, yet she had breathed life into the subject herself!

'He told me how she's happy to stay late at the office,' she said, light-hearted now. 'Quite a change.'

'There've been many changes since Gilberto departed the scene.'

Christa blinked. 'Gilberto's gone?'

'In January. For a time Ruth's world collapsed, but

hearts do heal, and Jefferson's been . . . encouraging. The pair of them always did get on well, but now they're almost inseparable.' Esther raised her face to the sun. 'I understood when you left before and, frankly, I wouldn't blame you if you decide to leave again. Whether you care to admit it or not, Jefferson's used you for a sucker since Day One.'

The Mayors, Mr and Mrs Everlasting Love, had split? Jeff had stepped in to comfort his secretary? Esther was advocating a second withdrawal? Everything had been thrown so fast and so furiously, Christa's head felt like a tossed salad.

'Jeff and Ruth are—are having an affair?' she said, in bewilderment. 'But she's over forty!'

'So? As for an actual affair, I wouldn't like to say how far things have gone, but,' her companion's mouth curved into a long, slow smile, 'the amount of time they spend closeted together at the office, in his car when he runs her home, et cetera, must have bred a certain awareness.'

Christa sat stock still. Esther's smile had been the sort of smile a Doberman gives just before going for the throat—and a dead giveaway. All of a sudden, and with startling clarity, she knew Jeff's sister-in-law was conducting a hate campaign against him—though she had no idea why. She removed her sunglasses. So many times she had tried to convince herself that the Brazilian woman had been addicted to fantasy, and now her spirits soared. Couldn't what had been said, both this morning and in the past, be rejected as figments of an over-active—and malignant—

imagination? Her spirits fell. Regrettably, those
fantasies had a disturbing habit of bumping against
fact.

'Oh, yes?' she said, turning to look at Marcus again.

Her companion refused to be deflected. 'For
months now your husband's been a regular visitor at
Ruth's house. If you don't believe me, ask Isabel,
Tony, anyone. Check it out.'

Christa longed to dismiss the charge as just another
pin being stuck into Jeff's waxen image, but Esther
sounded malevolently sure of herself. She inclined her
head. In deciding that the length of her husband's
working day eliminated the 'other woman', she had
forgotten a vital factor—that one woman had been
there all the time! And if she was ten years
older—maybe Ruth appealed to Jeff because she *was*
mature?

'You could get a flight in the morning,' Esther
suggested.

'Fly out tomorrow?'

Did Ruth like Barra da Tijuca?' Christa wondered
numbly. Had she chosen the leather sofa and chairs?
And the carpet? And the dining-suite?

'It's an idea.'

'I suppose so.'

'*Olá!*' her companion exclaimed, all of a sudden.
'You're back early.'

When Christa looked round, she found Jeff
standing behind her. Her heart missed a beat. Clad in
brief white shorts which emphasised the depth of his
tan, his long legs, his muscular thighs, he seemed

aggressively, excitingly male. But whose man was he? Hers—or someone else's?

'Once the Sao Paulo guy coughed up, I left,' he explained, and frowned across to where their son was tipping yet another sandpie from his bucket. 'Shouldn't Marcus be wearing a sunhat?'

'It's here.' Christa found the blue cotton cap. 'I meant to put it on him, but——' Her shrug acknowledged negligence.

'I'm going to work out on the parallel bars,' Esther said, as he went to attend to the little boy. She got up. 'See you later.'

'See you,' she muttered.

'OK, what's the she-devil been saying?' Jeff demanded, returning to sprawl beside Christa. 'And don't tell me nothing, because those eyes of yours——'

'What do you think she's said?' Christa retaliated, meeting a question with a question because she did not know what else to do.

Silently he studied her, as though he might learn the answer in the troubled blue of her gaze.

'Something about me? About how I'm a two-faced villain who's raised ambition to an art form and who'd stop at nothing if he felt it'd further his career?' A handful of sand was scooped up and dribbled out through his long, tanned fingers. 'She's right, I am ambitious—for Barssi's. And I admit that for the company's sake I would——' He shot her a frowning, sidelong glance. 'Christa, this is not a perfect world, and there are occasions when so long as no one gets hurt, I mean *really* hurt, the end justifies the means. I know you won't agree, but believe me——'

'No, no!' Christa broke in, terrified of what he might say next. Far from being fantasies, him zeroing in on Esther's insinuations had filled them with deadly damning substance, but she could not face a confession. Not now. Maybe not ever. If he admitted he had married her for mixed reasons, it would tear her apart. 'Esther was telling me about Ruth,' she said, choosing the lesser of two evils. 'I understand she's on her own now.'

'That's right,' he said curtly.

'You've——' Christa's heart contracted '—been comforting her?'

'It'd be more accurate to say we've comforted each other,' Jeff replied, his guarded expression making it plain there was a lot going on inside him which he was reluctant to talk about. 'One way or another.'

One way or another. There was a phrase to conjure with, Christa thought bleakly. 'You've—you've visited her at home?' she faltered.

'Yeah. Keep your cap on, Marcus,' he called, as the toddler's spadework dislodged his headgear and sent it spinning to the ground.

'But, *Papá*——!'

Jeff climbed to his feet. 'Suppose we go into the water?' he suggested.

The conversation had been terminated.

'What do you want with those?' Jeff enquired, when Christa walked into the bedroom that evening laden with pillows. 'I heard you telling my mother you'd sleep better with another one, but four——!'

She dropped the pillows on the bed and turned, ready for the skirmish she had anticipated. 'They're not for me to sleep on, they're to put between us. I don't want us to—to touch.'

He loosened his tie. 'Touch? What you mean is, you don't want us to make love. In other words, last night was a mistake and you regret it,' he said, the edge to his voice ominously clear.

Christa sighed. 'Not exactly.'

'And what does that mean?'

She cleared her throat. 'This morning you said we must talk and I agree, but before that happens I have a lot to straighten out in my mind.'

'Hot dog!'

'And I can't do that if——' Christa flushed. 'I need time to think with no distractions.'

'So after a night like last night I'm to be given the big freeze?' The silk tie was dragged from his collar and stretched tight between two hands, like a snake he was considering how best to strangle. 'I should have known by now that constancy doesn't figure too strongly in your bag of tricks.'

Her backbone straightened. 'Jefferson, I'm still willing to present a united front in public. It's just that in private——'

'In private we're going to lie on either side of a row of pillows!' he thundered. 'It amazes me you didn't walk in with a roll of bloody barbed wire!'

'Don't you yell at me!'

His jaw hardened to steel. 'I'll yell if I——'

Abruptly he broke off and raised two hands. 'OK, OK,' he said, breathing hard. 'I'll do whatever you wish. In the past you've accused me of not paying enough attention to what you want, so I'm taking notice now. However, I would like to point out that when it comes to driving a man to drink—and cold showers—lady, you're a natural!'

Christa felt a sudden stirring of compassion. 'I'm sorry.'

'Don't start apologising,' he rasped, then sighed. 'Would you prefer me to move into another room?'

'You'd do that?' she said, surprised. 'But I thought we wanted to keep your parents happy?'

'It's a matter of priorities.'

She considered the offer for a moment. 'I think, for their sake, you should stay.'

'How long do you reckon it'll take you to get everything straight in your mind?' Jeff enquired.

She pursed her lips. 'A week or so.'

'It's Vittorio's birthday a fortnight on Sunday, suppose we make that the deadline?'

Christa nodded. 'Sounds fine.'

CHAPTER EIGHT

ONE session of concentrated, cool-headed and objective thinking was all it took for Christa to work out her requirements where Marcus was concerned: she wanted her son to live with her, his father to have unrestricted access, joint decisions to be taken on his education, et cetera, et cetera. Each and every eventuality was carefully, and painfully, considered. For a day or two the matter was studiously left dormant to enable any neglected aspects to surface, but none did. Fully prepared, she could now approach Jeff—yet she marked time.

The snag was that although for a number of reasons, Ruth among them, a divorce seemed the practical answer, all her instincts cried out against one. Also, although it could be wishful thinking, she was not convinced that, deep down, Jeff wanted them to separate either. Conflicting voices jammed her head. If he was smitten with another woman, why had he been so desperate to make love to her? If he loved her, why had he regularly visited the other woman?

Christa built up endless arguments *for* staying together—and reduced them to rubble. Then she proceeded to do the same with arguments *against*. A week went by, and still her views were split, still

133

she dithered and held back.

'What'll you have?' Jeff enquired, and she roused herself from her musing.

'Pineapple juice, please.'

'And beer for me,' he told the waiter. 'I wonder how many drinks and ice-creams and cakes Marcus has consumed by now?' he mused, as the man walked away.

Christa made a face. 'I dread to think!'

It was Saturday afternoon and their son had accompanied his grandmother to the home of a family friend. The visit was, so Isabel insisted, a compassionate gesture towards a woman who lived alone and was starved of company and—heaven forbid!—had nothing whatsoever to do with her wishing to show off her grandson. Given time alone, Jeff had suggested they leave the city and head south to a quiet beach. For half an hour they had strolled between the palm trees until the heat had made a cool drink essential, and now they sat on the shady terrace of a bar which overlooked the blue sparkle of the ocean.

As they waited for their order, Christa sneaked a glance across the table. Was it chance that had had Jeff driving to this particular bay, or had he brought her because it was here he had proposed? Could this be a tentative step towards remembrance and . . . reconciliation? Or didn't he care? She sighed. Everything boiled down to how well she knew him, and, although once she would have blithely claimed to know him very well, now she wondered whether she had *ever* had much of an insight into what made him tick. She tugged her pink and gold ruched boob-tube a little higher at the armpits, and smoothed where it met her bare midriff. Her shorts were given a decisive tweak. This afternoon she would devote herself to getting to know him better.

'What made you decide to become a racing driver?' she enquired, when their drinks had arrived.

Jeff wiped froth from his mouth with the back of his hand. 'Why ask that all of a sudden?'

'I'm interested. OK, so you started driving go-karts when you were nine and cars were a hobby in your teens, but why take up racing professionally? You'd gone to college, come top of your year in business management then you changed course completely. Why? I assume it was part of a master plan, but——'

'Master plan? What the hell do you think I did, sit down on my first birthday and draft what I wanted from the next three score years and ten? I like to know where I'm going, but I'm not that much of a strategist!' Jeff protested. He stretched back to ease a packet of slim panatellas from the hip pocket of his jeans. 'No, taking up racing was a crazy move. The truth is,' he went on, as he selected a cigar, 'that although I made noises about being an adrenalin junkie and needing thrills, I only went into the sport because my father was so bloody determined I shouldn't.'

Christa gave a surprised laugh. 'You did it to rebel against Vittorio? I never knew that before.'

'You've never asked me before.'

'But you raced for six years.'

'That's how long it took me to wise up and realise that if I wasn't pleasing my father, I wasn't doing such a great job of delighting myself either.' He snapped his lighter and inhaled, narrowing his eyes against the blue-grey mist of smoke. 'From the day we were born, Vittorio had it planned that Tony and I would follow him into the business. At school my brother demonstrated an aptitude for maths, so—what d'you know?—it was decided he'd be the finance wizard, which left me earmarked for administration and marketing. We were never given a choice, either about whether we wanted to work for the company or what we'd do within it. When Tony left school he was despatched to study accountancy and——'

'But he didn't object?' Christa interrupted.

'No, figures are his kind of thing. It's people he doesn't handle too well.' Jeff frowned at the glowing tip of his cigar. 'And later I went to the States.'

'Did *you* object?'

'I didn't object to the course as such—from the first class on the first day it was obvious business management and I were well-matched—what I did object to was having it decided for me. I'd made my protests plain in a series of arguments when bits of the ceiling fell down,' he said pithily, 'but at nineteen I was no match for Vittorio. However, when I finished college I was twenty-three and a man, not a boy.'

Christa linked her fingers across a knee and smiled. 'You mean you'd lost your viginity?'

'I don't mean that at all!' he grated furiously.

His anger sat her back in her seat. She had merely been teasing him a little and had never expected such a violent reaction. Christa fidgeted with the gold pendant she wore around her neck. On reflection, it would have been wiser to avoid the subject of sex with all its attendant strains and stresses. Each night when they had gone to bed, they had lain close to each other—yet in splendid isolation. There had been no pillow barrier, but one was not required because Jeff had barely acknowledged her existence, let alone made an advance. Even his subconscious seemed to have absorbed her 'hands off' message, for not once in his sleep had he touched her. Yet, while he'd slept, she had lain awake for hours. While he'd barely moved, she had tossed and turned. Intensely aware of him, if he had stretched out one finger she would have responded by winding her body around his—and she suspected he knew as much. But his withdrawal had seemed self-assured and inviolate—until now.

'So, after six years you decided to pack in motor racing?' she prompted, and heard herself sound like a hostess on a TV chat show.

'There was more to it than that,' he said, his anger subsiding as quickly as it had erupted. 'To begin with I didn't have a sponsor, and it was ages before I managed to do more than scrape even. So as far as making a decent living goes, I wasn't. Also, although the team I drove for had workmanlike cars, they weren't race-winning cars.'

Christa's brows creased. 'You won races.'

'Some, but—and this isn't boasting—the only reason

the cars were quick was because I was quick, and because I had more than my fair share of what the Chinese call "joss". Other teams with superior machines asked me to join them, but the guy I was with had been good to me when I'd started, and it seemed like betrayal if I switched. For the final couple of years I needed to consciously inject interest and enthusiasm into my racing, and I didn't always make it. Another minus was the number of Grand Prix events which take place in exile,' Jeff went on, warming to his theme. 'I spent too much time lurking in hotel bedrooms in strange places, all on my own.' He drew on his cigar and squinted at her through the lazily curling smoke. 'If you now intend to remind me of those newspaper cuttings——'

'I don't.'

'Oh,' he said, in anticlimax. 'Anyway, the kind of women the circuits attract were another turn-off. Basically, you could divide them into two types, the brazen ones who oozed all over you—they came in boxes of a dozen—and those who played hard to get but who, in reality, would do anything with anyone. Whichever they were, all they were interested in was the image of a guy with a helmet, a fast car, the spurting bottle of champagne. I never met one who gave a damn about the real Jefferson Barssi.' He grinned. 'Which is what made it so great when you came along. You didn't know I'd been——' mocking inverted commas were sketched, '—a "famous racing driver", and when someone told you it made no difference. You liked me for me.' Abruptly the grin became a frown and he swerved. 'Those years at the wheel taught me a lot about myself and a lot about life. I learned to cope with pressure. I learned to think fast. And I learned there's no mileage in letting things upset you, that either you live with them or you change them.'

Christa's heart lurched. Did the 'live with them or change them' bit relate to her? she wondered.

'Is that so?' she murmured, very non-committal.

'*Yes.*' Jeff ground out the stub of his cigar. 'You remember what Esther said last week on the beach—about Tony and me?'

She frowned. 'No.'

'You do. You must,' he protested. 'You were upset enough at the time. Remember I spoke about being ambitious for Barssi & Company and how, so long as no one got hurt——'

She almost choked on a mouthful of pineapple juice. 'You were talking about—about your brother?' she gasped.

'Who else?'

'No one. Oh, no one,' she assured him quickly.

'You know how it's Vittorio's wish that when he dies Tony, as the elder son, will take over?' said Jeff. 'I can't allow it to happen. I want to . . . change things.'

Christa stared. 'You mean you intend to become the head of the company yourself?'

'If I can.' He lit another cigar. 'I must.'

'And what has docile, agreeable, compliant Tony ever done to you?' she demanded.

'Nothing. The trouble is, he's everything you say.'

'A soft target? One you know you can pick off without any trouble!'

Jeff flinched. 'This isn't a war, nor is it a power game. It's a question of whether or not Barssi & Company continues to thrive, to survive. If it doesn't, then not only will the Barssi family's living go by the board, but over six hundred employees and their families will be left wondering where their next crust's coming from.'

'Your take-over appears under the heading of philanthropy?' she scoffed.

'Christa, listen to me. Tony's a great guy and I love him dearly, but when it comes to the cut and thrust of business he doesn't have what it takes. He isn't commercially astute. He isn't forceful. He won't stand up and fight. You've seen how he is with Esther?' Jeff appealed. 'Whether he agrees with her or not, nine times out of ten what she says goes.'

'I suppose so,' she had to admit. 'I've always thought that Tony takes after your mother, whereas you take after your father.'

'I suspect that's a condemnation, but—yes, to an extent, I do.' He returned to the matter uppermost in his mind. 'As Tony allows his wife to walk all over him, so he does the same in business, but, like they say in the movies, it's a jungle out there. If the company's to maintain its place and its prosperity, we must be as sharp-witted, as determined, as aggressive as our competitors.'

'Tony's survived for—what, twelve years? So——'

'The only reason he's survived is because Vittorio's run things and run them tightly,' Jeff intervened. 'I don't deny Tony has his own responsibilities, but my father's always known what's been happening and has guided him accordingly. What I don't think he's realised is that while Tony's fine at carrying out orders, he's damn near incapable of giving them!' The frustrated fist he punched on the table had their glasses jumping, and made two youths who were sitting nearby turn round to stare. 'Another drink?' he demanded.

'Please. So although you reckon Tony isn't capable of taking charge, your father's happy?' Christa queried, when the waiter had brought a second round.

'He's never said anything to make me think otherwise,' Jeff agreed ruefully. 'But the trouble with the guy from Sao Paulo is just the latest example of Tony being too soft, too indecisive. he should have cut off his credit months ago, instead of which he does nothing and we end up being owed heaven knows how many *cruzeiros*.'

'And you sorted things out. Have you needed to sort out any other of his problems?'

'Many, over the years. Maybe my father isn't aware of it, but Tony is—and Esther.'

Christa frowned. 'This is why she's hostile towards you?'

'She sees me as a threat to Tony.'

'Which you are.'

'All I'm threatening is his projected position in the company.' Jeff expelled a tortured breath. 'I don't expect him to welcome the idea of stepping aside in favour of his younger brother, but if he continues on his merry way then Barssis' will fail. It won't happen overnight, but it will happen.'

Christa sipped her drink. When he had first broached taking control she had regarded it as an outrage, a gross imposition, a swindle; not any more. Now she understood why he needed to act and sympathised, but, more importantly, she also understood something else. Listening to him talk about his loyalty to the racing team, hearing how reluctant he was to disbar Tony, seeing his anguish, it had become clear that his ambition was controlled, unselfish, responsible. Jeff did not use or abuse people, and he had not used *her*. Christa felt a magical spurt of joy. Whatever Esther might claim, he had married her because he loved her—and for no other reason.

'Do you know for a fact that Tony would object if you became managing director?' she asked.

'No, but I do know Esther would be dead against it, which amounts to the same thing.'

'Couldn't he be nominal head and you run things all the same?' Christa suggested.

'I've considered that, but I can't see how it would work. People automatically go to the top when they're needing a major decision, and if I wasn't around and Tony made the wrong one it could very well be——' Jeff made a revolver with his fingers and placed them to his head.

She sighed. 'Your father's perceptive. I don't understand how he's failed to notice Tony's limitations.'

'He *was* perceptive, but he's been ill for a long time and if he did have reservations maybe now they don't seem so clear. Or maybe they don't matter. The eldest son stepping into his father's shoes is part of the fabric of family businesses in Brazil.'

'Pre-ordained?'

'Almost by papal decree.'

Christa folded her arms. 'You must speak to Vittorio,' she decided.

'How can I ask that he reconsider and state his position on something as emotive and serious as this, when day by day his health's deteriorating?' Jeff protested.

'It would be difficult,' she agreed.

At the beginning of the week Vittorio had again joined her and Marcus on the beach, but whereas he had coped easily with the first time outing, the second had been a hard-won victory of determination over ill health. The short walk had been slow, and on arrival the old man had found it impossible to sit at peace. After ten minutes he had suggested they return home. The following days had seen a marked deterioration, and now he rarely moved from his chair.

'Even if I did raise the subject, what the hell do I say?' Jeff appealed. 'Tony's the dutiful son. There was no argument, no rebellion, no six years of skidding around the world from one race track to the next for him. He went directly from college into the business, as good as gold, and has been there ever since. An unblemished record which Esther would be very quick to emphasise.'

'But you can't leave things until your father has . . . passed away,' Christa objected. 'He started the company and built it up to what it is today, so it's only right and proper he should be involved in what's going to happen next.'

Jeff inhaled and blew the smoke out slowly. 'You're right, and I would sure as hell prefer his agreement.'

'How would it be if I approached him?' she suggested. 'Vittorio and I have an understanding now——'

'I've noticed,' he commented drily.

'—and I could describe your fears, ask for his comments, but keep it all low-key. I'm sure he'd listen seriously to anything I had to say.'

Jeff fixed her with steady brown eyes. 'Like I'm listening seriously to you now?'

'New sensation, isn't it?' Christa said pertly. 'But I reckon me talking to your father is the answer.'

'Could be,' he agreed, smiling. 'Let me think about it for a couple of days, OK?' When she nodded, he clicked his fingers and sign-languaged to the waiter that he wanted to pay. 'Shall we go?'

The bill settled, they walked down to the sand. A hundred yards ahead, a group of teenagers were playing impromptu soccer, and as they passed the ball came skimming their way. In response to fervent shouts, Jeff stopped it and made ready to kick. It was then Christa noticed that the two boys from the bar were close behind. Earlier Jeff's table thumping had seemed to be the cause for them staring, but now she wondered if they could have recognised him. Certainly the taller of the two, a thick-set, swarthy individual in grubby shorts and a 'surfers do it standing up' T-shirt, looked keen to have a word, and as Jeff returned the ball the youth headed in his direction.

Asking questions had paid excellent dividends, Christa mused as she waited. Not only had those icky-picky doubts about the timing of their marriage been banished once and for all, but Jeff had opened himself up to her in a new and encouraging way. What was more, she had been able to offer reasoned and constructive help. So far, so good, but now—she took in an unsteady breath—she must press on and ask about Ruth.

'*Que horas sao?*' enquired the smaller and wirier of the two boys, appearing beside her.

Christa was looking at her watch to tell him the time, when suddenly he leapt forward and grabbed for her pendant. Her head jerked, she felt a razor-line burn at the back of her neck, then the chain snapped. A split second later the youth was off, running up the beach and towards the road. Desperately she tried to remember the Portuguese for 'stop, thief!' but surprise had struck her dumb and for a moment or two she stood there, a hand spread against her denuded throat.

'Hey!' she managed, at last.

Jeff swivelled, saw what had happened and, breaking from the other youth, headed off in pursuit.

Her instant gratitude rapidly switched to dismay. Along with the other safety instructions, Jeff had warned that, if you should be unlucky enough to be mugged in Brazil, the one thing *not* to do was make chase; because muggers carried knives. Yet here he was, sprinting like an athlete and hurling abuse.

'Jeff, come back! Let him go!' she yelled. The boy reached the road and five yards later he hit the tarmacadam too. 'The pendant doesn't matter.'

Flinging a furious look over his shoulder, Jeff sped on. Whether the pendant mattered or not, detaining his quarry did. Gradually the gap between hunted and hunter narrowed until only a stride separated them. Jeff was stretching out his arm, when suddenly an engine roared. Christa turned to find that the heavier youth had cut back to the bar and was making chase astride a huge black and battered Suzuki.

'Carlos!' he bellowed, swerving towards his accomplice.

As he drew level, the boy threw himself forward and the bike split behind him, missing Jeff by inches. In a skid and a screech of tyres, the motorcyclist swung round intent on rescue, but as Carlos attempted to hoist himself aboard Jeff lunged and he fell, knocking them both to the ground. Her breath stopped, Christa watched in horror as the machine executed a fast turn and headed straight towards the scrabble of bodies.

'Jeff, watch out!' she shouted, starting towards him.

The warning came too late. The boy managed to roll free, but when Jeff pushed himself up it was to take the full force of the front wheel against his shoulder.

He groaned, his face contorted with pain, and he fell back on to the road.

'Oh, Jeff, why did you have to be a hero?' Christa wailed, arriving as Carlos and partner sped to freedom. She dropped to her knees beside him. 'You could have been killed, you silly, brave, stupid man!'

He gazed up at her. 'Don't you care about the pendant?'

'No, no, I don't!' she cried, her eyes moving over him. In addition to his damaged shoulder, his arm had been scraped raw and blood was pouring from a cut on his brow. 'Do you think something's broken?' she asked fearfully.

'I care about that pendant,' Jeff muttered, 'even if you don't. I —'

He blacked out.

CHAPTER NINE

'MORE coffee, anyone?' asked Isabel, bustling into the living-room. 'I've just taken Father a second cup and I thought perhaps——'

Jeff looked up from the book he was reading to Marcus. 'Not for me.'

'Tea?'

'Nothing.'

'When you were small, you used to enjoy a glass of milk. Would you like me to——'

A muscle clenched in his jaw. 'I'm not thirsty.'

Isabel's smile went to the bureau, where Christa was writing postcards to Sylvie and her father.

'You'll have a cup, won't you?'

'No, thanks. Marcus doesn't need another drink either,' she added, stemming the query that loomed.

'Is it wise having Marcus on your knee?' his mother fretted, as Jeff started the story again. 'Little children easily grow restless, and if he reared up and knocked against you it could be painful.'

'Don't worry, my shoulder's well-protected,' he said, sliding his fingers into the open neck of his shirt to touch firm layers of white strapping. 'Paddington——' he began again.

'Dr Taveira's done a wonderful job,' Isabel babbled.

'Wasn't it fortunate his partner happened to be arriving at the beach when you fainted and could take you to hospital?'

'I passed out for two seconds,' Jeff replied brusquely, 'and I could have driven myself.'

A benign head was shaken. 'Impossible. You were in shock, and even though that bone splinter did stay put, your shoulder was severely bruised. You will take care of your *papá*, Marcus?' Isabel smiled. 'The doctor prescribed rest and quiet for one whole week.'

'Me will.' The little boy tapped the page. 'More!'

'You're certain there's nothing anyone needs?' Isabel enquired, looking hopefully around. 'No? Oh, well, for lunch today we'll be having——'

'Whatever it is, it'll be great,' Jeff assured her, and after a plumping up of a cushion, an opening of a window, she reluctantly departed. 'I swear that woman'll have me chewing the carpet before the day's out,' he muttered, as her footsteps retreated down the hall.

Christa grinned. 'She's only trying to help.'

'I know, but—heavens! These past three days are the first I've spent entirely in this house for years, and I swear I'd never realised until now what a fussy old hen she really is. She must have been in here chattering away at least six times this morning, and then she has the nerve to say I need quiet! You wouldn't do me a great favour and take over Paddington?' he asked, with a one-sided smile of entreaty. 'Tony assures me he's on top of things, but I'd like to call in at the office even so. It won't take long. If I phone for a cab now, I can be there and back in an hour.'

'I'll act as chauffeur,' Christa said promptly.

'You?'

'Me. You don't imagine you're the only person keen to bust out of here?' she demanded, when he looked dubious.

'Point taken. The three of us'll go—though in a cab.'

'I'd like to drive,' she told him.

'But——'

'How old do I need to get before you take what I say seriously?' she enquired. 'I'm capable of rolling down my window and raising fingers too, you know.'

Jeff laughed. 'Now you're talking like an adult! Let's go.'

The journey occurred without mishap, though Christa's vocabulary was enriched by several choice phrases which Sylvie had neglected to mention. Boosted by her newly begotten skill, she strode positively into the granite tower which housed Barssi & Company's offices, yet as the elevator rose so her confidence fell. The journey had not been made to escape from Isabel, nor to test her driving—though tackling the traffic was long overdue—she had come to see Ruth. Or, more precisely, she had come to see Ruth and Jeff together.

No mater what Esther might imply, despite what Jeff had verified, some inner quirk insisted she observe the interplay for herself. If she saw a mega-watt flow of electricity, it would be an exercise in

foolishness and unnecessary hurt, but—well, she
hadn't hanged herself so far, had she?

There was a moment as they walked along the
corridor when Christa felt tempted to turn tail and
run, but then Jeff opened a door and his secretary was
smiling a greeting. Each of them was welcomed and
exclaimed over in what appeared to be equal
proportions. She was so pleased to see Christa again.
Hadn't Marcus grown? What bad luck for Jeff to fall
foul of muggers! Surreptitious glances at the
commiserating redhead and her explaining boss failed
to reveal any spark, yet it was clear the friendly
working relationship had deepened into something far
more intimate.

Suddenly smiling became a strain and Christa
needed to fake her way through the conversation. For
her, a physical charge would be a vital requisite, but,
she acknowledged forlornly, her husband could think
otherwise. Indeed, after his experience with her, it
was possible he had avoided electricity like the plague!

The first flush of welcome over, Ruth provided a
short update on business. Jeff asked her to write a
letter or two, issued several other instructions, then
said he would have a word with his brother.

'Me see Uncle Tony,' begged Marcus and, casting
his eyes aloft in mock resignation, Jeff agreed.

Christa was set to join them, until Ruth insisted she
must stay and talk.

'We have so much to catch up on,' the redhead
smiled, drawing out a chair. 'I don't know if you're
aware of it,' she began, when father and son had

departed, 'but Jefferson has been so supportive. When my Gilberto——' She broke off to swallow and lower her head, when she raised it again her eyes were moist. 'Ever since my Gilberto——' One more she faltered.

'I was sorry to hear . . . what had happened,' Christa said into the silence. She did not know why she should feel sympathy for a woman who, having been abandoned by her own husband, had swiftly turned to hers, she only knew that she did. 'And surprised,' she added, as Ruth made valiant attempts at recovery.

'We were all surprised,' the secretary said, blotting away a tear. 'My Gilberto was so easy-going. The last person you'd expect to have had a heart attack.'

Christa stared. 'A heart attack?' she echoed.

'You didn't know the cause?'

Christa shook her head. I didn't know your husband had *died*! she thought, wondering how, why, she had taken Esther's 'departed' to mean desertion. She sighed. Gilberto Mayor's death was undoubtedly tragic and yet, as far as she was concerned, did it alter anything?

'Jeff explained how he'd—he'd been to your home,' she said, venturing on. She had wanted to see the relationship for herself, and now she decided she might as well hear what Ruth had to say about it.

'He told you. I wondered if he would. I *hoped* he would.' The redhead's hand fluttered to the frilled collar of her Victorian-style blouse. 'I don't wish to appear too familiar,' she said, 'but——' She sat straighter. 'When you left Rio, Jefferson appeared to take it in his stride. His high level of energy continued. He made shrewd decisions, was even-tempered, and gave the impression of being on top of things and totally in command of himself. It was a long time before I realised that here was someone who bled inside. Someone whose life had gone terribly wrong. Someone who had no idea what to do about it.' Her voice gained a drama reminiscent of Sylvie's. 'Behind the diffident manner existed a seething cauldron of doubts. It was then I——'

Christa's nails curled into her palms. Imagining she could listen to Ruth's account of the relationship had been a major misjudgement. To be regaled with tales of how the older woman had succoured this broken man and made him whole again would be like having a knife inside her, slowly turning.

'You don't need to tell me. I know you've helped him,' she interrupted, desperate to derail the conversation.

The secretary shook her head. 'The one who's helped Jefferson is Bruno.'

'Bruno?'

'My nephew. My sister is, regrettably, also a widow, and when Gilberto passed on we decided that she and her son should move in with me. Bruno's a couple of years older than Marcus, but he has the same mischievous brown eyes, the same impish grin, an identical urge to be up and doing. The first time they met, Jefferson remarked on their likeness, and after that——' Ruth smiled fondly '—you couldn't keep him away.'

Christa's heart took a sudden leap. 'He c-came to visit a—the little boy?' she stammered.

'Two or three times a week. Your husband might not admit it, even to himself, but he needed that child. Bruno represented a lifeline, one which connected him to Marcus, and through Marcus to you. Being with Bruno gave him the strength to continue, helped sustain the belief that some time, somehow, everything would come right again.'

'So Jeff didn't go to your house because he wanted to——' Christa blushed. Having started, it had become difficult to finish. 'To see you?' she completed awkwardly.

'Christa, your husband has been kind, thoughtful, responsive to my needs, both material and emotional, but as far as "seeing me" goes——' Ruth's mouth twitched. 'Apart from the fact I'm much too ancient, Jefferson has never "seen" another woman since you first set foot in Rio.'

'What do you say we give moving into Barra da Tijuca a spin?' said Jeff, as they drove back to Casa Libra. 'When I was with Tony I telephoned the electricians yet again, and I've managed to persuade them to take another crack at finding the fault.'

Christa pressed down her foot and executed a neat in-and-out manoeuvre which brought her to the front of a traffic queue. 'Persuade?' she said pertly.

'OK, so I said writs would be issued, heads would roll, and anarchy would reign if the damned power wasn't working by the end of the day.'

'All this to avoid being pressed to drink a second cup of coffee?' she enquired.

Jeff grinned. 'Everyone has their limits.'

Predictably, when his mother learned of their intention she was horrified. Suppose the fault could not be traced, what then? Isabel wanted to know. How would they manage without lights? Without a cooker? Without air-conditioning? Jeff's assurance that if all else failed he would insist on a temporary electricity supply only released a fresh wave of worries. Makeshift wires were bound to be dangerous, and what if someone received a shock? Or the apartment caught fire? Or the entire block went up in flames? Only Vittorio's order to let them be silenced her.

When they arrived at Barra da Tijuca the electrician and his mate were sodden with sweat, and as the hours passed they became limper. Only Jeff's mix of exhortations and thinly veiled threats kept them searching until, in the early evening, the defect was traced to a mesh of cables in the basement. A fast repair, a clicking of switches and—*sim, sim, sim!*—everything in Senhor Barssi's *apartamento* functioned.

Within minutes chilli con carne was simmering on the hob, an hour later they sat down to dinner, and by mid-evening Marcus was tucked up in bed.

'Champagne?' smiled Christa, coming out on to the balcony.

Deftly Jeff poured from the foaming bottle and handed her a glass. 'I figure we have two things to celebrate. Firstly our safe arrival,' he said, deadpan.

'I drove superbly!'

'There was a moment as you accelerated on Leblon when my whole life flashed before me. You won't take advantage of a wounded man?' he protested, lurching back to avoid being punched. 'And secondly, I wish to toast our deliverance from my mother. How you ever stood being in the house with her day after day amazes me. I realise that prior to you leaving she'd been getting on your nerves, but——'

'Prior to me leaving? She'd had me climbing the walls for eighteen months!'

'That long?' He frowned out at the night where a crescent moon shone silver arrows across an ink-black sea. 'Why didn't you tell me?'

Christa gave a small shrug. 'Because I don't go a bundle on complaining and because, in part, I was responsible for the way she treated me.'

'How?'

Resting an elbow on the balustrade, she listened for a moment to the whisper of the warm breeze among the greenery and the plash of waves on the beach below. 'From the start, Isabel welcomed me,' she began to explain. 'I didn't need to speak the same language to recognise her affection—it shone out. Falling in love with you was . . . overwhelming, but after so long without a mother and with a father who could only spare me the minimum of his time, to discover the package included someone like Isabel was—well, it came as a tremendous bonus. She gathered me up, gathered me in, and made me feel part of a family. When she cherished me, I loved it.'

'She did enough cherishing when we moved into Casa Libra,' Jeff remarked wryly.

'That's when it first started to irritate. However, it seemed petty to object and my objections weren't *that* great, so I kept quiet.' Christa sipped her champagne. 'But in time Marcus was born.'

A brow lifted. 'An event which sent my mother delirious with joy.'

'At first I welcomed her delight—that she should think Marcus was as wonderful as I did seemed incredibly flattering—but gradually it dawned on me that she expected to play an active role in his welfare.' Another sip was taken. 'I knew it was natural for her to want to help, but I began to resent it. I felt she was intruding into areas which belonged to me and my child. However, after I'd stayed silent for so long, uttering a forcible *no* had become a problem. Although I wanted Isabel to keep her distance I had no wish to hurt her, and so I went through the most extraordinary emotional contortions trying to satisfy both her needs and my own.' Christa sighed. 'Deferring to others saps the energy, but my lack of Portuguese often made deferring to Isabel a necessity. Whenever I required information about feeding, teething, or any of the hundred and one baby things, it had to be channelled through your mother, and so somehow it became her domain.'

Jeff rested a shoulder against the wall. 'And all this time you were becoming progressively more uptight?'

She nodded. 'I longed to make my own judgements, my own mistakes, but with Isabel, Vittorio and everyone else cooing over Marcus there didn't seem to be room for me to be involved. No one ever granted me much in the way of influence, much authority. I suppose I developed a kind of siege mentality,' she reflected. 'Certainly I felt you neglected me; that you were too keen on business.'

He straightened. 'I did and I was,' he agreed slowly. 'Getting the factory built on time, making certain production started by the agreed date, mattered so much, there was a time when I guess I lost sight of most everything else.' He massaged his jaw. 'But, hell, those were *your* computers.'

'Mine?' queried Christa, in surprise.

'Of course. That's why I was so determined everything should run according to plan.' His brown eyes met hers. 'I wanted you to be proud of me.'

Her heart clenched and suddenly she felt distraught.

'If only I'd known!'

'If only I'd realised how you felt about my mother,' he replied, with a wistful smile. He refilled their glasses. 'I knew you were eager for us to leave Casa Libra, but, heaven help me, I'd no idea you'd reached breaking point. If I had, I would never have agreed when Vittorio vetoed the move.'

'Vittorio?' Something snapped into position at the back of Christa's mind and she gazed at him in dismay. 'Oh, no! He vetoed it because of the cancer.'

Jeff nodded. 'For a week or two he'd been feeling lousy, and I guess he panicked. He buttonholed me one morning, and made some hysterical claim about us abandoning him in his hour of need, and begged me to agree to a postponement. Like a fool, I did.' He made a quick impatient gesture. 'I should have told you about his illness. I should have explained what made the factory so important.' For a few moments he stood glowering out into the darkness, then he drained his glass. 'I'm whacked,' he said abruptly. 'If you're happy with the main bedroom, I'll take the second one.'

Christa looked at him. She was the one who had requested no physical contact, and sleeping apart was merely an extension of this, yet she felt horribly *cut*. Why? she wondered, a split second later. Jeff was using his common sense. He would sleep much sounder without her moving around beside him, and hadn't his shoulder made his restless and disturbed her rest too? They would be far better off in separate beds, in separate rooms. They would. They would.

'Fine,' she agreed.

'Could you do something for me?' he enquired, as they walked across the living-room.

She pinned on a dazzling smile. 'You name it.'

Jeff's gaze travelled from her blonde head, over the swell of her breasts, down her torso, to her denim-clad limbs and her sandalled feet.

'Come with me to one of those motels where the beds vibrate and there are mirrors on the ceiling and they show blue videos?' A smile of self-derision twisted his features. 'No, in my state of health, I'd better settle for you taking off my shirt.'

As Christa eased the white cotton from his

shoulders, every nerve, every fibre in her body responded. Bandaged or not, weary or not, Jeff was a powerfully built male and his reference to Rio's unique motels where couples met for sessions of love, usually clandestine, had heightened her awareness of the sexuality kept so tightly under control.

'How's the injury?' she asked, ignoring the gleam of his golden skin and concentrating on the bandage which came up from his right armpit, crossed his chest to the bruised shoulder, then disappeared behind his back again.

'It's not such a big deal. I thought I might have problems opening the champagne, but I didn't.'

'No? Oh. Well. Goodnight,' she said, and pushed the shirt at him.

'Don't I get a kiss?' Jeff raised his good arm to move his fingers in a light caress across her cheek. 'Just one?'

Christa gazed at him in confusion. They had not touched for ten days, so why, minutes after he had banned her from his bed, must he suggest that they do so now? It made no sense. It wasn't fair. It ranked as sadism. When he bent it was to kiss her cheek, yet even so, the legs she stood on turned to jelly.

'If you need me in the night, give a yell,' she said, and instantly wondered what Freud would have made of *that* instruction.

'I will,' Jeff said gravely. 'What else are friends for?'

He did not require her attendance either that night or any subsequent one, yet Christa soon realised that

that was what they had become—friends. The days passed happily. Together they took Marcus to the beach, to the playground, and from time to time called in at Casa Libra to check on Vittorio. Wherever they went, whatever they did, it was as equals. Jeff listened to her, joked with her, showed himself to be on the same wavelength. She liked it. She liked him. She *loved* him, but then—for better, for worse, together or apart—she always had.

Embarking on that all-important discussion grew from a need into a pressure—yet paradoxically, the easier their relationship was, the harder it became to talk about the future. Christa could not explain why. Not only had Ruth ceased to be a factor, but her description of Jeff's distress—and fidelity—had raised high hopes. Their separation no longer seemed inevitable, and yet . . . Each evening she resolved to speak up the following morning, and each morning an agony of indecision kept her mute.

As her own silence worried her so, increasingly, did Jeff's. He must know his deadline was only a time limit and that talks could take place whenever and wherever, yet he never mentioned them. Why not? Was he also afraid of tempting providence, she wondered, or could he remain set on a divorce and have everything so sewn up that whatever she said was irrelevant? Adrift on a sea of contradictory feelings, Christa felt unreasonably cheered when she realised he had not referred to her offer to speak to Vittorio, either. If he was content to let that matter alone, maybe his silence had no significance? Maybe

Jeff was just generally living in limbo?

When Vittorio's birthday dawned, she awoke determined to speak *now;* then cowardice seeped in. Isabel had arranged a tea party and, Christa argued, surely the time for serious discussions was after they had visited Casa Libra? She went along prepared to simply socialise, but half-way through the afternoon her father-in-law appeared beside them.

'I'd like a quiet word with the two of you,' he said, and led the way to the study where they found Tony and Esther were waiting.

As Vittorio readied himself for what was clearly going to be an important announcement, Christa's heart fell. Over the past few days the decline in his health seemed to have been halted, but was he now about to reveal that he had only a few more days to live?

'As you all know,' he began, 'the intention was for Tony to preside over Barssi & Company after me.' His black eyes swung from his elder son to the younger. 'However, it's been decided that Jefferson will take control.'

Christa shot Jeff a startled look, and was assured by a barely perceptible shake of his head that he was as much in the dark as she.

'Jefferson is to be managing director?' Esther shrilled, leaping white-faced and furious to her feet. 'I guessed some sharp practice might take place, but I thought *you'd* have the sense to resist! Tony is your elder son, and as such it's his moral right to run the company.' Her voice rose to fishwife pitch. 'Tony has always understood he'll be the head and now you—you defraud him! I won't allow it! We'll sue! We'll—'

'Esther, it was Tony himself who asked that Jefferson should take over,' Vittorio informed her.

'What?' For a moment her mouth worked silently, then in a vicious swirl of skirt she spun to her husband. 'You requested it? You fool! You—'

'If he hadn't, I would have suggested the change myself,' said Vittorio, when Tony reddened and looked at his shoes. 'And made sure it was enforced.'

Silently Christa blessed her father-in-law for his forbearance. He had known his elder son's weaknesses, yet had been prepared to wait until he had recognised them himself.

'The company will flourish under Jeff. It would grind to a halt with me,' said Tony, finding his voice at last.

Esther's mouth made a thin gash of scarlet. 'Little brother told you that, I suppose? And you believed him?'

'Jeff didn't tell me anything.'

'Pouf! He's been working towards this since he first started with the company,' she said nastily. 'He doesn't drift along like you. He plots and schemes and *orchestrates* his life, and to hell with anyone else.'

'You're not only talking slander,' Jeff broke in, anger showing in the glitter of his eyes, 'you're talking utter nonsense.'

'The leopard's changed its spots?' his sister-in-law derided.

'Meaning?'

Her expression assumed a pinched triumph. 'That you married your wife in order to secure the Henley business!'

He shot Christa a swift, frowning glance. 'You *are* talking nonsense.'

'So the timing——'

She was cut off without preamble. 'Esther, the guy from UWC accused me of the same underhand trick, but what he didn't know and what you don't seem to be aware of either, is that although the contract between Barssis' and the Henley Group wasn't formally signed until after I'd proposed, it had been agreed much earlier.'

'More than a week,' Vittorio confirmed.

'You might find this hard to believe,' Jeff continued, 'but desperate as I was not to let Christa get away, ethics insisted I hold back.'

'So you didn't marry her on—on purpose?' his sister-in-law faltered.

'On purpose as in "to grab the business"? No.'

She glowered for a moment, then sat her hands on her hips. 'OK, man with all the answers,' she sneered, 'answer me this. What made you so determined to get your wife pregnant so quickly?'

To Christa's enormous surprise, Jeff frowned, hesitated, looked away. Marcus, it was obvious, *had* been conceived for a reason. Her shoulders straightened. Whatever it was, it did not matter. As he had once said, this wasn't a perfect world, and whatever had motivated him in the past was of no consequence. It was the present she cared about—and the future.

'I wanted a child,' he said lamely.

'And you got one. You sired a son, which is a darn sight more than Tony's ever managed to do!' Esther snapped, rounding on her husband again. 'When I married you, my family considered I'd bagged a prize. They thought I'd be the wife of a company chief and mother of his children, instead I end up with an infertile, two-bit accountant!'

'That's not true,' protested Tony, squirming with hurt and embarrassment. 'It isn't true at all.'

'You haven't given away your position as managing director?' she jeered.

'I've put the company, and our future affluence, into safe-keeping. And with regard to not having children, you know the specialist reckons the fault could be as much yours as mine,' he said, his cheeks growing even pinker. 'Perhaps if you called a halt to all that dieting and relaxed for once, we'd——'

'Relax?' Esther demanded, with an ugly shriek of laughter. 'How can I relax when my husband goes around undermining——'

'Why don't you adopt a child?' Christa interrupted, eager to rescue her brother-in-law. Esther had always been so emphatically against a family, it was a shock to realise it had not been true. But then, she thought wryly, the woman specialised in saying one thing and meaning another. 'Lots of people do,' she added.

'Yes, why not?' said Vittorio, recognising her question as an opportunity to calm the meeting down. 'That's what Isabel and I had in mind when she failed to conceive, then half-way through the arrangements she discovered she was expecting Tony. I've always been convinced it was her joy at the prospect of having someone else's baby to care for that enabled her to conceive a child of her own.'

'I've nothing against adoption,' Tony declared, his face brightening.

Stranded by the switch in the conversation, Esther sat down again. 'I suppose——' she began.

'Consider it,' Vittorio rapped, 'and consider what Tony's said about Jefferson guaranteeing *your* affluence.' He turned to his younger son. 'Although Tony and I are agreed you should run the company, we've yet to hear if you're willing.'

'A smile appeared in the corner of Jeff's mouth. 'I get to decide?'

'Only so long as your decision's the right one,' his father chuckled.

'I'm agreeable.'

'Thanks,' said Tony, as the meeting broke up. He shook Jeff's hand. 'Now I can sleep easy again.'

'How about starting your new duties tomorrow?' Vittorio enquired, when Tony and Esther had departed. 'I'd be grateful if the change-over could take place as soon as possible.' He noticed Jeff was frowning. 'Is your shoulder still painful? Would you prefer to wait a while.'

'My shoulder's fine.'

'Tomorrow, then?'

Jeff nodded. 'Tomorrow.'

CHAPTER TEN

BY THE TIME Christa put Marcus to bed that evening, she was in a fine state of trepidation. All day she had been sensitive to the relentless ticking of the clock, and was now awesomely aware that zero hour had arrived. If only she hadn't worked herself into such a do-or-die corner! If only she could have been brave earlier! If only——Returning to the living-room, she perched herself on the edge of the sofa, said a silent prayer, and began.

'With regard to the future. I'd like to open our discussion by saying——'

Jeff glanced up from the paperback he was reading. 'Not tonight.'

'Excuse me?'

'I'm not in the mood,' he said politely, and returned to his book.

Christa sat there, transfixed. Now she had finally mounted the rostrum, her audience had no interest in her recital? The let-down was numbing. Admittedly the session in the study had provided him with plenty to think about, and she had noticed that, despite him chatting to relatives and being generally good-humoured, his frown had never seemed far away; but not in the mood? He *had* to be. Their discussion was of monumental importance—to him, to her, to Marcus.

She straightened. 'Jeff, I——'

This time he did not even look up. 'We'll talk in the morning.'

Christa stared at the top of his dark head, then located a paperback too. She could recognise a final rejection when she heard one! Attempts were made to read, but the once page-turning biography had lost its appeal. Nerves ajangle, she went out to the balcony and gazed at the sea, then returned to the sofa again. Back and forth she roamed, until Jeff suggested they batten the apartment down for the night.

'I'm taking this off,' he said, as he walked into his room. He wrenched open his shirt and tugged at the shoulder bandage. 'I'm fed up with the damn thing.'

Christa hovered in the doorway. 'Want me to help?'

'No.' He yanked at the white ties, but instead of loosening the knot he tightened it. For a moment he scowled down. 'Please,' he said.

His silence and upright stance made his impatience plain. Jeff, she knew, would have much preferred to have managed alone, and when her unpicking became the removal of layer upon layer of strapping, she began to wish he had too. To be exposing his chest, inch by slow inch, seemed like a disturbingly erotic striptease.

'Better?' Christa enquired, industriously coiling the bandage into a neat roll.

Jeff flexed his shoulder, rolled and relaxed it again, revelling in the freedom. 'Much. Thanks.'

'It hasn't withered from lack of use?' she demanded,

the display of naked masculinity making her feel prickly and at odds.

'Not this particular muscle, no.' His hand closed around the door-handle. 'Sleep well.'

Christa turned her head away, afraid he might glimpse her pain. Every night he had kissed her, and even though they had been brief, brotherly kisses on the cheek she had treasured them as gestures of affection. But there was no affection now, just the wish for her to go—quickly.

'And you,' she said.

Lying in bed with her hands clasped behind her head, she brooded; about Jeff's dismissal, about the scene at Casa Libra, about the future. They would talk in the morning, he had said, but the morning lay eight long hours away. And in the morning Jeff took up his new responsibilities. Christa frowned. Delaying talks until tomorrow was not a good idea. She thrust back the sheet and made for the door. There were times in life when you needed to be bold and determined, come what may. She would go and tell him how much she loved him, and ask, plead, beg, that they stay together for ever and ever. Amen.

Barefoot, she padded along the hall.

'Are you awake?' she asked, never doubting for one moment that he would be. 'Sorry to barge in like this, but I really do need to talk.'

Silence. His back towards her, Jeff lay on his side covered by a single sheet. In the shadows, the shape he made looked stiff and strangely huddled at the same time.

'No,' he said, after an age.

'Jeff——'

'Go away.'

Christa stood firm. She had something to say and she intended to say it. 'It's important we——'

'You've kept me waiting two weeks, another few more hours aren't going to make any bloody difference,' he muttered, in a twisted voice she had never heard him use before.

'I apologise for that, but——'

'Leave me *alone*!'

He had not turned, had not moved so much as an inch, yet there was something about the lie of his head on the pillow and the hunch of him which spoke of matters gone horribly amiss.

'Is your shoulder hurting?' she asked. 'Was removing the bandage a mistake? Are you worried about taking control tomorrow?' she appealed, when she received no reply. The desire to help carried her closer to the bed. 'What's wrong?'

In a surge of torso and sheet, he sat up. 'Get the hell out of here!' he thundered.

'Oh, Jeff!' she faltered, gazing at him in dismay. His lashes were wet and down one tanned cheek she could see the damp trail of a tear. 'Oh, Jeff,' she repeated.

He pushed both hands through his hair and sat there for a minute or two, head bent. Then he blinked, sniffed, wiped his cheek with the back of his wrist.

'Didn't you know that men are allowed to sob these days?' he enquired. The smile he attempted sat bitterly on his mouth. 'Politicians, athletes, businessmen, we're weeping all over the place.'

'What's the matter?'

He looked up. 'You don't know? Hell!' His laugh was flat and humourless. 'It's us.'

'Us?'

'Yes, us!' he slammed back, finding anger from somewhere. 'I thought I could swing it and make everything OK.'

Christa's heart leapt. 'You mean——'

'It's not going to happen,' he said, before she could get any further. 'Ever since I arrived at the cottage and found Marcus in the care of that Sylvie woman, I've been acting like a fool. No, before that. Long before that. It's no wonder you feel——'

'Shall I tell you how I feel?'

'There's no need to spell it out, thanks,' he rasped. 'I know.'

'I don't think you do.' She took a step forward and sat on the bed. Not too close to him. Not too far away. 'This past fortnight——'

'This past fortnight we've gotten along fine, but it doesn't mean a thing. All our——' Jeff searched for the word '—chumminess shows is that we're adult human beings who know how to play the game.'

Her skin went cold. A moment ago she had been convinced they were going to live happily ever after, now . . .

'Game?' she queried cautiously.

'That's what this is. But everyone gets tired of playing after a while, and it's sure as hell this particular frolic isn't going to last. I know you'll leave

Rio again—only the next time it'll be for good.'

'No!'

'This afternoon when Esther claimed I'd married you in order to swing the business deal, I saw your face,' he said heavily. 'I saw a flicker of something—something which said you were tempted to believe her.'

'Wrong tense,' Christa retorted. 'The flicker said I *had* been tempted to believe her. But not any more.'

Jeff hissed out an impatient breath. 'I heard what you said on the beach, dammit!'

'I never said I was going.'

'You were thinking about it.'

She cast her mind back. 'I was thinking about what Esther had said.'

'It's the same thing.'

'It's not!'

'Christa, you stayed in England for six months—six whole months! I asked you to come back, but would you? Would you, hell! Now if you felt like that——'

'I didn't make the journey because Marcus wasn't fit enough.'

He gave a snort of disgust. 'Marcus had had a cold. One lousy cold!'

'It was bronchitis,' she said uncomfortably, 'and the measles——' Her voice petered away.

'What about them?'

'I told you he'd had a mild dose, but the truth is he—he nearly died. Marcus hadn't had time to recover from the bronchitis when he became infected,' she explained, as he looked at her in horror, 'and it hit him extra hard. He had to be rushed into hospital, and there was one dreadful night when——' Her fingers curled and uncurled. 'All I could do was pray. I know I should have told you, and I wanted to, but I felt so ashamed.'

Jeff frowned. 'For pete's sake, why?'

'Marcus had always been such a livewire. People were constantly admiring his chubby cheeks and commenting on his good health; but that was when your mother was around.' Christa swallowed. 'Then the moment he's in my sole care, he falls ill.'

'It was coincidence. Maybe the result of swapping one climate for another. It had nothing to do with you.'

'I was responsible for the climate change,' she pointed out. 'However, fear of being thought a failure kept me quiet then, and subsequently stopped me returning to Rio until Marcus was one hundred per cent fit.' Her chin lifted. 'Right or wrong, I refused to reappear with a thin, sickly child and get stuck with the 'inadequate' label for evermore!'

Jeff considered what she had said, then sighed. 'You must have gone through hell, coping with his illness alone.'

'It was a harrowing experience,' she agreed. 'During that night when he was so sick, I felt as if I aged ten years.'

'Honey,' he murmured, and placed his hand over hers. 'As we're talking about Marcus, there's something I want to explain,' he said, after a moment. 'The reason I didn't give you much choice about whether or not you became pregnant——'

'You didn't give me *any* choice!'

'—was because I was as scared as hell I might be sterile.'

Christa gave a disbelieving laugh. 'Sterile is the last thing you are!'

'Yes, thank heaven. But it took my parents ten years before they produced a child, and I knew Tony and Esther were having all kinds of trouble. On that basis, it seemed lack of fecundity could be a family failing. I should have told you before we were married, but everything happened in such a rush and somehow I never got around to it.' Jeff frowned. 'Maybe I didn't get around to it because I was afraid if I said something I'd lose you,' he reflected. 'I don't know. Anyway, I couldn't bear the prospect of waiting the two years you wanted and then discovering it was no go.'

'I forgive you. Marcus is the second best thing that ever happened to me.'

'Second? Then—then you were planning to come back to me?' Jeff said stiltedly.

'Always.'

'Honey!' he murmured, and gave a huge sigh of relief. 'I do love you.'

He drew her into his arms and, as he held her close and told her of his adoration, all the hurt, the uncertainty, the worries of the past six months suddenly welled up inside her and Christa blinked.

'Oh, heavens,' she said, 'now it's my turn to cry.'

For a while she wept against his shoulder and Jeff stroked her hair.

'Will you also forgive me for taking Marcus away?' he asked, when the tears had stopped. 'I know you reckon it wasn't necessary, but it was—at least, it seemed so at the time,' he amended. 'You see, when I received your letter asking for a discussion in England I anticipated problems.'

She drew back. 'Like what?'

'Being asked to agree terms with a divorce lawyer.'

'But why? Jeff, I asked if we could sort things out, I never mentioned ending anything!'

'No, but your letter spotlighted the mess we were in and—and you don't imagine I was going to sit back and let that Alan guy muscle in?' he demanded, abruptly ablaze with indignant fire.

'Alan?'

'You'd written a letter to Esther and said how kind he'd been, building shelves. I saw them when I was at the cottage,' Jeff said disgustedly. 'Your neighbour made a point of stressing what strong, sturdy, state-of-the-art structures they were!'

Christa giggled. 'Sylvie would. She's full of wifely pride.'

His brows rose. 'Sylvie is Alan's wife?'

'Yes.'

'Then you weren't——'

'No.'

'Why did I take any notice of Esther's innuendoes?' Jeff asked, shaking a despairing head.

'Because you're human, like me. There was a time,' she said slowly, 'when, thanks to Esther, I thought you and Ruth were having an affair.'

Jeff swore, hard and long. 'You wouldn't like to come into bed and tell me all about it?' he suggested. 'Hell, your feet are freezing!' he complained, as she slid in beside him.

Christa made demure eyes. 'If you'd rather we didn't touch, we can always put a pillow between us.'

'Just you try it!' he growled, and kissed her. 'Right,' he said, when she was breathless and properly subdued, 'tell me about this romance I was supposed to be conducting.'

The story took time. 'Ruth reckoned Bruno was a source of strength,' Christa said, reaching the conversation at the office.

Jeff nodded. 'That kid gave me a wonderful amount of comfort—and some pain. He used to climb on his mother's knee and wrap his arms around her neck, just like Marcus does with you,' he explained, when she looked curious. 'It choked me up.' A breath was expelled. 'And my sister-in-law implied that I was visiting Ruth for illicit reasons?'

'She implied it, but——' Christa wrinkled her nose. 'One of the difficulties with Esther is that whatever tale she tells she appears to regard it as true herself, which gives it extra credence.'

'A woman with a jaundiced view of life,' he remarked crustily. 'Though I guess growing up in the *flavellas* would tend to breed doubt and distrust in anyone. Earlier you said you'd half believed Esther's idea that I'd married you for business reasons,' he continued. 'Did you honestly think I could be such a——' His voice trailed away.

'Jeff, don't be hurt,' she begged. 'We barely knew each other when we got married, and we were from worlds apart.' Linking her fingers with his, she started at the early days of their marriage and soberly detailed the doubts Esther had raised, the uncertainty, the grievances. Nothing was left out. Everything was explained. Finally, she grinned. 'However, now I know you have far too much integrity to ever consider such a dastardly act!'

'How about your father?' he enquired, a hint of laughter coming into his voice. 'Do you think he has integrity too?'

She looked at him puzzled. 'Yes.'

'Honey, where you and I were concerned his integrity is nil. It was your father who arranged for you to spend a month in Rio. It was your father who insisted I skip meetings in order to take his daughter sightseeing. I liked what I saw, it's true, but your father did his bit as matchmaker.'

'To secure the deal?' asked Christa, enthralled by this account of her father's skulduggery.

'Old George ain't no slouch. He recognised that a tie-up with Barssis guaranteed excellent returns for the Henley Group.' Jeff hesitated. 'But I suspect his interest goes further.'

'In what way?'

'He doesn't have a male heir prepared to take on the business, and it'll be another twenty-five years before Marcus is in the running.'

'And he thinks you're smart,' she slid in. 'Has Dad

said anything definite?'

'No, but he's made pointed references to me moving on to something bigger. Quizzed me about how I'd feel about living in England.'

'You said?' she queried.

'I said fine.'

For a moment Christa's mind travelled into the future—such a promising future—then she retreated to the past. 'You reckoned taking Marcus was necessary *at the time*, do I take it you had second thoughts?'

'And how!' groaned Jeff. 'It seemed a great idea when I cooked it up—I knew you'd come after Marcus and it took you away from Alan—but half-way across the Atlantic I recognised all I'd done was turn you into my enemy. And, even worse, I was doing exactly what Vittorio would have done.'

'That didn't appeal?'

'No way. After you left Rio I spent a lot of time thinking about where I'd gone wrong and——' his mouth made a downturn, '—I accepted that I'd acted the conquistador too.'

Christa laughed. 'Your thought processes were sabotaged at an early age.'

'Maybe, yet I was determined our relationship wouldn't be like my parents'. I knew it couldn't be. I knew you were a different kind of woman from Isabel.'

'And you're a different man from your father.'

Gravely, Jeff nodded. 'Remember I said

dependency frightens him? I think, for a while, it frightened *me*.' His arm tightened around her. 'The only thing that puts the fear of God into me now is the thought of the woman I depend on leaving me.'

'She'll never do that,' Christa murmured, and he kissed her again.

'By the time you arrived in Rio, I was in a dreadful state,' he continued, a little while later. 'I hadn't a clue what I should say, what I should do, so one minute I was doing my best to get you into bed, and the next I heard myself shouting at you.'

'Then you announced that you'd brought me here because of your father.'

'It was a slapbang reaction. You'd spurned me and I—I just needed to hit back.'

'So was his illness a factor?' asked Christa.

'A secondary one.' Jeff fell silent, then roused himself. 'When we did make love it seemed there was hope, only when I suggested we talk you stalled. From then on signals that you'd given up on our relationship seemed to come thick and fast, to be clinched by you not caring about losing the pendant.'

'I did care, only I cared more about losing you,' she protested.

'I realise that now, but at the time all I could focus on was that it had been my gift to you, so you dismissing it seemed like you were dismissing me.'

'Never!'

Jeff took hold of a wayward strand of tawny hair and tucked it behind her ear.

'Only two people who love each other could punish each other so much,' he murmured, and suddenly they were clinging, mouths locked together.

He drew her down from the pillow until they were lying entwined, torso pressed against torso, heated limb wrapped around heated limb.

'No fancy pyjamas?' she enquired.

'Would you kindly remove your hand, madam?'

The tip of her tongue protruded from between her teeth. 'I thought you liked it when I stroked your thigh?'

'It is somewhat . . . stimulating. The story goes that in Brazil there was no racial harmony until the Portuguese learned to make love in a hammock,' said Jeff, rolling them over until his full weight was pressing her down. 'It seems to me we needed to live apart and come back together again in order to find our harmony.'

'You could be right,' she murmured, as his lips caressed hers in a kiss which was slow and deep, his tongue exploring the edge of her teeth, the silken walls of her mouth, the heat of her tongue.

She sighed, her hands moving restlessly across his broad shoulders, a little groan of pleasure emerging as his fingers plucked at the coffee-coloured satin and he drew it from her body. He kissed her again and murmured his love, slowly trailing his fingertips over her face, across her shoulder down to the taut peaks of her breasts. Lazily, tantalisingly, he traced circles around one swollen aureole and the other, then he brought his hand back to her face.

'Suck it,' he murmured, sliding a finger between her lips.

Christa drew it into her mouth, tasting it, caressing his finger until he said 'Enough.' His hand returned to her breast. There was a moment when he contented himself enscribing moist circles, but then his finger was rubbing across her nipples at first in catlike flicks, then harder and harder until she arched her back and gasped in delight.

'Again,' Jeff murmured, and this time when she had licked his finger he slid his hand down to the secret, silken peak of flesh that nestled between her thighs. Softly but relentlessly, he stroked and stroked and stroked until her head was dizzy, and her limbs weak, and every cell of her body was inflamed.

His head came to her breast, his mouth exciting the pert pink nipples as completely as his finger had done. He moved down, and as his tongue caressed the nerve centre of her being Christa's hips began to move. Her senses swam and she was adrift, her body throbbing and rising to meet his. He entered her, his hands returning to her breasts to roll and pinch her nipples in a frenetic rhythm which matched the relentless thrust of his hips.

'Yes,' Jeff muttered. 'Oh, yes!'

His rhythm broke and for a long, intense moment he arched above her, his skin shiny with perspiration, the hard muscles of his chest bathed in moonlight.

'Yes,' he said again, and he took her.

CHAPTER ELEVEN

'HAVE you seen Marcus?' Isabel enquired, anxiety lining her brow. 'He seems to have gone missing.'

Christa halted her conversation with an elderly Barssi uncle, and smiled. 'He's somewhere around.'

'I haven't seen him since we were in church,' her mother-in-law fretted, dark eyes sifting through the friends and relatives scattered around the living-room and on the balcony beyond. 'He did come back?'

'In the car with Jeff and me.'

'Lovely food,' praised the uncle, helping himself to what was, if anyone had counted, his sixth vol-au-vent. He admired the selection of pâtés and meats, quiches, pies, savoury rices and salads laid out on the buffet table. 'You're very clever, preparing a spread like this yourself, and you're very clever to have such a well-behaved daughter. At every other christening I've attended the infant's screamed so loud you couldn't hear yourself think, but Victoria was as good as gold.'

'She's named in memory of Vittorio,' Isabel informed him, as though the fact had a direct bearing on her granddaughter's behaviour. As the baby had not cried, neither did she now as she remembered her beloved husband; though her eyes grew misty.

Vittorio had left strict instructions that she was not to mourn. He would be waiting for her in heaven, and in the meantime she must be happy. 'He'd have been so proud. It's such a pity he died not knowing that within a year he'd have one new grandchild and another on the way.'

The uncle pricked up his ears. 'Another?'

'Oh, dear!' Isabel's hand flew to her mouth and she looked at Christa in blushing dismay. 'I wasn't supposed to say.'

'You'll have to tell that husband of yours to leave you alone,' the uncle teased, brown-button eyes sparkling. 'Though I confess if I were in Jefferson's shoes I'd——'

'Good heavens, Victoria's only two months old. It isn't Christa who's pregnant,' Isabel rebuked primly. She leant forward to hiss into his ear. 'It's Esther.'

The uncle exhibited droll surprise.

'Her condition was only confirmed yesterday, so she's still getting used to the idea,' Isabel continued, in a piercing stage whisper which alerted at least half a dozen other guests. 'Tony wants her to stop work straight away, but she insists she'll carry on for a while. She even says she might go back to her job once the baby's born. If she did, I'd be delighted to help. I often looked after Marcus when he was tiny, so——'

'If you'll excuse me,' Christa interrupted, 'I'll go and find him.'

The uncle reached for another vol-au-vent.

'Lovely food,' he said again. He watched her thread her way through the crush, a slim figure in oyster-coloured silk. 'Lovely girl too.'

Interruptions from her guests meant it was another ten minutes before Christa was free to locate her son. Reaching the hallway, she heard the murmur of voices in the bedroom which had been turned into a lemon and white nursery.

'You were the same size once,' Jeff was saying, as she opened the door.

'Little as Tory?' Marcus said doubtfully. His arm stuck through the cot bars, the two-year-old held his sister's hand.

'So was your *Papá*,' said Christa, walking in.

'Amazing, isn't it?' Jeff grinned, as incredulous eyes travelled all the way up his six foot three inches.

'I left Victoria in here so that she could go to sleep,' she pointed out gently.

'Tory not tired,' said Marcus, and the baby kicked her fat legs and gurgled in agreement.

'How about you, honey?' Jeff asked, putting his arm around Christa's waist. He kissed her brow. 'You've been on the go since six this morning.'

She smiled up at him. 'I'm good for another few hours yet.'

'OK, but if you feel like collapsing tell me and I'll send the mob out there home.'

It was mid-evening before the last stragglers left, and another hour before Marcus and Victoria were finally settled down for the night. Christa kicked off her high heels and stretched out on the soft leather sofa.

'Thanks,' she said, as Jeff handed her a glass of wine

and sat down beside her. 'I need this.'

'And I need my beautiful wife who made today possible.'

'I didn't do it all on my own,' she laughed. 'There was another person involved.'

Jeff turned his head to look at the void behind him. 'Me? But I didn't plan the menu, buy the food, and spend days skidding around on an invisible skateboard preparing it.'

'You did have something to do with Victoria being here—if I remember correctly?'

'You do.' He reached across to the coffee-table and passed her a small dark blue velvet box. 'I spent almost a year tramping around jewellers' shops to find a replacement, but finally I had one made.'

Christa gazed down at a pendant that nestled on pale crushed silk. A golden oval, it contained a delicately worked plus and minus sign. 'Jeff, it's the same as the one that was stolen!' she exclaimed.

'You like it?'

'It's beautiful.' She waited as he fastened the catch at the back of her neck, then lifted the pendant admiringly. 'Thank you.'

'Thank you,' he said softly. 'Thank you for Marcus and for Victoria but, most of all, thank you for being you.' He kissed her. 'You remember what the pendant means?'

A feeling of unbearable happiness brought a lump to her throat.

'I love you more than yesterday but less than tomorrow,' she said chokily.

'And I do,' murmured Jeff, drawing her close. 'Christa, I do.'

MILLS & BOON®

Makes any time special

Copyright © Harlequin Enterprises Limited 1997
All rights reserved

Enjoy a romantic novel from
Mills & Boon®

Presents™ *Enchanted*™ *Temptation®*

Historical Romance™ *Medical Romance*™

MILLS & BOON®

Makes any time special™

Bestselling themed romances brought back to you by popular demand

Each month By Request brings you three full–length novels in one beautiful volume featuring the best of the best.

So if you missed a favourite Romance the first time around, here is your chance to relive the magic from some of our most popular authors.

Look out for
Close Proximity in May 1999
featuring Charlotte Lamb,
Margaret Way and Lindsay Armstrong

*Available at most branches of WH Smith, Tesco,
Asda, Martins, Borders, Easons,
Volume One/James Thin
and most good paperback bookshops*

MILLS & BOON®

Next Month's Romance Titles

♡

Each month you can choose from a wide variety of romance novels from Mills & Boon®. Below are the new titles to look out for next month from the Presents™ and Enchanted™ series.

Presents™

THE SPANISH GROOM	Lynne Graham
HER GUILTY SECRET	Anne Mather
THE PATERNITY AFFAIR	Robyn Donald
MARRIAGE ON THE EDGE	Sandra Marton
THE UNEXPECTED BABY	Diana Hamilton
VIRGIN MISTRESS	Kay Thorpe
MAKESHIFT MARRIAGE	Daphne Clair
SATURDAY'S BRIDE	Kate Walker

Enchanted™

AN INNOCENT BRIDE	Betty Neels
NELL'S COWBOY	Debbie Macomber
DADDY AND DAUGHTERS	Barbara McMahon
MARRYING WILLIAM	Trisha David
HIS GIRL MONDAY TO FRIDAY	Linda Miles
BRIDE INCLUDED	Janelle Denison
OUTBACK WIFE AND MOTHER	Barbara Hannay
HAVE BABY, WILL MARRY	Christie Ridgway

On sale from 7th May 1999

H1 9904

Available at most branches of WH Smith, Tesco, Asda, Martins, Borders, Easons, Volume One/James Thin and most good paperback bookshops

MILLS & BOON®

Medical Romance™

COMING NEXT MONTH

VILLAGE PARTNERS by Laura MacDonald

Dr Sara Denton tried to forget Dr Alex Mason, but it didn't work. Then she went to her uncle's and found Alex was a partner at the general practice! And Alex *really* wanted her to stay...

ONE OF A KIND by Alison Roberts

Dr Sam Marshall, fresh from Australia, was certainly unique! Sister Kate Campbell, with an A&E department to run at the busy London hospital, had no time to spare, but Sam was persistent!

MARRYING HER PARTNER by Jennifer Taylor
A Country Practice—the first of four books.

Dr Elizabeth Allen wasn't comfortable with change, but when Dr James Sinclair arrived at the Lake District practice, change was inevitable!

ONE OF THE FAMILY by Meredith Webber

Nurse Sarah Tremaine wanted to adopt baby Sam, but first she had to get permission from the child's uncle. But Dr Adam Fletcher didn't know he had a nephew...

Available from 7th May 1999

Available at most branches of WH Smith, Tesco, Asda, Martins, Borders, Easons, Volume One/James Thin and most good paperback bookshops

MILLS & BOON®

Historical Romance™

Coming next month

MISTRESS OF MADDERLEA
by Mary Nichols
A Regency delight!

Miss Sophie Roswell switched places with her cousin
Charlotte for the Season, and only realised what a big
mistake that was when eligible *parti* Richard, Viscount
Braybrooke, came into her life…

———◆———

BLACKWOOD'S LADY
by Gail Whitiker
A Regency delight!

It was time David, Marquis of Blackwood, set up his nursery,
and Lady Nicola Wyndham fitted the bill as a possible wife.
But she had a passion she couldn't reveal to David…

On sale from 7th May 1999

*Available at most branches of WH Smith, Tesco, Asda,
Martins, Borders, Easons, Volume One/James Thin
and most good paperback bookshops*

Spoil yourself next month
with these four novels from

Temptation®

DIAL A HERO by JoAnn Ross

Hero For Hire

Sexy charmer Lucas Kincaid had quit the bodyguard business—
just before he was pulled back in for one last assignment.
Somebody wanted to hurt author Grace Fairfield, whose steamy
love scenes had nothing on the sparks flying between her and
Lucas! Too bad it was his duty never to leave her side…

THE WRONG MAN IN WYOMING by Kristine Rolofson

Bachelors and Booties

Baby bottles, nappies, sleepless nights…Jed Monroe was
convinced he wasn't daddy material. But when beautiful Abby
Andrews was stranded on his ranch with her kids, he found
himself getting up at night to help her with the baby. Or maybe it
was just to catch her in her nightgown and persuade her to come
to his bed!

THE LAST BACHELOR by Carolyn Andrews

Mac Delaney couldn't believe it. All over town, bachelors were
dropping like flies. But not this bachelor—until he ran into
smart, brave, sexy Dr Francesca Carmichael! Now he was ready
to kiss the single life goodbye—that's if his chosen bride didn't
turn him down.

TAKEN! by Lori Foster

Blaze

If he'd thought she'd come quietly, security expert Dillon Jones
wouldn't have used his special skills to kidnap her. But Virginia
Johnson was a fighter, and Dillon had a black eye to prove it. He
couldn't help wondering how she would act in the throes of
passion…not that his code of honour would let him find out…

MILLS & BOON®

Nearly
Weds!

From your favourite romance authors:

Betty Neels
Making Sure of Sarah

Carole Mortimer
The Man She'll Marry

Penny Jordan
They're Wed Again!

Enjoy an eventful trip to the altar with
three new wedding stories—when
nearly weds become *newly weds!*

Available from 19th March 1999

CATHERINE LANIGAN

tender MALICE

When Karen invented a revolutionary computer program, her life changed forever. A co-worker goes missing and her roommate is threatened.

Who can she trust?

Is it the man with whom she has become involved, or her new business partner?

MIRA®

Available from 23rd April

R.J. KAISER

Easy Virtue

A showgirl, a minister and an unsolved murder!

When her father was convicted of a violent murder she knew he didn't commit, Mary Margaret vowed to clear his name. She joins forces with Reverend Dane Barrett, and bit by bit they uncover the veil of mystery surrounding her father's case—enough to clear his name and expose the real killer.

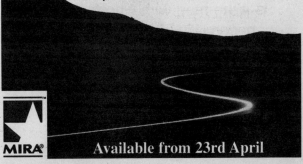

MIRA®

Available from 23rd April

HELEN R. MYERS

Come Sundown

In the steamy heat of Parish, Mississippi, there is a new chief of police. Ben Rader is here to shape up the department, and first on the list is the investigation of a mysterious death.

But things are not what they appear to be. Come Sundown things change in Parish...

MIRA®

Available from 23rd April

Who would you trust with your life?

THE BEST OF ENEMIES

Think again.

TAYLOR SMITH

Linked to a terrorist bombing, a young student disappears. Only her tutor believes in the girl's innocence and is determined to find her before she is silenced forever.

"Smith evokes a full array of heart-felt emotions and taps into that deep-seated fear that neither life nor love is predictable."

—Publishers Weekly

1-55166-277-9
MIRA® AVAILABLE NOW IN PAPERBACK

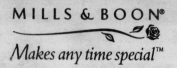

MILLS & BOON®

Makes any time special™

The Regency Collection

Mills & Boon® is delighted to bring back, for a limited period, 12 of our favourite Regency Romances for you to enjoy.

These special books will be available for you to collect each month from May, and with two full-length Historical Romance™ novels in each volume they are great value at only £4.99.

Volume One available from 7th May